Fantastical Visions IV

I0526197

Edited by
W. H. HORNER

Illustrated by
Stephanie Pui-Mun Law

**Fantasist
Enterprises**

Wilmington, Delaware

Fantasist Enterprises
PO Box 9381
Wilmington, DE 19809
www.FEBooks.net

Designed by W. H. Horner Editorial & Design

Fantastical Visions IV
Copyright © 2009 by Fantasist Enterprises
ISBN 10: 0-9713608-7-1
ISBN 13: 978-0-9713608-7-7

First printing: June 2009

10 9 8 7 6 5 4 3 2 1

This book is available for wholesale through the publisher and through Ingram Book Group. It can be ordered for retail at most booksellers, both online and off, and is available from the publisher's website.

Fantasist Enterprises grants a discount on the purchase of three or more copies of single titles. For further details, please send an e-mail to payments@fantasistent. com, or write to the publisher at the address above, care of "Bulk Orders."

Please interact with us on the web at the following websites:

The FE Forum:
http://www.fantasistent.com/FORUM/

FaceBook:
http://www.facebook.com/pages/Fantasist-Enterprises/65438463671

MySpace:
http://www.myspace.com/fantasist

Twitter:
http://twitter.com/fantasistent

To the First Writes,
for reenergizing my sense of purpose.

Contents

Introduction   ix
W. H. Horner

Evelyn   1
Michail Velichansky

Imaginix   31
Maggie Slater

The Mermaid's Silver Pool   51
Jeff R. Campbell

Abandoned Responsibility   59
G. Scott Huggins

Gratitude   77
Margaret Yang

The Benefits of Public Transportation   95
Todd Austin Hunt

The Song that Made Hell Hell   107
Greg Beatty

How Savio Arcaini Came by His Sword   115
M. T. Reiten

The Corn Bear   135
Michael Penncavage

The Desert Island Fifty   145
Jason S. Ridler

The Pit Fighter   157
Alex Jackson

Contents

A Plant's Scream   177
Christine Welcome

Healing Hands   189
Aliette de Bodard

Dragonfly Savior   213
David Walton

Deathless in Manhattan   237
Hank Quense

A Night on Pope Lake   251
James R. Cain

Renewal   263
Robyn A. Hay

Chaos Theory   277
Brandon Alspaugh

About the Contributors   290

Introduction

W. H. Horner

It's hard to believe that it's been ten years since I first set up shop on the internet, and began accepting submissions for the very first *Fantastical Visions*. Oh how things have changed, and I don't just mean the website.

Looking back, I think of myself as a babe in the woods at that point. I had yet to graduate from college and had never worked for a publishing house. I was still learning the fundamentals of good writing, and I certainly knew very little about graphic design and layout.

But what I did have was a passion for stories and a passion for helping authors tell them as best as our two skill-sets allow. I still have those passions and they have kept me going over the years and driven me to constantly learn and improve my work.

Completing college, working for a midsized publisher, and earning my master's degree in writing popular fiction certainly helped me grow as an editor and publisher, but I want to give special thanks to the authors I've worked with over the years. I learned something about writing, editing, and producing books with each title Fantasist Enterprises published, thanks to the very smart and talented authors whose work graces those pages.

I am constantly humbled and challenged by the faith that authors place in me when they agree to be published by FE. It's been a difficult few years, and I've asked for a great deal of patience from authors while I've pushed a number of books through delays to the light at the end of the publishing tunnel. And though it takes a great amount of time and effort on both my part and the part of the authors, I believe that one of my greatest responsibilities is to make sure that the fiction I publish is of impeccable quality. Sometimes that means a half dozen editorial passes on a story. And even though some authors admit to grumpiness later, they usually also admit that the story is one they remain proud of—and that they learned a great deal from the experience.

That is one of my chief joys. If I managed to teach an author something—

if their subsequent writing is just a little bit better after they worked with me—then I feel that I've accomplished something important. Something that is valuable to the author and to our culture. That is the purpose of a publisher: to be gatekeepers, to direct the cultural dialogue by lending perceived authority to the voices selected for publication, and by doing so, work towards changing the hearts and minds of readers.

I have always believed in the transformative power of short fiction. Short stories, after all, are inherently about transformation. That power in a small package is what draws me to the form, and will continue to hold my interest even as FE begins to explore new ground.

The past year has been an exciting one. FE finally moved into the territory of longer works with Lawrence C. Connolly's *Veins*, and we've taken baby steps into the music industry with his accompanying soundtrack. This year will see the publication of two more anthologies, plus our first single-author collection, *Visions*, also by Connolly.

It is my hope to work with additional authors on novel and collection projects over the coming years, as well as to continue exploring the realm of companion music. Certainly, I have my sights on other media as well, but we'll just have to work up to that. FE has a lot of ground to cover, but I believe that we're making wonderful strides and that people are beginning to recognize that fact.

I certainly put the authors in this book through their paces over the past few months, and I appreciate their patience in working with me. *Fantastical Visions IV* has had an unusual history already, considering the fact that I selected these stories for publication more than four years ago. In a way, those delays allowed the book to mature. I'm certainly a stronger editor than I was when I first picked these stories, and the authors have definitely grown in the intervening years. It shows in the quality of the finished products. While some of the stories required very little attention, others went through a series of transformations to become something stronger and more beautiful. What started as a book of which I could have been proud, turned into something that leaves me nearly breathless with the amount of depth and soul it contains.

The book you are now holding is one of the strongest yet to come out of FE. I'm especially happy that it is a Fantastical Visions because it takes me back to where this adventure started. I always saw the series as something on which to cut my teeth, as well as a vehicle for new and up-and-coming authors to showcase their work—and what we have with this book is a beautiful showcase of talent: eighteen powerful stories and the magical art of Stephanie Pui-Mun Law. I look forward to the coming months and the recognition these talented artists will certainly receive.

Keep your eyes out for the names listed in the table of contents, I expect big things from them.

W. H. Horner
Wilmington, DE
June 23, 2009

Evelyn

Michail Velichansky

When Mommy came home, Evelyn ran to her crying, "Kitty's gone! I can't find him anywhere!"

"I'm sorry, sweetie. Mommy's very tired right now. I'm sure your kitty just went out to play. He'll probably be back soon."

"But-but-but he went out yesterday, and his food's still in the bowl, and . . . and what if he doesn't come back this time?" Her lip quivered. She wanted Mommy to make things better.

"Mommy needs to sleep. Mommy has another night shift in six hours."

Evelyn grabbed hold of Mommy's arm. "But Kitty's gone! We have to find him, or he might get hurt!"

"Be quiet," Mommy said, slapping Evelyn's hand aside. "Or you'll wake Daddy." Daddy was being funny again. He walked funny, and spoke funny, and smelled funny. He laughed a lot. "Now, let Mommy go to bed, okay? Mommy's had a long day." She lay down on the couch and wrapped herself in yesterday's (and all the other days') sheets, closed her eyes, and said sleepily, "Goodnight Jeannie. Goodnight Mom."

Evelyn tugged at Mommy's shirt, but it did no good. So she went outside to search. The heat of the day hit her face like a wall and made it hard to breathe. The air rippled, and the asphalt looked like it was covered with oil. Where had Kitty gone? He always came home after going outside. Evelyn wished she hadn't let him out, that she had hid him instead. But Daddy had been angry. Usually Kitty came back after a few hours, once Daddy was asleep again.

She looked around. Her street was on a hill with houses on both sides. Some hid behind chain-link fences. Some had trimmed lawns with bright, green grass; others had thick, wild grass, or brown, dying grass. Here, a rusted lawnmower. There, a disassembled car. Dogs barked in the distance. Children's laugher rolled down the streets, high-pitched and cruel.

Evelyn flinched and bit her lip. She hated laughter.

She had to find Kitty. She had to. What would Kitty do without her? What would she do without him?

"Kitty?" she whispered, so soft she barely heard it. Children's voices drew closer.

Maybe Kitty's in the secret place! Outside, beneath her room's broken window was a loose board that let her underneath the house. She swung it aside and crawled in. It was dark and wet. There were things moving down there and making noises. Not-nice noises. Lots-of-eyes noises, creeping-crawling noises. It was where Evelyn went when she wanted to hide.

"I'm not tasty," she said, in case they forgot. She hugged her knees. "Kitty? Are you in here?"

"No kitties down here," said a voice surrounding her.

"Are . . . are you sure?"

"Meow," the voice said. "Meeeeooooow. Hear any kitties answering?"

A squeaky voice said, "Kitty? You mean cat? No, no cats. I'd smell a cat. Smell cat on you, and smell cat in the house, but no cat down here. Not now. Unless he's hiding. Sometimes he hides where I can't smell him. Not nice kitty."

"Yes, yes," said the first voice. "Kitty plays with little gray friends, and then more food for us. Always more food for us."

"Do you know where he went?" Evelyn asked.

"No," said the crawling voice.

"No," said the squeaky voice. "But maybe you don't want a kitty anymore? No more kitties with sharp claws to tear nice friendly mouse? You can give me treats and I'll be your friend."

The other voice laughed a scuttling, squirming laugh. "They give us treats all the time. So many treats!"

"I want to find my kitty. He needs me," Evelyn said.

"Don't worry," said the squeaky voice. "I'll be fine. Still have plenty to eat, didn't need your treats anyway. You're just a stupid girl anyway. I bet your kitty doesn't even want you to find him, he probably wanted to get away from you." It wasn't true. Kitty would never leave her. He was her best friend. He was her only friend.

The other voice laughed. It seemed closer now. Evelyn scrunched herself in, tried to make herself smaller. There was a smell around her: the way it always smelled in the kitchen, especially at night when the lights came on. "Don't cry. Maybe you ask the cats where your kitty went? Cats might know.

Not always friendly, not even with each other, but they might know."

"Ask . . . other kitties about my kitty?"

"Sure. Ask them. Find your kitty. Kitty will play with little gray friends and leave something for us? And maybe you'll leave little treats for your friends too? Lots of treats for us, lots of treats above and below. So we can have millions and millions of little babies, yes! Just like you. Millions and millions and millions!"

Evelyn scurried out from under the house. The street was quiet now. She was glad; the voice frightened her even when it was being nice. Still, she whispered, "Thank you," before running down the road in search of other cats.

"Kitty?" she hissed now and then. "Kitty? Where are you? Has anybody seen my kitty?" The road swung around. Her house's wasted lawn and shaded windows disappeared behind houses just as bleak. Dogs chained up in yards growled and barked at her as she passed. Here and there cats sunned themselves on the sidewalk, but they scattered when she approached. Finally she spotted an orange cat on the roof of an old truck, too high for her to reach. She approached slowly.

"Please," she called out. "I'm trying to find my kitty."

The cat stared down at her, yawning.

"Please? It's very *alone* . . . without him."

"What's his name?"

Evelyn had to think. She had always called him Kitty, but he had told her his real name once. "Tom," she said. "Tom Robin. He was gray and black and—"

The orange cat hissed.

"—he had . . . a scar under his eye. . . ."

"I know of Tom Robin. He's a bandit and a murderer."

"No!" Evelyn cried. "He's the sweetest kitty ever!"

"You shouldn't look for Tom Robin. I don't think you would be pleased to find him. He's best forgotten. There will be other pets for you, little girl."

Evelyn's eyes watered, but she did not let herself cry. Crying was bad. Daddy hated it when she cried.

"Kitty isn't a pet," she said, staring down at the ground. "Kitty is my friend." *My only friend.*

The orange cat meowed. It stretched and scratched at the metal roof. Evelyn grit her teeth against the sound. "He's dangerous, you know. But if you truly wish to find him, speak to the Council. They may help you. But they're danger—" The orange cat hissed and arched its back, looking past Evelyn.

Then it jumped off the truck and darted away.

"Wait!" Evelyn cried. "Please don't go! What about my kitty?"

"What about your kitty?" asked a voice behind her, thin as razor blades.

"Yes, tell us," said another voice.

Evelyn turned around. Two boys towered over her. Tall and lean, they both had thin, dirty faces with eyes that never blinked, and torn, stained clothing. They never stopped smiling, mouths open too wide and showing sharp white teeth. Only their hair color was different: one had black hair, the other harsh, burned blond. They held crusted knives in their hands. The laugh they shared was high and cruel.

"I . . . I lost my kitty," Evelyn mumbled, backing away.

"She lost her kitty," said the one with black hair.

"Have we found her kitty?" asked the one with blond hair.

They moved to either side of her.

"We found a kitty before, yes we did."

"Oh yes."

"Wa-was it mine?" Evelyn asked.

"Bring it out—"

"—and we'll see."

The one with blond hair reached behind him, grinning, and pulled out something gray and furry-soft. Evelyn jumped back with a yelp, but the one with black hair pushed her forward again.

"Was this your kitty?"

"It must have lost its fur."

Underneath, the cat's fur was still wet with blood.

"You shouldn't have done that," Evelyn said, hands clenched in fists. "You're very bad!"

The blond licked his lips and asked his twin, "Are we very bad?"

"Didn't we find her kitty for her, red all over?"

"That's not my kitty," she said. "My kitty's big and black, and he'd scratch you."

The one with blonde hair hissed, and the one with black hair snapped his teeth in front of her face.

"Not yours?"

"Not hers?"

They laughed again, and started to skip around her. She tried to run, but wherever she went, one of them was there, pushing her and chortling. She kicked and bit, but they were bigger and stronger, and seemed not to mind it when her teeth tore through their skin. They knocked her down and danced around her, singing, "Where has it gone then? Where has it gone then?"

When they tired of their game they each gave her a final kick.

"Maybe you'll visit the forest sometime?" asked the black-haired twin.

"Maybe we'll skin you, too."

They hissed and stabbed their knives in her direction, then ran on down the street. Their laughter echoed.

Evelyn hugged herself where she sat, hurting, on the ground. She wanted to cry, to run, to lie down and sleep. But it was always hard for her to sleep without Kitty. He'd lay on her all warm, without a care. He would purr until her whole body felt it, and then she almost couldn't hear Mommy and Daddy screaming.

"Hst! Robin's friend! Hey little girl!" Something orange stalked the shadows in the green of a small bush. "If you still want to talk to the Council, take a left from the big road. If it's sunny out, that's where they'll be, and many others beside. Be wary of them, and of your Tom Robin."

The road wound through rows of squat houses. There were hearts and obscene stick-people etched into the broken cement. Then the road dead-ended at a rotting fence. Behind it the forest loomed, dark and sudden. There were houses on either side of the road, all of them abandoned. The sun beat down harshly and the asphalt was hot to the touch. Evelyn's feet were sweaty in her shoes. She was frightened.

The fourth house had a large sheet of metal on the lawn. It sparkled in the sunlight. Cats lounged all over it. They paid Evelyn no attention as she approached. Warm sun, warm metal, warm fur.

"Excuse me," she said. "I-I'm trying to find my kitty. He's lost, and I can't find him. He needs me." The cats said nothing. Evelyn tried to think of what to say. "His name is Tom Robin."

A hiss went up. Eyes turned on her, orange, green, and yellow. Night prowler eyes, hunter eyes. The cats stood, their heads low between their shoulder blades. A lean cat missing an ear stepped forward. He looked haughty and terrible to Evelyn, nothing like her kitty.

"So you're the one who's been hiding him. Tom Robin is dead, ape-child. Leave now, before we take your face." He leaped. Claws sliced through her cheek. They felt cold. "Leave now!"

Evelyn stumbled back, her cheek burning. Cats' eyes followed her as she turned and ran. Tears rolled down her face. Salt bit into the scratches, like gasoline tossed onto a fire. But it was not her cheek that made her cry.

The floor of the forest was damp. Still Evelyn did not move. Sniffling, she ran a hand across her nose and wiped it on her already stained shirt. She held her breath to make herself stop crying.

She didn't want to move. She didn't know *why* to move.

"Poor Kitty," she whispered. "Poor Evelyn. . . ." She stroked her own hair clumsily, the way Mommy had a long time ago.

Then Evelyn heard a faint rustling. Something breathed nearby—*sniff, sniff.* A black nose appeared around a tree, then a brown muzzle and small black eyes. *Sniff, sniff.* The dog slunk closer. Sticks were tangled in its matted fur, and it was covered in leaves. Normally, Evelyn would have run—she knew strange dogs could hurt you, no matter what Daddy said. But there was nowhere to go.

"Who are you?" the dog growled. "You with the cats?"

"No. I hate them, mean kitties. I *hate* them."

Sniff, sniff. "You smell like cat."

"Was my kitty, and now he's gone." She held her breath till her face felt swollen.

The dog turned his head to one side, then to another. "Where'd he go?"

Evelyn pointed in the direction she had run from. "Bad kitties made him be gone. I was looking for him. Went to bad kitties to ask where he was, and they said, 'No more Kitty. Kitty's gone.' Before that, maybe I could find him, but they made him be gone."

The dog sniffed her again. He licked his lips. "You smell like food. I haven't eaten in three days. All the young squirrels went away, and there's hardly any old ones left. You wouldn't have any food on you? A little meat and bone? Master used to give me meat and bone. . . ."

Evelyn shook her head.

The dog muttered, "If I were a wolf, I'd have a pack. If I had a pack, I'd go hunt. And if I could hunt, I wouldn't be hungry. If I weren't hungry, I would grow strong. If I grew strong, I'd grow fast, I'd grow big. If I grew big, I'd be a wolf. If I were a wolf . . ." He stared at Evelyn, growling. It sounded deeper, as though it came from a much bigger dog. He looked bigger, too. His mouth pulled back to show brutal fangs. Evelyn's heart beat faster. But she felt too tired to run. She scrunched herself up and waited.

The growl faded. The dog's teeth became dull again. For a second it seemed he had remembered something, but now it was gone. "Maybe I could help you, if you bring me some food?" He placed his head on her knees. "Maybe I know where your kitty is? Just a little bit of food, little bit of meat and bone. . . ."

"You know where my kitty is? You can make him be not gone?"

The dog whined and stared up at her with filmy brown eyes.

"All right," she said. "I'll bring you food if you can help me find my kitty." The dog wagged his tail, and Evelyn patted him on the head. She was frightened. But Kitty wasn't gone anymore. The nice dog had brought him back, she could find him now.

As she walked away, the dog muttered, "Master told me to watch the cats, said they were evil, witches . . . I watch. There's no food. The squirrels are gone, the cats too dangerous. There used to be birds to listen to, but they've all changed to something else now. Where did they all go? Even the cats don't know. But they don't even know why their queen won't wake."

Evelyn climbed over the rotting fence that was meant to keep the forest out, avoiding the cats. A stagnant breeze blew against her face, stinging her cheek. Somewhere a newborn screamed. Somewhere a dog howled. Soon she stood in front of her house. She put her head against the door and listened for screams. Then she opened it and stepped inside.

"Jeannie? Jeannie, is that you?" Mommy's voice was like wrung laundry. Evelyn wanted to say something, but Mommy still slept. She tip-toed into the kitchen, hoping neither Mommy nor Daddy woke. The fridge was almost empty, but she found an old piece of ham—mostly fat—and a half-eaten burger. One of the vegetable bins was missing. The other had a plastic bottle filled with Daddy's medicine. Without it, he would lie in bed or sometimes on the floor, groaning and vomiting. Evelyn set the food next to the sink and poured the liquid down the drain. The smell made her gag, and fear knotted her belly. What if he saw her? What if Mommy saw? Evelyn knew it was wrong to get rid of Daddy's medicine, that people needed their medicine. Only someone very bad would rather someone stay sick. She screwed the top back on and returned the bottle to the vegetable bin.

When she looked up again she saw a cockroach crawling on the hamburger. It was big and brown with red wings. Evelyn jumped back. Another appeared, and another.

"For us?" asked a thousand voices from the sink, and a bitter, noxious smell overcame the medicine's.

Evelyn grabbed the ham and held it away from the sink. "No," she said. "For someone else."

"That's all right," the voices said. "Plenty around. Food everywhere. Find your kitty?"

"Not yet. But I will. Very soon."

"Yes, good. And you'll remember your friends? Open door to the cold place? Yes, and feed your friends who helped you search."

"But that's *our* food," Evelyn said.

"So much? For only three? Down here are millions and millions . . . would you like to see?" Roaches swarmed out of the sink. Evelyn screamed. She turned on the water, and ran out of the kitchen.

"Tell the cats if they need a new queen, we can spare a few!"

Behind her, a thousand voices laughed.

"Jeannie, don't go. . . ." Mommy was talking in her sleep again. "Please, Jeannie. It's not so bad. I . . . I promise things will get better."

A voice came unbidden to Evelyn, a memory she didn't want to remember. A soft voice. *I have to go. The birds, they sing so pretty. They're calling, Mommy. I have to go.*

"Please, Jeannie. . . ."

Slowly, Evelyn walked up to her mommy. She bent down and kissed Mommy's cheek. It was cold and clammy, and her eyes darted beneath their lids.

"I have to find Kitty," Evelyn whispered. "I can't let him be gone again. I can't. He's all I have." Saying it made his absence that much worse.

"Please, Jeannie," Mommy whispered. "Please don't. You're all—"

Evelyn ran out the door.

The dog grabbed the ham, drool running down the sides of his mouth. He lay on his belly, chewing on the fat. "Meat and bone," he said, still holding the latter in his mouth. "Nothing better than meat and bone."

"You said you knew where my kitty was."

The dog's tail stopped wagging. "I think, maybe. No guarantees, you know. But there's a place that cats go when—well, a place they go to sometimes. A secret place. I can take you there."

Evelyn looked up. The sun was setting. "Let's go now, okay?"

"Um . . . save this for later, then." The dog began to dig. "Can't leave it out for the cats. Worse things, too." Evelyn stared off to the side politely as he buried the bone. Nervous, she tugged at her hair.

The dog barked. "Follow me," he said, and lowered his nose to the ground. He sniffed as he padded between the trees. He walked quickly. The forest became thicker. The ground was covered in small, mean bushes covered in thorns. Pale roots stuck out of the ground. Dragonflies buzzed around them.

The dog stopped. "It's just ahead."

Evelyn walked on, but he didn't follow. "Come on," she said. "If my kitty's there, we have to find him."

"I can't go there. That's a cat place."

"But I have to find my kitty."

The dog whined.

Evelyn sniffled and said, "Thank you, Doggy." Then she was running past short, twisted trees with ash-gray bark. She entered a clearing. Everywhere lay fragile bones, whole skeletons. She tried not to look at them. Tried not to see the cats that hadn't finished rotting yet. A wind blew at her from all directions, howling in her ears. The smell made her throw up. She wiped her mouth on her shirt.

"Kitty?"

She stumbled further into the clearing. Her voice was weak.

"Kitty? Are you here?" Fat black flies buzzed drunkenly. Maggots squirmed over lumps of cat-flesh.

"Tom?"

"I remember you." The voice was raw and broken where once it had been deep and smooth. But the laugh was still full of joy and malice. A cat's laugh was a special thing, her kitty had once told her, shared only among cats. It sounded like the wail of stones when a fierce wind blew.

"Tom Kitty!" Evelyn ran toward the voice.

The sight hit her like a fist. Kitty lay on the ground, his fur matted with blood. A scratch ran across his face. Pus oozed from one eye. She crawled over to him and hugged him. Tears streamed down her face and she didn't care. She took no notice of the blood soaking into her shirt, of sticky fur in her hands.

"You're hurt," she whispered. "I'll get you out of here, take you home. Mommy will help you."

He laughed again. "How? She's asleep, and nothing wakes her. Nor is there anything she or you could do. Still, I am glad to see you, Evey-girl."

Evelyn stroked Tom's head. "You're hurting. There must be something. Where did you go? I looked everywhere, and the cats told me . . ."

"That I was dead?"

Evelyn nodded. "B-but you'll be okay now."

"I *am* dead," Tom Robin said. "Or I will be. There's nothing can be done about it."

"You can't die. I found you."

"Oh, but I can and I will, little Evey-girl. Even if you took me away and healed my wounds, I'd die." He yawned, showing off his teeth. "This is where cats come to die. If a cat spends any time here, he *will* die. And I've been here for too long."

"But you can't die. I looked and looked and I *found* you."

"Did you think that would make everything better?"

"It has too. Doesn't it?"

Tom Robin laughed. "I was dead the minute they captured me. They'd have never let me go, and I'd tell them nothing, so they tore at me and left me here to die. There was never anything you could have done."

Evelyn shook.

"I've still some time, Evey. Talk to me. Tell me how you found this place."

So Evelyn talked, telling him everything that had happened just as she always had. He purred. She toyed with his ear.

"You've surprised me, Evelyn," Tom Robin said when she finished. "I think there's something I'd like you to do for me."

Evelyn smiled. Her mouth quivered. It would be all right. If she found Kitty, it had to be all right. She nodded.

Tom Robin's muscles twitched with pain. He closed his good eye. "Do you remember the black cat you met, the one missing an ear?"

"He wasn't nice. He tried to make you go away."

"Yes. He's the one that put me here, him and that menagerie he calls a council."

"Why?"

"They think I did something, something that they didn't like. But they don't really understand, not yet. His name is Morgo. I want you to give that name to the two children you met."

"But—"

"Don't worry. They're friends of mine, native to this place. They have been useful to me. Once you've given them the name, there is a place I want you to go. I have a present for you there."

Evelyn listened hard as he described the path she should take. No one had ever given her a present before.

"Go now. Bring back what I've described and you will have your present."

She scrambled up. "Thank you Tom Kitty, love you Kitty."

"Go and do this for your Kitty if you love him," Tom Robin said. "And go fast."

She tripped over bones, then ran back into the forest. Her head felt light. Things would work out. They had to. She thought about her present.

"Did you find him?"

Surprised, Evelyn stumbled and fell to her knees.

The dog nuzzled her gently. "You okay?"

There was a lump in Evelyn's throat. "Yes. Fine."

"Found him?" the dog asked, curiosity and confusion in his voice.

"Yes. Yes!" Evelyn smiled and hugged the dog around the neck. She scratched him; he growled and wagged his tail. She whispered, "Thank you thank you thank you, so very much. Nice Doggy. Good Doggy. Would you like to come with me? I need to get back out of the forest. Come with me?"

"Yeah. Yeah, I'll come. And maybe we can get a little more food? A little more meat and bone?"

Evelyn wiped the tears from her face. It felt good to smile. "I'll see what we have left."

The forest ended, and they walked over the sheet-metal in the yard. The dog sniffed the air and growled. "Smells like cat," he said. The asphalt was still warm from the sun, and the air was thick as the heat rose. A breeze carried a hint of night's cool air. A few streetlights still came on, dim in the evening light.

"Eat first, yes?" The dog's ears were pressed against his head and his tail hung still.

"I don't know," Evelyn said. "I don't know where Kitty's friends are. We can go home, they might be on the way." She put her hand on his head so that they walked together.

Kids ran by them: shirtless, shoeless, yelling and throwing rocks. Yet the streets felt empty and lonely. Evelyn's shoes made no sound on the ground. The dog wheezed. Evelyn's house was a squat, dark thing with electric-yellow light seeping through the curtains. Close by someone screamed; metallic laughter followed. She walked a little further and found the twins. A boy lay on the ground between them. They kicked him, and he cried. No light glinted on their knives. Around them, a circle of children watched.

"I have to talk to them," Evelyn said.

"To who?"

She pointed.

"They've got knives," the dog said.

"Kitty knows them." It sounded like a question.

"Why don't we get some food, and maybe later—"

"But Kitty asked me to. I said I would."

The twins danced around the boy, holding hands and singing nonsense. Evelyn thought she heard a sucking sound, like some creature feeding. The twins giggled and walked away. Behind them, the boy stood, only to be pushed down by the other children.

Evelyn ran after Kitty's friends. "Wait!"

They stopped and turned on her. "She's come back then, has she?" said the one with black hair.

"Has she found her little kitty?"

Evelyn glanced around and saw that the dog was gone. The two boys drew closer; she tried not to look them in the eyes. "I found him, and . . . and he wants you to do something for him."

"Does he, now?" They clicked their teeth. "Who is he then?"

"T-T-Tom Robin," Evelyn said. "He said he knew you—" but they'd already hissed, drawing back their knives. They didn't stop smiling.

"We know him."

"What does he want?"

"Th-there's a kitty here. Not Tom Kitty—a mean black kitty missing an ear. M-Morgo. My kitty wanted me to tell you that."

"We know Morgo. Dangerous, Morgo," said the boy with blond hair.

"But we owe the Robin."

They touched their knives together. Gray metal scraped softly against gray metal.

"We'll do this."

"Since you know him, you can go."

"Maybe later you'll come back?"

"Come back and see your Morgo."

"Goodbye Robin's friend."

They laughed and ran through someone's yard and vaulted over a fence to vanish in the shadows.

Slowly, Evelyn walked back to her house.

"I'm sorry," the dog said, appearing at her side. "They didn't smell right."

"I'm hungry," Evelyn said absently.

"Should . . . should I come in?" the dog asked.

"I don't think Daddy would like it," Evelyn said. "He doesn't like animals very much. And he's funny now. I'll be back soon."

Inside, static flickered on the television, casting the room in nauseous, squirming light. Evelyn passed the couch where Mommy had slept. The blanket lay crumpled on the floor. The light in the kitchen buzzed over her head. The fridge was empty, but she found an old box of cereal in the cupboard. She sniffed. There was food, delicious food, something fried, with spices. But it came from Daddy's room. The cupboard door closed with a wooden *thunk*.

"So there you are."

Evelyn cringed.

"Turn around when I talk to you!"

She did. Her Daddy wore jeans that hung loose on his hips and nothing else. He was a small man, all bone and hard muscle. His skin was pale like a lizard's and he smelled of vomit.

"That bitch mother of yours didn't make you dinner again. Where've you been?"

Evelyn said nothing. She barely heard him. She tugged painfully at her hair and thought of Kitty.

"—all over the place, doing god knows what, like a fucking cockroach. That worthless mother of yours should—"

Daddy kept changing in size. He grew large, too large, then shrank. He was so small now. She could pick him up in her hands.

"—should take all you fuckin' brats and teach you respect. Fuckin' *respect*. Just run around all the time in everyone's way, like that no good—"

Daddy banged his hand on the counter as he yelled. He could barely reach it. Evelyn grabbed the box of cereal and ran, her Daddy's shouts drowned out by the television's drone. The sun sank lower in the sky. The dog ran next to her.

The dog panted. "Did you . . . get any food?"

"Just this," she said. She opened the box of cereal, and ate the flakes one by one. They were mushy. The dog left, then came back with his bone.

"No problem," he said. "Still have my bone. More than I've had for a while."

Nearby, a cricket chirped. The bone cracked between the dog's teeth. A pale gibbous moon shone between the leaves; the brightest stars twinkled in the purple sky. Evelyn thought about her bed at home, but found it less appealing than the ground. Under her breath, she whispered Tom Robin's directions so she wouldn't forget.

"This isn't too bad, huh?" the dog said. "Little bit of meat and bone, and . . . well, it feels nice now, doesn't it?" He scratched himself. "I can smell anything that comes up here, too, so it should be pretty safe. You can sleep. If you like." There was an interesting smell just to his left, and he planted his nose in it.

Evelyn jerked up. "But I don't want to sleep yet. I have to go get something." She blinked the sleep out of her eyes. "Come on. We gotta go get my present." She scratched his belly for a moment. Then they stood, and Evelyn led the way. Soon the excitement died down, and she felt afraid and tired. Night came early to the forest, though the last remains of daylight still lingered in the sky. Darkness stretched between the trees, quiet and menacing.

"Tell me a story," Evelyn whispered.

"What? Um. I'm not really good at making—"

"Please? Just while we walk." Evelyn thought she remembered, once, her mother telling Jeannie a story while Evelyn lay in her Mommy's arms. Sometimes, stories made the night less scary.

"All right. I'll try." The dog walked in silence for a while. When he spoke again his voice was slower, steadier. "There was once a great queen of the cats, descended from those queens who ruled long ago in the many sunlit cities along the River of Life. She ruled well, and the cats prospered. She lived in a glass palace that shined with the light of a thousand reflected suns; when she was in heat, the cats wailed beneath her balcony, drowning out all other sounds—while she sat, regal, staring up into the sun. And sometimes she would choose a suitor, and their screams would roll over the city so that no one slept."

As he spoke, they made their way through the swamp. A friar's lantern flitted about in the distance, its light soft and eerie. Evelyn was afraid and excited; carried by the dog's words, her mind jumped from the thick swamp-darkness to great queens and sunlit cities.

"One day, though, her advisors and slaves found her asleep, and when they tried to wake her, she would not stir. Nothing they tried worked. Their queen was gone. Yet she was not dead: she breathed, and ate when fed, and dreamed strange dreams.

"For years the cats lived like this. Many tried to wake her in different ways, but neither traveling wise men, nor gypsies, nor hairless cats from the East had any luck. Many took personal meanings in the queen's sleep, believing it to be one omen or another, and none agreed. Some took it upon themselves to discover the villains behind it, and many creatures died in the night surrounded by sharp claws and yellow eyes. Many wars were started, and still the queen slept."

They left the swamp. Trees grew thick about them. Daisies sprouted from their trunks, translucent in the moonlight. Mushrooms sparkled as they walked past. No insects buzzed here; no rodents scurried through the brush.

"Finally, the queen's subjects and advisors got together and decided that they could not go on without a ruler, so they stopped feeding their queen, stopped setting milk in front of her. The queen's body withered and shrunk, until she had no muscles left, and only bones could be felt beneath her thin, ragged fur—but still she lived.

"One of the queen's many daughters was next in line, and it was she who ordered that the queen be killed. Without any real reluctance, the order was obeyed. All night the queen bled from her eyes and mouth and from her many wounds, until all her lives were spent and her shriveled body ceased to breath."

They walked through a grove of bamboo in shallow, filthy water. Many shafts were broken, as though something had forced a path through. Some ended in jagged points where they'd been broken.

"They left the body where they had killed it, in a secret place where cats go to die. The queen's daughter was pleased, for she was strong and wise and ruthless. She felt that she would make a good queen, and that she had done right in murdering her mother. Her mother would have done the same. She celebrated for days in the old queen's palace while a crowd waited outside to see their ruler. Finally, she walked out onto the balcony and proclaimed herself the new queen. A cheer went up, for the cats had been without a queen for years, and some part of them that even they do not truly understand longed for a queen to rule them.

"But the cheer changed to a multitude of screams; everywhere fur bristled and tails puffed.

"'Imposter!' they cried.

"Those at the front leapt up onto girders and fences, onto window sills and balconies, up telephone poles and fire-escapes. Lightning fast they moved, and before she could react, they were on the balcony with her. Her guards helped to cast her down among the crowd, and with their teeth and claws they tore her apart.

"For somehow, they had known—had *felt*—that she was not their queen. Ever since, the same has happened to all who tried."

The dog looked up at Evelyn and wagged his tail.

"Thank you," she said, scratching him behind the ear lightly. "It . . . it wasn't very nice. Do you think they'll find it again? Whatever it is the cats lost."

"Probably not," the dog said. "Cats aren't very good at finding things. You need a dog for that."

A creek burbled ahead of them.

"We're almost there," Evelyn said.

"Smells strange here." The dog's tail slowed. "Can't quite make it out. . . ."

Excited, Evelyn hurried on.

The dog growled into the shadows. "Doesn't smell right. Something lives there." Still, he followed her.

Ahead of them stood a small, squat bridge, its stones all covered in moss. Water bubbled underneath. "There!" Evelyn cried. She ran towards it. The dog crept after, head low to the ground, snapping his teeth at the smell. Evelyn climbed down into the water. It rose up to her chest, and was so cold that her teeth chattered as she made her way toward the bridge's underbelly. Something cracked under her feet. Crimson spots shimmered in the darkness ahead of her. She crawled under the bridge and reached for them. They were buried in a slimy, rotting mass of leaves and fur and hair. Shuddering, Evelyn dug through it till the spots merged into a single light. It was egg-shaped, larger than her head, warm and soft and very, very smooth. She cradled it in her arms as she crawled back.

The dog was edging towards the bridge, tearing the ground up as he went. His growl had turned to a whine. He sprang back when Evelyn walked out. "What is it?" he asked.

"It's a present," Evelyn whispered. "Right where Kitty said it would be. Tom Kitty gave it to me. A present for Evelyn." Her fingers shook as she petted the thing in her hands. "Pretty."

"Maybe we shouldn't stay here?" the dog said. "Please?"

"All right," Evelyn said, staring down into her present, into shades of red that flowed like lava. She stood, though she could not remember sitting down. She followed the dog back into the forest.

"It still smells," the dog muttered. "Your present smells like . . . I don't know. Maybe you should put it away? It's too bright."

Evelyn covered as much of the orb as she could with her shirt. She made sure she could still touch its surface with her fingertips. She felt happy and exhausted.

"Let's stop," she said.

The dog sniffed. "Little bit further."

"Where are we going?"

"We should get away. I don't like it there."

But she couldn't walk any further. Her feet dragged on the ground, snagging on roots.

"Just a little bit further?" the dog begged, nudging her with his cold nose. "Just away a little?"

Evelyn nodded and tried to walk. The water in the bamboo lake woke her for a little while. When they stepped out, she sat down in a nook among the tree roots. Her eyes closed. She woke once as bamboo poles clattered down over the roots. The dog spaced the bamboo out so that it made a sort of roof. "You can sleep now," the dog said. "I think it's safe."

He lay down next to her, his fur and body warm. But Evelyn turned away, curling up around her present. "Thank you," she whispered happily. The swirling lava left strange afterimages in the darkness when she closed her eyes.

Evelyn dreamed:

She dreamed that she was running, fast, impossibly fast. Around her everything was a rainbow of smells for which she had no names. What joy! Sprinting, leaping from place to place, up onto roofs and down again. The joy vanished when she heard the voices and smelled the harsh, coppery smell. She remembered who she was running *from*.

Now it was terror that drove her. She felt the pain in her muscles, felt her heart pump violently. Their breaths hissing behind her. She leapt from roof to fence, then down to pavement. She tried to cut to the forest, but the thing jumped out in front of her, screeching in a frequency Evelyn had never heard. It slashed at her. She jumped away. The second creature came up the opposite side as she hit asphalt, and now she was trapped out in the open. Their laughter was cruel and ancient. Fear gripped her heart, such fear as she had never known and was ashamed to feel. She hissed back at them, but what came out was a pathetic mewling, like a kitten's. For the first time, she feared she could not outrun them.

She ran now out of desperation. Her claws cracked on the asphalt, but she no longer cared. Then a knife sank into her side. Blood choked off her scream. Another slash, and her throat spilled blood over the pavement.

She watched them skin her corpse.

She watched them eat her.

She watched them make a toy out of her bones.

In the gray world of dream and death, they were shadows, empty nothings. They walked away hand in hand.

She thought a dream-thought that went: Maybe it's everything else that's shadow, and they are real.

Evelyn woke choking, trying to scream and breathe at the same time. She held her present close to her and whimpered. It hummed inside her head. She kissed it, sniffled, and went back to sleep.

It was still night when Evelyn woke again. Something moved, sloshing through the water. Stalks of bamboo clunked together. The dog sat nearby, growling softly. The sounds faded. Evelyn checked to make sure Kitty's present was still there, and began to fall asleep again. Suddenly there came a horrible wail—a sound that tore the air and ran down her spine. Somewhere in the forest two pitiful voices howled. Evelyn clutched at her present, until finally a thin rain drowned the sound.

Evelyn woke wet, cold, and hungry. Her body hurt from sleeping on the ground, and she still felt tired. She rubbed the sand out of her eyes.

The sky was gray and hazy. The smell of new rain and wet leaves was all around. She made sure she had her present and peeked out between the bamboo poles. The forest looked as though it had been washed clean of the darkness. Shivering, Evelyn sat back down. The dog put his nose under Evelyn's arms, pressing his head against her side. His fur dripped, matted to his body. He looked thin and old, and his fur smelled. Trying to warm herself, Evelyn hugged her present.

"It smells strange, like the two kids with knives," the dog said. "What kind of present is it?"

"I . . . I don't know. But it's for me, and it's very warm and pretty."

The dog whimpered. "All rested now? We should go. We're too close to the bridge." He nosed his way through the bamboo.

"I'm hungry," Evelyn said. The dog licked his muzzle in agreement. But

they had no way of getting food, so they walked on. Evelyn said, "We have to go see Kitty. He told me to come back to him after I got his present from the bridge."

The swamp was swollen with rain, and they had to find a way around it. The dog muttered to himself, but Evelyn didn't listen. She felt happy holding her present. The sky was dirty gray—she wished the sun would come out so that the sky could feel happy too. But even the rain wasn't so bad.

"I'll wait," the dog said when they reached the graveyard. "Have to wait, don't I? Of course I do. I'll wait."

Evelyn paid no attention to skeletons or bodies, nor to the reek of wet compost as she ran. Tom Robin lay in the same place. She set her present down and kissed him.

"Thank you so much Kitty, it's so pretty, I—"

"Did you do what I asked you to do?"

Evelyn nodded happily.

"Did you sleep well?" he asked, a purr in his voice.

"Y-yes. I think so," Evelyn lied. She smiled again. "It felt a little warm at night, and I felt better even though it was dark and scary."

Tom Robin laughed. "You did well, my Evey. Now it's time for you to open your present. I wish to see the look on your face before I die."

She stared at the red thing in front of her. "What do I do?"

"Did you guess what it is, Evey? It's an egg, the offspring of two very ancient creatures. You've met them. But it is more than that as well—I placed something in it. Something that I want you to have. Break it open and see."

"All right!" She tried to open it with her hands, but though the surface was soft she could not break it. She felt around and found a rock amongst the bones. With her fingernails she worked it out of the dirt.

She stared into the egg again, then glanced at Tom.

"Go ahead," he said. "It's yours. Open it."

Slowly, Evelyn lifted the rock and brought it down on the egg. The rock broke it with a soft thud. The egg hissed. Something oozed out, a thin stream of foul-smelling oil. Tom purred louder. Swallowing her nausea, Evelyn jammed her finger into the tear and pulled. She cringed at the sound the egg-flesh made as it was torn apart. Rot spilled onto the ground. Whatever had been alive inside lived no longer. But then something rose up, like an oil slick floating in the air, all shimmering light and painful colors. She felt as though she'd never seen real colors before, and she reached out a quivering hand to touch it.

Her fingertips tingled. She wanted to run *fast, through the jungles and plains, chasing after the mouse and the rat, after the sun and the moon, sleek muscles propelling her forward, claws slipping through prey and foe and lover.*

"It is the soul of the queen of cats," Tom Robin said. "Years ago, I seduced her and stole it from her. I hid it in many places, close to me and far from me—places like that egg, where it could feed and stay alive. That is a wonderful present for you, little Evelyn. Pick it up."

Evelyn brought her hands together beneath the soul. She felt nothing, but the soul was there, sharp and shimmering, playing in her hands. Its chaotic motions mesmerized her. Around her, the world seemed less beautiful, seemed to fade and die. There was something terrible in it that frightened her. Yet even the terrifying sharpness of its light, and its strange, alien motions were beautiful. It was this, she knew, that had warmed her at night.

"Drink it," Tom Robin said. His voice sent currents running through the soul.

Evelyn tried to speak but found that her voice had abandoned her. The terror she felt seemed better than any joy.

"Drink it, my Evelyn. Drink it and your soul will be tainted by the soul of the queen of cats, and you will be beautiful and terrible."

So beautiful . . . for me. . . . Thank you, Tom Kitty.

She lifted the soul to her mouth, and drank.

At first she only tasted a hint of something sweet, like honeysuckle. Then she took a breath, and it filled her nose, smelling of incense and desert, hot jungle and cool summer nights. It smelled of fear. She breathed out, and continued to drink. Her eyes were closed, but the soul was like a sun stuck under her eyelids. Her throat burned and the screams of cats mating filled her ears.

And then it all became white noise. She neither felt, nor saw, nor smelled, nor heard, nor tasted. Evelyn floated in the emptiness, unsure of time or place, unsure of who she was. Then she heard distant laughter, and opened her eyes. Everything was gray and dim, yet at the same time she saw things clearer. Evelyn stroked Tom Robin's fur. "It's wonderful," she said, though she was unsure why she had said it.

"You're welcome." His laughter weakened and his body quaked. Evelyn watched, running her hand along his once-sleek fur, over new wounds and old scars. His heart beat fast against her palm, but his breathing was uneven. His purr no longer sounded pleasant.

"I think it's coming now," he said. "Time for me to go."

Evelyn snapped out of her reverie. "Go where?"

"To rot, Evey. To my grave. I am dying, finally. This was the last of them—no lives left. I'll be just like all the others, just bones piled up in one place so that the ants and maggots have their fill."

"You can't die." Evelyn's voice flared. "You won't die. I won't let you."

Tom Robin glanced up at her, and some of his strength seemed to return. "You're right. I won't die. Not completely, not like the rest of them. Because they'll remember me. You'll be my legacy, and you won't let them forget, will you, my Evelyn? But I would stay longer if I could. I would stay forever, for as long as I could hold on to this life with tooth and claw. I would play with all the worlds as though they were mice, and in the end . . . I would watch it all burn. . . ." His voice sank. He tried to speak again, but only meowed pathetically. Blood oozed from his wounds, but there was no force behind it.

"No! No, you can't die!" Evelyn commanded him in vain. "You can't die! I won't let you!" Her stomach twisted into knots. She wanted to run, to kill, to . . . *something.*

She wrapped her arms around Tom Robin and held him tightly.

"I'm dying," he whispered. There was disbelief in his voice.

"Please. Please don't." She tried not to cry, tried to swallow the tears, sobbing and hiccupping into the cat's bloody fur. "I love you."

Her kitty's chest rose slowly, lifting her head. He had always been hard, all muscle and scar tissue. Except his belly. That had always been soft.

"Goodbye, Evelyn." His voice had become small and weak and frightened. "I think I loved you as much as I ever loved anyone. You will be the best of all my tricks." He shuddered, and lay still.

Quietly, Evelyn lifted her head. She took her hands off the cat. She clenched her teeth until her head shook from the strain, and she made the tears not be. She walked back to the trees and searched until she found some moss. She wiped the blood off her hands.

Then she sat and stared at the red streaks.

After a while, Evelyn knew what she would do.

Calmly, Evelyn walked back to her kitty. She gathered up the eggshells. Where once they had been a deep, bright red, now they were dull, absorbing light where once they had given it off. The liquid that had spilled from them had dried.

"Goodbye Kitty," Evelyn said.

Walking away, she did not wonder whether she had left anything behind.

The dog scrambled to his feet when he saw her, tail wagging. She set the egg-shells down in front of her. "Take these to the place we slept last night. Cover them with bamboo. Use small pieces—I'll need to lift them."

The dog stared at her, and at the broken things at her feet. His tail slowed. "I don't like it."

"Please? For me?" Evelyn kissed him just above the nose and scratched his neck. "You'll do it for me? Of course you will, because you're a good doggy."

"All right," he said.

"Hide and wait for me there."

"You're not coming?" the dog asked. He put his nose against her hand.

"I can't. I have to do something. You're helping me." She pointed in the direction she wanted him to go. The dog sniffed the eggshells and whimpered. Evelyn turned away, watching out of the corner of her eye. Muttering to himself, the dog gripped the eggshells in his jaws and walked into the forest.

When she could not see him anymore, Evelyn walked off in her own direction, cutting through a yard to avoid the other cats. She listened for the screams of children.

Evelyn heard laughter, but did not hear what she sought. She kept walking.

She found them in the last place she looked, sitting on the steps of her house. They sat unmoving, their heads hanging down. Two sets of wild hair, black and blond. They held hands, the one with blond hair having to reach across his chest. They still held knives in their left hands. Their clothes torn, their skin encrusted with mud, a small lump lay between them on the steps. They watched Evelyn with bloodshot eyes as she walked up the cracked sidewalk.

"Did it like we said," the one with black hair spat.

"Paid Robin back," said the other. He picked up the lump, threw it at Evelyn. She caught it, and its own weight caused it to unwrap. It was a coat of black fur. It was still moist.

Somewhere inside herself Evelyn felt sick. But it was like standing on one side of a pane of glass and having someone yell on the other side. She examined the fur. Gently, she touched the fingertips of her right hand to the scratch on her cheek.

You would have died anyway, she thought.

"Thank you," Evelyn said.

"Pleased?" asked the one with blond hair.

"Was not easy."

"Maybe Robin owes *us* now."

"Take us to him."

"All right," Evelyn said. "This way." They hopped up and stood on either side of her. She led the way. Inside, she felt a cold, brutal fury. They had killed a cat. They had ruined something that belonged to her.

"We have to go around the long way, or else we'd have to go past the council."

The one with black hair nodded. "Wouldn't want to hurt any kitties—"

"—would we?" the other finished.

They followed Evelyn into the forest. Soon the ground became soft under their feet. The smell of swamp-water wafted over them like a rotting caress. Next to Evelyn the children smiled—like a child's parody of a hyena, or a hyena's parody of a child. Their faces were thin and stretched, the outline of bones clearly visible. Their left arms ran down past their knees and ended in long, wicked claws. They were naked. Their skin was a sunken green, but their bellies were milky and transparent like the belly of a fish. In their mouths were double rows of small, sharp teeth.

One of them had blond hair running up its back, coarse as copper wire. The other had hair as dark as onyx.

Evelyn did not let herself scream, or run, or cry. The fear was no longer the whole of her. She took refuge in the part of her that no longer felt the fear, the place where her present dwelt. Evelyn stared straight ahead as they passed the place that led to the cat's graveyard.

Out of the swamp, and through the forest's deeps, past trees covered in parasitic daisies, the bamboo grove came into view, and the black-haired creature hissed through its teeth.

"This way," Evelyn said, leading them to the place where she had slept the night before. They knocked their teeth together rhythmically as they walked. She felt one of them reach behind her to touch the other.

The tree Evelyn was heading towards was close. Its roots stuck out of the cut-off hill, through the air and down into the lower earth like a bent and twisted cage, part of which was covered with bamboo. As her eyes focused, Evelyn allowed herself a little smile. "Kitty? Kitty, where are you?"

"Come out Robin," one of the creatures hissed.

"We need information and revenge."

"H-he was here." Evelyn set the fur she was carrying down, and began to pick up pieces of bamboo and throw them aside as though confused. In the few seconds she held them, she examined each piece. Her whole body felt hard, compressed, muscles swollen with blood.

Thunk, another piece thrown aside.

"Where is he?" the one with blond hair asked.

Evelyn lifted another piece of bamboo, one with a jagged end, and stood aside.

"Take us to him, now."

"Or we will skin you, now." Their claws were mesmerizing as they waved them through the air.

From somewhere close, there was a yelp, and the two creatures turned.

"Kitty!" Evelyn cried, as though she had found something. The black-haired creature followed Evelyn's gaze into the nook beneath the tree. It screamed, and it was the same scream she had heard the night before. It leapt down among the roots, frothing at the mouth. The blond-haired creature followed, wailing.

Down in the nook, laid out carefully to show off the dry, rotten insides, were the remains of Evelyn's present. The creatures fell on their knees, they pulled each other's hair, raked each other's flesh with broken claws.

"Dead!" they screamed.

"Murdered!"

"Death. Revenge. Skin to blood to meat to bone to dust."

They turned to look at Evelyn, their eyes glistening, dark orbs set into skull faces.

Through one of those eyes Evelyn drove the bamboo. The creature whimpered dully, and fluid sputtered out over the makeshift spear.

Evelyn threw herself back just as the black-haired creature lunged. Claws grazed her side. Hot blood poured down over her leg.

She forced herself up, then fell back hard as the creature leaped on top of her, burying its claws into her shoulders. It opened its mouth. Hot spittle dripped down on her face. A part of her could only stare at rows of teeth. The rest kicked and twisted to try and keep its mouth away.

Something snarled, and the creature threw itself backward. Its claws slid out of Evelyn's shoulder. The dog had sunk his teeth into the creature's neck. He hung on, scratching with his claws. The creature thrashed about, clawing at the dog's flanks. Evelyn threw herself against it. Everything was a tangle of hair and fur. The stink of sweat and wet dog assaulted her nose and made her wilder.

All the while the one-eyed creature wailed.

The smells and sounds, the pain, the feelings of her muscles—the way they rejoiced in the motion, as though they were moving for the first time—the madness that danced before her eyes like lava—all drove Evelyn on. She laughed at all of it, laughed as she bit green flesh and something oily filled her mouth, as the creature tried to escape and tore out one of her teeth. Their blood mixed and tasted thick and sweet in her mouth. It was a cat's laugh, and a cat's laugh was special. It mixed with screams and snarls, with the hiss of indrawn breath.

The creature weakened, its strength spilled into the shallow water. The dog stood over it, jaws locked over its neck. It squirmed uselessly. A bubbling sound escaped its throat.

"Down," Evelyn gasped. "Down!" The dog looked up at her, perplexed. Then he let go and backed away.

Evelyn grabbed a piece of bamboo, dug it into the ground, and pulled herself up.

"Stay," she commanded. The creature crawled, leaving a filmy trail behind it. Using the bamboo for support, Evelyn walked closer. She watched it crawl into the ditch where the eggshells lay. It tried to say something, but instead clear, oily filth speckled green and white poured down its chin.

Next to it, the one-eyed thing gurgled to itself. It tried to pull the bamboo out of its eye, but its fingers didn't work properly anymore. Drool ran down its chin; its good eye rolled.

Black-hair tried to sit up, and fell. For a second it was still, and then it reached out and pawed at the eggshells. Then it grabbed its mate and held it, held it tight, though the blond-haired creature screeched idiotically and batted at the other with its paws.

The dog snarled, "We can finish them now."

"Leave them," Evelyn said. For a second, the dog glared at her. Then he sat down, turning away from the scene below, and from Evelyn. Evelyn said nothing. For an hour she watched as the creatures died. She smiled, and it was a terrible smile.

But Evelyn knew: They had killed cats, and cats were hers alone.

She no longer remembered that she had not always known this.

When their wounds ceased to ooze, Evelyn crawled down to them. Her hands trembled from weakness, but she made them work: she grabbed the hair on each of the creature's head and scalped them with their own claws. She had to pull hard to tear off the sticky mess.

When she was finished, Evelyn said, "You can have the rest. Plenty of meat and bone."

The dog said nothing.

Evelyn shrugged and picked up the fur. "Come on," she said, and began, laboriously, to walk back. The dog followed. Outside the swamp, he stopped.

"Come," Evelyn said. "Come Doggy."

The dog trembled. "No."

Evelyn frowned.

He wouldn't meet her gaze. "That," he said. "What we did. I . . . I didn't like it."

"What do you mean? We had to do it. They did bad things. Nasty things." Her voice softened: "We did it together."

"No! That . . . that was a cat thing. You toyed with them. You watched."

"I made them pay," she said, confused. She didn't understand what he was saying and ignored the nagging feeling that maybe she should.

The dog whimpered.

"We did it," Evelyn said. "I found my kitty, and I made the mean things pay. Now I'll go back to the cats, and you'll come with me. We'll—"

"I won't. No more cat things. No more cats."

"But . . . but there's plenty of meat and bone. The cats know where. Come."

"Won't."

"Come!"

The dog's growl was weak and pathetic.

"No cats," the dog muttered to himself. "Bad kitties, fucking kitties." He slumped down on the ground. He sneezed several times. "No meat and bone, not like that . . . not like mean kitties."

"Please?" she whispered, too soft for him to hear. Then she jerked up straight. "Stay, if that's what you want," she said. And walked away.

Behind her the dog spoke to himself, biting off his own words. "*If I were a wolf*—"

Evelyn did not turn around. There was no voice behind the glass. It wasn't crying, and she didn't have to listen.

Evelyn walked through the forest alone, carrying the hair and fur. Often, she stopped to rest, taking small joy in picking daisies out of the trees and tearing off the clear, glassy petals. She walked through the swamp, to the place where she had eaten the day before. The terrible beauty wrapped about her ignored that she was dirty and hurt, that she smelled like she'd crawled through a swamp and slept next to a mangy dog.

Evelyn walked out of the forest and saw the cats lounging on the lawn. The metal lay cold and useless without the sun. She could see now that they were nervous and agitated, could see all the fears their feline glamour hid. Then she walked up to them and threw down the bloody scalps, let the fur unroll.

The cats hissed.

She hissed back. Then she straightened, looking down on the cats and meeting their gaze.

She smiled. "I'm your new queen."

Somewhere, the clouds parted and sunlight streamed through. Somewhere, thunder rolled. From the forest came a weak, lonely howl. And the cats turned their bellies up as though to warm themselves on her, offering Evelyn their cruel and beautiful lives.

Imaginix

Maggie Slater

Christof was a creator, and though he hid behind the worn walls of his shop, no one ever forgot. Over the years, he must have become rich; his clients were numerous and ridiculously wealthy. Not many people had Christof's gift of creation, and to obtain a fantasy, who wouldn't pay a king's ransom?

But he was growing old. His whiskers trailed thin and white from his chin and beneath his long nose, and his eyes were tucked inside many folds of skin, though they were as sharp as a raven's. That must have been why he noticed Torin, why he had pulled him off the streets where he begged, and put him up in his own small cottage, connected directly to the workshop. Torin was young, younger than an apprentice should be at sixteen, and although he had the gift, he hadn't seen enough to become a good creator, at least that's what the neighboring shopkeepers thought. All the same, they couldn't argue with Christof. And so, Torin stayed.

It was early in the morning when Torin awoke, the pink tint of sunrise just peeking over the hills. The previous night had been unbearably hot, making the sheets stick to his skin and tangle around him. Sleep had come hard but he remembered dreaming, which was a problem. As he peeled himself free of the sheets, still damp with his own sweat, the boy saw the creature in the corner, scuffling about. It had the ears of a rabbit, but the nose of a fox; its tail was long with a tuft of fur at the end.

When his bare feet touched the ground, the creature spun around and tilted its head, the confused expression on its face making the boy laugh. It raised itself up on its hind legs—huge like a jackrabbit's—and sniffed the air for a moment, before dropping back to the ground in order to scratch itself. Torin sighed, and with a wave of his hand, he erased the creature.

The room was too quiet now, and from downstairs came the sounds of the old man working. His curiosity aroused, Torin tiptoed to the top step and lay down, letting his head dip below it in order to look into the shop below. The old creator sat on a stool, surrounded by shelves of ghostly objects waiting to be detailed and solidified, motioning changes to the imagination sculpture before him. The creation was a horse, though only the front half was finished. The other half was "penciled in," as the old man liked to say when describing the faint, pale lines that outlined the figure like a drawing. Only once he filled in all the organs and bones and muscles would he add the hair, slowly working from the inside out until he was ready to declare the work finished, and thus make it solid and as real as anything.

The horse was for a young merchant who wanted a strong and swift steed that could carry him and his precious wares to far-off destinations. As far as Torin could tell, the horse looked magnificent. Christof added each detail like a master painter, moving his hands like brush strokes while the horse's finished front snorted and pawed the ground. The unfinished half moved also, but sometimes the light wouldn't catch the lines, making it invisible to any eye other than Christof's. After all, he was a painter of the mind.

The old man must have felt eyes upon him; years of sensitivity to detail had not gone without affecting his everyday life. He looked up and met Torin's gaze with a smile. "Come down, boy," he said, snapping his fingers as he spoke, which immediately made the imaginix horse freeze in place, protecting it from accidental changes. "You're still working on that sword, aren't you? Have you finished the hilt yet?"

"No, sir," Torin said, coming down the stairs. "I'm having a little trouble on the inlaid diamonds. I don't seem able to replicate the shine of them."

"Hmm." The old man nodded. "Diamonds are very tricky indeed. Perhaps I should have given you a project with sapphires instead. Bring it here, I'll show you how to do diamonds." He waved toward the shelves where all the unfinished pieces were stored.

Torin went over and gingerly lifted the sketched form of the long sword. It was light to the touch as it was still only an imaginix. Only when Christof made it real would its blade be ready to strike down foes. He carried it over to his low work stool, allowing it to hover a few feet from him so he could take in the whole image at once. Christof snapped his fingers and brought the horse over to the corner, where he froze it again, now that it was out of the way. Then he pulled his stool up next to Torin.

"Now," he said, adjusting his spectacles, "the first thing to do when dealing with a diamond is to make sure you know the shape and cut of it. That's very important because it will dictate the rest of the design." He snapped his fingers, unfreezing the sword. Then he motioned it closer as he inspected Torin's work. "This isn't bad, but you've overcomplicated it a bit. You need only six edges, instead of nine. That will shine perfectly well for the likes of this lord." He erased several of the edges and polished the shape.

Torin flushed at his messy handiwork, wishing his strokes were as confident as the master's.

"Start by creating a temporary light source. It won't be there forever, you'll erase it eventually, but for now, you just need a pattern to follow." The old man made a swift circular motion with his left hand and a small ball of light appeared. "Now follow the rays of light." He traced one of the beams, enhancing it as he went. Touching the sketched diamond, Christof began drawing out glimmers of all sorts of colors, faint hints to strong shines. Torin watched with amazement as the diamond began to look real and truly valuable.

"Now, dust it with shine like so. . . ." The old man made a few slight gestures and the diamond gleamed in its setting. "There we are. A diamond. Now try fixing up the gold trimming, here. It looks a little dull. I think you could put in a bit more shine, and try to polish it nicely when you're done. You'd be surprised how much of a difference it makes on the final product."

With that the old man smiled, the corners of his eyes wrinkling into a thousand little crow's feet while beneath the heavy lids his piercing eyes glimmered. Torin couldn't help but smile back before turning to the hilt of the sword.

It was a long, complex undertaking, and every so often Torin would find his attention drifting off to watch Christof work on some new item. At first, it was a feathered headdress for a rich woman in the town. Then it was a crown, so elegant and regal it could be for none other than the king. After working on the crown, Christof went into the kitchen on the other side of the shop to make himself some tea.

As Torin sat, still working on the tendrils of gold trim running around the sides of the hilt, his eyes drifted to the back of the shop, and to the locked door. Behind it, he knew, were all of Christof's private projects. Torin couldn't help but think of all the wonders the old man must create back there.

Just a few months ago, he had gotten a glimpse of one.

An elderly gentleman, dressed in rich fabrics, furs, and gold entered the shop and asked for Christof personally. "This is a task for the master," he said, his double chin rippling as he glared down at Torin. Christof took the gentleman into the back room and stayed there for the whole afternoon. Nearing sunset, the door to the back room opened and the elderly gentleman exited, walking briskly, his face flushed a deep red.

For nearly a week, Christof only came out of the back room for a meal here and there, and at the end of it, he was so exhausted that he collapsed in his bed and slept for two days. Torin lay awake at night, wondering what the elderly gentleman had ordered. It must be something spectacular, he thought, trying to picture all the greatest things he could imagine while small, unpolished images of those things popped into the air above his head. They hovered there in the dim light until Torin wiped them away and forced himself to sleep.

Exactly two weeks after he had come, the elderly gentleman returned, bringing with him a young man, probably his son. The son held his chin high and walked with a swagger. Christof escorted them both into the back room, and they stayed there for several hours. At times, raised voices echoed through the door.

Finally, Torin's heart leapt as he heard the hinges creak. He stood to the side of the shop, trying to make himself as small and inconspicuous as possible, so that he might get a glimpse of the special item. But it was no item at all. When the young man walked out of the back room, a beautiful girl with a smile like an angel and hair like a raven's wing clasped his arm and looked up at him with deep, emerald eyes. Torin held his breath watching her walk by, her feet small and delicate in soft slippers that peeked out from beneath her finely embroidered gown. She was breathtakingly beautiful and her admiring eyes never once left the young man's face, and with that, he seemed very pleased.

The elderly man, now practically bubbling over with good cheer, shook Christof's hand and gave him a purse of money. "Marvelous job, sir!" he said, beaming. "I never thought she'd turn out so well! You are truly a magician! She has just a touch of my wife in her, but she's a thousand times more beautiful. And her disposition! Perfect!" He continued on, spouting compliments like a fountain until he, his son, and his son's new wife stepped out of the shop and rode away.

Christof stood on the doorstep under the wooden sign as it swung stiffly in the breeze, creaking a melancholy sound. Torin watched him for some time, and when he turned to leave the old man alone, Christof said suddenly, "My boy, never take a job that requires you to shape a person's very existence. It is too great a weight on the conscience." And with a heavy sigh, the old creator walked into the back room of the shop and didn't come out for the rest of the night.

Torin's curiosity about the mysterious room grew. Christof spent more time in it than ever before, even sleeping there some nights. No one had commissioned a private item for several weeks, so if Christof were working on something, it must be for himself, and therefore, must be the most exciting and exquisite thing in the entire world.

When the creator came downstairs late that afternoon, he was yawning. Christof rarely took naps; the only time he did was when he planned on working through the night.

Tonight he would work in the back room.

All the possibilities conjured up by Torin's curiosity popped into the air around his head, and though he tried to wipe them away before Christof noticed, nothing escaped the old man's sharp eyes.

"What were you thinking about, boy?" A smirk danced across Christof's lips as he moved toward the door. "Not trying to figure out what I'm working on, are you?"

Relieved that he wasn't angry, Torin smiled back. "It must be something wonderful," he murmured, his voice tinged with awe.

"Indeed," the old creator said with a solemn nod. "Indeed." And then he walked into the back room, closing the door swiftly behind him.

Torin didn't sleep at all that night, and the images that appeared over his bed did little to appease his curiosity. Around daybreak, he heard the old man come up the stairs yawning heavily as he moved into his room and went to bed. With nerves itching in his legs, Torin got up in the dim light and tiptoed downstairs, forcing himself to turn away from the door to the back room and walk into the kitchen. He took up the wooden bucket by the oven and went outside to pour out the old water from the day before. Then he went over to the well behind the shop to draw some water for tea. Perhaps if he had it ready by the time the master awoke, he would get a hint at what was in the back room.

As he turned away from the well, his hands clutching the wet handle of the heavy bucket, Torin heard a sound come from the back of the shop. Then, quite suddenly, the shutters to the back room opened from the inside, and a girl's face looked out at him.

"Hello," she said. Her smile was a little crooked, though not unpleasant. Her hair, curly and chestnut colored, danced about her face.

"What are you doing back there?" Torin whispered. "No one's supposed to be back there!"

The girl looked surprised. "Oh. I didn't know." Her gold-brown eyes watched him with curiosity. "Who are you?"

"I'm Torin. I'm Master Christof's apprentice."

The girl looked thoughtful for a moment, looking up at nothing. Then she nodded and looked back at him. "Torin, then. I'll remember you."

"Pardon?"

"Shhh!" the girl said, pressing a slim finger to her lips. "You'll wake up my father!"

"Who's your father?" Torin asked, taking a few steps closer to the window.

Her lion-like eyes twinkled with mischief. "Wouldn't you like to know?" With a giggle, she reached out her slender arms and closed the shutters. A moment later, the light in the back room went out, and Torin didn't hear anything more.

Christof came down around noon, yawning as usual. He took a cup of tea and sat at the table, musing silently to himself as he stared off into space. Torin watched him carefully and decided it was best to tell him about the girl who had been in the back room. He feared that he had somehow inadvertently created her in the early hours, and if one of his creations was running about in places it shouldn't be, the master ought to know about it. She was a surprisingly good creation, though, and for a moment he felt rather proud of himself.

"Sir," he said at last, "I fear a dream of mine took on a life of its own."

"Oh, is that so?" Christof said, not sounding terribly interested.

"Yes, sir. I got up early this morning and I saw a girl looking out the back window of your private workroom."

"You what?" The old man jumped to his feet. "Oh, blast me!" he muttered, rushing out of the kitchen toward the back room. The old man disappeared inside and slammed the door. A moment later, Torin heard a snap, and then Christof emerged again, wiping his brow with a handkerchief.

Torin watched the old man pour himself some tea and step outside. Something was wrong; Christof never forgot to freeze an item. Torin's face must have betrayed what he was thinking, or perhaps it was the small image of the creator snapping his fingers, that caught the old man's eyes when he came back in.

"You need to learn to control your projections," Christof said, "or everyone will see what you're thinking." Then he swallowed the rest of his tea, dregs and all, and went into the main workroom to finish the horse.

Torin spent the rest of the day slaving over a pair of silver and opal earrings for a wealthy young lady in the neighboring town. At first, the old man had seemed distracted, pausing every few details to stand up, step back, and glare at the unfinished horse before settling back to work with a huff of irritation. But after some time, Christof relaxed, and even occasionally came by to examine Torin's work, grunting approval at his special touches.

By noon, Christof had finished the horse project, and the owner—the wealthy young merchant—came by the shop to collect it. Torin was surprised by how sad he was to see the horse go. The finished product was the most magnificent beast he'd ever seen, worthy enough to be a king's steed. As the horse trotted off with its owner, Christof disappeared into the back room, gone for another night.

Torin ate dinner alone in the kitchen with only the candlelight and a small creature from his mind to keep him company. The tiny toad danced about on two feet, doing all sorts of silly antics that made him laugh. Finally, though, he erased the creature and trudged up the stairs to his room.

The season had turned and fall was fast approaching; a cool, scented breeze of ripening apples and dried leaves blew in his window, sending a chill through the thin fabric of his nightshirt. Pulling the sheet and blanket up to his chin, Torin did not find it difficult to fall asleep.

In the middle of the night, he awoke as something lightly pressed upon the bed beside his feet. Torin blinked a few times and then saw the girl from the window sitting on his bed. She smiled the same crooked smile, which now struck him as exceptionally charming.

"Hello," she said, her voice sounding a little lighter and much sweeter. "I told you I wouldn't forget you."

"What are you doing here?" Torin asked. "I thought Christof froze you. Or erased you." He tried to remember if he'd been thinking about her, and wondered if the girl was only another one of his thoughts projected while he slept.

Apparently, he forgot to control his imagination again, for a small image of her appeared. Her eyebrows rose and then she giggled, her voice dancing like raindrops on flower petals. "My, you are a silly boy!" She tilted her head to one side and looked at him for a long time. Then she said suddenly, "What does it mean when a boy says a girl is pretty?"

Torin sat up. "What?"

"What's it mean?" She rose and walked over to his meager bookshelf, looking thoughtful, her bottom lip protruding slightly. "I heard a boy say that to a girl in the street just behind the workshop. He gave her flowers, too." As she spoke, she touched the spines of the books, and Torin winced at the dust that came off on her fingers.

"Well . . ." Torin pulled the blankets up about his waist, embarrassed knowing that he had no pants on to speak of. "It means that he found her attractive. You know, he likes her . . . he thinks she looks good." After the comment had escaped his lips, he felt very foolish, so he added quickly, "If your eyes sparkle like stars, then your eyes are pretty. Like that."

She studied the ceiling with a pensive frown. Then the girl smiled her crooked smile and leaned toward him slightly, her eyes dancing as if she wanted to laugh but held it back. "Do you think I'm pretty?" A faint blush spread across her cheeks.

Torin felt his face catch fire, and he glanced away. "I—I think so," he said, shrugging and nodding at the same time.

She muffled a giggle behind her hand. From the next room, Christof murmured in his sleep, and the girl looked over toward the door. "I'm afraid I'm going to wake the poor dear," she whispered. "I'll have to speak with you another time, Torin." She took a step toward the door and then stopped suddenly, turning to look at him with one eyebrow raised. "Do you really think I'm pretty? You're not just saying that?"

Torin shook his head. "No, of course not."

The girl smiled and quite to his surprise, she moved close to him and gave him a peck on the cheek. When she pulled away, her blush had returned. "That's what the girl in the street did. She said he was her sweetheart."

"Am I your sweetheart?" Torin asked, his face and ears burning.

"Oh, I hope you don't mind," the girl said, putting one of her slender hands to her cheek. The white linen dress she wore swished in the silence. It was so plain, but it made her face and hair look all the more lovely.

"Not at all. But I don't even know your name."

"Hmm." Her thoughtful expression spread across her face. "That's funny, neither do I!" Then she giggled and disappeared out the door.

No matter how hard he tried, Torin found his focus interrupted constantly by thoughts of the girl in the back room. All his gold trims and dressings turned to coppery chestnut and all the opals and emeralds turned to amber like her eyes.

That night, Torin sat up and waited for the girl to come back. The horizon was tinged with pink by the time he finally fell into deep sleep, dreaming about the girl with no name.

The morning came with a shock. Two large hands shook him roughly from sleep and he opened his eyes to see Christof's face an inch from his own. The old man's fingers dug into his arms, but before Torin could stammer a word, Christof shook him again and growled, "You've been working on her, haven't you, you idiot! You haven't even learned how to control your own thoughts, how could you think of touching my project?"

"Sir! Working on who, sir?"

The old creator cast a suspicious eye on him. "Don't try to trick me, boy! A creator always knows every detail of his works! I know that child inside and out, and I remember creating everything about her. She has the heart of an angel and the curiosity of a kitten, but she's smart as a scholar! But you . . ." He wagged his finger as Torin lay back on his elbows, mouth gaping. "You changed something about her! Now all she does is pile her hair on top of her head and make faces in anything that will reflect her image! She talks about beauty constantly, and you changed her hair! You made it brighter, shinier. Her eyes sparkle more, and on top of that, she's got on a new dress! And you even made her figure fill it! She should never wear a dress like that!"

Torin's face burned at the accusation and at the image that suddenly appeared in his mind. Unfortunately, it also materialized in the air not far from his head.

The old creator's eyes narrowed and his face turned a bright red. "Just as I suspected!" He erased the image with a brusque swipe of his hand. Then Christof leaned very close to Torin, his nose snorting hot, tea-scented breath into his face. "Now you listen here," he said, his bushy eyebrows pulled so low on his forehead that his eyes weren't even visible. "You keep your mind off of her! I won't have a young whelp mixing things up on me, you hear?"

Then with a tremendous huff, Christof turned on his heels and marched down the stairs, grumbling about mirrors appearing out of nowhere. For the rest of the day, Torin guarded his thoughts carefully, unsure of how he'd managed to get himself into such a predicament. Instead, he trained all his energies on the work that hovered before him. Occasionally, he let his eyes glance over at the door to the back room, and each time, he was met with a cold glare from the master.

For three days, Christof stayed away from the back room, watching Torin like a ram eyeing a prowling wolf. But at last, the old creator's mood softened, and one afternoon he came over to inspect Torin's work. Torin sat on his stool, beaming at his masterpiece. He had slaved for hours on the beautiful new sword, and it was undoubtedly the best imaginix he had ever created.

"That's not bad," Christof said, his voice hinting that it left something to be desired. The old man lifted a hand to his chin and stroked his beard for some time, looking very hard at the sword while his bushy eyebrows arched in concern. "Torin . . ."

Torin winced. Conversations that began with a direct address always ended up becoming a long reprimand.

". . . did you try your best on this piece?"

Torin leapt to his feet. "Of course I did! I put my all into it! Can't you see the diamonds? The glint of the gold? The straight edge of the blade?"

The creator stood quietly, gazing at the sword while he nodded agreement. "I don't mean to say that it doesn't look beautiful. But you're missing something."

The old man seated himself on the stool. "This sword of yours, it's flat. It has no character."

"What does that—"

The old man held up his hand, and then, with a few quick strokes, Christof drew up a new sword and filled in the basic structure of the blade, a task that had taken Torin much of the afternoon. "No real objects are without character. As creators, we must carefully craft that into our imaginix. Let me show you what I mean."

Christof sketched a book in the air. "Take this book for example. It is new; the cover is bright and unblemished. The pages have yet to be spread apart and no eyes have ever touched the words before. Feel how it begs someone to discover it. It looks for someone curious enough to pull back the cover and sit amazed for hours and hours, unable to put it down. Inside, it must have some great secrets that will fascinate a great many readers to come, but what it really wants is that first reader, the first one whose eyes will widen with surprise and glee. But here . . ." The creator drew up a second book, filled in the appearance and let it hang beside the first. "How does this one make you feel?"

Torin looked at both books. The first called to him, and his hands ached to reach out and touch it, to fold open the cover and let it enchant him as Christof had described. The second book did nothing; it was neither enchanting nor exciting even though it had no visible differences from the first. "It doesn't make me feel anything. . . ."

"That is what character is. The first book has depth. The second one is only a shell. Now, take your sword." He turned back to Torin's sword. "It is for Lord Blackworthe's son, is it not?"

"Yes." Inside, the burn of shame ate away at Torin's composure. It felt like the creator had run the imaginix sword right through him.

"Do not think your work is bad," Christof said gently, "but you must try to give your work character. You have a good eye and can reproduce visual items very well, but they lack depth. Watch."

Christof began to work on the second sword, visually nothing more than a hunk of unpolished metal. "What does a sword mean to a young man? You must know the purpose of this item inside and out."

The image didn't change in front of his eyes, it was still very plain, and Torin couldn't see when the old man began tailoring the character of the sword, but he could feel the change immediately. He felt the urge to take hold of the simple hilt and raise it above his head, the weight of the metal pushing down in his palm, reminding him of the security it provided. He was noble and true, skilled at manipulating the blade. He could feel eyes on him, admiring him and revering him. The sword made him feel like a hero.

"You can feel the difference, then?" Christof asked, and Torin turned to look at his own lifeless creation.

With a sniff, the creator wiped away the simple blade he'd used as an example, and Torin winced as the feeling of heroic pride vanished, leaving him cold and more aware of his abysmal failure now than ever.

"Why did you erase it?" Torin cried. "It was perfect!"

The old creator grinned in a kind but joking manner as he rose to his feet and moved across the workroom. "It's not my project. Besides, you need to learn how to do this."

Torin scowled. "I don't know how to add character to a full piece."

"You can," the old man said as he climbed the stairs to his room for the night, "but it's very difficult. It might be best to start over."

Torin slumped onto his stool with a heavy heart, looking with bleary eyes at the sword that still hung in the air. When the muffled thud of the bedroom door closing reached his ears, he folded his arms on his knees and tried desperately to fight off his tears of frustration.

The door to the back room opened softly, and before he knew it, the girl was kneeling beside him, pressing her cool hands against his cheeks. "What's wrong?" she asked.

"Nothing," Torin said, brushing her away. "What are you doing out here? I thought Christof froze you."

The girl chuckled. "Well, that's silly. He can't freeze me. I won't let him."

"I don't think you have much of a choice," he said with a scoff.

Standing up, the girl put her hands on her hips and tilted her head to one side. "Why not? I can change things, too, you know. Just like my father." Then she smiled and blushed. "Do you like my hair? I tinted it a little brighter red. I think it compliments my dress, don't you?"

Torin looked up and heaved a sigh as he looked at her curling red hair and the yellow dress she now wore. It was true that the dress was prettier than the old linen one, and what the creator had said about her figure was true also, but he felt cross and frowned. "And Christof tells me that *my* work lacks depth!"

The girl froze in place, staring at him, and for a moment, he thought he'd actually done something to her. But quite abruptly, tears sprang into her eyes and she bit her lip. "How can you say that? You told me I was pretty! Isn't that what you want me to be?"

He tried to stop himself, but his foul mood had already taken over his mouth. "You're nothing but a shell, aren't you? All that talk of character, personality in work—he doesn't even do that himself! He's just trying to make everything more difficult for me. Go away, I have to start this sword all over again, and I don't have time to be bothered!"

The squeak that escaped her lips made him turn around, but he only caught a glimpse of her as she ran to the back room and closed the door. Torin sighed as his heart sank lower, but he shook it off, and with a swipe of his hand, erased the sword. It would be punishment enough to stay up all night to work until it was perfect. He'd apologize later.

Sunlight poured in through the windows of the shop, heating Torin's back as he lay slumped over his knees on his work stool. The half-finished sword glistened in the light as it hovered in the air behind the thin screen of dust that drifted to the ground in the early morning silence.

Christof shuffled through the workshop to the back room, and Torin didn't flinch when the hinges on the door squeaked. A moment later, the master burst back into the workshop with a cry, stirring the dust with his heavy steps while his eyes darted about, settling at last on Torin who awoke with a start. The old man rushed over to him and took him by the shoulders. "Where is she?" he demanded. "Where's my daughter?"

"Who?"

"My daughter! My creation! What have you done with her?"

Torin stared at the old man, and as he did, the similarities between the girl from the back room and Christof suddenly struck him. Certainly, she was younger and a girl, but now he understood. "I haven't done anything with her, sir," he said.

The old man frowned at him, studying his face, but at last he put his hands on his head and groaned with despair. He shuffled into the kitchen and sank to a chair beside the table, wilting before Torin's eyes. "Is it possible that I erased her without thinking?" His voice was weak and he gazed at nothing.

Torin's heart skipped a beat. "But I saw her last night!" he cried. "She came out to see me, and I—" He swallowed hard, thinking of what he had said to her. "She was here!"

Without telling them what to do, his feet rushed him into the back room, and Christof made no protest. A shelf to one side held a few uncompleted items that glistened in the dim light, but besides two high-backed chairs and a taller work stool, the room was mostly empty. Torin ran to the open window in the back and stared out at the street behind the workshop, but there was no trace of the girl.

"Not all that hard work! Not my sweet, innocent child!" The creator moaned as Torin returned. The expression on the old man's face made him sick to his stomach.

"We must look for her!" Torin said. He bolted through the kitchen, to the street. "She hasn't been gone long. She must be near!"

"But what if she's erased? How will we know?" The old man pulled at his beard. Tears filled the creases of his face as he let out a low groan. "I could never make anyone like her again! It's impossible! She'll be gone forever!"

Torin's heart pounded as he flew out of the shop, frantically dodging the crowds of people just emerging from their homes for the new day. He searched everywhere, down all the paths and roads, and in all the shops, asking anyone who stopped long enough to listen whether they'd seen a young girl with chestnut hair and lion-like eyes pass by. No one had. He searched until he was exhausted, and finally, in despair, Torin walked slowly back to the shop. The glorious orange light of the sunset spilled over everything and warmed his face, but it brought no cheer to his heart. His feet were too heavy to carry him up the few steps into the shop, so he sank down onto them and propped up his chin with his hands.

What if he had erased her during the night when he'd meant to erase a poorly started sword? Torin groaned and let his hands drop so that his head could droop. "This is all my fault."

His eyes began watering as he thought about her crooked little smile and her sparkling eyes. He choked at the memory of her slipping into his room and giving him a kiss on the cheek. He fought back the trembles in his breath and stood up, wiping away the tears. Then swallowing the rest of his sorrow as best he could, he walked silently into the shop.

The old creator still sat at the table, his head cradled in his hands, and when he saw that Torin had returned alone, the old man put his head down on his arms and cried, unashamed.

The old creator closed his shop, and sat alone in his back room for two weeks.

But at the end of those two weeks, he emerged, drifting like a ghost. Torin's eyelids fluttered from half sleep at the sound of Christof's door opening, and he sat up as the creator walked into the kitchen, his face long and worn.

"Is there anything I can get for you, sir?" Torin asked, afraid to raise his voice above a low whisper.

"No." A pair of tired eyes looked over at him. "Have you been sleeping poorly?"

Torin flushed, but nodded. "Yes, sir. Bad dreams, mostly. . . ." he said, hoping it would be enough to satisfy the old man. It was, and Christof shuffled through the workroom and slipped upstairs. Torin leaned his arms on the kitchen table and sighed. How could he tell the old man that he'd spent his nights wide awake, vainly attempting to recreate the girl with the crooked smile? How could he admit his failure?

He remembered every detail of her face, every twinkle in her eye, but it wasn't enough. Her image could stand there looking at him, but it wasn't the same. "I'll always be a bad creator," he whispered into the silent room, "because I can't see anything but the surface."

A knock on the shop door wracked his already aching head. With a frown, Torin went over and cracked it open. Through the slit, he saw a young woman standing on the front step. She was dressed like every other girl in town, with a wine-colored shawl draped around her shoulders and over her head, covering her braided hair. She crossed her arms and leaned back with her chin level to the ground. She looked him right in the eye as she spoke. "I've come to see the creator."

"We're closed," Torin muttered, and tried to shut the door, but her hand stopped it.

"But it's a weekday," she said. "Let me in."

"I said we're closed, miss." His eyes narrowed. Who did she think she was, barging in on him in his misery?

"I'm not going to wait here forever. Let me in!" She pushed the door open with surprising force and brushed past him into the workshop.

"Hey, you can't go up there!" He caught her arm as she reached the first step of the stairs. "Who do you think you are?"

"I don't believe it."

The two of them looked up at the top of the stairs where Christof stood, his face one of utter amazement. Then his mouth spread into a smile and he hurried down the stairs faster than Torin had ever seen the old man move. The creator took the girl by the shoulders and looked her over. "What's happened to you?"

"Aren't you even going to welcome me home, Father?" she asked, grinning a crooked smile. Torin's heart sank into his stomach as she glanced over at him and winked.

"But your hair, it's like unpolished copper! And your clothes! How did this happen? Who did this to you? Where have you been?" The old man's bushy eyebrows drew down into a frown as he held her at arm's length, still glaring at the changes.

"No one did this to me, Father! I did this myself. You always saw me taking over your business someday, but in order to do that, I'd have to be a creator, so I am! You made me one." She smiled and looked over at Torin, who had slowly backed towards the kitchen. "Torin, don't you recognize me?"

"You've changed," was all he managed to get out in a rasping voice.

She turned to her father and gave him a big hug before leading him toward the kitchen table. "I promise, Father. I'll explain everything. Oh, I do hope you're not too angry with me for running off, but you see . . . I had to. I needed to find out who I am."

"I made you who you are! I could have told you if you'd just asked," Christof muttered, sitting down in the chair. "You didn't need to change anything!"

The girl pushed back her shawl and began making a pot of tea. "And you did a wonderful job, but you see, I needed to become myself. You know, the person I'll be for the rest of my life. Doesn't that make any sense?"

The old man grumbled, and the girl laughed. Torin felt out of place, like a frozen imaginix in a room of real things. When neither father nor daughter was looking, he slipped out the door and walked toward the edge of town.

There, the hill swept down to the huge grass plains rippling in the wind below. He sank to the ground and looked out across the land, leaning his chin on his knees as he sighed. The wind blew against his face, cooling it, but inside he still felt the hollow ache of shame. She'd seen more, experienced more, lived and grown into a complex, real person, but he . . . what was he? He hadn't even recognized her.

"I'm nothing but a child," he said, burying his face in his arms. "I'll never be a good creator. I don't have the skill."

"Don't say that," a soft voice said behind him. His face flushed and he refused to turn his head to look at Christof's daughter as she sat down next to him. "Why are you so hard on yourself? What's wrong?"

She tried to rest a hand on his shoulder, but he shrugged it off, and immediately felt bad about it. "I was wrong when I told you that you had no depth. I'm the one who can't see beyond the surface. How can I be a good creator if I can never get past the obvious?"

The girl sighed and lay back in the grass, staring up at the sky. "You'll learn."

"Will I?" He frowned. "I can't even make a simple sword right. I said those things to you because I was ashamed of myself." Torin reached out and plucked a blade of grass, fingering it absently as he sighed. "I feel awful about what I said to you. I'm so sorry. . . ."

He glanced over at her and saw her smile. Sitting up, she crossed her arms over her knees and laid her head down on them as she watched him. Her dark copper braid fell down to the side and the breeze pulled on it gently. "You were mean to me then, but don't feel too bad," she said. "You made me think about it. From what I've seen of people, I don't think anyone really knows if they lack depth or not unless someone points it out. You pointed it out to me, and you were right. I was only what my father had made me, or what I thought you wanted me to be. I realized that wasn't enough, so I left in order to figure out who *I* wanted to be, and in the process, I found a lot of things I wanted to change. I liked being more independent and able to form my own opinions of things without relying on my father's thoughts. I liked looking at things critically and I liked being a little impulsive." Her smile faded, and when she continued, her face was solemn. "I'm lucky, though. Being a creator *and* an imaginix, I can change all those things in an instant. For you it will take a little more time and effort."

Torin sighed, but as he sat, an idea was forming in his mind. It frightened him a little, but the excitement of it made his hair stand on end. So much of his life was devoted to becoming a creator. What time had he devoted to becoming himself?

"I'm going to leave for a while," he said at last.

Christof's daughter laughed—not a giggle like before, but a soft, hearty laugh—and pointed at the image floating in the air not far from them. "I know." A miniature Torin stood clasping a cloth sack and a walking staff, puffing out his chest with pride, emitting a strong sense of adventure.

With an embarrassed chuckle, Torin wiped it away. "I guess Christof was right about me needing to control my thoughts better. . . ." He sighed and looked over at her, almost jumping when he realized how close she was, leaning in toward him.

"I guess you're not so bad at creating character after all," she said, her smile as crooked as ever. "I got a chill from that adventurous spirit."

Then, quite suddenly, she threw her arms around his neck and kissed him. A blast of stars shimmered around them, and when she pulled away, her cheeks were flushed. Torin felt a little dizzy, and his lips tingled.

"Well," she said as she stood up, brushing a strand of hair from her face, "I'll go get your things together!"

"Wait!" Torin jumped up and caught her wrist, just as she began to run toward the house. Chuckling, she turned around slowly, her lion-like eyes bearing spark of pride he hadn't recognized before. "I still don't know your name."

"Well . . ." Her bottom lip protruded slightly as she tilted her head. "I thought it'd be best to name myself after my father, since he created me. So I suppose my name will be Christle."

"I'll miss you, Christle." Torin stooped to lean his forehead against hers.

She sighed and his heartbeat raced as she pressed closer to him. "Come home quickly."

"I'll return as soon as I can," he said, and smiled.

The Mermaid's Silver Pool

Jeff R. Campbell

We don't speak of that day, not to strangers, not even among ourselves. The funeral, the boy, the flash of silver magic—no one expects to find themselves in the middle of such going-ons. It's the stuff of old sailors' tales, told by a night-time fire, when darkness scrapes at the door and folk are willing to believe any foolishness. Some'll shrug and tell you it happened too fast to be sure of anything, others just look away and claim not to recall. But I remember. No, to be honest 'remember' isn't the word for what I suffer. What I saw that day burns in my thoughts still.

Seems a strange place to begin, but the tale belongs as much to Lockee as it does the others. Lockee had been a boy with an ear for tales, hauling in each word and stowing it in his thoughts. They say Lockee knew four ghost stories before he learned his first knot. When other lads Lockee's age were taking up nets and finding young wives Lockee took himself out to the tall ships and a sailor's life. Few expected him to ever return but, many years later, age and a snapped leg heaved him ashore. No one sailors forever. Lockee limped his way back home; his head stuffed with tales from distant shores. He shared those stories with any willing to listen. The unwilling, if they were trapped in earshot, had to hear them too. Lockee had never been a man to hoard comfort; a sailor's life is a harsh one and those tales had been Lockee's succour. A frightened man takes heart from tales of courage; a bored sailor is soothed by stories of wonder. Best not to consider the tales of lonely seafarers. For years Lockee offered his crew-mates the solace of a well-told story. He saw no reason to change his ways just because fate washed him aground.

Then there was Holk, whose funeral none but I will speak of. A fine fisher, a faithful husband and a good father to his boy. Even before he was lost there were few who'd speak a bad word of Holk. His fair features and easy charm had been the talk of maids up and down the shore but whatever mischief there might have been ended when he spoke his vows as a husband. Marriage agreed with Holk, as did fatherhood. He was a happy, contented man well aware of all waiting for him ashore; so when Holk's skiff didn't return that morning, folks started to fret. Morning stretched to noon and the fishers found some reason to leave harbour. They pulled oars or stretched sail, eyes peering into the afternoon glare until they found his empty boat. His nets were still in the water. They pulled the nets in and, to their relief, found them heavy with nothing but fish. There was no sign of Holk, though the skiff bore no signs of misfortune. As the sun fell into the far waters, painting the sky red, the searchers returned with nothing but an empty boat and some fish.

Day followed day, ships went out to fish and to search but nothing more was found. Enid, Holk's wife, waited hopefully on the pier. Each day, when the last ship returned, she made the long walk up to the house Holk had built for them, her face wet with tears. Two weeks passed before the fishers pulled Holk's skiff over to his pier and awkwardly presented it to Dav, Holk's only child.

Dav had always been big for his age, a solemn, quiet boy often called on to watch over his playmates. A responsible lad with his father's features, his mother's deep, expressive eyes and a deliberate way all his own. Just thirteen seasons, but the boy was already taller than many of the men. Standing there, taking the skiff's rope, there were few who could meet the pain in the boy's eyes. While there's never a good time to be without a father, all agreed such a loss suffered at Dav's tender age was a tragedy.

Passing the fishing boat to Dav was the signal the village had waited for; what hope they'd held for Holk's return was gone. Next morning Enid did not come down to the pier to watch the ships. The home she'd shared with Holk was draped in dark cloth and the windows blackened. In keeping with custom, a young maid was sent on a pale horse to fetch back a priest. A suit of Holk's clothes was laid out on a table in the parlour, there being no body to grieve over. A grave was dug, albeit a shallow one. The ground is stony and, with no body to carry, the tomb needed only a slight keel.

The sad day arrived. We gathered at noon, after the fishing was done and folk had a chance to scrub and dress in their finest. Gloom filled Holk's house, men and women walked into a home where only memories were bright. Women made their way to the kitchen, to keep their hands busy and to comfort Enid. Men shuffled into the parlour, to gaze with long faces at the empty suit of clothes and to sip home-brew. Outside, in the sunshine and breeze, children played. Dav sat in the parlour's corner, quiet as ever. Before long the spectre of the empty suit pressed on the men's spirits and, avoiding Dav's eye, they cast about for some means of shrugging off their unaccustomed solemnity. So it was they found Lockee.

"What was it Lockee? Sea-dragon? Ghost of the deep?"

"Aye, titter if you like but your jest scrapes truth." He ought to have known better, ought to have been more respectful, but Lockee could never resist an ear bent his way. "Never found his body, did you? Sea takes who it will, but, when the deep's finished with them, it tosses back a token. Not Holk though, no sign of him, almost as if whatever took him ain't finished with him yet."

"Go on Lockee," one of the men said. "Sea took him, that's all."

"Most likely." Lockee nodded. "Most likely that's all that happened. Sea takes who it will, no man stays master of the waves forever. I will say this though: Holk was as fine a fisher as ever I saw. Watched him row out of the harbour that day and if you'd told me then he'd not be coming back I'd not have believed you. Waves had some leap to them but I'd seen Holk come back from far worse. It's a shame, what else is there to say?"

Sipping his drink, Lockee let his hook lie until he felt them ready. For all his faults, Lockee knew how to tell a story. "Of course, could be more to it than we suppose. Could be Holk was taken by something other than the sea."

"Something like a shark?" Someone asked.

"Not a shark," Lockee scoffed. "Shark would leave a mark, you know that. No, it would have to be something more, something magical."

"A sea-dragon! I knew it!"

"No, you addle-minded chucklehead! Think a sea-dragon would leave a skiff unmarked?"

"What then? Don't be shy with it Lockee."

"You all knew Holk, knew him when he was a new man and not yet married. You've cause to remember the fuss the maids made over him, some of you found wives trailing in his wake."

There were smiles then, memories as warm as the liquor they sipped. "What of it Lockee?" one of the men asked.

"Just this: Swimming in the cold of the ocean are creatures hunting for men such as Holk. To them, such men are treasures to be hoarded. Could be one such creature took Holk, carried him down to their city on the sea-bed."

"What kind of creature Lockee?"

"A mermaid." Lockee savoured their rapt attention as he sipped his drink.

"A what? You mean one of them seal-women?"

"What?" Lockee sputtered. "That's a Selkie, for pity's sake. No, a mermaid.

A woman above, a fish below. They live on the ocean bottom, in the deepest part of the sea. Coming up to hunt, peering through the waves, searching for men like Holk."

"What would a mermaid want with Holk?" An unfortunate, naive voice wondered aloud, to the amusement of many. Flushed, embarrassed by the snickering, the man persisted. "What I mean is, if she's a fish below—"

"A mermaid is a beautiful creature," Lockee said. "They say the sight of a mermaid knocks the breath from a man. Fair skin, voices like a song, hair with a lustre not even gold can match. To see them is to lose your heart. Once, when I was sailoring, I saw a man jump from the tall rigging and fall into the waves. Mate said the man had seen a mermaid and, even from up in the sails, he leapt down to be with her, made reckless with desire."

A hush fell over us all. Instead of grief, our heads filled with imaginings of beautiful women dressed as a fish (which is to say, not dressed at all). Our thoughts were far from the darkened room in which we stood, out among the waves and the creatures glimmering beneath them.

Then someone asked, "That what happened to Holk? You reckon he jumped into the sea?"

"No."

Just one word, not even spoken loudly, but it hauled us back, pulled us hard into that blackened parlour. Dav's voice, Holk's son, reminding us where and why we gathered. The tale's spell was broken. Shamed, the men turned and drifted away from Lockee.

"My father would not have jumped from his boat," Dav said, his voice firm. "He loved my mother, and she's beauty and magic enough for any man."

"You're right, of course," Lockee said. As the others turned away, Lockee stepped right up to Dav as if he'd said nothing wrong. "Holk would not have jumped. Likely the mermaid leapt from the water as dolphins do. Jumped out of the water and snatched up Holk in her arms, carrying him down to her city."

We winced to hear Lockee carry on so, meeting with the boy's grief with such foolishness, but it was his way. A sailor's comfort, the solace of a tale, it was all Lockee had to offer.

"It's a beautiful city Dav, or so they say. Gates of copper, stripped from the hulls of sunken ships—"

"My father would come back to us. If he lived, he'd come back to us."

Lockee shook his head. "Lad, it's the very bottom of the ocean! Those maids, to them he's a treasure, they'd never bring him back."

"He'd come back." There was no doubt in Dav's voice. "He'd come back or he'd die trying. He loved my mother."

"Oh lad, don't you see?" A lesser, more reasonable man would have backed away, would have left the boy to his grief. Lockee was not that man. He'd never been one to hoard comfort. Surely it was better to think of Holk alive and adored by beautiful sea-maids than to think of his cold, bloated corpse drifting in the waves, pecked at by fish. Lockee was trying to help in the only way he knew.

"Don't you see? Down there, in the magic of that place, all those mermaids seem like your mother to him. That's the secret of their magic, the secret of their great beauty."

Dav said nothing. You could see the boy wrestling with Lockee's tale, like a fish struggling to escape a closing net but finding no opening. Dav's brows knitted together, his fists clenched and he closed his eyes tight to try and keep down his tears. As Lockee watched, the young man's composure broke and he was a boy of thirteen seasons, a boy who would never see his father again.

"Lad?" Lockee stared in horror at the change his tale had wrought in the self-possessed boy.

"Can they look like me?" Dav asked, his voice breaking. "Down there in that city, can they look like me? Is that why Da's not come back?"

Hard to say at that moment whose face was more stricken, Dav's or Lockee's. Lockee had meant no harm. His tales were all the comfort he had to offer. The boy had seen straight through his tale though, seen through it to the pain on the other side. Lockee couldn't bear it, couldn't stand up to it. He'd wanted to help, instead his story had wounded the lad. He searched his thoughts, looking for some tale that could mend what he'd broken, but he found nothing.

With no tale to repeat, Lockee did as he'd never done before. He told a story he'd not heard, gave a tale it's first telling. It sprung from him as if it had lain there all along, the truest tale he'd ever spoken.

Putting his arm around the lad, Lockee pulled him closer, speaking in a low voice, intending his words for the boy only. "Down there, in the deepest part of their city, where the ocean's magic is strongest, there's a pool of liquid silver so pure it reflects all the world. Every day your father walks to that pool, dips his hand in it and watches the reflection. You know what he sees? You. Wherever you are, whatever you're doing, he'll be watching. And when hard times come, as they come to every man, just close your eyes a moment and you'll feel him there, reaching through that pool of silver and laying his hand on your shoulder."

At that moment, the women came out of the kitchen, moving chairs and arranging things. The priest had arrived. The service was starting. Dav was called to his mother's side. He moved away from Lockee but not before Lockee had seen his tale take hold. There was a—well, peace would be too strong a word for what settled Dav's features. Still, the boy's tears stopped and his chin shifted as if he'd found some new determination. The priest stood over the empty clothes, speaking the solemn words. Despite her resolve Enid wept to hear a priest speak for the man she'd loved. Dav offered her his hand, sitting there so quietly, his eyes closed and his head bent as if waiting for the service to end.

None of us, not even Lockee, understood what the boy was really waiting for.

The priest was more than halfway through the service when it happened. Suddenly Dav was on his feet, twisting around, his arms reaching out. His chair fell over with a clatter and a bang. The gathered mourners gasped, his mother started, but Dav noticed none of it. His eyes were wild as he leapt up, arms outstretched, his customary caution forgotten. He jumped, grasping for something, and he found it. For an instant Dav hung in the air, pulling with all his might against something unseen, something that wasn't there.

There was a flash, a dazzling silver flash that burned its ghost onto the watching eyes. Dav fell heavily, but, as we blinked away the spectres dancing across our vision, it was plain Dav had not fallen alone. The boy had his hands fastened on someone, a naked man who lay on the floor as dazzled as any of us.

His eyes unfocused, Holk looked about as if lost. Dav had waited for the phantom touch promised by Lockee's story and, when he felt his father's hand reach through the silver pool, he'd seized it.

Folk fell over themselves in their rush to back away from the resurrected fisher who'd fallen into our midst. The priest fell beneath the table. Lockee sat in his chair, his jaw fallen almost to the floor. As her neighbours fled, Enid reached out to her husband, uncertain what to expect. Her hand touched his skin, he turned and looked at her, then he smiled. He breathed her name and he no longer seemed lost. Enid fell forward, into his warm embrace. With a smile Dav released his father. Enid's voice filled the room, a sound joyous enough to banish fear. Those who fled paused.

A horrible shriek sounded from outside the darkened home, terrible enough to tremble even the stoutest of hearts. Those who had rushed away from Holk now rushed away from the horrible wailing. Enid and Holk fell silent, still embracing but frightened. Only Dav seemed unaffected. The boy stood, walked calmly to the door and threw it open. Stooping in that deliberate way of his,

Dav picked up a fist-sized stone and hurled it down into the harbour waves.

"Get out!" Dav hollered. "Get out! He's no need for such as you!"

He stooped, picked up another stone and hurled it. Panic had thrown some of us near the door. We followed Dav out into the day's glare. What we saw felled us, knocked the breath from us. Down in the water of the harbour something floated on the waves, something that shone with a lustre not even gold could match.

Dav marched down to the water, yelling and throwing stones. One splashed right next to the sea-maid. My heart skipped as the beautiful vision disappeared beneath the waves. To my relief she surfaced again a little way off. She shrieked a second time, the sound shrivelling the courage of all who heard it. All but Dav. He picked up another stone and threw again.

And then it was gone.

We picked ourselves up, unable to speak. I'd torn the knees out of my best trousers; I wasn't the only one to do so. Lockee was there, his mouth still hanging open and his eyes as wide as the ocean itself. Inside, Holk was dressing in the suit of clothes they'd meant to bury in his place.

Needless to say, Holk was never allowed out on the sea again. Dav fishes for his family now, and a fine job he does too. Holk wanders over to Lockee's place and the two men drink tea and share a companionable silence as they wait for the boy to return. No one speaks of that day. Not Dav, not Holk, not even Lockee.

There are times though, times when I'm out alone in my boat pulling in my nets, when I look down into the water and see a flash of—something. It tears at me and, though I can't swim a stroke, I want to jump in and chase it, chase it down to the deepest part of the ocean. I'd gladly drown if I knew I'd glimpse again what I saw on the day of Holk's funeral. But then the flash is gone and I stand alone in my boat, feeling like a coward. Yet a day may come when I don't come back, a day when my boat is found empty on the sea. If that should happen, remember this tale and know that I died in pursuit of beauty, a contented man.

Abandoned Responsibility

G. Scott Huggins

E yes!"

The muffled shout bounced outside the trance Responsibility used when she had to do weaving. The word searched for something to connect to as she moved four fingers in rhythm: over-under-under-over. . . .

Then she recognized the voice. The sailcloth fell from her fingers as she rose.

"I need eyes!" The shout was closer now, and the trapdoor in the bottom of her cell rattled and folded up to admit a slim figure in a black cloak. Zhad bounded in, his hair, face and eyes white as clouds beneath his hood. Those sightless orbs wavered and fixed on her. "Look out starboard, Respy," he gasped, "and tell me what you see."

She turned to the slit of the starboard window. The ship was turned spinward, and the red-yellow-white spike of the sun glared in her face so that even her slitted eyes needed a moment to adjust. She extended a wingtip backwards for Zhad, who took it. She pulled him to her, until his hands were on her shoulders.

"Well, what is it?" he asked. "All I could hear was that some kind of boat was in the water, but no one was saying what. Inconsiderate lot that they are."

That explained the excitement. Meetings on the Great Ocean were rare, and usually cause for celebration, trading . . . or fighting. Responsibility picked out the cause of the uproar.

"There's a boat. Bright yellow. It looks as if it's . . . made of pillows?" She had never seen such a boat. It floated like cork, a flea next to the great, flattened curve of *Ekkaia's* hull. A shape lay on it. A man in blue clothing with—red hair. Hair the color of the sunspike at its base. Pirate.

"Pirate?" She hadn't realized she'd spoken the word aloud, but the shock on Zhad's face told her differently. "How many?" Zhad asked. "I didn't hear battle stations sounded. Are you sure?"

"Just one, if he is a pirate. I'm not sure," she lied. "Let's take a closer look." She pulled him toward the hatch. He came reluctantly, obviously torn between curiosity and fear.

"Are you sure you want to risk it? If Haraad catches us—maybe I'd better just climb down. . . ."

"It might be over by then. Besides, everyone who's on deck is looking over the side. If there's ever a time we can get down and back up without being noticed, it's now. If we're lucky."

And it had been long since her last flight; long and too long.

"Sure, Respy, no one ever notices you," Zhad said.

Responsibility flushed. "We got away with it once."

"Once. When we both climbed down. At midnight. And old Goff was on watch. Who sees about as well as I do." Zhad's albinism had blinded him when he was three. The Great Ocean was not forgiving of differences. But then, neither were *Ekkaia's* crew, particularly.

"Are you coming or not?" she said, a little too sharply, sitting on the rim of the trapdoor.

For answer, he scrambled down behind her and wrapped his pale legs around her green, scaled ones. Then he threw his arms about her neck. "I really hate this part," he muttered.

She dropped.

They fell free for less than a second before her wings snapped out and the wind nearly tore her bones apart. The pain was glorious. Twin rivers of fire reached from wingtips to shoulders to ribs as they dropped: a fast spiral around Ekkaia's naked mainmast. A hundred feet of freedom from her cell—a converted crow's nest—to the deck.

Usually, people were waiting for her when she did this. To take her by the wings and escort her back up to the cell for a week of no exercise or visitors (as if anyone but Zhad ever came to see her). This time, she had judged correctly. Everyone was looking over the side at the pirate.

She tried to slow more, to prolong the glide, but Zhad's weight on her back dragged at her.

Even without him, she could not have flown, and the injustice of this still tore at her. As a child she had promised herself that when she was grown she would fly away, like her mother, and never see *Ekkaia* again. Bad enough to be a freak, dusted with emerald scales all over. Bad enough to have spider-veined wings in place of arms. Bad enough to be the only half-human, half-dragon in the whole Great Disc of the World, but to be so here . . . and not even to be able to fly away. Oh, she was light enough. Her bones were hollow, or so the ship's doctors had said. She could glide for minutes at a time; but always, she sank lower and lower, eventually ending up back on the deck where her mother had set her.

The story had been told to her since she understood words. How near the beginning of *Ekkaia's* voyage, a dragon had appeared and left her. The dragon said she had great need and would hold *Ekkaia* responsible for her when she returned. Her mother had left nothing else. No clothing, no secret talisman—not even a name. And so they called her Responsibility, lest any other name displease the dragon. And they kept her in her high cell, lest any harm come to her. They took great pains to see that she stayed healthy. Even *Ekkaia's* bulk and arsenal was no match for a dragon.

But for now—nearly twenty seconds—she was free. No longer Responsibility, but Arz . . . Ezr . . . the name failed her. Was it a fragmented memory? Or was she just stupid, like Jaal down in the cattle decks, whose parents had died when he was two, and who kept prattling on about how his real parents were a pirate king and queen? All things considered, she supposed it would be miraculous if she were sane.

She swerved. The deck of the ship shifted, and a cabin slid beneath them. She hit the roof, and hard, dull bars of pain drove up her shins. She and Zhad staggered apart.

From the top of this deckhouse she could see over the heads of the assembled crew and the other gawkers. As the word spread, more people swarmed out of the hatches to catch a glimpse of the stranger. The crowd was impossibly thick to starboard, and Responsibility wondered if it were possible to capsize a Century Ship.

She thought it unlikely. They were two miles long and nearly a quarter that wide. Each one was cut from the trunk of a single Grove Tree. But if it did happen . . . she shuddered at the thought of being lost in a hundred thousand miles of ocean. As this man had been.

"I can't see much, but they've got him over the side, now. They're in the way, but he doesn't look good. He must have been out there a long time. The pillow boat is up, too, but it looks like all the feathers got dumped out of it. He has red hair, but it's too short for a pirate. . . ."

"He's a pirate all right," said a deep voice behind them.

Responsibility jumped and whirled. Zhad never moved.

"Good afternoon, Cana," he said. "I thought it was you." Nothing ever surprised Zhad. This didn't deter Cana in the least.

"Suppose it had been Haraad?" the big black man said, his voice rumbling. "You'd have your back as red as your eyes, Zhad. As for Responsibility . . ."

She felt her heart sink.

"No exercise for you for a week," Cana said. "Be grateful I don't make it two. No, don't even start. It's not worth my meat ration for a month to be caught helping you. Luckily for you, it's not worth it to me to miss this by escorting your ass back up to your nest."

Responsibility felt the strange urge to scream and smile at the same time. More than any other officer on the ship, Cana had been a sort of father figure. Not that he took any special time with her, but he was in favor of ending her imprisonment. "A dragon is no fool," he'd said. "Her mother knew the risks on a Century Ship. Let her live; don't stunt her growth. That might anger the dragon as much as her death." The rest of the officers had overruled him. No one liked having a scaly, deformed Sword of Dragonfire hanging over their ship, and shutting her up made them able to forget. Still, Responsibility felt a sort of . . . respect for the big man.

Zhad was talking.

"If you'd been Haraad—" he snorted "—I'd have heard you the second you stepped on the ladder. But you couldn't have been, because Haraad's over there." He pointed. The blond, darkly tanned first mate moved through the crowd. Sometimes Zhad's sense of direction was eerie.

Two sailors held the pirate as he staggered over the remains of his boat. He found his footing and took a long pull from the waterflask at his hip. Then he straightened as Haraad broke through the semicircle.

"Ah, Captain." The pirate bowed. His accent was crisp and strange, and the crowd hushed as they strained to listen. "I thank you for your hospitality—"

Haraad cut him off with his usual tact. "The captain . . . has better things to do. I'm his son. And we aren't rescuing you, pirate."

The stranger's odds would have been better a year ago, with the captain, but he had taken sick. Haraad was just enough of a sailor to see *Ekkaia* safely back to the Grove. But there was no way for this man to know that.

The stranger's face fell. "I was afraid of that," he said calmly. "I don't suppose you'd believe me if I told you that our, ah . . . situation . . . has changed?"

The crowd laughed, Haraad loudest of all. It was an oily, ugly sound. But even Responsibility felt the laughter well up in her for an instant. Pirates change? One might as well ask the sunspike to move! Ever since the First Fleet split, the Near Islands had been rife with pirates. It did not look good for the pirate, alone on a Century Ship.

Alone. She almost felt sympathy, then quashed it. Let *him* know how it feels before he dies.

"Yes, I'm sure this is a change for you," Haraad said, smiling. "A change for us, too. One we'll enjoy more than you will."

"The change is greater than you know. There are no more Free Navies. The Consortium has come."

Now the sound that went through the crew was one of fear and anger. Anger that this man really was a pirate; only they referred to themselves as the Free Navies. And the name of the Consortium alone was enough to inspire fear.

None of *Ekkaia's* crew had ever encountered the Consortium. It was a legend. The Consortium were the best swordsmen on the Ocean, though they almost had no need of swords. They were said to have ships that moved without sails; to know spells that would make their enemies explode. They froze dragons into shapes of metal and rode them, so it was said. Froze *dragons*. Responsibility felt her own blood chill. Perhaps that was what had happened to her mother.

If the Near Islands had fallen, then the Consortium was close. And even if they had done *Ekkaia's* crew a great favor by exterminating the pirates . . . at least pirates were known.

But Haraad only grinned. "You think us fools, eh?"

Before the stranger could reply, one of the two sailors took a long, curved bundle wrapped in rags from the shapeless mass that had once been a boat. Haraad took it and unwound the strips of cloth. Then he gaped. The crowd shrank back.

"Omnisword," Responsibility gasped, and felt Zhad stiffen beside her.

The weapon's primary blade was a yard long, with a wicked curve near the end. In spite of this, it was double-edged. A secondary blade protruded a foot from the end of the hilt. Even the shearing-guard's edge was sharp: double crescents of metal over the two-handed grip.

They had never seen one before. But everyone on the ship knew they were looking at the dreaded weapon of the Consortium.

"Your name?"

"Lieutenant Asnai Moshaiu. Consortium Navy. I said the Consortium had come. . . ." He smiled without humor.

"Consortium." Haraad sneered, strode to the middle of the deck, and brought the sword over his head. With one stroke, he buried the curved point at the base of the mast. It sank deep, the curve of the blade disappearing within the deck. Haraad looked taken aback, but continued.

"One sword doesn't frighten me. To me you're another lying pirate. To the Cage with him!" There was another ugly laugh—if a bit less certain—and all eyes looked to the top of the foremast, where two sailors were already beginning their climb. Something that had been a man sat in the tiny cage fixed to the masthead. It was quite dead. Another sailor approached and handed Moshaiu the traditional jug of water and loaf of bread. If the sentence of death fazed him, he didn't show it, but simply allowed himself to be led. As he passed beneath their deckhouse, he looked up, and Responsibility found herself for the first time with a clear view of his face.

It was like looking in the stillest pool. A magic pool that showed a too-perfect copy of her face. It was scaleless and tanned to perfection; subtly heavier, and with round eyes that widened in shock as they met her slitted ones. Moshaiu stopped so abruptly that his escorts shoved him two steps forward. Recognition. He opened his mouth . . . and a saber hilt felled him to the deck, gasping.

"So he likes old Respy." Someone sniggered. "If Consortium women are that ugly, we might all die of fright!" There was another wave of laughter. Responsibility did not hear.

Haraad looked up and saw her; his face flushed dark. "Twenty lashes to her," he said, pointing. "Then get her back above, Mr. Cana!" He anxiously looked skyward. Satisfied that nothing more threatening than clouds hung there, he fingered the rod that hung at his belt. He carried it always, since assuming the power of captain: "Haraad's Rod" was a joke where he could not hear. Responsibility never laughed.

She simply sat there until Cana picked her up and carried her to Haraad.

After Cana left, her breathing was so ragged and loud that she barely heard the click of the lock as she fought not to sob. The spike shone through her window, faded from the white-yellow-red of its sun aspect to the silver and soft gold of its moon aspect, but her body was alive with brown streaks of fire where the slender rod had hit her.

It was amazing what you could do to someone and not actually damage her. A bitter smile played on her face, over her sharp teeth; for all Haraad's fury in beating her, he never quite shed the mask of fear. He would never be rid of the doubt that one day Responsibility's mother would return. He looked at her more anxiously now than before. This was the part of the ocean that *Ekkaia* had been crossing on its outward voyage, when Responsibility had been left on board. No Century Ship could really stay out for a century. Nineteen years later, *Ekkaia's* voyage was almost over. Soon she would be at the Grove.

Haraad's fear was cold comfort. Responsibility had long since given up believing her mother would ever return, but could it be coincidence that this stranger had appeared? Now? With effort, she picked up her tin cup. An easy task for anyone else, difficult for her. Her wings were twice as long as the arms they replaced, and the two ridiculous-looking finger stubs halfway down each leading edge were almost useless. The bottom of the cup was as clear as a lady's makeup mirror.

She saw the same face she had always seen below hair black as the night sea. Fine-cut and freakish. Light traceries of scales so fine as to be almost invisible covered her features, thickening as they ran down her neck. And except for the scales, she saw a face identical to that of the man also locked in a cage, the one person who had ever looked at her with something besides pity or fear.

Two weeks, Haraad had said. He'd be dead by the time she could get out again.

She lay back and watched the stars twinkle fitfully through the thatched roof. The thatched roof that just barely kept out the rain. She had never wanted to find out how much worse it would be if she punched a hole in it. There was no place she could go when the *Ekkaia* was at sea, and no port where anyone would be friendlier than her shipmates. But suddenly, she had a place to go, even if it was still on the ship, and she laughed at her folly. The sound was so loud in the tight room that she reflexively stifled it in case anyone else heard.

An hour later, balancing unsteadily in the high winds around the crumpled roof on top of her cell, she was no longer laughing. The roof had been stronger than it looked, and her wingtips were raw and bloody. Only her elbow grip on the thick central spire of the mast kept her from being blown off.

From here, *Ekkaia* was a forest of sails, all taut and billowed by the ship's winddrivers. The real wind pressed feebly against them, blowing, as it always did, toward the spike; sunspike or moonspike, it made no difference. High above, the kite sails fluttered, anchoring them against it in the high winds.

Below, the sea licked its lips, hungry.

The Cage dangled within her line of sight. Nearly half a mile away. She'd never make it.

Her roof was gone. She had no choice. For the first time in years, she lifted up a silent prayer to her mother, wherever she might be. Then, using all her strength, she launched herself into the air.

And she was free again. The night wind seemed to sing as it enveloped her, throwing her toward the moonspike. She fought back, angling into the breeze, turning into the blast from the winddrivers. She caught one and soared up, up over the starboard mizzen.

She was flying. The name welled up unbidden in her, and she almost shouted, *Ezra*, *Ayzir*, but again, it would not come clear.

Her momentum flagged, and she looked to the bows. She was out of the path of the artificial wind, and already far too low. Any minute now, one of the watch would look up and see her. . . .

"The-e-e-e-r-r-m-a-l-s!"

The shout pierced the night. It almost sounded like music. Was that him? She looked to the Cage. It was the pirate. He was shouting at her. Repeating. But what did that strange word mean?

He burst into full song. A trained tenor carried through the night, singing the most unlikely lyrics. "Thermals, dammit! The kitchens, the kitchens, O-ve-r the kitchens! Over-the-kitchens there lived a maid-a bright and chee-ry fairy-maid . . ." He looked away and trailed off into nonsense.

"Shut up, you blasted pirate!" a watchman called.

The kitchens? Why the kitchens? But her spiral was inexorably descending and could only end with her capture. She wove between the port and starboard mizzens. The smell of fresh bread filled the air around her. Behind her she could hear Moshaiu remonstrating:

"But good sir, I have nothing else to do with my time, and you have already killed me . . ." Moshaiu's voice rang out mocking from his cage. Drawing attention away from her. She swept in over the chimneys.

And gasped as a column of hot air rocketed her upwards. She nearly lost control and plunged downward, but her wings held, aching with overuse. She fought to stay in the warm air, tightening her spiral as much as she dared. The ship whirled about her. . . .

Beneath her.

She was frozen in wonder. She was at least twice the height of the mainmast!

And the foremast was below her. She knew what to do. She glided down, backed wing, and grabbed onto the bars of the Cage as if she'd been doing it all her life. Quickly, she clung on to the bars, chest heaving with exertion.

"You had me worried there a minute . . . Azriyqam."

She nearly fell off the mast. The name reverberated through her head like a soft hammer. *Azriyqam.*

"Who are you? How do you know me?" She was amazed at the steadiness of her own voice.

His wolfish grin faded. Then, for the first time, she heard uncertainty in his voice. "Don't you know?"

Despite the risk, she leaned back and peeked downwards. "Know what?"

Was that pity in his face? "No, you really don't. All this time, I thought you must . . . and it's obvious you recognized me, so—"

"I recognized *me*," she blurted.

The grin returned, a little. "We do favor our father."

Responsibility—*Azriyqam?*—almost plummeted to the deck. What was he saying?

"I know this is unbelievable to you, but I'm your brother," he said, watching her face. "Half-brother. Gods, I never imagined. . . . Well, it's a long story. . . ."

"We have plenty of time," she found herself saying harshly. "Until someone looks up here, anyway, and then we don't have any, and I've been waiting for twenty years for this story, so make it good!" She bared her sharp teeth. At that moment she imagined herself capable of biting through the iron of the cage. Her four knuckles whitened on the bars, but she never thought about letting go.

"You haven't foreseen a damn thing, have you? In fact, you've barely flown until tonight. You didn't even know how to use thermal columns for lift. Oh, Shaaliym," he said softly, "what have we done?"

"Stop talking to yourself and start talking to me!" she whispered fiercely. "Or I'll kill you right now!"

"Considering that your lack of knowledge almost certainly means you haven't brought a key with you, I might be wise to take you up on that offer, given the alternative." His eyes were empty, and Responsibility knew it was beyond her power to make him say anything. He was, after all, already dead. In two days, he would be screaming for death. Until thirst closed his throat forever. Until exhaustion robbed his limbs of strength and the gulls began to. . . .

She closed her eyes against the vision. But he merely sighed, and his courage

seemed to return. "You deserve more of us. Where to begin?

"Our family rules Halskette—one of what you call the Near Islands."

She gaped at him.

"No, quite literally, *our* family. It's a twin throne—dragon and human. The intermarriage helps keep the kingdom together. Every ruler has two—at least two—consorts. One dragon, and one human. The purebred children—like me—maintain the succession; the halfbreeds are councilors. Mediators. Wizards. Dragons foresee; humans invent; halfbreeds usually do some of both."

Responsibility's head whirled. Halfbreeds? More like her? She was the only one . . . wasn't she? But the stranger—her brother?—was continuing.

"When the Consortium attacked, Father was taken by surprise in one of his border towns, and Shaaliym—your mother—fled with you."

"And she just left me here." A lifetime of anger was building—a solid mass behind Responsibility's eyes and lodged in her throat.

"She didn't have a choice." Asnai's eyes met her own, unblinking. "The Consortium has . . . their own style of magic. They're almost all human and they don't like halfbreeds. Everyone in the Twin Kingdoms thought that the halfbreeds would be slaughtered if the Consortium won. And your mother had foreseen that you and I would meet at sea. She must have thought that we'd be the last two of our line. No one knew then how overextended the Consortium was, nor that we could possibly ally with them, no matter how shakily."

"She could have kept me with her. You could have come looking."

"Well, dammit, what do you think I was doing?"

Responsibility jerked back from the fierce anger in his voice.

"You mean—you came here expecting to find me?" The thought was too horrible. Too big. She had never thought to be looked for, never watched over, except in the hopeless, little-girl fantasies of every orphan. But the fantasy was true. And now it would truly die.

"I can't think of anyplace I would have expected to find you less." He laughed grimly. "I certainly never thought Shaaliym would have put you on a Century Ship! I suppose she thought I could get you off one fairly easily; we pirates do have a reputation . . . but it's certainly the last place anyone would look.

"Everyone knew Shaaliym's foreseeing. She never came back, and so, when I was of age, I took a place in the Consortium Navy. Father . . . loved Shaaliym very much."

"And you expected me to know all this?"

"Some. Enough that you'd be expecting me. All halfdragons can foresee to some extent. I guess that answers the question as to whether foreseeing is instinctive or learned. . . ." He sighed and touched his hands to her fingers. "I can't believe I've found you, Azriyqam. I mean, I always knew, but . . . it's rather like coming face to face with a minor legend."

Responsibility was too startled to laugh. Then Asnai's face fell. "Unfortunately, I rather thought that your mother or you would take it from here. Or that I'd actually have a ship of my own, as opposed to being shipwrecked. I suppose it's only a matter of time before someone spots us and puts you back in your cell."

"Or puts you both in *your* cell, you idiots," a low voice whispered below them. "You know what the penalty is for helping someone in the Cage?"

Responsibility nearly jumped out of her skin. "Zhad?" How dare he interrupt! No, wait. His very sensible concerns began to penetrate her fog.

"Who else? Now let's get out of here before we're all three forced to share that thing."

It was too much to handle at once, and she found herself focusing on the obvious: "How did you get up here?"

"Rule number one: being blind is almost as good as being invisible. No one ever suspects you of anything except idiocy. Seeing as I spend a good deal of time with you, Madame Azriyqam, I suppose I can't blame them."

The name sounded strange from Zhad, but there was no time to comment.

"This is my brother, Zhad; I'm not leaving yet, I don't care if they do put me up here with him!"

"Yeah, yeah, so I heard; who's asking you to leave him? Pass this up." A key jangled.

Asnai reached down for it. "More pleased than you know to meet you, Zhad. Azriyqam, your friend is smarter than either of us." The Cage flew open. "Now how do we get past the guard?"

Zhad huffed impatiently. "What guard? Why guard you? No one likes you, so who'd risk helping you? The watchmen look out, not in. Unless you attract their attention. Let's go!"

The climb down seemed the longest in Responsibility's life, but they finally touched deck and shrank into a doorway. "Now what?"

"Now we go fetch your brother's boat and . . ."

Asnai put a hand on Zhad's shoulder.

He started to shake it off, then stopped. "What?"

"That boat was punctured by your helpful crew. Besides, even Consortium lifeboats just float. We'd be picked up at dawn."

An awful silence drifted over the three of them.

Zhad's brash demeanor had evaporated. "But I thought, you . . ." He looked ready to cry.

"Wait. Where are the lifeboats?" Asnai asked.

"All along the hull, port and starboard," Responsibility said. "But only the big ones have sails. Any we could lower would only have oars."

"That's all right. Can we get a winddriver?"

Zhad started to laugh hysterically. "Nothing's fastened down firmer than a winddriver, you moron! You'd need a day with all kinds of tools; I know. I've heard them complaining about changing them. Besides, she just told you they don't have sails!"

"Trust me, Zhad. If they change them, are there spares?"

Zhad's breathing eased. "Yes."

"Can you get me one?"

"I suppose. They aren't big."

"Good. Go. Azriyqam and I will get the boat ready."

Zhad disappeared into the night.

"You're just giving him false hope," Responsibility said. "There are watchmen all along the edge of the deck."

"Actually, I have an idea about that."

The sailor on duty yelled and jumped a foot when she fluttered down right next to him. Instantly, shouts of query raced along the decks of the *Ekkaia*, and the two nearest sailors came running.

"OOOOO-KAAAYYYYY!" the first man shouted. "Just Responsibility!" Then he turned on her as the other two came up. "What are you doing out of your cage, little bird?" he said with a nasty grin.

"I thought you were locked up," said another. "Wouldn't want to anger Mommy, now, would we?"

Responsibility remembered every contemptuous glare she had ever received and channeled it at the sailor. "My mother is already greatly displeased." She spread her arms wide. Her wings. They stared. "And she hears you."

Was it a twitch, or did one of them look nervously skyward? She thought she had used such threats far too often as a little girl for them to be really effective. But they were now in the same seas where her mother had first appeared. . . .

"Yeah, right," the first man said. Then something large dropped down, almost on top of them. The sailor and his companion froze, cowering. Responsibility flattened and rolled out of the way. Asnai stood over her, omnisword already whistling through the first sailor's neck. The man at his back drew his sabre and gurgled in agony as Asnai lunged backwards, piercing his chest with the shorter blade.

The third man had his sword out to parry . . . and looked very surprised when Asnai reversed his swing and brought the pommel blade around to crush his skull, as if with a battleaxe. The three had made no sound. Around the curve of the hull, there were no shouts of alarm. And there was a hole three sailors wide in *Ekkaia's* port watch.

After lowering the boat, Responsibility and Asnai made their way back to the mainmast. "He's not here," Asnai said.

"Yes he is. He's just about as good at not being seen as he is at not seeing."

Asnai still jumped when Zhad dropped between them from the lower spar. "Nice to see you still have faith in me, oh highly connected one," he said, bowing to Responsibility. "I don't know what you'll do with this and no sail." He took the winddriver—a bulky construction of polished wood and stone covered in arcane symbols—from between two large boxes where it had lain concealed and gave it to Asnai.

Asnai looked it over, then rammed the hilt blade of the omnisword down into a pair of runes. They shattered, leaving empty holes where they had been inlaid.

"And so much for the reaction-damping spell. Just like old Free Navy days." He grinned. "Zhad, remind me to acquaint you with the Laws of Motion some time. Benefits of a Consortium education. Now see if you two can scare up some food and water. Then join me. Five minutes. No more." He was gone.

They almost made it.

They were halfway across the open deck when the shout went up. "Boarders!"

Responsibility and Zhad froze, not needing to speak. The guard had changed. They dropped the supplies. Zhad hesitated.

"It's open ground, Zhad, run!" They ran.

The cries echoed around them. "Boarders! Portside amidships! Boarders! Boarders!" The deck began to ring with the soft thunder of men running. Pounding feet fell behind them. From the corner of her eye, Responsibility saw another sailor turn in pursuit.

And then there were figures in front of them. Two. Four. A dozen. They stopped, ten feet from the side. All eyes were fixed on them, and on the three dead bodies they hadn't had time to hide. The circle closed in.

"Stop!" she cried, spreading her wings out to their full extent. The sailors hesitated, sabers drawn. In the dim light, they had not recognized her.

"Responsibility? You?" Cana stepped forward from his place at the edge of the deck. "I'd never have believed . . ." His voice hardened. "Why?"

The disappointment in the big man's voice hurt more than she thought it ever could. But before she answered, Haraad stepped up beside him.

"Because she's a pirate-loving traitor." All eyes looked toward the foremast, though it was out of sight. "Yes, he's gone," Haraad shouted. "And here are his accomplices. The only question is, where is he?" He stepped forward, menacing. Responsibility willed herself not to look over the side.

"You do not dare hurt me," she called, so everyone would hear. "My mother will take a terrible vengeance on this ship if I am harmed."

A murmur of unease drifted through the sailors. But Haraad's voice was steady and dead. "If your mother had wanted you unharmed she would have been back long ago."

"Are you certain of that?" she said, forcing herself to step forward and meet his eyes. "How certain are you?"

He blinked!

"Do you see my face? Do you remember the pirate's? My mother foresaw that my brother and I would meet here. My mother foresaw this moment. Perhaps she is planning a family reunion."

Haraad stepped back. He had seen the resemblance. The sailors murmured. Still, Haraad hadn't taken his eyes off her. She couldn't keep this up much longer. What was Asnai doing?

"Perhaps she was testing you. Perhaps she is testing me. Perhaps—"

The winddriver started up with a booming roar.

"Mother! You have come for your daughter at last!"

They couldn't help it. Every eye shot fearfully to the sky. No one was watching her.

As Responsibility, she had never offered violence to anyone. She had never dared.

Azriyqam lashed out. Her wings had twice the reach of a man's arms. Her left wing buried its horny tip in Haraad's throat. Her right cut into Cana's thigh, and she winced with the big man as he fell, breathing a silent apology.

"Zhad, on my back!" The slight figure crashed into her and held on. She let the momentum carry her past the two bleeding men. Then she was over the side, and falling, falling toward Asnai's waiting boat. By the time anyone thought to call for bows, they were well out of range, *Ekkaia* dwindling in the distance, the winddriver's magical jet kicking up water behind them.

"No supplies, eh?" Asnai deadpanned. "It's going to be a long, dry voyage home." The moonspike was beginning to lighten, turning its colors to that of sun. Asnai steered them toward it.

"Home?" Azriyqam said as she watched *Ekkaia* vanish astern. The end of her captivity had come. She had gotten—in a way—the vengeance she had always wanted.

The end of the world had come. She had never thought beyond that. Somehow, she had assumed that everything would simply . . . stop. She hoped Cana was all right. "Home?" she said again. "Where is it?"

Zhad took her shoulders in his hands. "Home is where it's always been," he said softly. "It's just that we've never been there."

Azriyqam felt herself nodding. Somehow, it would be enough.

Gratitude

Margaret Yang

Klaus and I had been lovers for nearly two months when he had his ninth heart attack. This one came soon after dawn, as he was rising for the day. I was boiling water at the hearth when I heard Klaus gasp and fall back on the bed. I ran to his room and saw him clutching his chest and moaning, one pale, plump, hairy leg sticking absurdly in the air, red slipper still dangling from his foot.

I crawled across the high bed and held him as well as I could, although my arms could never come close to encircling his girth. "Just breathe, Klaus. All will be well. Breathe."

"Hurts," Klaus gasped.

"I know, darling, I know. I will make you something for the pain when it is over. Just breathe with me." I inhaled deeply to show him how. "Look at me, Klaus. Look at me." I held him and breathed with him until finally, after what seemed like hours, he no longer clutched at his chest as if he would tear it open. His face, which had gone as white as his beard, regained some rosy color as the blood returned.

Sitting up as if nothing had happened, Klaus began his morning ritual of coughing and spitting. With his heart still weak, it took him longer than usual to rid himself of the night's phlegm. I sat behind him, patting his back while he hacked and wheezed, willing the lungs to clear themselves.

When he was down to rumbling and throat clearing, I told him I would prepare a special tea. Klaus just nodded as I left for the kitchen. I took a handful each of lindenflower and elderflower and added them to the boiling water, along with willow bark for the pain. I hadn't any angelica, or strong peppers, so I put in some juniper to help his blood circulate, along with a fresh radish—sliced thin—to strengthen his heart. When the tea had steeped well, I added a generous measure of honey to cover the odors, and to appeal to Klaus's sweet tooth. I wanted to be sure he actually drank it.

I poured it all into a large mug, then opened the kitchen door and set it outside to cool. On the ground outside the door was a basket of fresh eggs and a small crock. I opened the crock and sniffed the dried flowers inside. Red clover. That, I assumed, was for me. The eggs, a gift for Klaus. I gathered both crock and basket and brought them inside, along with the tea.

When I returned to his room, Klaus was settled back on the pillows, happily smoking his pipe. I handed him the heavy mug. He set down the pipe and took the mug in both hands. "Thank you, Rheva. Thank you."

"It is my gift to you," I said, completing my part of the ritual. "No thanks are necessary."

Klaus lowered his eyes with a small smirk, as if he found my way of giving quaint. Perhaps to him, it was. He gulped half the tea, then reached for his pipe.

I sat opposite him on the bed, tucking up my legs and resting my chin on my knees. "Must you?" I asked. "Smoking does you no good. These attacks, they are coming more frequently."

Klaus gestured with his pipe. "I endure them."

"But they cause you such pain! And you are weak for days after. I fear that one day, it may kill you."

Klaus laughed, his naked belly shaking with his mirth. "My dear girl, you will be in your grave, your bones rotting, and I will still be here, as jolly as ever."

"Yes, you will," I said. "Turning your airways inside out every morning in coughing fits that last longer and longer each day."

Klaus reached over and stroked my cheek. "Are you speaking as my healer, my dear?"

I swatted his hand away. "I care about you too much to see you suffer so."

He leaned back and took another drag at his pipe. "Giving up my smoke would cause me worse suffering."

I narrowed my eyes at him. Klaus sat back on his pillows, alternately sipping tea and taking puffs of his pipe, completely content with the world. I shook my head at my foolishness. I should have known better than to argue. Nothing ever upset him. Nothing at all. Not even that which would have killed a mortal man.

I rolled off the oversized bed, threw on my new blue cloak, and reached for my boots.

Klaus regarded me casually. "Are you going out?"

"My garden needs tending," I said.

"You will return later, will you not?"

"Perhaps."

My dismissive tone didn't bother him, either. He merely took another drag on his pipe and smiled. "Very well. I may be in the stables today."

I slipped out through the kitchen door, taking some cheese and a handful of raisins for my breakfast. I could have gone back and thanked Klaus for them, but I did not feel like giving gratitude that day. I strode purposefully away from his house, cradling the red clover under my arm like an infant. By now, the sun was already well above the horizon, and I had work waiting for me at home. There were weeds to pull, rosemary and sage to harvest, and if Klaus was going to continue to smoke that disgusting pipe, I also had to gather more wintergreen leaves.

Of course, if it hadn't been for Klaus's smoking—and its ill effects—I never would have met him in the first place.

He had come to me one late summer day when I was working in the storage shed behind my cottage, hanging bunches of dill and basil from the rafters to dry. Standing on tiptoe atop the tall stool, I didn't see Klaus walk in until he got my attention by barking out a loud cough, startling me off my perch.

He caught me as I fell, setting me on my feet and apologizing for giving me a fright. He told me that the cough was the reason for his visit, as he'd heard I could cure anyone of anything through my teas and tinctures.

"I doubt I can cure everything, m'lord," I said. "Perhaps you are thinking of Nola, who lives across the river. She can make—"

"You are called Rheva, are you not?"

"I am, m'lord."

"Then you are the one I've heard tell of. And you must call me Klaus."

"Very well, Klaus." The name—so foreign, so unique—felt dangerous on my tongue. I moved my stool near the open door, where the light was better, and invited him to sit. I moved away, busying myself in the farthest corner of the shed, my thoughts dizzying in their rush to be heard. Klaus? Here? It was like a fairy story told to a child: exciting, yet completely unreal. When my hands had stopped shaking and my breathing had returned to normal, I crept forward to where Klaus still sat, patiently waiting.

"This problem," I said. "You've had it long?"

"Quite a long time. But it's been worse since midsummer." He stroked one side of his snowy beard. Up close and in bright light, he didn't appear as old as I'd first assumed. Certainly he was *old*, in the way that immortals are, but the skin around his eyes was smooth and unwrinkled, and his hands appeared soft and unblemished.

"Have you taken anything for the cough?" I asked.

He nodded. "I was given something. Horehound and licorice drops, I believe. The taste is pleasing, but no matter how many I consume—"

"Oh! No, no, that will not do." Everyone thought they could make healing concoctions. Few could. That magic was all but lost. "The horehound is useless, and the licorice is dangerous in large amounts. It leads to weakness and high blood pressure, sometimes even sexual difficulties." I clapped a hand over my mouth, feeling my face go hot. Did I just actually say that? To *him*? I stepped back, retreating into the shadows.

Klaus stood and followed. I pressed my back against the far wall of the shed. Klaus stood directly before me. "In humans too?" he asked, completely composed.

I ducked my head, glad for the dim light. "Well, I'm unsure. I understand the anatomies are . . . similar . . . so I assume . . ." I suddenly saw that I was staring at the place right below his belt buckle, and quickly returned my gaze to his face. I did not have to tilt my chin up far to look at him. He was not the giant I'd assumed him to be. Of course, my family is tall. My brother, Jak, stood nearly five feet. "I will make you a tea," I said, fleeing to the opposite wall, where jars of dry herbs and fresh honey stood on shelves. "Much better than candies. But I will need to gather pine needles and wintergreen."

Klaus threw his head back and laughed: a hearty, masculine laugh that collapsed into wheezing at the end. "You have all this, here, but no pine needles? Pine grows everywhere."

"Exactly why I do not store it, m'lord. I gather it as needed."

He nodded as he gave me a measuring look. "I will help. And my name is Klaus."

He came to me often after that, usually for more tea. On such occasions, he'd present fistfuls of pine needles and wintergreen leaves already picked. Or he came with other gifts: giant wheels of cheese, loaves of bread, ribbons for my hair. On the day he presented me with a tiny box holding two dozen precious cloves, my gratitude overflowed and I kissed him over and over, like a small bird pecking at his cheeks, his neck, his lips.

Now, as I stepped around puddles in the lane, I was glad that I had not worn Klaus's latest gift. Soft slippers were fine to wear to a feast, but my old boots were more suited to a damp day. My new cloak was equally impractical, but also irresistible.

The quickest way home was to follow the village wall. As I passed the

factory gates, I wrinkled my nose at the foul odor. They were making paper again. Next week, it would be paints in vivid reds, screaming yellows, and other childish colors. I took shallow breaths through my mouth until I was well past the village and had turned into the rutted lane between cottages that led to mine.

I was just reaching for the latch on my door when I saw Shirl, my dearest friend, burst out of her own door across the lane. She was followed closely by Tavel, and Tavel's little sister, Trix.

They clustered on my doorstep, the tops of their heads no higher than my shoulder. Shirl had used ribbons to plait her hair into a complex weave that showed off the exquisite point of her ears. Her dark grey cloak was freshly washed and mended, and I wondered if she was in love again. Tavel wore her usual solemn look. She seemed to take everything seriously, while Trix, three years younger, never took them seriously enough.

"Good day, Rheva," my friends said almost at once.

"Good day to you." I turned to Tavel. "And how is your mother? Does she sleep well these nights?

Tavel nodded soberly. "The valerian you gave her does help."

"But she complains it smells of father's old socks!" Trix giggled behind her hand.

I laughed. "Next time, I will add lavender to cover the odor. And you Shirl? How are your crops? We have had much rain of late."

"Never mind that," Shirl said, swaying from foot to foot with impatience. "What about *him?*"

"Him?" I said. "Him who? Do you mean Klaus?"

"Yes!" they chorused.

"Is it true what they say?" Trix asked. "That he can keep giving pleasure an entire night?"

I smiled, shaking my head. "No. He is ordinary."

"He is far from ordinary," Shirl said.

"Very well. He's immortal. But otherwise, quite normal."

"But what about . . ." Shirl trailed off, embarrassed.

"Well perhaps—*perhaps*—due to long experience, he is a bit more *accomplished* than most—"

"I knew it!" Trix squealed. She poked a sharp elbow at Tavel. "I told you so!"

Tavel merely stared at me with that grim look of hers. I knew what she was thinking. Why me? Why did Klaus, who could have anyone he wanted, choose me? Certainly there were elves prettier and more clever than I. But it was me he wanted, so I shrugged and tried not to question my good fortune. To be sleeping with Klaus was like sleeping with Aubrey, the legendary elf-king. It was like sleeping with a god. If a god asks you to be with him, you don't say no. You thank your lucky stars and open your legs.

"I nearly forgot," Tavel said, digging through the basket on her arm. "Mother said to give you this." She held out three fat beeswax candles and a honey crock. "And she says to come by for a large bag of apples."

"Thank you, Tavel. Thank you for this gift."

"It is my gift to you. No thanks are necessary."

Even Trix was silent during the giving ritual, although Tavel spoke the words quickly, as if she wanted to get it over with. I bowed my head, uncomfortable with my friend's generosity, when I obviously needed it the least. Looking down, I was glad that I'd left my new shoes at Klaus's house. My old boots were only slightly less shabby than theirs. But there was nothing I could do about my new cloak. Its kitten-like softness all but purred in the sunlight. Trix's cloak, in particular, was almost more patch than cloth. Why hadn't anyone noticed? Why hadn't anyone given her wool for a new one? Of course, *I'd* noticed. Now that I had two cloaks, it was right to give her my old one. Yet, perhaps, with Trix's fair skin and blue eyes, my new one would suit her better.

Before I could decide, the door burst open behind me. "Where have you been?" my elder brother demanded. "Oh! Good day, ladies. Finished with your prattle?"

"Good day, Jak," my friends mumbled. They quickly said their goodbyes and melted away: Shirl to her own cottage, Tavel and Trix continuing down the lane.

"I said, where have you been?"

I pushed past Jak and through the door. Since our parents died, Jak thought of me as his charge, even though I did the caretaking more often. I set the candles, honey, and red clover on the table in the center of the room. "You know exactly where I've been."

Jak slouched in the corner, folding his sinewy arms across his chest. He usually spent his days gathering wood in the forests. He was quick as well as strong, and gathered much in a short time. Nearly every dwelling on our lane was kept warm by Jak's gifts. He spent the rest of his days in the archives, reading dusty tomes that no one else had time for. Jak tapped his foot impatiently. "So, did you ask him?"

"Not yet."

"Why not?"

"I haven't found a way, yet." I draped my beautiful cloak across a chair. It looked odd there, the soft wool too fine to belong to the same owner as the rough, pine-branch chair. I should have given this cloak to Trix when I had the chance.

"You must find a way." Jak loomed over me.

"Why?" I asked. "Why do you want to work for someone you despise so?"

"I only want to work for him for a short while." Jak reached out a finger and touched the edge of my cloak. "Anyway, it seems to have turned out all right for you."

I stared at Jak, my mouth open. "I don't work for Klaus!"

"You don't?"

"No." I grabbed the broom and started sweeping the hearth. Jak always left things in such a mess when I was away. "Besides, it's not that simple. Stablehands are born into the job, inheriting it from their fathers and mothers."

"Surely the ruler of the land can make an exception for me."

"Klaus does not rule this land! He passes no laws. He has no authority. He doesn't even live in the village."

Jak slapped the table in front of him. "It matters not where he lives. The entire land revolves around him. He is central to everything we do. He even expects tribute."

I swept ashes into the farthest corner of the hearth. "We do not pay tribute. We give *gifts*. How else will the factory workers and stablehands be fed? Be clothed?"

Jak threw himself into a chair. "Ah, he's got you fooled as well."

"How dare you?" I gripped the broom in both hands, willing myself not to fling it at his head. "A gift is sacred. You don't disparage a gift."

Jak's heavy eyebrows came together as he gave a snort of disgust. "Factory workers and stablehands have the best of everything while others starve."

I gasped. "Nobody starves here!"

"Don't you remember, when we were children, the hungry months between the dwindling of winter's stores and the first fruits of spring?"

"Those are lean times for everyone, everywhere."

Jak raised his eyebrows. "Everyone? Even those inside the village walls? What do you suppose they eat?" He leaned forward with a nasty grin. "What do you suppose *you* will eat this winter, little sister?"

I slammed the broom down, the handle clattering on the hearthstones. "Stop it right now, Jak. I will hear no more of this nonsense. I have herbs to gather." I marched to the shelf on the opposite wall and snatched up my largest basket, then crossed to the door and flung it open. "And if you expect me to cook you a meal tonight, you'd best do some gathering of your own."

It wasn't until some days later that I found the courage—and a reason—to ask Klaus to make Jak a stablehand. I stood near the hearth in Klaus's kitchen, stirring thyme and rosemary into a stew for our supper. The herbs were for flavor as well as health. I'd added every ingredient I could think of to strengthen his heart: carrot, barley, radish, leek. I'd even slipped in a small amount of hawthorn to help his blood circulate.

Klaus stood behind me and put his arms around my waist, nuzzling my neck. "Mmm, that smells wonderful, Rheva."

"I hope it will be." I took the pot off the fire.

"You do not have to cook for me, you know."

"I know."

Wherever Klaus went, he found a welcoming home, and was served a warm meal. When I was young, mother always made an extra portion of food, just in case. But Klaus never came to our cottage. He didn't know what he missed. Mother's food was the most delicious in the land. I'd learned all of my herb lore, both for cooking and for medicine, from her.

Klaus kissed me once more. "Thank you for cooking, Rheva."

"It is my gift to you," I said. "No thanks are necessary." I felt so happy and safe in Klaus's arms, I almost asked about Jak right then. But before I could, Klaus pulled away and started slicing bread to go with our stew.

"Let us eat quickly then," Klaus said. "After, I must go see a small boy named Homm."

"Homm? I do not believe I know him."

"His parents supervise the factory. Homm was playing with some other boys and hurt himself falling from the village wall."

"Is he hurt badly?"

"Not badly." Klaus ladled stew into bowls and led me to the table. "He has an injured arm." Klaus spooned up some stew, smacking his lips and smiling. "Delicious."

"Shall I accompany you?" I asked. "I may be of some help."

"That would be a great kindness."

As we ate, I thought about Klaus and his own kindness. If he arrived at the child's home at suppertime, the boy's parents would naturally want to feed him. By arriving later, he would free the parents from that obligation, and allow them to concentrate on their son.

After supper, we walked the short distance to the village. I seldom passed through the gates. It wasn't forbidden, I simply did not often have a reason to enter.

The cottages near the outskirts were very much like those outside the village. As we walked, I began to notice small differences: roof thatch woven tighter, front steps standing straighter, more windows, some with curtains. The lane was wider here, with more space between dwellings.

We turned down another lane, wider yet, and walked farther into the heart of the village. Klaus knocked at the door of a house far larger and grander than his own, and Homm's parents ushered us into a room with a polished stone floor and sturdy wooden chairs covered in soft cushions. Lamps and candles burned everywhere, as if oil and beeswax were unlimited, casting the room in harsh shadows.

Sitting on a chair, surrounded by plump pillows, sat a child of six or seven, who I assumed to be Homm. His younger siblings crowded around Klaus, giggling and jostling for hugs. Klaus pulled bags of candy from his pockets and handed them about, saving the largest for Homm. The mother allowed the little ones to give Klaus their thanks, then shooed them away.

Klaus knelt by Homm's chair. "Think you're one of my caribou now, do you my lad?" Klaus chuckled. "Think you can fly?"

"I'm sure now that I can't," Homm said glumly.

Klaus laughed harder. "Be glad, young one. I've brought the best healer in the land. She will cure your hurts so quickly you will think it magic."

I nodded silently. Natural magic was practically the only kind left.

Homm rolled his eyes toward me. Still, I said nothing, feeling woefully out of place in this splendid house. I'd always known that factory workers lived well. I'd thought the gifts they gave when they came for my herbs were fine indeed. Looking around, I now realized that they thought me worthy of mere tokens.

Homm's mother bade me sit next to her. I felt unsteady on the delicate cushion, as if I would slide off. I adjusted myself carefully, while looking at Homm's mother out of the corner of my eye. She seemed dressed for a feast, although this was not a festival day. Her shoes looked brand-new, and she wore a string of pink beads wrapped around her neck, another at her wrist.

She smiled at me. "I'm so glad you came, Rheva."

"Have you put anything on his arm?" I asked. "Or given him any medicine?"

"No. We did not know what medicine to give."

I slipped off the cushion, more sure of myself now. I approached Homm, who looked up at me with solemn eyes. I gently examined his arm, which was swollen and bruised, but not broken. I told Homm's mother which herbs to put into a poultice, and which to make into a tea.

Homm's mother thanked me in the traditional way, and prompted Homm to do likewise. I assured them that no thanks were necessary.

After that, there was not much more to say. Klaus joked with Homm for a few moments and played with the younger children, but we soon took our leave.

Later, in bed, I rested my head on Klaus's chest and listened to his heart. It sounded strong and healthy. Perhaps my stews and concoctions were doing more good than even I'd hoped. Klaus rested comfortably on the pillows, absently rubbing my back. Now was my chance to ask about Jak. I took a deep breath and willed courage for myself. This shouldn't be so very difficult. Humans, I knew, asked for things all the time. Klaus received hundreds of letters each year from children asking for toys. They didn't seem to find this behavior at all shocking. But we were different. Asking for something was so completely foreign, I didn't know if I could do it.

Still, for Jak's sake, I had to try. I thought about the house we'd visited today, the life a factory worker lived. If Jak became a stablehand and moved inside the village, he would be so rich and happy that he'd forget all about wanting to leave.

I took a deep breath and squeezed Klaus tight. "I want to ask you something."

"Anything, my love," Klaus said sleepily.

"I want to ask you *for* something."

Now I had his attention. "Yes? What is it?"

"It's about Jak. He's . . . he has a great need." No, that wasn't right at all. There had to be a better way. "He very much wishes to serve you." Better. I lifted my head to look at Klaus in the fading light, hoping to see his reaction before proceeding. He simply looked at me curiously. Even so, the words would not come. "Jak is very hard-working and very good with animals," I blurted. "His fondest wish is to become a stablehand and work with the caribou." There. It was done. I held my breath, waiting.

"Whatever for?" Klaus asked. "It's a horrid job. Messy."

"He seems not to mind filth," I said. That much was true, anyway. "Can you do this for him?" I looked into Klaus's eyes, forcing myself to speak, despite my shaking voice. "For me? Please?"

Klaus nodded. "Done! If it means that much to you, you may fetch him in the morning, and I will show him what to do."

"Truly?" I scanned his face to see if this was one of his many jests, but it was too dark, and I did not dare light a candle.

"Truly," Klaus said. "Anything for you. I adore giving you gifts, Rheva. You are always so pleased to get them."

"Oh thank you, Klaus! Thank you!"

He reached for his pipe and tobacco, and shambled off to the kitchen to light it at the hearth. He came back a moment later and bounced on the high bed, bringing the distasteful smell of burning tobacco with him. "And now, Rheva? Shall I give you another gift?" He pressed his body against mine.

"Ah, the pipe!" I said, taking it out of his hand. "You'll set us both alight."

Klaus tried to kiss me, but I gave him only my cheek. "Do you know any herbs good for burns?" he said as I set his pipe aside. He ran his hands down my legs and up between them. "Or for setting someone on fire with passion?"

"Is there nothing you take seriously?"

"Nothing."

"Sometimes I think you should go play with toys instead of giving them away."

"A grand idea," Klaus said. "But I'd rather play with you."

I relaxed into his embrace and kissed him back. After all, Klaus was quite generous in the bedroom too.

The closer we came to Yule, the more Jak talked of leaving. He acted as if he were actually going somewhere. Right up to winter solstice, I made every effort to talk sense into him. "I thought you were happy as a stablehand," I said. "You're so good with the caribou."

"Naturally," Jak said. "Gaining their trust is as vital as gaining Klaus's."

"And you have. Klaus speaks well of you." I thought the praise would appease him, allow him to give up this ridiculous fantasy of leaving.

Jak merely raised his eyebrows and reached for the raisins I'd set aside for the special pudding. I snatched them away and added them to the pot. "Attempting to leave is pure folly," I said.

"The barrier between worlds is open but one night a year," Jak said. "If I don't leave at Yule, I shall have to shovel caribou dung for another twelve months. They stink now, in the cold. Can you imagine the stench in the heat of summer?"

"It's all but impossible to cross to the human world," I said. "The veil between worlds is narrow, and even Klaus must fly to breach it."

Jak said nothing, slouched in his usual sullen posture against the wall, arms crossed over chest. He had no idea how the world of humans worked. I knew, because I'd asked Klaus once. For humans, nothing was given freely. Everything was bought by the sweat of one's own brow. Klaus had simply shrugged when I said that it sounded unbearably lonely. As much as Jak annoyed me sometimes, I could not wish for him such a bleak existence.

I finished stirring the pudding, then wrapped it in a thin cloth and set it carefully in a shallow pot of water to steam over the fire. I had to balance one end on a brick, since the cooking pot had a broken handle. I remembered mother breaking it when I was small, spilling hot soup all over the floor, Jak telling her not to cry while helping her clean it up.

"What of the letters?" Jak said suddenly. "Letters reach us from the human world."

I laughed. "Are you as small as a letter now, Jak? As thin as parchment? Besides, those letters come *to* our world, not from it. And do you have any idea where Klaus must cross the barrier each year? Where the veil is thinnest? A frozen wasteland in the far north!"

"Truly?" Jak asked. "Or is that just what he wants you to believe?"

I turned my back and got out ingredients for the honey cakes, stirring flour, oats and nuts together. I fetched another bowl to dilute the honey with milk.

Jak reached for the spoon. "Here, let me do that." He poured a sizable measure of honey into the bowl and started adding milk.

"Don't add too much at once," I said. "It will make lumps."

"I know," Jak said. "I remember making this dish with mother."

I smiled. "And you made it lumpy every time."

"I'm better now," Jak said, stirring in mere drops of milk. At that rate, it would take him all day, but the honey would be smooth indeed. He added another drop and churned the honey thoughtfully. "Did you ever wonder why Klaus remains here among us?"

"Please, Jak. Let's just cook."

"I am cooking," he said, stirring harder. "But aren't you at least curious? Why not fly abroad at Yule and remain among the humans?"

"Come now, Jak. You know why." Every elf in the land knew about the curse. Five centuries ago, when the veil between the worlds was thinner, a human—Klaus—somehow entered our world. Being ignorant of our ways, he accepted every gift offered, giving scant little in return. Aubrey, the elf-king, grew so angry at this that he cursed Klaus, making him practice constant generosity. If that weren't enough, he also cursed poor Klaus with immortality, making sure his example would live on forever. It was something the elf-king thought humans should learn. From what I knew of the world of humans, Aubrey was right.

"How do you know he was cursed?" Jak asked. "Perhaps it's just a tale told to us as children. To make us behave."

"What?" I took two steps back from the table, as if to distance myself from Jak's words. "How can you say that?"

Jak calmly lifted the spoon from the honey to check its thickness. He added more milk. "Why will you believe the story of the curse, but not believe me when I say I will leave?"

"Ah, Jak. You make my ears hurt. I will listen to no more of this. Give me that bowl. I'll finish the honey cakes myself."

Jak folded both arms protectively around the milk and honey. "Very well, very well. I'm sorry. I meant no disrespect."

I doubted that, but I let him continue stirring while I beat two eggs to add to the batter.

"Suppose Klaus really was cursed," Jak said.

"Suppose?"

"Very well. He was cursed. But years ago, when he started giving gifts, he just gave sweets or a few coins to people he knew. Except it wasn't good enough. His appetite for generosity has grown, and now it is out of control. Humans expect his gifts. All he does is feed the greed of human children, undoing everything that Aubrey strove for." Jak pushed the bowl toward me. "There. It's done."

I reached across the table and grabbed the bowl, thoroughly sick of his insolence. I emptied the honey into the flour mixture, and banged the bowl on the table. "I don't understand you at all, Jak. You dislike Klaus so much, yet you actually think he can help you escape."

"No, little sister," Jak said. "It is *because* of Klaus that I want to escape."

And escape Jak did, just as he said he would.

I went to Klaus's house before dawn on Yule morning, wrapped in my warm blue cloak against the winter chill. I cleaned out the hearth and laid a fresh fire, thinking a warm and cozy home the perfect gift for his return.

I expected to find Klaus exhausted from his night's travel. He did not, of course, visit every human child. Parents had always given gifts in his name. But each year, a few believers received a Yuletide surprise. Klaus traveled far in the human world to make his deliveries. I thought I would see a weary old man, but Klaus was a firebrand, storming into his house.

"You!" he shouted, pointing a finger at me. "You!"

I leapt up from the hearth, still holding a handful of kindling. "What? What is it, Klaus?"

"I can't believe you'd do this to me! After all I've given you!"

"What?" I asked. Splinters from the wood dug into my hand as I gripped the kindling tighter. "What have I done?"

"I should have known better. Your brother was too eager, too quick to take responsibility with the caribou. Letting him distribute the load on the sleigh was a huge mistake. It was too easy for him to leave off my best gifts and substitute himself."

So he'd done it. He'd actually done it. I stood mute at the fire, not knowing what to say.

Klaus took off his boots and hurled them across the room. "I should have known you two were planning something the moment you asked me to make Jak a stablehand. An elf, *asking* for things! But I let him into the village because I knew how important this was to you, Rheva. I helped Jak at every turn. And this is the thanks I get. Out!" He pointed to the door. "Get out!"

I couldn't move if I tried. It was all so shocking. Klaus? Angry? I'd never seen him frown, much less yell. And why was he angry with *me*?

"After all I've done for you," Klaus bellowed. "After all I've done! I can tolerate a lot, Rheva, but ingrates are not welcome in my house."

Ingrate? What did gratitude have to do with anything? And then, suddenly, like a spark leaping from the fire, I saw the truth. The story was indeed true—all of it—but one piece was missing. One essential piece. The elf-king's curse had nothing to do with generosity, because you cannot make humans generous. It was far, far worse. Aubrey had cursed Klaus with an insatiable need. More than sweets, more than his pipe, more than anything, Klaus craved gratitude.

He sagged into a chair, covered his face with his hands, and wept like a child. "Poor Jak," he moaned. "Poor, poor Jak. He will be lost, a stranger among those not his kind, doomed to remain there forever. How could you

Rheva? How could you let him do that?"

I could endure Klaus's sorrow even less than his anger. I threw the kindling into the flames and ran to him, putting my arms around his neck. "I am sorry, Klaus. I am so, so sorry. I didn't know! I never believed he'd truly—"

Klaus flung my arms off. "I said, get out. Ungrateful little wench. Out!" He stomped to the door and flung it wide. "Now!"

I fled into the cold, leaving everything behind, even my beautiful new cloak.

The next time I saw my cloak, it was wrapped securely around the shoulders of my friend Trix. The soft slippers were also no longer mine, being planted squarely on Trix's small feet. She stood in the middle of the lane, talking to Shirl. Trix didn't seem to mind the early spring slush on her fine shoes.

When she saw me approach, Trix walked in the other direction, head down, face flushed. I don't know why. To my mind, Trix and Klaus made a fine couple. Trix was younger, poorer, and more easily impressed than I was. Surely she would be grateful to him for a longer time.

Shirl saw me and waved me over. She gestured to Trix's back, now far down the lane. "She was trying to talk me into planting tobacco," Shirl said. "You know, for his pipe."

I gasped. "She *asked* you?"

"No, of course not, but I understood what she wanted. Oh!" Shirl reached into her apron pocket. "But I have a gift for you." She handed me a folded piece of paper. It was the thinnest, most delicate page I'd ever seen. If I held it to the light, I could see right through it.

"It's beautiful. Thank you, Shirl. Thank you for this gift."

"It is my gift to you. No thanks are necessary. Open it!"

I unfolded the paper and found a letter, one that resembled any other begging letter from a human child. But the handwriting was large and erratic and extremely familiar. "Dear Sir," it read. "I have been a very good boy this year. I have done everything I promised I'd do. Please send me a new tire for my bicycle and a warm coat, as winters are cold here in Sweden." Sweden? I tried to remember conversations with Klaus. Was Sweden a good place? I hoped so. I raced through the rest of the letter. "My little sister likes to pretend she can cook. She needs a new cooking pot, as the handle of hers is broken." The letter was signed "Jakson." My father had been named Jak as well.

I looked up at Shirl, who beamed. "Where did you get this?"

Shirl waved my question away. "Someone in the factory gave it to Flocka, who gave it to my cousin Julo, who gave it to my mother. Everyone knows that Jak stowed away at Yule, and we've all been waiting for some word from him. This is his, isn't it?"

I nodded, clutching the precious letter to my chest. "Thank you for this, Shirl."

"I told you, no thanks are necessary." She embraced me. "And now I must get to my planting."

I took leave of Shirl and we went our separate ways: her to the fields, and me to the woods. I needed to gather more wintergreen and pine needles. If Shirl truly would plant tobacco, Klaus would need more—much more—of my special tea.

The Benefits of Public Transportation

Todd Austin Hunt

Thornberry tried to keep his eyes on his hands, which were folded in his lap, but the tusks of his interviewer were too gruesomely fascinating to ignore. They curved up from Mr. Rosaday's mouth a full five inches. Streams of chicken-fat saliva dropped from the tips like water from a melting icicle and splattered the piled skin of his neck.

Mr. Rosaday grunted then grabbed another chicken leg from the shrinking heap on his desk. He shoved it into his mouth. The sound of crunching bones made Thornberry's eyelids shudder. Rosaday swallowed and stabbed a greasy finger into Thornberry's resume, adding yet another smudge.

"Huh," Mr. Rosaday said. "Huh. You have nothing here. Absolutely nothing." With a flick of his wrist, he tossed the resume into Thornberry's face. His black eyes careened in their sockets, as if trying to find something useful on Thornberry. He scoffed, which caused a bubble of snot to form around his snout. "I don't understand how you *ever* found work, Mr. Thornberry. You have no qualifications. You have no talents. Your experience is drivel, and, quite frankly, I cannot stand to look at you while I eat." Mr. Rosaday pointed to the door. "Please leave."

Thornberry nodded and picked up his dirty resume. Mr. Rosaday continued chewing. Thornberry tried to stand up straight as he left, but his shoulders were too heavy with the burden of what his wife was going to say once he got to their flat.

"He was *right!* You are nothing, Nigel. How long do you think we can live on *my* savings? I'm weary of you walking through that door with bad news." Virginia sat at the head of the kitchen table, her face furiously red. Thornberry blocked out her voice and wondered why he had ever married this pig. Virginia had a svelte figure, but her head was pink, round, hairless and fat. *Well,* he thought. *She does have some hair. Hanging from her chin and ears.*

"Are you listening to a damn word I say?" she shouted, which caused her jowls to shake. "Our babies deserve only the best, but the way you're going, we'll never be able to save enough to get both of them into university."

Thornberry sighed. The babies sat on the sofa in the adjoining living room, watching their favorite video. He had lost count of the times he had kept himself from grimacing at the sight of the boys. Paulie and Gary were identical twins, identical blue eyes peering voraciously at the television screen, identical creamy-white tapered scalps peaking identical chubby segmented bodies. *Why are my sons grub worms?*

Paulie and Gary held hands and chuckled at the video, which played the same short, confusing scene over and over again. It showed a darkened room where two crouching, shadowed forms played with spherical objects on the floor. The figures froze less than a minute into their play, then scurried out of the picture, leaving the tiny spheres all over the place. A moment later a larger figure came into the room, falling down and lying there for a few seconds until the whole thing restarted. Paulie and Gary giggled gleefully.

Thornberry got up and pounded the OFF switch. "What *is* this, Virginia? Why do they always watch this?"

Paulie and Gary made keening noises behind him.

Virginia looked away and said, "Oh, it's just something that all the kiddies like to watch nowadays. Leave the babies alone! Let them watch."

Thornberry stared at her for a second then shrugged. He grabbed his coat from the tree and muttered, "I'm going out for a bit."

The closed door only muffled Virginia's whine. "Don't you dare drink any of that gin!"

"I don't know what I'm going to do, Angel. I realize it's important that I find a job soon, but I can't understand *why* it's important. Every day I feel like a stranger within my own family." Thornberry took a long swallow of his Greene King Indian Pale Ale. "And . . ."

"And what?" Angel asked. She sat on the other side of the plush booth, dressed as usual in her white seraphim robes. The golden pipe-cleaner wings and halo jiggled slightly with her movements.

Thornberry glanced around, nervous. The Shakespeare's Head was crowded, but the patrons seemed absorbed in their own talk. "I . . . I think they hate me."

Angel replied by folding his hand in both of hers. Her smooth brow remained unruffled, but the woman's pink lips pressed tightly together.

"My wife is a sow and my sons are larvae, and they hate me. You can see why I'm not that motivated. I can't understand how this happened to me. Was I blind?"

"You let them use you, but I know you're not blind."

Thornberry pulled his hand from the embrace. "I'm not sure about that. I don't *have* any talents worthy of fetching me work. I'm a husk of something I've long forgotten."

Angel shook her head and slipped a pen from her robes. She wrote an address on a serviette and tapped it with a golden fingernail. "His name is Sport. He developed this technology expressly for someone like you. I want you to go see him; I've already talked to him about your problem."

Thornberry examined the name of the establishment: Center of Magnified Abilities. "What does this 'Sport' do?"

"He scans your mind for one strong talent, then magnifies it tenfold. Once he does this, you'll have no trouble finding what you're looking for."

"How come I've not read about this in the papers?"

Angel made an impatient face. "It's a customized technology, and he only assists those I suggest. Please trust me, Nigel. I *only* have your best interests at heart. You'll see."

"He doesn't use any medicine?"

"No. You have nothing to worry about, silly." Angel's cheerfulness disappeared and she reached over the table, grabbing his face in her warm hands. "You can't wait to see him, though, you *must* visit him tonight."

"Tonight? The place is open? It's nine-thirty."

"This chance is the only one you'll get. You don't have much time before all job opportunities are closed down. The Center for Magnified Abilities is the singular path to success." Pulling his head close, she kissed him on both cheeks. "How I love and miss you, brother."

Wings bouncing, she walked out of the pub into Kingsway, vanishing in the pedestrian traffic. Her words had caused an unexpected pain in Thornberry's stomach, which confused him. Before he could ponder what she said, a man walked by, whispering in his ear, "Look how he's shrunk these past few weeks. He's handsome like I remember."

Virginia's voice.

Thornberry spun. "Here, sir. What was that trick?" But the man had faded around a corner.

Thornberry rubbed the paper between thumb and forefinger, looking into his beer. The whole situation was absurd, preposterous. But how sane was his life right now, anyway? Men mimicking his wife and disappearing. Even if his family hated him, he was responsible for supporting them. That's what good fathers and husbands did.

Touching his cell phone through his coat, he considered calling home. For a moment. Virginia would merely talk him out of it. Thornberry memorized the address, folded the paper and put it in his pocket. Abandoning his IPA in fear of further hallucinations, he left in search of Sport.

When the Routemaster bus arrived at his destination, he stood on the bottom step staring dumbly at the churning mass of people being sucked down the gullet of the Finchley Road Underground Station. He checked Angel's handwriting for the tenth time, but the address was correct.

This has to be a mistake.

A hand hit him hard on the back, knocking him off the step. The serviette fluttered to the pavement. He whirled around.

"What's wrong with you, you bloody wanker? First you stand in the way of everyone's trying to get somewhere; now you're spreading your filthy rubbish around. Don't you see the bin?"

It was the conductor. The man wore a paisley suit instead of the traditional uniform. His barrel chest was frightfully huge, which was offset by a scrawny neck and a punk haircut dyed a brilliant red. Automatically, Thornberry said, "Sorry." He bent over to pick up the paper, but the conductor stepped off the bus and shoved him to the ground. Dozens of legs found detours around his startled form.

"What is it you're so sorry about, wanker? When are you going to spit out that teat and start talking?"

Thornberry rose to his feet, infuriated. "I've had quite enough of this. . . ."

The punk-conductor laughed and slapped him with the back of his jeweled hand. Touching his burning cheek, Thornberry growled and balled a fist. He crunched his knuckles against the conductor's nose and was startled by the hot burst of blood that splashed his fingers. His body tensed for a counterattack, but the man grinned at him. Blood from the pulpy nose flowed down, painting his teeth.

"I think this is the right stop," the punk said. "You have a nice day." He boarded the bus, which stood still for a moment while Mr. Rosaday's voice emerged from its intercom speakers.

"You wasted your charm on that one, sweet. He looks no different to me, only he's even less a man now." The bus roared away, enveloping Thornberry in a huge cloud of exhaust, and he bent over in a coughing spasm.

A hand touched his shoulder. "Are you okay, Mr. Thornberry?" The voice came from a young man, dressed in a fluorescent green football jersey, black Umbros, shin pads, and razor cleats. His face was lean and handsome, comfortable with smiles. One thick eyebrow rose at least an inch above the other. He carried a small sign. "One meets the strangest people in a big city like London. Strange people who do the most bizarre things. I just take it for granted, now. It's good of you to defend yourself. Makes a better man."

Thornberry wiped blood from his knuckles with a handkerchief. "I think I'm going crazy. I'm hearing voices. Did you hear that from the bus?" He took a second look at the outfit. "Are you . . . Sport?"

What a ridiculous name. What isn't ridiculous?

"Yes and yes. You need not worry, though, these things *are* being said." They shook hands, and Sport held the sign up. Center of Magnified Abilities was written in thick black strokes. "Angel described every notch and crevice of your face."

Thornberry pointed to the stairs leading down onto the tube platforms. "Where's your office, er, headquarters? Angel must have made an error."

"No. She led you to the right place." He flourished his hand to the red circle bisected by the blue line just outside the station. "I like to think of it as an office evolved, for I know no stasis. It's in constant motion." Sport cleared his throat. "Are you ready to begin the process?"

Spheres of fear were gathering in Thornberry's chest, coming together to coalesce into a heavy stone weighing him down. *Why am I doing this? This is a boy, a football player, not a doctor. How can he possibly help me, anyway? I have no talents to magnify.*

Sport's blue eyes gazed at him in a way akin to Angel, as if he understood every doubt and fear in Thornberry's mind and wanted desperately to dissolve them.

"Do you trust Angel, Mr. Thornberry?"

"I do trust her." Thornberry rubbed his eyes with his thumbs. "But, honestly, I can't tell you *why* I trust her."

"Trust is enough. This will change your life. For the better." Sport gestured to the entrance with his head. "Follow me?"

Thornberry glanced to the long stretch of Finchley Road curving away to the right, flanked by leaning three-story buildings. He liked to think that Paulie and Gary and Virginia were worried about him, but he knew it wasn't true. Maybe doing this would make him someone to worry about.

"Lead the way," he said.

They pushed through the throng flowing around the entrance. As usual, everyone kept their heads down, intent upon their own business. Upon reaching the turnstile blocking the stairs descending to the platform, Thornberry reached into a pocket for his Travelcard, but Sport inserted his and the three-pronged stile completely retracted into the machine. Sport walked through and grinned at Thornberry's surprised expression.

"Office privileges," Sport said. "Come on."

Thornberry watched the prongs emerge from the machine as they proceeded right to the Jubilee platform. The silence assaulted him stronger than any noise ever could. They were alone. He looked around in alarm. Although the fluorescent ceiling lights and the green instructions on the ticket-machine terminals shone on, the station was barren. A pornographic magazine lay on the floor just outside the newsstand. A breeze whistled through the station, riffling the glossy pages of the skin book.

The lust of ghosts.

"Where did everyone go?"

A faraway rumbling sound grew closer and louder, startling Thornberry in the wake of the ominous hush. Sport grabbed his arm and pulled him to the stairs. "There's no time. We have to catch this train. It won't wait long and it's the last train available." The rumbling intensified as they rushed down to the southbound platform, almost tumbling down head over heel. The train roared into the terminal just as Thornberry leaped from the last step. He almost missed the train's destination label at the front:

St. Thomas' 347

He didn't recognize the street, and began to ask Sport where it was, but the doors hissed open and the football player pushed him inside the rear car. The doors slammed shut too fast, catching Sport's left ankle, and didn't rebound. The train began to move. The platform edge would shear off his foot.

"Untie your shoe!" Thornberry shouted.

Sport quickly pulled at the lace, loosening the binding. The smell of burning rubber filled the air as the concrete sidings ate at the cleats. Thornberry grabbed the young man's shoulders and yanked him into the car. His foot slipped out of the shoe and Sport fell on top of Thornberry. The shoe danced and jerked wildly as the edge feverishly devoured it.

Sport stood up, giving Thornberry a helping hand. The young man leaned over and whispered in his ear. "Thank you." Swiveling rapidly, he picked up what looked like a motorcycle helmet from one of the dingy seats. The helmet was black, with a dark visor at the front. One purple dial decorated its side. "Put this on."

"What is it?"

"It's called the Talentometer. It will locate your strongest ability and expand it tenfold."

Thornberry looked at it doubtfully. "I'm not sure . . ."

"Mr. Thornberry, it's too late to back out of this now. Failure to go through with this will only be devastating. We don't have long. This train goes straight to Piccadilly Circus with no stops." Sport held the helmet out to him, indicating that if it was going to be done, it had to be his choice.

He grabbed the Talentometer and placed it on his head. The smell of vinyl was strong. The visor over his eyes entirely blocked off his vision. Sport took his hand and guided him to a seat.

"Are you ready?" Sport asked. He sounded as if he were in a different room. Thornberry nodded. Sport turned the dial on the helmet's surface, which made a loud clicking sound. Expecting slight pain, or noise, or something, Thornberry winced. Nothing happened at first. Gradually, he felt the beginnings of a small vibration around his scalp. It tickled at first, but his skin soon lost its sensitivity. Sport was quiet beside him, so he became vividly aware of the noise of the train through the tunnels. It was moving faster than he had ever experienced. The usual steady clacks of the rails sounded like the hurried beats of an excited heart. The sound lulled him into dozing thoughts.

He stood in knee-high grass at the corner of what looked like a giant black barn. Wrinkling his nose at the stench of pigshit, he walked around the corner and almost fell into a feeding trough. Somebody lay in the trough, and he gasped when he recognized it was himself. Snuffling noises made him look up. Virginia and Mr. Rosaday crawled on their hands and knees toward the trough. They grunted at the body inside, and each bent over and took a large bite out of his chest. Mouths full, two maggots emerged from Virginia's snout and dropped to the body. The maggots each crawled to a wound and buried themselves in the flesh. Virginia and Mr. Rosaday opened their mouths, and the taken flesh remolded itself over the wounds perfectly. Their eyes rose and froze on Thornberry.

". . . Circus, Mr. Thornberry. We've arrived at Piccadilly Circus."

Thornberry reached to remove the helmet, but Sport restrained his hands.

"Not quite yet," Sport said.

"Did it do anything? The vibration made me fall asleep and I had a weird dream, but I don't feel any different."

Sport gripped his shoulder. "Your ability is seeing."

"Seeing? I already had excellent vision. I don't understand."

"Not seeing so much in the physical sense as the psychological. We've magnified your ability to perceive and understand situations in a way that no one can match, allowing you to take control of your life in a way you never thought possible. This is the only time you'll ever have to visit the Center. I don't want you to remove the Talentometer until we've reached the surface." Sport stood, pulling Thornberry up with him. "Put your hand on my shoulder, and I'll lead you out of the Underground. It's time to leave."

Before the doors of the car hissed shut, the high-strung, whimpering voices of Paulie and Gary came from the inside, "Let's us go home, mum."

"Yes, we wants to play."

Thornberry halted and began to turn around, but Sport seized his shoulder. "Pay that no mind. Follow me."

Reluctant and bewildered, Thornberry followed Sport out of the car and out of the station. As they rose up on the escalator, the lively sounds of Piccadilly Circus grew louder. The noises were comforting after the mysterious absence of people. He was excited about discovering the change that had taken place within him.

They emerged from the enclosure of the station into the warm summer night. The collective hum of thousands of people talking made him smile. Horns honking, drunk laughter, tires screeching: all of it was wonderful.

Sport patted him on the back. "Here we go, Mr. Thornberry."

The young man removed the helmet. The air felt sweet on his sweaty face and neck. The intrusion of the powerful lights in the square dazzled him; he squinted at Sport for a few moments then his eyes adjusted.

The world became quiet.

Sport's features had changed. He still wore the football uniform, but he was taller and slightly obese. His thick, sandy hair had thinned out and grayed on an egg-shaped head. The smile-creases at the corner of the eyes were devoured by dark oily circles. The skin was pockmarked from years of outrageous acne, and his ears had become smaller, jutting out as if afraid of the head. The eyes, though, were the same illuminating blue, and his nose was straight and fine as before.

Thornberry stood shocked as he gazed into the face of Nigel Thornberry.

"What . . . what?" he sputtered.

Sport-turned-Thornberry only nodded his head and made another flourish at the expanse of Piccadilly Circus. Every single voice was stifled, and every single face was that of Nigel Thornberry. He began to shake as the multitude of himself stared back at him in expectant silence. Standing behind Sport was a version of himself dressed in Angel's garments. That one raised his fingers to lips and sent him a kiss. Beside him were four versions of himself holding hands. They were dressed as Mr. Rosaday, Virginia, Paulie, and Gary.

Mr. Rosaday spoke. "Hush your mouths, boys. And spill a bit more of those tears, as the doctor's soon to be here."

Paulie said, "Where's the plug at?"

Gary said, "Yeah. How do they pull it if it ain't there?"

Virginia: "There's no real plug, sweetlings. Now, be my crying babies."

As one, they pointed to the vast advertising screen overlooking the Circus.

Paulie and Gary's favorite video was playing on the giant screen, but this time, everything was brightly clear and in color. The room was a kitchen. Two chubby little boys laughed and wheezed as they played with marbles on the tiled floor.

Paulie and Gary.

One flicked a marble and said, "Big Fat Nigel's gonna get mad if he catches us playing on the floor again."

The other snickered. "It doesn't matter. He's at work. He can't do anything about it, anyway. If he yells at us like he did before, mum'll just tell Grandpy, then he won't have no job. Besides, last time when he fell it was funny."

"Yeah, let's not clean up."

I did fall once.

A sound of a door shutting came from beyond the kitchen. "Virginia?" His voice.

The boys froze for a moment, then rushed out of the room.

"Virginia?" He watched himself emerge into the kitchen, calling his wife's name then slipping on the marbles. He fell, the back of his head crashing too hard on the tiles, bursting open. The screen went blank.

I fell twice. The second time I didn't get up.

The Thornberry dressed as Sport caught his attention. He fixed him in place with a serious gaze, then said quietly, "Thornberry, it's time for you to get up. You can see now; you can see what you need, and more important, *who* you don't need. They've already given up on you. It's time for you to get up."

After a few seconds of quiet, he heard the amazing sound of a thousand people simultaneously inhaling, followed by the incredible chorus of his own voice magnified:

"It's time for you to get up, Thornberry."

His ears opened up before his eyes. Virginia was bawling, which was accompanied by the orchestrated sniffling of Paulie and Gary. Over this, his father-in-law, Rosaday, murmured ridiculous condolences.

A strange voice said, "There's nothing else we can do, Mrs. Thornberry. I think you've made the right choice."

Thornberry opened his eyes and first saw the picture on the table beside his bed. He always kept it close. The picture displayed his little brother and sister before they had been killed in an accident in the Underground. James wore his football uniform; his arm was around Erica's shoulders, whose angel wings jutted into James's ear. It obviously tickled, by the enormity of the smile. He had played a game that day, and she performed in a school play. It was difficult sometimes to remember them wearing anything else. Thornberry felt blessed that he had been able to see both.

Angel and Sport, ghosts of my mind. I miss them so.

Looking up, he saw the owner of the strange voice. A doctor. The rest of them were all huddled together, oblivious of his open eyes. Although he felt very weak, he yanked the respirator from his mouth. When he cleared his throat, Virginia shrieked so loud that Paulie and Gary, remnants of an earlier union, began to cry in earnest.

Good.

"I'm assuming I'm at St. Thomas' Hospital, Doctor?"

The doctor nodded, stunned to gestures only.

"Room 347?"

Another nod.

Mr. Rosaday's large, purple mouth hung wide open.

"Doctor, I'm very curious. Would you tell me, kindly, by what manner they've said I fell and slipped into this coma? Because, quite frankly, I need a good laugh and I'm most impatient to share with you what really happened."

When Virginia fell, it sounded like a stack of newspapers dropped on the floor of his attic, never to be read again.

"Virginia?" Mr. Rosaday slapped her pale cheeks. "Virginia?"

Thornberry laughed. It felt good to laugh.

"I imagine," he said, "that the sound of my voice gave her a delicate shock."

The Song that Made Hell Hell

Greg Beatty

As I stepped into the boat, all I heard was dripping from Charon's stilled oars. I asked what waited beyond the river. He did not answer. If he had not waited to row until I had stepped aboard, I might not have been there at all. Such was life. Such is death.

The steady creak and splash of the oars went on forever. Each drop of Styx thrown into the air hung there until forgotten, bathed in the mist from Lethe just beyond. Memories of my life did the same: each stroke brought the past into consciousness, then it fell away and evaporated. I forgot what I had been. I forgot my fear of the lands beyond death, at least until Charon raised his hooded head. I heard nothing, but I saw him listen long enough for us to drift in the river of forgetfulness. We had spun twice round before the ancient oarsman bent to his task with new vigor.

Curious. Who hurries in the underworld? Then I heard it, soaring over the agitated splashing of Charon's oars. Music. Not the music of the gods, which lulls us into vulnerability, nor the music of the spheres, which makes men geometers and sophists. This was the music of life, played upon a lyre. The hand that played it was rich with talent, and the lyre might have been forged by Hephaestus himself, but it was a living hand.

This is how I knew. Rather than summoning visions of golden rain or crystal spheres, this song carried life, life and memories of life. I saw my mother's face purple as she strained to bring forth my brother Diomedes, dead now these fourteen years from a spear thrust. I smelled the breeze that carries salt fish and weary men home from the sea. And I felt love again, love in its many petaled variations. My first horse. Nikos, the slave I freed for valor and embraced as a second self. And above them all, fair Kalista. I stammered again the greeting I had mangled when we first met. I had stood in the gateway, bound by duty to greet her father, only to have one glimpse of her blind me like sun upon a shield. Thankfully, aged Nestor was still a man who remembered—

A whisper moved through the song. It mixed with the Styx's splash upon the rocks, shaping a susurration of warning and wonder.

. . . pheus, Orpheus, Orpheus.

I had heard of Orpheus. Even barbarians knew that his songs make warriors weep, and brought offers of love from men and women alike. Now, as we came to the unlit shores, Charon fought for a place to land his boat. The dead, who are ever and always alone, crowded together to whisper of Orpheus, the greatest musician.

When I stepped off the boat I learned why. The whispers were uneven, but worn smooth, like scraps of cloth passed hand to hand. For a woman. The gods let him. Eurydice. For Eurydice. You must see her. Orpheus yet lives. His song persuaded the gods.

I first thought that there was some great mystery, and that the other dead were trying to piece together Orpheus's reason for being there while still alive. When I looked my first dead man in the face, I knew they whispered for another reason. The dead spoke in scraps because the whole cloth was too rich with awe. To speak it was to burst asunder with the purest envy: that of the dead for the living.

And more: the envy of the ordinary for the extraordinary. Think, if you will, of what makes men content with their position in life. We are born rich or poor, slave or free, and for the most part we remain so. We are content with these inequalities because of the two greater equalities that yoke us all: we do not choose our places in life, and we all pass through the light but once before entering the eternal shadow.

Now the dead clustered in tight and breathless clumps upon the shore and watched the cosmos change. Death is bitter enough when it comes alike for all men, but death is bitter beyond belief when it comes for all men except one. Before, only the demi-divine lummox Heracles had come to the underworld and left again, and Heracles was too thick for any man to envy. When Orpheus walked among the dead, he played songs that called us impotently back to life. He was still strong, he was still proud, and he loved. And, though Orpheus was but a man, his passage among us was a sign that he was better than we were. Better than I was.

Music was the sail that pulled Orpheus forward, a chord at a time. Love stretched from his fingers to Eurydice in sweet and tangible arcs. It anchored in her beauty, a beauty I could now barely see, obscured as it was by a second circle of breathless attending dead. Sailors say Egyptians believe their souls are weighed after death. Good is heaped in one pan, evil in the other. If the evil sinks, a dog god eats their tainted souls.

I have never envied the decadent Egyptians until now. What gnawed my dead and boneless soul was nothing so fair as a measuring god. It was envy. Around me, the other dead shifted at its bite.

I knew why. Virtue is a game open to all alike, a third shared equality. But who among us is powerful enough to challenge death? Who is beautiful enough to deserve it? And who is so loved?

The most beautiful music in the worlds continued. It hurt everyone who heard it except the lover and the loved. As Orpheus neared the shores of the underworld, he grew visibly content with his achievement. His fingers plucked the strings idly, as if at play. Eurydice followed in silent, remembering hope. With each step, color returned to her face. My nails found my own cheeks, where they raked long furrows of despair, but no blood blossomed to distract me.

Instead, I watched them walk on, the superior lover rescuing his fair beloved from the eternal shade. I listened to music I could never, ever, make. I hated Orpheus for making it, and Eurydice for deserving it. But more, I hated myself for not being worthy. Around them, the dead grew angry. We began to push and shout, and that made us angrier still, for very little strength remains to the dead. Our roar was only a breeze in the night, but Orpheus had a musician's ears, and he heard everything.

Orpheus heard Panderus shout, and he heard Gyges shout, and I saw him hear me shout. He heard all of us spit pale, sinewless words of hatred. And Orpheus smiled. Every noise is an instrument to a gift like his. My hate became harmony, and for this I hated him more.

But dead men know one thing above all else: the fate they share with other dead. This thread, not so fine, not so pure, but much, much older than Orpheus's melody, ran from every dead man's mouth to Eurydice's ears. She knew that she was dead, and so she listened to the resentment of the dead rather than holding fast to the chords of love.

Like any great performer, Orpheus knew when he had lost his audience.

He continued to walk towards life and daylight, driving crowds of the dead before him like a wake before the prow of a boat. But his contentment was gone. Instead, desperation drove his fingers, making his music leap and soar like a Cretan bull dancer, in arcs that impressed us one and all, but in movements that implied inevitability. And there is only one inevitability.

There is a story about a satyr named Marsyas who found a flute in the forest and challenged Apollo to a contest. He lost, of course, and Apollo had him flayed alive for his overwhelming pride. Orpheus played better than either the satyr or the god. We wept as we cursed him; we cursed him because we wept, we dead, who had left tears behind us with our hearts' blood. And we cursed him for bringing beauty and hope into our shadowed lands.

And we grew silent, because for all of his greatness, we dead knew something Orpheus had never had to learn. One can challenge the gods. Country folk mutter that Marsyas actually won his contest with Apollo, but that the Muses conspired against him. The worst that can happen when one challenges the gods is death. Death is no penalty. Death is a certainty. Death comes for all men.

What happens, though, when you challenge death? What is the penalty? We knew, and we watched the truth penetrate Orpheus's song. When you challenge death, life becomes the penalty. We dead grew silent then, and watched two things war in the shadow of death: Orpheus's song, and Orpheus's doubt.

His song was championed by love, life, beauty, talent, genius, and glory. His doubt needed no champions. Every light casts a shadow; doubt grows in all of them. We dead watched doubt rise to fray the edges of his song. A great sigh rose up, and Orpheus did not incorporate it into his song. That made us sigh again. Earlier, he would have made music from those sad sounds. Now they sliced through his song like winter winds.

Orpheus heard his gap, and he stumbled. The lyre sprang from his hands and he fell. Everything changed. Panderus leapt to save the precious lyre, and Gyges and I braced ourselves to catch the musician.

He fell through us, of course. What support can the dead give? I do not know what pained him most: the bite of the black rocks of Hades into the flesh of his knees, or the jangle of his lyre upon the stones. The dead flocked to him, reaching weak-thewed hands to help him stand.

Other dead, too distant to reach him, took up the shards of his song and lifted it high into the dark air. Do you know what it sounds like when the dead echo beauty? When ten, a hundred, a thousand breathless throats—none of whom have a fraction of your gift—sing your song of life's beauty, while you wipe the blood from your knees and try not to surrender to despair?

I knew then why Orpheus had been allowed to come into the underworld, and, like all foreknowledge, it made my condition more bitter, not less. I watched him clutch at his lyre. I watched him raise his hand to test the strings, and I saw his heartstring snap.

Instead of playing, Orpheus laid one palm flat upon the strings and turned towards Eurydice.

We tried to stop him, we dead who knew. We crowded in front of him, and in front of her, so that no god could say he had turned to see his beloved. But Orpheus looked with the eyes of love, and he picked Eurydice out among all the myriad dead.

Orpheus got to see her for the length of one breath only. Then Eurydice was gone, as if his pained exhalation, the only breath in all of Hades, had blown her out like an oil lamp. Orpheus reached out to her, but all this did was send his lyre bouncing off a rock and into the Lethe, where it was as forgotten as the dead themselves. For a moment, the color that his song had brought to her cheeks hung in the air, a ghost of a ghost, then it too was gone.

Orpheus gathered himself as best he could, calling Eurydice back to him, to love, and to life with voice, clapped hand, stomped feet, and desperate whistling. Each tack he took, we dead took with him, ghostly echoes stamping and calling in pale and accidental parody of his love song.

We sang with Orpheus until his throat grew dry from lack of wine and his voice cracked. We sang as his voice faded, until he sang worse than even the dead. And we walked behind him, a myriad inferior shadows, when he finally gave up and tried to cast himself in the Lethe.

Death is cruel. All that happened was that the waters receded, so that forgetfulness fled from him. Orpheus licked the rocks of Hades until his tongue painted them red with blood, but for him there was no blessed oblivion, no more than there was for us. The only thing we dead have managed to forget since that day is the precise route that Orpheus took as he returned to life.

We can find the thin spots in our prison. We find chinks in the fortress walls of death, places like Delphi and Epidaurus and High Market Cemetery and New Orleans, places where our voices drift through in our faint and breathless song. Sometimes we find those gates of horn and ivory through which dreams are sent, and we send our ugly, inferior copies of his song to those we left behind. When they hear us, they wake crying. Sometimes we cry too, the dry and pathetic tears of the dead. Then, for a time, we forget where the gates are found, until our need grows great again, and we sing for love once more.

We curse Orpheus, we dead in our impotent anger, for bringing hope back to us. Hades hurts us more, now that we hope. But we remember him too, and we sing his song. It is the only remnant of the world of life that many of the dead know; some drank of Lethe too deeply. But even those oblivious dead weep at his song.

When we remember life, we know now that it is not fair. We know that we were not loved as Eurydice was loved. We know we do not have the gifts that made Orpheus great. We know all of this, and again, it is bitter.

But we sing his song in a great chorus of the dead, and we are getting better. Before Orpheus came to torture us with hope, Hades was just dark. It is his song that made Hell hurt. But. But. But.

But we remember what he sounded like. We remember that Orpheus almost brought her back—and what his face looked like when she was gone. And, while all of this knowledge is bitter, it is also sweet. His is the song that made Hell Hell, but it is also the only honey we know. Here in the dark, bounded by a river of oblivion, in a place where the only marker of time is the splash of Charon's coming and going, we sing. And we are getting better.

Put a hand to your ear.

Listen.

I promise you that in every dream, every echo, and every breeze that rustles tall grasses, you will hear the song of the dead, crying their love for those who still live. We dead sing for you, as you will sing for those you love, in time.

How Savio Arcaini Came by His Sword

M. T. Reiten

Pietro followed his master, Savio Arcaini, into the shadowed cemetery perched on the craggy hill above the small stone chapel. Savio held up a silver chain dangling a glass ball the size of a grape, which illuminated the headstones and whipping rain with a faint blue glow. He pointed at a fresh hump of earth, melting out streams of mud. "Dig here."

The wind and rain did not deter Savio, though Pietro wished he were in bed, as would any right-minded man who had a room waiting on a blustery night like this. Their accommodations, paid for with Savio's coins, lay three miles away down a winding road in the small village of Trissino. The downward trail would prove more challenging when they returned from this distressing outing. Pietro wished he were back in the wheat fields and river valleys near the city of his birth, Ferraria, rather than traipsing along roads barely fit for goats. All he would gain for this night would be a broken leg. Of this Pietro was sure. Or perhaps twitching with a cracked neck at the bottom of a cliff. Or consumption would set in and claim his life less swiftly—he was already soaked to the bone.

Savio's snapping fingers pulled Pietro back to his immediate misery. Savio Arcaini was hardly what one pictured as a philosopher—a youngish man to be considered a master by most reckonings, tall, assured and well dressed. Savio could barely grow a beard, only a trimmed hint of a mustache on his upper lip and a bristling swatch of whiskers on his sharp chin. But his attitude fit that of a studied philosopher and alchemist.

Pietro stuck the shovel into the dirt. The edges of the grave continuously collapsed as he dug. He uncovered the lid of an unadorned wood casket after an hour of labor. When Pietro struggled out, mud coated him from the elbows down.

"Well?" Savio asked. The rain beaded up and ran from his woolen cloak in a most unnatural way. "Open it."

Pietro had apprenticed to the philosopher and alchemist because he had thought it should be easy work, reading books and fiddling with concoctions, answering unknowable questions with confounding riddles. But those would be tests of skill and wit, not trials to be overcome by brute endurance and great quantities of needless suffering.

After a moment of hesitation, Pietro slipped back into the grave and pried at the top of the simple pine casket with the tip of the shovel. The wet wood splintered around the nails as he lifted the lid. For the moment, Pietro was glad for the rain as it kept the stench of death from his nose.

Savio bent down, his glowing sphere illuminating the contents. A pretty young woman's body lay inside. Her best dress of white silk, probably her intended wedding gown, began to grow damp from spattering rain. Chunks of soil dribbled into the casket, dislodged from beneath Savio's boots at the edge of the hole.

He produced another glass globe, slightly smaller than the one providing light, from inside his cloak. The glass sphere had a tiny ring of iron imbedded in its surface with a delicate nub of glass protruding from the center of the ring. He held the sphere by the dead girl's face and broke the nub with a gloved finger. The globe popped hollowly and hissed, sucking the spirit of the girl inside, trapping her essence by arcane art and the physics of the aether. It began to shimmer with a faint blue light.

Pietro glanced at the small marble headstone. Maria Cantabello had been of a well-to-do family. He crossed himself, closed her casket, and began filling the grave back in.

"Why, Master, do we come out on a night like this?" Savio, as a philosopher, usually entertained Pietro's questions, rarely beating him for insolence except at appropriate public affairs where it was expected. "Why not a clear night so we do not drown on top of this hill?"

"I must take this particular spirit three days after the body was laid to rest. Not two or four days, but three." Savio examined his newly acquired glowing orb. "Good fortune brought the storm, so no one will see what we do from the chapel."

Pietro scraped the last of the dirt over the grave, glad to be finished. "Perhaps if the priests wouldn't approve, we shouldn't be doing this?"

"The priests haven't the imagination to see how this will change the world. They remain in the past, held by church tradition and superstition about desecrating hallowed ground." Savio threw back the hood of his cloak and launched into one of his orations. The wind lashed at his long black hair and the sphere cast his features into a shadowy caricature, all nose and chin. "When I was at Bologna, we cut apart corpses just to see how the human machine was strung together. To see how this jar of clay was formed. There it was acceptable as furthering medicine. Even the most feeble-witted can play out in their mind how medicine can aid and succor them. Ask a man with a toothache if he believes in the science of medicine and he will be swift to answer and beg for the results, no thought to the defiled bones and organs of those who came before."

Savio whipped his gloved hand toward the sky. Rain droplets slashed from his long fingers as they traced through the air like a rapier blade. "Too few have the capacity to conceive how spectral engineering will make the whole of their lives better, not just soothe a dyspeptic stomach or dispel the ague. I shall change the world."

Pietro leaned against the shovel. The only change he wanted was to be warm and dry. He straightened up as Savio's attention turned away from his grand vision and back onto his apprentice.

"Perhaps now would be a good time to return to the village?" Pietro asked with forlorn hope.

"This is not a good time. You have another grave to uncover. Eight and a half years ago, this one's maternal aunt died." Savio held up his newly filled spirit orb and walked toward another corner of the cemetery. "Do you know what that means?"

"It means I shall have to dig through hardened earth." Pietro trailed after his master, dragging the shovel.

"Do the sums and you will see why we have come here tonight. Just over three thousand days ago her maiden aunt was buried. Three days and three thousand days, you see. Both corpses are of the same sex, similar age, same family, same church, and same ground. The only difference between the two is the time since death. A subject like this is so hard to find."

"Her name is Maria," Pietro said, not sure why he corrected his master.

"I've heard that before." Savio gave a dismissive wave of his hand. He pulled his hood over his head as he stopped beside another small headstone. "They're all called Maria."

The earth in the second grave proved hard-packed and resulted in strenuous digging for Pietro, but he uncovered the decaying coffin. After opening it, Pietro saw in the faint light of Savio's orb, that eight years had removed most of the flesh, obscuring any family resemblance to the first corpse of the evening. Savio popped another orb near the empty, skeletal smile of the dead aunt and ensnared the spirit with a hiss of rushing aether. Pietro refilled the grave and they left the cemetery. The final orb was slow to light, matching the blue glow of the others only as they were halfway down the hilltop.

Back in Ferraria, Savio trained ghosts in the cellar of his house by application of sparks produced from an amber and silk friction wheel. He might have had other techniques, but Pietro never saw them. During training sessions, such as that night, Savio banished Pietro to the tiny glassblowing shop he kept on the second floor of his house and ordered him to study.

"Pietro!" Savio called from the cellar.

Pietro woke from a light doze in the shop. A book on astronomy lay open on his lap, turned to the first page of tiny print. He set aside the small volume and went downstairs.

Racks of the luminescent spirit orbs lined the cellar, arranged carefully in sections on the walls, as if they were prized bottles of wine. The cellar had once been dark, lit only by flickering candles, but now a swirling glimmer emanated from hundreds of orbs. They ranged in size from that of an orange or small flask to tiny baubles no larger than delicate Venetian beads. Each orb had a small ring of iron like the dark iris of an incandescent, disembodied eyeball.

A small printing press sat in one corner, a remnant of Savio's failed experiment to have ghosts set moveable type. The friction wheel was placed in its mahogany and brass storage box in the opposite corner. A slab of marble on iron posts served as a high table in the center of the cellar with a tall chair next to it. Savio scribbled fervently in his record, looking up as Pietro descended the squeaky stairs.

"I've trained them all to the same task and recorded their abilities." Savio pointed at his table where a stand for an orb sat next to a line of graduated weights. The smallest masses were grains of sand ranging upward in weight to bent strips of gold foil and finally to metal type characters. His book of notes lay open to arcane scrawls of mathematics and carefully rendered tables. "I have shown an inverse relationship between the time the spirit spent tied to its corpse and the strength of an orb. This behavior holds over the span of hours. However, the orbs we recovered from Trissino test to the same meager ability. Three days or three thousand days makes little difference. From my measurements, I venture that the comfort of last rites and a grave in hallowed ground hastens the loss of contact with the corporeal realm."

"So we must rob heathen tombs?" Pietro asked, fearing a longer, more dangerous journey in the days ahead.

"Do pay attention, you dull excuse for a scholar, or I shall send you to Bologna to lay in the surgical theater as an anatomy aid for the fumble-fingered simpletons." Savio was in a good mood to waste such a long insult on Pietro. "What other conclusion can you draw from these results?"

"The freshly dead are best, but they go stale quickly."

"So you do listen, but you have yet to think."

"But, Master, with due respect, should we talk of them as if they were so much old bread?"

"What would those ghosts be doing if I hadn't collected them? Waiting in their graves for the Second Coming. Forgetting all that it was to be alive. The touch of a kiss, the sound of a song, the whimsy of a jest shared between lovers. And is not Sloth one of the deadly sins? Should they just lay about in their coffins, wallowing like an idle apprentice in his bed past dawn?"

"Truly, I do not know," Pietro said.

"To harness the strength of the dead, I have fashioned this!" Savio reached beneath the table, pulled out a rapier and unsheathed it. The blade struck the chains where an oil lamp once had hung from the ceiling. The chains swung, links rasping, like a lank pendulum.

"You have fashioned a sword?" Pietro stepped back, not for fear of his life, but for fear of the unpredictable nature of Savio and the knowledge that his master was, even by his own account, a poor fencer.

A broad metal cup covered the cross guard on the hilt. This utilitarian style was unlike the graceful bands of metal forming a cage around the hand that Pietro had seen on noblemen's swords before. The blade tapered to a wicked, narrow point, a yard of steel with one purpose, killing.

"Look." Savio flipped the rapier around, pointing the hilt toward Pietro. Savio pulled it back as Pietro reached for the grip. "You look with your eyes, not with your fingers."

Inside the cup hilt, a pair of the smaller spirit orbs was wired to the blade like luminous sapphires in a delicate setting.

Savio continued. "I had a cutler assemble the rapier, but I have added orbs to enhance the blade's usefulness."

"What can a ghost do for a duelist? Spirits to keep the blade sharp? Perhaps to polish away rust?" Pietro knew the woeful limitations of ghosts' ability to influence the physical world.

"Pietro Degli Espositi," Savio said, shaking his head. He re-cased the rapier and hung it from his belt. "I keep you close because you may yet have the imagination to appreciate my designs. Come with me and you shall see how my plan unfolds over a glass of wine. Bring the architect's orb."

Pietro decided that he would listen to a donkey braying if he had wine to drink. From the racks, he retrieved the orb occupied by the ghost of Brunelleschi, and eagerly followed his master into the dark streets of Ferraria.

"I don't know what you're talking about. Dueling is against church canon and against the duchy's laws." The man Savio claimed was Vicento Malignari stared into his dented pewter mug. The few other patrons in the public house avoided the table.

Duelists, according to the stories Pietro had heard, were supposed to be dashing figures, concerned about the honor of their ladies, the integrity of their word, and the propriety of their actions. Malignari had a broad ugly mouth, like a cow's, and he had no trouble growing a beard. His cheeks and chin bristled with black and gray whiskers. He wore a buff leather doublet, brightly dyed in purple and yellow, but his shirt beneath was ragged and stained at the sleeves. His gloves, tucked into his belt, were thick brown gauntlets, more likely to be found on a farmhand than a well-bred gentleman.

"I am not a priest, nor am I one of the duke's men." Savio made a pouring gesture toward the coarse man's mug.

Pietro stepped forward from the wall where Savio had stationed him, and poured a quarter cup of red wine from the large bottle—stingy since the unused portion of the bottle was promised to him as a reward for keeping silent.

Malignari stared at Savio with heavy lidded eyes. He took a drink and then asked, "Why then do you want to know if I'm planning a duel?"

"I am a trainer of ghosts and wish to assist you in your next contest of arms."

"Ghosts?" Malignari barked out a laugh. "Like the tales of haunted castles my *nonna* would tell me as a child?"

"Do you know how difficult it is to have a spirit abandon the earthly vessel of the body after death? No. Stories of hauntings are made and promoted for reasons known only to the living." Savio placed the architect's orb on the table. He took a saltcellar from a hidden pocket and dropped a large pinch next to the glowing orb. He offered a magnifying glass to the duelist. "Watch what can be done."

A small cathedral built from the grains of salt slowly formed on the table, like a fairy castle of ice. The ghost of the architect made spires and arching domes that rivaled in miniature the most fantastic structures of Venice, Florence, or Rome.

"And how can this magician's trick aid me?" Malignari ignored the glass and wiped the salt onto the floor.

Savio forced a smile, though to Pietro it had the same warmth as a crocodile's grin. "You, sir, have knowledge of the fighting arts far exceeding my own, but may I ask how much steel is between a fatal thrust and a parried blade?"

"It depends." Malignari held his scarred hands over the table with his index fingers apart. He moved them closer together as he spoke. "Four inches. An inch. A hair's breadth."

Savio drew the rapier. The two orbs set within the basket hilt shed a ghostly radiance. He offered it to Malignari. "I have bound spirits to this blade. Have you heard of Liberi and Renzo Pelligrino. . . ?"

Malignari frowned at the rapier, but he leaned forward. "I didn't know Liberi had died."

"These trapped ghosts enhance the hand that wields the blade. That hair's breadth will turn the point every time with reflexes not slowed by mortal flesh. And the expertly guided inch will find your opponent's heart with vision that sees beyond living sight."

"I trained under the Swabian himself. What do I need with a sorcerer's plaything?"

"Why are you here in Ferarria and not Venice? Are others regarded more dangerous to cross a blade with than yourself?" Savio motioned for Pietro to fill the swordsman's cup again.

Peitro grudgingly filled the mug. Malignari seemed to have an unquenchable thirst.

"You tempt fate by taunting me." Malignari's left hand closed into a fist even as he raised his right with the mug to his lips.

"Money is lost at death to creditors and family to spend as they may. No one will ask where they came upon the gold. While those who come after you may wear your famous reputation like a cloak, it will always remain your name. Vicento Malignari, the finest fencer in northern *Italia*."

"In all *Italia*," Malignari mumbled with venom in his voice.

"In all of Europe," Savio said like a gambler raising the stakes, eager to hear the current hand of cards called.

"Then I will test your blade before agreeing to anything." Malignari took the rapier and exchanged it for his own. He tossed his old sword at Pietro. "Have your boy mind my weapon."

Pietro caught Malignari's battered rapier and nearly dropped the wine bottle. He trailed after Malignari and Savio as they went into the foggy streets. When he was certain that no one was looking, he took swigs of the rich Sangiovese and wiped the mouth of the bottle on his sleeve.

Pietro stood next to Savio in the shadowed doorway at the top of the short flight of stairs. They kept still and quiet, as Malignari demanded. A flicker of candlelight spilled from an opened door further up the straight alleyway. A man stepped out of the back entrance to a fine mansion that belonged to a minor nobleman in the Este's court. He absently brushed at his sleeves, adjusted his laced shirt cuffs, and started into the darkness with a confident stride as the door shut behind him. An odd hour to be venturing out alone, Pietro thought.

Malignari stood at the base of the stairs. He set his mug on the cobblestones as the footfalls of the approaching stranger grew louder. Malignari shouted, "Foul cur, I shall have satisfaction. You have slept with my betrothed, Romilda!"

The gentleman stopped, his face shadowed by his floppy plumed hat and his black velvet clothes blended with the darkness. "You mistake me for someone else."

"You are Nunzio the Tax Collector." Malignari took two staggering steps to his right. "You have sullied Romilda this very night as I waited for you."

"You, my good fellow, appear to be drunk," Nunzio the Tax Collector said evenly. But he did sweep his cape aside exposing the hilt of a dueling sword. "I do not know Romilda in that way."

"Now you call me a liar?" Malignari asked in a growl. "Will your insults never end, Jew?"

"Your mouth may betray your heart to my steel," Nunzio said, the heat of a growing temper flaring into his words. "Apologize for your hasty words and we can walk away with no harm done."

"I would sooner kiss a bull's *testicoli* than offer an apology to you."

Nunzio drew his rapier. He leveled the point at Malignari's throat.

Malignari's new blade appeared, beat the threatening rapier away, and whistled through the air in a flourish. Malignari cast aside the empty sheathe and dropped into an en guard stance. The blue glow from the basket hilt illuminated his forearm and cast dancing shadows on the crowded walls. The mask of drunkenness lifted. "Have on, Jew!"

The rapiers rang and flickered in the pale ghost light. Pietro leaned forward to see the forced duel, but Savio pulled him back by the tail of his shirt. Through the railing, Pietro could barely follow the action: beat thrust parry riposte. Then Malignari's blade sank a foot of steel into Nunzio's torso, splitting lung, bloodying velvet tunic.

"What ungodly thing is that?" Nunzio the Tax Collector collapsed and slid off Malignari's sword.

Savio bounded down the stairs and kneeled by the fallen official. He produced an empty orb and waited for Nunzio to drown in his own blood. Savio broke the glass sphere open before his subject had finished dying. A gurgling cry rose from Nunzio's corpse as his spirit was ripped away and crushed into the orb. The glassy sphere burned as bright as a lantern, revealing the avaricious visage of Savio Arcaini staring into its gleaming center with a face as pale as bone and eyes as black as ink.

Pietro had quietly descended the stairs and stood next to Malignari. His master slipped the newly acquired orb into one of his many hidden pockets, returning the alleyway to darkness. Malignari took the remaining wine from Pietro and drank directly from the bottle. Savio joined them at the base of the stairs.

"You've regained your betrothed's honor," Pietro said to Malignari.

"Forgive my servant for speaking out of turn." Savio cuffed Pietro in the back of the head with the flat of his hand.

"My betrothed? I have never seen this Romilda. A wealthy friend who owed taxes asked me to prevent this Nunzio from collecting." Malignari snorted at Pietro's wide-eyed stare. "Some advice, boy. You don't face your enemy with courtesy or kindness, but with steel and a hard heart."

"And the blade?" Savio asked.

"It fights well." Malignari handed the empty bottle to Pietro.

Savio and Pietro attended five more duels that Malignari arranged throughout the next weeks. Brutal and short affairs, Malignari grew more approving of his ghostly rapier as he spitted old sworn and new swearing enemies.

Pietro answered a pounding at the door. Malignari stood on the steps, cheeks flushed and breathing hard as if he had just dashed to the alchemist's house.

"Get your master and his baubles," he growled. "I have a duel."

"In broad daylight?" Pietro glanced up at the midday sun.

Malignari gripped Pietro's arm, pinching skin beneath his shirt with a tight grip, and gave him a rough shove back into the house. "Do as I say before I give you my boot."

Minutes later, Pietro struggled to keep pace with his master and the duelist as they worked their way into the shop-lined streets of the old city, just off the main plaza. They bowed heads for a momentary whisper, and then Savio turned aside to inspect a pewtersmith's display. Pietro hesitated, but a gruff command from Malignari and a curt nod from his master sent him into the crowd after the duelist. They came to a rough halt outside the crumbling façade of a bakery.

"See the fair-haired fop in the new hat?" Malignari asked as he passed a tiny silver coin through the window to the baker. "Nicolo Venturi. Walks as if he owned Ferarria?"

Pietro did see a slender, beardless man in a fine outfit wandering down the street several buildings away. He wore a puffed-sleeve jerkin with slashes of red and gold and matching pumpkin breeches over his hose in the gaudy style of a Swiss mercenary, momentarily the fashion in Venice. A velvet cape of deepest crimson draped over his left shoulder, he strutted past a few ladies, honored them with a rakish bow, and readjusted what obviously was a blade at his hip, feebly concealed beneath his cape. He continued his parade toward where Pietro and Malignari stood.

"Hold." Malignari shoved his leather coin purse into Pietro's hand as he reached for a round loaf of bread from the baker.

The heavy sack of coin consumed all of Pietro's attention. The cool weight in his hand felt like how he imagined a breast to feel, if a bit lumpy, but with the promise of freedom and power rather than a sinful pleasure. He gave it an experimental heft, wondering the ratio of silver *denari* to gold *ducats* inside.

Abruptly, Malignari shouldered Pietro into the path of the Venetian rake. Stumbling, Pietro brushed past the young man who spun aside to give him ample room to fall. The rich velvety cape whipped across Pietro's face before his cheek hit the mud and the cobblestones knocked his breath away.

"I'll not have you mistreat my man like that," Malignari said loud enough to draw attention.

"Your *boy* fell into me." In a slightly more hushed tone, the rake turned his attention to Pietro. "You should have more care than to stumble into dangerous men." He showed the hilt of his sword briefly and smiled. He offered his gloved hand to assist Pietro to his feet.

Pietro took his help and staggered upright. "Thank you, sir."

The fair-haired duelist was not much older than himself and about the same height. He smelled of lavender and grinned slyly as though he knew funny secrets. He turned to continue up the street.

"What is this?" Malignari lunged, laying his hands on the young man's torso. He produced his tooled leather coin purse and jingled it above his head for the gathering crowd to see.

Pietro looked down at his own hands in surprise and back at Malignari. When had he lost the purse?

"That is not mine." The young rake smoothed his clothes from the rough handling. "I'll not have—"

"No, it is *my* purse, but it was in *your* shirt!"

"I am a Venturi; I have no need to steal."

Malignari broke into an ugly smile, but his hooded eyes narrowed and burned. His breathing grew deep and his voice dropped an octave. Malignari's joy and rage intermingled before his duels. "So you thieve for sport?"

"I should cut you down for such slander." Venturi pulled aside his cape to fully bare the hilt of his rapier. "What fool has his boy carry his purse?"

"I am a fool, now, yet you accuse me of slander? Do you not recognize me, Venturi? Do you not know Vicento Malignari?"

Venturi's eyes grew wide. His right hand went to his sword and his left freed his cape from his neck, as lithe as a dancer. The cape fluttered in an arc as he skipped back, clearing more space in the street. It partially wrapped around his off arm to hang like a net as both duelists' blades slid free of their cases. "I train under the Swabian," Venturi said.

"I know." Malignari shrugged, unconcerned, and attacked.

Pietro watched the fight with a growing sense of disgust, pressing back into the crowd. No pretense of honor lay behind this fight. Their thin blades rang: parry, riposte, thrust. Malignari lacked the younger man's grace, but he had strength behind his wrist. Venturi beat, disengaged, and threw himself into a lunge. Malignari barely got his rapier up in time, steel skittering across steel, and the young rake's tip bit through the shoulder of his doublet. Venturi caught up Malignari's blade in his cape and lunged toward the older man's belly. Malignari dropped to a crouch, tugging on the cape, and the rake's blade went off mark. Venturi lurched forward and Malignari's gleaming rapier tip tore from within the folds of the ensnaring cape. Malignari shoved his blade into Venturi's throat.

Venturi dropped his blade and held his hands to his neck as frothy blood dribbled between his fingers. He stumbled dizzily to his knees. Pietro found himself staring into dying eyes as the young rake lifted an imploring hand, glove smeared with blood, to be helped to his feet. Before Pietro could react, Savio pushed him aside.

"I am a physician," Savio said, easing Venturi to the ground. An empty glass orb expertly appeared in his hand, concealed from casual view, as he feigned professional concern.

Pietro heard the now familiar pop and hiss as Savio stole the ghost. Venturi's body spasmed and then lay still. The brilliance of the noonday sun washed out the faint blue glow.

Savio shook his head sadly, palming the orb, and crossed himself. "I fear he needs a priest."

"That, my dear Malignari, was far too public a display." Savio sat in a chair in his seldom-used parlor.

Across from him, Vicento Malignari smelled drunk. "It had to be public. I broke no canon by dueling, because I defended myself against a thief. He bared steel first. The duke's men understood that it was just another bastard Venetian who lacked the sense to stay in Venice."

Savio said nothing, but glanced impatiently toward the entrance to his cellar.

"I felt the cool hand of Liberi in that last parry." Malignari wiggled a finger through the puncture in his doublet that had barely missed his right shoulder and would have ended the fight. "Now is the time. I will send word to my archrival. I have bested his finest student, his heir, and he must come to collect the body. We will meet at the Po on the road to Venice five nights from now. You will witness my laying an old score to rest. Take good notes, scribbler, and put me in the history books."

Savio nodded in distraction, pleased with his new ghosts and the results of the measurements he had performed in the preceding weeks, but clearly annoyed at this interruption. Engrossed, he had neglected Pietro's studies for his time in the cellar, but Pietro had yet to bring it to Savio's preoccupied attention.

"So give us some wine to celebrate my fame. I cannot exist on air like you, philosopher." Malignari barked out a laugh.

"I am certainly making no progress sitting here, so we might as well indulge." Savio snapped his fingers at Pietro and motioned to the cellar. "The Valpolicella."

Pietro wanted to protest treating this killer as a guest, especially at the cost of a bottle from a sorely diminished stock, but he turned to fetch the wine, throwing a half-concealed glare at Malignari. Apparently this was all he was good for now, carrying things silently from one place to another. After the fight, Savio had Pietro deliver the body to the cathedral, and the journey to lay the young man's empty corpse onto the marble floor haunted him. Taking ghosts of people who were already dead seemed more like harvesting, if somewhat more sacrilegious than taking a scythe to wheat, but what Pietro had witnessed in the past several weeks was a most personal theft and murder. Perhaps he had required the full light of day to see his master's actions for what they were, but he was duty bound by oath and station even if relegated to a mere servant. Yet Savio Arcaini had not delivered a single mortal blow. The foul slayings had begun once Malignari had taken up that rapier guided by ghostly hands.

Pietro descended the creaking stairs into the laboratory, unusually empty of the philosopher, but filled with his leavings: half-eaten bread, three open ink pots, a sheaf of curling parchment, a cheese gone moldy next to an ivory and brass abacus. A threadbare coat hung from the printing press and the friction wheel sat on the table out of its box.

He stood in the serene blue luminescence of over five hundred orbs. Five hundred spirits confined to spheres, the culmination of five hundred lives, lit the cellar from the wine rack adapted to store the philosopher's subjects. Pietro shrugged and turned away. At least Savio no longer used candles, so Pietro no longer had to scrape up the wax drippings that had once spattered the stone floor and marble tabletop.

Pietro grabbed the last Valpolicella and blew clinging dust from the bottle. Perhaps Savio could train a ghost to clean dust, one tedious speck at a time? A practical application of their meager touch on the physical world. But according to Savio the best abilities came from ghosts performing tasks close to their living passions and Pietro doubted any spirits on the rack had a consuming obsession with tidying up.

Pietro found himself staring at the orb occupied by the ghost of the young girl, Maria from Trissino. What had her passions been? Undoubtedly not cleaning. Or dueling.

With a quick glance at the stairway, Pietro grabbed the two Trissino orbs and slipped them under his shirt. He leapt up the stairs, bottle in hand, certain of what he was going to do, but uncertain as to how.

On the appointed day of the following week, they journeyed by foot to the inn at the old Roman bridge on the south shore of the River Po, a few miles outside of Ferraria. The afternoon was clear and bright among the open fields of wheat, but when they rested in the cool common room of the inn, Malignari took no wine for his normal thirst. Instead, he had one draught of watery beer and then waited in silence, his hand resting on the hilt of the ghostly rapier. His fingers tapped impatiently on the cool, glass orbs in the hilt.

"More beer? Some wine?" Pietro tried not to stare at Malignari, but the duelist had barely moved from his slouch since they had arrived. The sun had begun to set and Pietro was afraid he would have no chance to swap the orbs. If this was any other evening, Malignari would have left several times to empty his bladder, giving Pietro abundant opportunity.

"No." Malignari continued his brooding.

A few patrons wandered in as the evening advanced, but they avoided the dim corner of the room where Malignari and Savio sat. Pietro would have joined a group of laughing young men, freshly out of the fields, who gathered at a far table if Savio would have allowed it. Instead, Pietro sat with his chin on his crossed arms resting on the table, blinking away the sleep of boredom, to keep his vigil on the blade an arm's reach away. He almost wished that he had brought a book to study like Savio had, hunched in the corner with candle and a faint bluish glimmer.

Eventually, Malignari stood, stretched, and scratched himself in a most ungentlemanly fashion. He set the blade against the wall and began to walk to the door.

"Should you not take your rapier?" Savio asked, barely looking up from his book.

Pietro snapped awake as the duelist hesitated.

Malignari shook his head. "A dagger will do. I'm only going to relieve myself, not attend a duel. Mind my weapon, boy."

Once Malignari left and Savio returned to his reading, Pietro leaned across the bench. He popped the orbs from their clasps and lurched to catch the rapier before it slid to the ground. He glanced over at Savio, but his master gave no sign of noticing his movement. Pietro placed the Trissino orbs in the hilt and sat up, heart racing and palms damp.

Savio turned a page.

At midnight, rubbing sleep from his eyes, Pietro stumbled out to the foot of the ancient stone bridge. Lanterns shed light on the arches that spanned the wide river. Malignari massaged his hand and paced with a fervent energy. Savio stood as still as a stork beneath the faint yellow radiance of the lantern flame.

Two figures came over the bridge. As they drew closer, Pietro saw that the one on the left had a neatly trimmed beard and long golden hair of the same honeyed color as the young Venturi that Malignari had cut down in Ferraria. He moved gracefully as if he were in the middle of a ballroom, not closing to an arranged duel. On the right, walked an older, squatter man wearing a traveling cape and an unadorned jerkin, cut in a style popular well before Pietro was born. The older man had none of the overt feline grace of his companion, yet there was a sublime effortlessness to his steps. At first, Pietro thought the older man was a servant to the nobleman, but they both wore rapiers and gauntlets. Stopping ten paces away, the older man took off his floppy hat, exposing his bald head, and traveling cape, exposing his round belly. He handed his removed garments to the fair-haired duelist.

"Hanko, you came." Malignari handed his cloak to Pietro, mirroring the older man's casual actions.

"I did." Hanko had a thick Bavarian accent. "I never miss a lesson."

"Yes, yes." Malignari sounded annoyed. "This is Savio Arcaini, my second, and his servant."

Hanko presented the gentleman standing on his right. "Vicento, you remember Nicolo Venturi? He was just a boy when you saw him last. He will be my second, ensuring honor is met."

"Time does pass and it levies a toll," Malignari said with a curt nod. "I did not recognize Nicolo grown."

"This duel is rightfully mine for Domenico," Nicolo said. "I received word of my youngest brother, you honorless—"

"Enough, Nico. This dispute is first between Vicento and me." Hanko placed a hand on the younger man's shoulder.

Pietro heard Savio whisper. "I should have brought an extra orb."

"Shall our seconds observe propriety and meet?" Hanko asked.

Malignari shook his head violently and drew the rapier. "No need. Only your blood will settle this."

"So be it." Hanko shrugged and freed his weapon, an unassuming rapier with a brass swept hilt and pommel. He pointed at the glow coming from his opponent's sword. "What is that, Vicento? Trapped fireflies?"

"It's a beacon to hell, which is where I will send you." Malignari rendered a mocking salute with his rapier. The ugly smile spread across Malignari's face, hideous in the blue glimmer cast from the bound spirits.

"You always sought a tricky weapon, didn't you? I thought you would have learned from that wavy-bladed flamberge rapier in Vienna. A poor craftsman expects new tools to improve his skill."

The swordsmen faced each other on the even ground just off the bridge and settled into guard, weapons up, barely crossing tips. Slight movements of the hips or wrist by one made the other shift back or forward an inch. To Pietro, the action was as dull as watching the posturing of chess players.

With unhurried ease, Hanko beat Malignari's blade and disengaged, dropping the point below Malignari's guard. Hanko thrust and Malignari parried with a slight turn of the wrist. The blades slid along each other in a hiss of steel-on-steel. Malignari's smile fell away as the tip of Hanko's rapier disappeared into his breast, appearing again from the armpit of his off-hand side. Hanko withdrew the blade as swiftly as he had plunged it through Malignari. The fight was finished.

"Pierced lung and severed aorta," Savio said next to Pietro. "Judging from the angle."

Pietro nodded and swallowed.

Malignari pressed his left hand against his chest and sat down. He looked into the glow from the orbs on the rapier, astonished and confused. He looked up with the vacant expression found on the head of a slaughtered calf. Breathing heavy, he slumped to the side in a small, but growing, puddle of his own blood.

Hanko lowered his blade from guarded position. "Over-confidence has finally killed you, poor Vicento. Just a hair's breadth more and my point would have missed."

"What was his quarrel with you?" Nicolo asked, holding out the older man's sheath and a piece of cloth.

"I do not even remember." Hanko cleaned his blade on the small square of oily felt. He returned the cased rapier to the leather carrier on his belt and retrieved his hat and cape from Nicolo. "We had best be going. I do not like traveling at night."

"Signore Arcaini, can you tell me where I can find my brother?" Nicolo Venturi asked as Savio approached the fallen duelist.

"His body lies in the cathedral." Savio knelt by Malignari.

"My thanks." Nicolo turned to Hanko. Without further word, the Venetians continued down the road to Ferraria.

Pietro trotted over to his master. He hoped his voice sounded more surprised than guilty when he asked his carefully prepared question. "How did the ghosts of Liberi and Pelligrini let this happen?"

"Liberi is still alive as far as I know, and I have never possessed Pelligrini's ghost. The original orbs were of the untrainable sort, the product of early experiments. Good at shedding light, nothing more."

"You deceived him? You let your man Malignari lose!"

"When one experiment is finished, you move on to the next, enlightened." He freed the glowing orbs from the clasps on the rapier and handed them to Pietro. "Be certain to place these back in their proper slots. The Trissino ghosts, if I'm not mistaken. And I shall have to school you on proper sleight of hand."

"You knew?"

"My plodding little turnip, I don't care who wins or loses. I gain a fresh strong orb either way." He bent over Malignari's face with an empty orb and broke the nub. The duelist's body twitched as his ghost was drawn into the sphere. "I now have collected a swordsman's spirit and I have a fine sword in which to place it."

The Corn Bear

Michael Penncavage

The road cut a straight swath through the fields. Extending to the horizon in all directions, the rows of corn created an endless sea of lush greens and pale yellows. A warm breeze washed over the area, causing the husks to bend in unison, paying homage to the sun.

The conditions were perfect as the Pennington Peddlers Cycling Group sped along the recently paved country road. Infrequent hills and a lazy, westerly wind made for ideal cycling conditions. They had chosen this route the same way as the others—by tacking a map onto the wall and tossing a dart at it. They went wherever the dart landed.

This month it was Roger's turn. Having barely ever handled a dart before, the throw was awkward. It struck the top of the map, making his companions collectively groan. They all lived in the southern part of the state. Getting to their destination was going to be a *long* drive.

It was agreed Roger would do some serious practice before it was his turn again.

The morning dew was fast evaporating when the dozen riders that made up the Pennington Peddlers arrived at the Dusty Creek Motor Inn. Drew had plotted a sixty-mile course that would wind them through the countryside before placing them back at the motel.

The group quickly got ready. Bicycle gears and derailleurs were oiled, tires were inflated, spokes checked, water bottles filled, and by nine-thirty, the Dusty Creek Inn was a mere pinpoint in the distance behind them.

None of them had ever traveled to this part of the state before. And for good reason. Corn, barns, corn, cattle, corn, pigs, and more corn were the area's mainstay—a complete contrast to the more metropolitan south. Real estate was cheap and a typical farmer owned countless miles of fourth-, fifth-, and sixth-generation land. Property lines were nonexistent, making it impossible for anyone but the owners to determine where one man's land ended and another's began.

It was a virtual sea of corn, the road parting the way as if it had become Moses, the riders the Israelites, and the corn the Red Sea.

Three hours into the ride, Roger glanced at his watch. He smiled as he downshifted and pedaled harder, taking advantage of the slight decline in the road. His speedometer read 27 mph and he was barely breathing hard. Earlier in the morning he had worried about making everyone drive so far, but now, after they were on the road and making great time, he didn't feel as bad.

A strange rumble passed through the air. Roger glanced down at his tires, thinking that he had gotten a flat. To his relief they were fine. He turned his head so that the wind wasn't blowing in his ears and listened. He heard it again, sounding like some sort of fog-horn.

"You hear that?" he asked his girlfriend Laurie who pedaled by him.

"Only thing I hear is the rumble of my stomach. I'm starved!"

They passed a faded metal sign slightly after noon. It bled rust from buck-shot holes.

TOWN LIMITS

WOODRUFF

POPULATION: 452

A few minutes later they rode into town. Woodruff consisted of a bar, feed store, gas station, and little else. There were remnants of other abandoned buildings but they had become so weather-beaten from the bitter winters and searing summers that it was impossible to tell what they had once been.

The group stopped in front of the bar. It was so battered that it seemed like one more windstorm would be all that it needed to bring it down. A wood sign swung above the door: *Jake's.*

"Let's have lunch here," Stewart said as he propped his cycle against a nearby railing.

"In there?" His girlfriend, Sarah, looked at him as if he were joking. "No thanks. I packed a lunch."

Stewart groaned as he pulled off his helmet and fastened it to the handle-bars. "Oats and bananas? No thanks. I'm more in the mood for a hamburger. We've got so many miles to go that we'll burn off anything we eat, no matter how greasy it is." Stewart pulled his empty bottle from its cage. "I'm out of water, anyway. If we eat in there, we can have the bartender refill our bottles."

Sarah took the lunch out from her bike bag. "Do what you want. Just don't look to me for antacids when you get heartburn going up the next hill."

It took a minute for their eyes to adjust to the bar's murky interior. The lights were on but they did nothing to reduce the gloom. The curtains were fastened so tight over the windows that it could have been night outside. Up in the rafters, a smoke-encrusted fan slowly turned, doing little to reduce the stifling heat in the room. A pool table sat in the back, the once-green felt top looking as if it had not been replaced in several decades. Black-and-white photos of people dressed in long-outdated clothes lined the walls. A small trophy case was off to one corner, the glass so dusty that its contents could barely be seen. A lack of tables meant dinner crowds were not a major source of revenue. It did not appear that Jake's got much of *any* crowd since four of the barstools had their seats torn off and did not look as if they were being missed.

A short, thin man who looked between 90 and 100 years old emerged through a back door, carrying a crate of beer that looked impossibly heavy for him. With surprising ease, he hefted the crate onto the bar-top, making the bottles within clank together noisily.

"Afternoon. I'm Jake." He smiled, displaying his three stained teeth. "Hope you weren't waiting long. I was down in the cellar."

"Do you serve lunch?" Stewart asked.

Jake pondered the question as if it were one he wasn't regularly asked. "Yes. Though we have a limited menu."

Sarah snickered and received a kick from Stewart underneath the bar.

Drew removed his cycling gloves. "What do you have?"

Scratching his beard, Jake thought about this for a moment. "Let's see. I could put on some cheeseburgers or hotdogs if you like. I think we have some of them buffalo wings left in the freezer."

"Anything else?" Sarah asked.

"Afraid not. Though I got ten different beers on tap if you want something to drink," he said grinning.

They grinned back at him.

Fifteen minutes later Jake came back from the kitchen with a tray full of food. "I had some fries back there too. You sure none of you ladies would like something to eat?"

Sarah put down her glass of water. "No, thanks."

Jake nodded as he poured another pint for Roger. "It's sure a hot one to-day, isn't it?"

"Yes," Laurie said, giving Roger a concerned look. "And *you* shouldn't be drinking so much alcohol. You're going to dehydrate."

"She's right, buddy," Drew said as he took a bite from his burger. "We've got a lot of miles left to bike. There isn't any sag-wagon to come along and get you if you start cramping up."

Roger ignored them, finished his beer, and signaled to Jake for another. "Relax. There are lots of carbohydrates in beer." He looked to Stewart and grinned. "And it's common knowledge that a high carbohydrate diet is vital for people who do a lot of exercise. Besides, as long as I drink some water with each beer, I'll be fine."

A pout formed on Laurie's face. "I don't care. That's your last one."

Jake handed Roger another beer. "Y'all are bicyclers?"

"That's right," Drew said. "We're touring the area for the day."

Jake leaned against the bar. "Back in the day, I used to scoot all over the place with my bicycle. Of course that was a long time ago. Before cars were much in fashion around these parts." He cleared away the dirty dishes and placed them into the wash basin. "I trust you're all keeping clear of them Corn Bears?"

Stewart looked at him strangely as if he had misheard the man. "I'm sorry . . . the what?"

Jake produced a towel from underneath the counter and began wiping the bar-top. "The Corn Bear, son. No one's ever told you about them?" The group gave him blank stares. Jake stopped wiping and grinned again. "Well, I reckon it's a good thing you stopped in at Jake's then."

Roger looked at the old man as if he had been doing more than just gathering bottles down in the cellar. "What exactly is a *Corn Bear*?"

"The Corn Bear is . . . well, I'm not really sure what it is. They live in the cornfields. Everyone who grows up in these parts knows about them."

"What do they look like?" Stewart asked, trying desperately to keep a straight face.

"Big and wide." Jake used his hands to show the width.

"Cows are big and wide," Drew said.

"And they live in the corn?" Laurie asked. "What happens after the weather gets cold?"

"Legend says that it dies when the crops are harvested and is born anew with each spring thaw. Its strength comes from the crops—the higher the corn grows, the stronger and larger it gets." Jake poured himself a beer from the tap. "And I can't recall a season that the corn has grown so high as this season."

"Have you ever seen one?"

"Only once. I was driving along not far from here when I saw something dart across the road ahead of me. It was gone in a flash and for a minute I thought it was the heat reflecting off the road, playing tricks on me. I got out of my car and walked into the grass. About twenty feet off the road, just inside the first row of corn, was a spot where a few of the stalks had been crushed and flattened out. Then, deep in the cornfield I heard a sound so terrible that it made me jump into the truck, take off, and never look back." In one gulp, Jake drained half the mug's contents. "I always kept one eye on the cornfield after that."

"It could have been a wolf," Drew said.

"Coyotes don't venture to this area until well into the winter."

"Have these . . . *Corn Bears* been known to eat people?" Sarah tried to keep a straight face.

"No one's sure." Jake began filling up their water bottles from the bar's spigot. "Occasionally the police find a motorist's car off to the side of the road, abandoned."

Drew tugged on his cycling gloves. "Yeah, but that's because the serial killer probably got them."

Sarah hit him across his arm. "That's a horrible thing to say!"

"Okay, seriously. Maybe the car broke down and the driver abandoned the vehicle."

"I suppose," Jake said, scribbling out the lunch bill onto a slip of paper. "But I've always made it my policy to keep a rifle in the truck's gun rack just in case."

They passed around the bill. The five hamburgers cost a total of fifteen dollars. Sarah grinned as she waved the bill at Roger. "Hey, Roger, your beer tab was the same as the food!"

Roger looked at his empty beer glass and silently burped.

They paid the bill, left a generous tip, and headed out.

The day grew hot as the group began the return portion of the trip. The unmerciful sun made them drain their water bottles. The breeze, no longer at their backs, made it feel like they were pedaling through water. Even the cars, which were usually an annoyance, had disappeared, leaving the riders alone to the road, the sun, and the wind.

And most of all, the corn.

To help fight the wind resistance they cycled in a pace-line, the lead taking the brunt of the wind, allowing those behind to benefit from the slipstream. It helped until the wind, as if sensing it was being tricked, began to blow harder. Calves burned from lactic acid buildup and chests grew heavy from labored breathing. Weariness set in and their pace faltered. They looked for a place to take a break, to get them out of the sun, to help catch their breath, but no shade could be found. Not a tree, bush, or even a tall weed was in view to offer them refuge.

Nothing but the corn. And for a rider, the muddy ground only served one purpose.

Roger slowed as he coasted over to the road's shoulder.

Drew pulled up alongside of him. "Don't tell me you have to go to the bathroom again? That's the fourth time in two hours! I told you not to drink all of those beers! You're going to shrivel up into a prune if you keep peeing as this rate."

Roger felt as if his friend might be right. Between the burgers and the beers, his legs had become leaden sinkers, his mouth a cotton factory, and his lips dried worms. "Don't worry. I'll catch up," he said, walking through the first row.

The corn towered above him and the stalks grew so thick that they felt like prison bars. The farmer had planted the seeds in straight lines, perfectly spaced, making the corn stalks look like soldiers in perfect formation.

Roger walked in deep, making sure that a passing motorist—or worse, a cop—wouldn't see him. He wasn't sure if it was a fining offence, but knowing his luck, it probably was.

The immense corn leaves, eager to absorb as much of the sun as possible, created a natural canopy. As a result, most of the rays did not reach the ground, which made the air cool and the ground moist.

Finishing his business, Roger closed his eyes and leaned against a stalk, grateful that it was able to support his weight. The cool, moist air felt refreshing. He dreaded going back out into the sun.

A sudden rustling broke the silence. Roger opened his eyes and was roused from his daze as he tried to determine which direction it had come from. The rustling happened again and he looked to his left. . . .

Nothing. He let out a sigh of relief. *Just the wind blowing through the leaves.* A bead of sweat dribbled down his forehead and off his nose. Jake's tall tales were playing tricks with his mind. He turned quickly and strode through the corn towards the road.

However, after a dozen rows, he hadn't reached the edge. Roger retraced his steps. Pushing aside the stalks, he walked back through the corn, looking for the marker he had left. But after walking the same distance, he didn't come across the puddle.

Panic seized him.

He was lost.

Roger cursed himself for being so careless. Every moment he spent wandering around, his friends were slowly distancing themselves from him.

He tried listening for passing cars to help him find the right direction. All that he heard was his rapid breathing and his heart pounding in his ears.

He began walking, hoping he was now going in the right direction. *I must have just walked farther into the field than I thought.* With each step his bicycle shoes sank deep into the mud, making a sucking noise as he yanked them out.

The same fog-horn sound from before reverberated through the air. It was louder this time and seemed so out of place that it sent a shiver up between his shoulder blades.

He realized that whatever was making the noise was in the cornfield as well.

The corn rustled and shook violently near him. The air grew foul, smelling of musk and decay.

It's a dog.

No. Not a dog.

It was something much worse.

The approaching roar of a car engine made his heart skip a beat. *The road.* He *was* heading in the right direction. Roger ran faster, not bothering to push aside the stalks. The corn battered and cut him as he stormed through. He felt a trickle, which he knew wasn't sweat, run down his temple.

Through the vegetation Roger caught a glimpse of something metallic. *The bicycle.* A moment later he saw the black shimmer of the road through the stalks. He was almost there.

Something snagged his leg. He spun around to keep his balance, his momentum propelling him out of the corn and onto the grassy shoulder that separated the field from the road.

He lay on the grass for a moment, trying desperately to catch his breath.

A gash crossed his thigh. Fortunately, the wound wasn't deep but it was significant enough that his leg was smeared in blood.

After a moment he realized that whatever was within the corn was not coming any closer. Either it couldn't or wouldn't venture out into the sunlight. The cornfield, as immense as it was, was its prison.

Roger sighed in relief.

He had escaped.

He turned to his bicycle when he heard the shuffling of feet up by the roadside. He squinted and saw Jake approaching. A rifle was slung over his shoulder. "Get yourself into a bit of trouble, there?" he said. "Damn, you look worse than a fellow I once saw attacked by a Doberman."

"It's . . . right there . . . inside the corn," Roger gasped, pointing.

Jake looked past him and into the field.

Roger took a step forward. Jake leveled the rifle at him. Roger stopped short and instinctually backtracked. "What the hell are you doing?"

"Did I or did I not warn you to stay out of the cornfields?"

"It . . . I had to go to the . . ." Roger lost his train of thought as he stared at the rifle.

Jake spat onto the ground. "You go running into the field, excite my baby, make him think it's feeding time and then decide to just run away? Don't you think that's a little unfair?"

The corn rustled again. The air became even more foul than before.

A shadow rose behind Roger and he realized he had taken too many steps backwards.

Jake watched as Roger was pulled through the corn. A short, pathetic scream sounded. The stalks swayed as the Corn Bear dragged its prey deep within the field.

Silence followed.

Jake threw his rifle up on the gun rack, looking up and down the road.

Not a car in sight.

Jake hoisted himself into the cab, hit the ignition, and drove off.

In the weeds, Roger's bicycle still lay, its rear wheel spinning freely in the warm summer air.

The Desert Island Fifty

Jason S. Ridler

Dan warmed his hands over the steaming pile of fries, gravy, and cheese curds. "Screw Quebec," he said. "Harvey's makes the best poutine in the universe."

"You'd know," Charlie said. "You've been eating it for ten years."

"Our tenth anniversary."

"Yup," Charlie said as he rammed another fry in his mouth.

At sixteen they'd both slung burgers there, but the job was so beneath the two budding rock stars that Charlie and Dan both told their boss to cram it after two months, vowing to eat there once a year using the money their band made. Three years later, Charlie traded in his Gibson SG for a computer, but the tradition stuck.

"Novel done?" Dan said, shoveling poutine into his maw.

"Almost," Charlie lied. He'd finished the title: *Kiss My Heart as it Breathes*, but that was it. He *did* have ten years worth of great titles. His current favorites were *Thunder in the Bone* and *When the Void Sings, I Cry*. He wanted to be a writer so bad, but the muse never sang. And now he knew why. "How's Clocktower Blue doing?" he said, switching gears.

"Good. We're rockabilly now. New name, too, The Desert Island Five, after the old conversation starter, the five books, albums, whatever, that you'd be happy with on a desert island."

"Great name."

"Yeah, we used to play DI5 here *a lot*, heh. Bet I can still name your five favorite books."

Charlie laughed. "No chance."

Dan spoke mechanically. "Um, *Death Bird Stories* ... Co-co, *Dis-Possessed* ... *Savage Season*, and ... oh, yeah, *End* ... *Ender's Game*."

"Bravo," Charlie said, knowing he couldn't name one thing on any of Dan's crappy lists. "What tunes you doing now?"

"Carl Perkins, Collins Kids, Joe Memphis. We've got real gigs now! No more being paid in beer, thank Christ. And we're doing the blues festival in K-Town this year, too."

"Wow, things are really happening," Charlie said, stifling his jealousy.

"Alright, I guess." Dan licked the gravy off his front teeth and gave Charlie a wide stare. "What crawled up your ass and died?"

"I'm just thinking. Did you think we'd be here at twenty six?"

"No, I thought we'd be touring with Nirvana. They're history, I play bars, you write novels. Shit happens."

Charlie's fingers twitched. "But it should be good shit happening. We should be getting our big break. We're supposed to be *important* now."

Dan furrowed his eyebrows. "What?"

"I've been reading a lot of writers' biographies," Charlie said. "All my heroes had started writing their great works by now, some at *nineteen*. Back then I strove to be an alcoholic lead guitarist."

"Well, your stomach couldn't handle *that*, Sir Pukes A Lot."

Charlie snickered. "Funny."

"So, what made these guys great?"

Charlie sighed. "They all had cool lives. They were raised on EC comics and radio serials like the *Shadow*. They'd fought in wars, or worked crazy jobs, or run with street gangs, or traveled the world with just a knife and a bottle of moonshine. What great novelist ever worked at Harvey's or Loeb?"

"You?"

"Ha, I'm a joke without a punch line."

"Well, *that* was pretty clever."

"I stole it from Harlan Ellison." Charlie grunted. "I should be on panels and discussion groups by now, doing book tours and signings, but I can't because all I've had to work with is my own life; a resume of suburban boredom, and the *last* thing I want to be is Douglas Coupland."

"I thought you liked him."

"I like Douglas Adams."

"Right, the Hitchhiker guy. Hilarious."

"And he wrote scripts for the *Doctor Who* radio show. Shit, what can I offer? The summer we played Punkfest and that nut case in the audience requested 'Sugar Sugar' after every song? That's just depressing."

"I'm sure your book's gonna be great."

"But that's it. It'll be my book, and I suck."

Dan scratched his head with both hands. "So *get* some experiences. Do some crazy shit so you can write your crazy book."

"*That's not it!* I can't do anything to be the novelist I want to be because I would have to be someone else to do it. I'm past that stage where any real writer has cut their teeth before creating their life's work. I don't have the summers where I only read Hemingway, mastering the bare bones of the plain style, or learned the craft of humour from being a stagehand at the Shaw festival. I'm past the watermark for generating cool experiences. I'm stuck being me."

"Why the hell do you have to have these experiences anyway? Aren't you fantasy, horror types supposed to make shit up?"

"All fiction is lies."

"There you go."

"See? I stole *that* line from Kurt Vonnegut, a World War Two vet."

Dan took a big, slow breath. "Ok, ok. So, then, why don't you write about the band? Hell, you started Clocktower Blue, and we did tons of crazy crap. Just change the names so we don't get the Mounties on our asses."

"Those memories suck. No one wants to read about suburban kids who aspired to be Hüsker Dü and ended up as the opening act to Dan Ackroyd's Blues Brothers' carnival of snores in Kingston."

Dan got up and jammed his empty container in the trash so fast Charlie thought he'd punched a hole in the wall. "Thanks, *friend.*"

"I'm just saying what I feel."

"We'll either change or suck on a turd. I was going to ask you to play rhythm with us, but I guess that's beneath you now. News flash, Chuck, misery doesn't love company, you self-defeating fuck." Dan bolted through the door like a wounded rhino.

Slowly, Charlie scrunched his burger wrapper into a ball so tiny and tight it might as well have been a bullet. A man, no bigger than a ten-year-old boy, approached. He was as craggy as a mountain and tipped his fedora before he spoke.

"Pardon me, but did I hear correctly, you're a writer?"

"Uh . . . well, sorta."

"Well, that's just great. The world needs books. Too much bad stuff on TV."

"Right. Can I help you with something?"

"Oh, I thought I'd ask if *you* wanted help. I work in the publishing world."

"No shit?"

"Please, I can't abide swearing. May I sit?"

"Sorry, sure."

The old man sat. "Martin Hecatomb." He extended his hand.

"Charlie Pritchard." They shook. The man's hand was iced skin, harder than leather. Moron needed to buy some gloves.

"See, Mr. Pritchard, although I'm not one to pry, I couldn't help overhearing your dilemma, and, well, I'm willing to fix it for you."

"You could get my novel published? I'm almost done—"

Mr. Hecatomb smiled. "No. But by your own admission, how good could it be, even if it were completed? As you said, a novel expresses the life of the writer. And you haven't had much of a life, have you?"

Hearing it from someone else made Charlie want to kick teeth. He fought for something in his head to throw at the little shit, some awesome piece of evidence, but it all faded into a sour moment.

Mr. Hecatomb spoke jauntily. "But I *can* increase the talent in you."

Charlie snorted. "A training course? Look, the best thing a writers group ever got me was a blow job from some hippie chick who believed in unicorns."

Mr. Hecatomb laughed and covered his mouth. "Mr. Pritchard, please!"

"Sorry."

He adjusted his tie as if he needed the knot to breathe. "This is not a writers group. I'm offering you a chance to write the books you crave, without effort. All it requires is a bit of paperwork and I guarantee your next works will be awe-inspiring."

"And?"

"Sorry?"

"Well, I'm not keen on process, but how much does it cost?"

"Nothing from you. Absolutely free. You won't have to take anything or sign anything. All you have to be is willing to receive whatever we send you, no questions asked. A handshake will be our confirmation." He took out a note pad and pen from his jacket pocket and placed them in front of Charlie. "Please put your name and address here. After that, all I need is a list of all your favorite authors, ones that you respect and admire and wish you could write like. We'll formulate your regiment from this data."

"Sure," Charlie said, confused, hopeful and desperate. "And what happens then?"

"You'll produce the books you want."

"Just like that?"

"Think of it as magic, if it makes it easier."

Easy was Charlie's speed, effortless his style. He started writing down his favorite authors.

"But, Mr. Pritchard, they must be living authors."

"Why?"

Mr. Hecatomb grinned. "It has to do with intellectual property and all that. Using the dead is more troublesome and less cost effective. Don't fret; all of this is to protect you from harm."

Charlie laughed. "Mister, if want me to sign in blood—"

"No need. Just get as many names down as you can."

Charlie started with his desert-island-five and then some, but at thirty he drew a blank. Then he thought of all the blurbs he'd wanted to read on the back of his own books and the writer's block fizzled. "Pritchard's work reads like Margaret Atwood on acid!" "Forget Barker, Rice and King, Pritchard is the new Dean of Horror." Or, his personal favorite, "Pritchard has the grace of Amy Tan, the heart of Lewis Shiner, and the soul of Grace Amundson." And that did it. He capped the list at fifty. His wrist hurt. It was the most writing he'd done in years.

They shook hands, a gentleman's agreement to receive whatever would be sent, and the chill in the old man's hand tingled in Charlie's finger bones. Mr. Hecatomb told him it would take seven days for the work to get done. He suggested Charlie get lots of sleep, then try to write his next novel after a week. "It will be quite an experience." He gave him his phone number, should there be any trouble.

"Sure thing," Charlie said, laughing to himself as Mr. Hecatomb left. "Freaky bastard."

A week passed. Charlie forgot about the old man and the list. One night, bored with the rerun of *Friends* on TV, he felt an itch in his finger. He started plugging away under the title *Kiss My Heart as it Breathes*.

It was godlike. Every word came out like a bullet, and he wrote with machine gun speed, so fast that he barely knew where he was going with every paragraph but confident as steel that it was in the right direction. And the work wasn't pulphouse drek; this was literature, sublime enough to give Harold Bloom a hard-on for life. He finished it in four weeks, fingers frozen from exhaustion, and was fired from Loeb for missing shifts.

He was scared to read it, but when he did he cried. It read like a novel. It felt like a novel. Hell, it smelled like a novel! He read it again and again completely oblivious to the fact that every page was a surprise, as if someone else had sweated through the pages.

When he reached "The End" for the third time, he closed his eyes to consider it in all its glory.

And the story evaporated from memory.

Every time.

Nothing stuck. There were flashes of brilliance, moments of spiritual wonder and epiphanies of the heart, and he knew this was the best book he had ever read. . . .

But every reading left him blank, his memory bankrupt of the experience.

The next day he got the letter from Hecatomb Agencies. It gave instructions on where to send the draft. He mailed it off. Looking at it made him sick.

Soon, the contract came. It made Stephen King's advance for *Carrie* look like a contributor's copy. But he had to write two more books. Then he could renew for a lifetime contract.

The books were in him. He could feel them in his blood, waiting to burst out through his fingers, hiding in his thoughts until he actually put them to paper, and he knew if he typed they'd spring out like hell unleashed. This time, he told himself, it will be different. This time I'll remember.

He signed the deal, opened his computer file, and started writing beneath his favorite titles.

He didn't sleep for days. He lived on Girl Guide cookies and RC Cola. He finished one novel in three weeks, the other in two. In the white heat of creation he felt divinity run through every cell and fiber of his fuzzy soul; he damn well glowed in the dark as he let the words flow into *Thunder in the Bone* and *When the Void Sings, I Cry.*

The dry blood on his gums cracked fresh as he finished the last page, smiled, and passed out. When he woke up stinking of shit-stained underwear and killer gingivitis he reached for the manuscripts and started reading. He was in love. The words sang off the page and into his heart like rolling thunder. Then he reached "The End."

Time held its breath.

"What was the name of my protagonist?" he said, words like rank leaves on his lips.

A dead black space hung in his mind where the memory should have been.

"Damn!" he threw the pages against the floor of his stained apartment. All he could remember were the titles, those rotten, stupid titles that he'd had for years.

He sent the manuscripts to the publisher and stopped writing.

He lived well for a while, paid his rent for a few months in advance, got his teeth fixed, and bought some clothes that didn't smell like a week-old corpse. His fingers itched but he didn't go near the computer. He just watched old movies.

Months later the books were published in succession. Each one a bestseller and award winner. He got invitations to parties. He was called this century's Theodore Sturgeon, a postmodern Robertson Davies. Hollywood types wanted to know whom he'd choose to play *hush* in the movie version of *Kiss My Heart*.

The name of the character never stuck.

He stopped answering the phone, never went to the release parties, ignored the invitation to chair a panel at Cambridge on the renaissance of fantastic literature. He'd only written the work, what the hell did he know?

A high school photo of him got out, so to avoid scrutiny he grew a beard. He put on the old leather jacket from his Clocktower Blue days and wandered into a bookstore. He picked up the hardcover copy of *Kiss My Heart as it Breathes* from the wall covered in his work. His mouth went dry looking at the cover. There was a handsome man wearing a trench coat, the world behind him a blur of colors and beads of light. He traced the title with his cold index finger before opening it.

He read the first page. Closed the book.

"Damn."

The clerk behind the desk, a teen with third degree acne, gave him a worried look. "Can I help you?"

"You read this?" Charlie said.

"Who hasn't? That book kicked ass."

"Really?"

"Totally. A buddy of mine told me I'd be hooked from the first sentence, and it's true. I couldn't *stop* reading it. Don't let the crappy title fool you."

Slowly, as calmly as he could, Charlie walked over to the cash desk and handed over the book.

"My eyes are kinda bad. Could you read me the first sentence?"

"Sure! Any chance to read Pritchard." A hollow sense of pride nibbled Charlie's heart.

The kid opened the book and read, and Charlie beamed until the words evaporated from his mind like tears in the desert.

"Isn't that amazing? How does he do it?"

"I wish I knew."

Charlie bought his own book with the money it generated, not wanting either. "What . . . kind of book is it?"

The kid's mouth gaped open as he searched for the words. "It's hard to describe Pritchard's stuff because it's just so . . . so crazy it's genius. A modern day quest, but not predictable, and scary as hell sometimes. But the characters rule. Especially *hush*, who is totally kick-ass. How he *hush* with the *hush* changed my life."

Charlie nodded, anger squeezing his jaw shut.

"Don't laugh," the teen said, "but I wanna be a writer just like Pritchard."

"*No you don't*," Charlie said.

"You're just saying that because you haven't read him."

"No," Charlie said, feeling a guilty tug, "what I mean is you should learn from the masters. You should read Ray Bradbury, Stephen King, and—"

"Yeah, right! All those fogies retired. *No one* reads them. Next to Pritchard they look like the Teletubbies."

The bottom of Charlie Pritchard's world dropped like a hangman's trapdoor. He bought a dozen newspapers and sure enough it was true. All fifty, no matter where they were on the planet, had stopped writing. Some had started new professions; others said they had taken ill, some were suffering amnesia. Others refused to be interviewed. One of them wrote an apologetic letter to her fans stating that her imagination had suffered a stroke.

The Desert Island Fifty had stopped writing.

He called Hecatomb.

"You've gotta stop it."

"But, you're on a roll."

"I know . . . what you've done to those writers. You're killing my heroes!"

"Finally woke up, did you? C'mon Charlie. Does it matter? People love what's coming out of you."

"Whatever the hell it is, it ain't mine. It's a lie. It's evil and I don't want to do this anymore!"

"Deal with it, Charlie. You still have at least forty some books in you from what we've siphoned. You're becoming the man of letters you've pined for, and all for a few days of bliss as the work we've engineered runs through you. It's win-win for you, Charlie. No work and all fame."

"I can't read it!"

"That wasn't part of the deal."

Charlie grunted. "How the hell did you do it?"

"You weren't keen on process before."

"Tell me!"

"It's against policy, but I have faith in you. Each of your books is a gestalt of divine imaginative power from the raw knack of the great dreamers, twisted into a shape of our choosing, and poured through you, our ark and facilitator. We impregnate your empty dreams."

"I'm gonna be sick."

"That list was incredible, Charlie. You picked the dreamers who really have *heart and soul*. Terrific! You did with one book what we estimated would take a trilogy! You should be proud, son."

"Of what? I didn't do anything!"

"But you did. Without you the wheels wouldn't be moving. People are losing interest in TV, the Internet, shifting their lustful eyes toward the novels coming through you. When *Thunder in the Bone* came out in February, ten people in Toronto died of exposure waiting in line for the store to open. It's happening, Charlie."

"What's happening?"

"Sacrifice! They're dying for your words! And when enough of them collapse in line-ups at signings, starve themselves between book releases, and die waiting for you to show up at their schools, phase one will be done, and you'll be empty. Rich and so very empty. And you'll make another list, and we'll fill your near-bottomless hole with the remaining fantastic voices. Thanks to your emptiness, the imagination of the world will be a single song sooner than expected, all rivals siphoned of their gift into our ark."

"Why are you doing this?"

"We are the enemy of change, Charlie, and imagination is a revolution song. We've fought it for years to no avail. So, we changed tactics. We've siphoned the dreams of the best and most noble revolutionaries, creating what will be one impossible dream that we shall all dance in at night and reflect on in the morning. This dream is singular and will drown out all others by its sheer power, and soon no one will pay attention to the new dreamers. Those young revolutionaries will perish in silence as we all hum our overwhelming song for forever and a day. Bliss on earth.

"All we needed was an inside man, a Judas to accept the offer, someone oblivious to the heart of the enemy's tales, someone selfish, lazy, barren of talent: And there you sat, Charlie, a fan with dreams of glory without sacrifice. As empty as a new Trojan horse, ready to be filled with dreams contorted to our purpose, and destined to do the job, no questions asked. All you had to do was point, and we siphoned, and filled you beyond our own expectations.

"You're remarkable, Charlie. In the hands of fifty of the greatest living dreamers you never once saw the message beyond the tale. Not once were you inspired to write your own truth. You were everything we could have hoped for in a writer!"

Charlie hung up and screamed. He felt the books in his blood, the itch in his fingers. He blacked out from the pain in his head.

He woke the next morning and prepared to kill himself. The new contract was in the mailbox, but beside it was a letter from Schenectady, New York that took the Valium out of his mouth.

It was from a writer. He knew what Charlie was up to. He knew all about Mr. Hecatomb and the invisible string that Charlie's poisonous books were weaving through the world, tying people to his every page like a noose. And he knew about the writers Charlie had crippled: he too had been on the list, but Charlie had misspelled his name, giving him a chance to escape. He said this happens once every few hundred years, a battle in a war that never ends. That Charlie wasn't the alpha and he wouldn't be the omega. And while he chastised Charlie for being a no-talent rube (so brutally, in fact, that Charlie almost put the pills back under his tongue), he also gave him a sliver of hope to save the authors he'd abused and stop Hecatomb's plan.

The envelope also contained a black quill owned by the Marquis De Sade, instructions, and a warning.

Charlie wipes the tears from his eyes. He is at the Harvey's where he had met Mr. Hecatomb exactly one year ago. Dan has not shown up for the eleventh reunion, but that was to be expected.

Here he will write a story, a truthful one, the only one he has in him: a story of blindness, plagiarism, stupidity, and the rape of creativity. And it will end with an apology for which there can be no forgiveness.

It will be written fifty times, one copy for each of the fifty whose lives were bludgeoned by his cowardice: every word written with his blood. The quill is sharp and never dulls.

With every letter completed, the spell breaks and what was stolen is returned. He feels the power exit his blood and return home as the quill's red tip marks the page. And with every copy, the poison of Hecatomb's manipulations becomes manifest, and a year is bitten off of Charlie's life.

Every page turns his beard gray and shrivels his sore, liver-spotted hands. By the forty-ninth letter he can barely move or see. But he doesn't stop. He'll pay the price.

He will be seventy-seven when he has finished, sitting at Harvey's, covered in hundreds of tiny wounds, dying where he had sworn he'd never work again.

Charlie realizes what it means to be a writer. It hurts but he smiles, and starts another page.

The Pit Fighter

Alex Jackson

Gumm dug his feet in, stood bolt upright, straining his body against the twine that bound him to the wooden pole. The pole shifted in the sand. Sweat crawled down his shaven head. He was remarkably strong for a little man.

Then he stopped and looked up over the stone walls of the pit, his black eyes glistening in the lamplight. He could take the time to look into the audience. His opponent, a meaty southerner with a tangle of red locks, was badly beaten and hung limply from the pole to which he was tied. Welts had begun to form about the southerner's face, a string of foam dangled from a swollen lower lip.

As Gumm stared up at me, a shifting haze seemed to hang before his face as though he were looking up at me from underwater. And my heart beat high in my chest as his voice rasped inside my head.

How sad you are now. How unfortunate. Watch closely.

I found myself looking at the floor, my head shaking back and forth. I heard the sounds of flesh smacking flesh. When I looked up, Gumm was pounding his opponent's face with his fists. The stout southerner's head bobbed about as if he were a doll in the hands of an overzealous child. Flecks of blood streaked Gumm's arms and face. I hated pugilism. But more than that, I loathed Hortice Gumm.

My father had always held to the notion that pit fighters were worse than whores. He told me this at least once a day. Because when I was a child, years before servitude and familiarity dulled my taste for it, I spoke of nothing but the Pit and the colorful fighters who dueled for their lives in the great stone hole.

Thus I was thrilled when I met Dahl, who shared my fascination with the Pit. From the time of my father's death to my fourteenth summer, Dahl had been my closest friend. In the autumn of that year, he went missing.

After the old man died, I became a servant at Roal's Den. I met Dahl while on an errand at the tailor's where he apprenticed. Over time we became friends.

We were about the same age and sometimes people would say that we looked like brothers, though his hair was brown and mine jet. Unlike me, Dahl was cocky and often seemed to me to be a bit older than he was.

At the end of the market week, the two of us would walk down to the old stone bridge that leads out of the city to the mainland. I could always manage to steal some food and a sack of wine from the Den's stocks, and we would sit out there by the water and drink and talk.

It often seemed to me at the time that Dahl had a keen insight into people. I remember him telling me: "Every man wishes he were a pit fighter, Urias, whether he admits it or not. That's why people love it, because if they had their druthers, they'd be knocking other men's heads for coin, I can assure you."

That was Dahl. He was old for his age, which is why I couldn't understand how he ever became enthralled by someone like Hortice Gumm. I saw through Gumm right away.

We were at the center of the city for the Harvest Bazaar on the night that Gumm appeared. Dahl and I had bought a pair of leather bracers—the kind archers wear to protect their wrists. We bought them from this ancient bowyer-fletcher at the bazaar. We didn't have enough money for two pairs so we split one.

A lot of folks our age were down by the Channel Bridge that night, crowded around a huge fire and drinking wine. Among them was Hortice Gumm. What immediately struck me as odd, but apparently wasn't at all strange to Dahl, was his age. The man had seen thirty summers at least. The oldest among us had not seen twenty. He wore a pit fighter's black jerkin, his head powdered with stubble as if he had just been released from the dungeons at Scaithe. Several missing teeth left black gaps in his grin.

He was talking to a group of boys when I first saw him—flashing a Silverguard dagger and recounting some story. His frame jerked and quivered when he spoke, as though something inside him was trying to wriggle its way free. Immediately, I wondered to myself: Why is this grown man bent on impressing a group of children? But beside this, there was a sense—a feeling I got when I looked at him. Something about him made my skin crawl. It's hard to explain, but I felt that way as soon as I saw him. Dahl did not.

I must have noticed Dahl's interest in the pit fighter and was trying to hold his attention. I don't remember what I was talking about, only that when I looked up to see if he was listening, he was hovering outside the circle that had formed around Gumm. He stood there grinning and nodding his head as though he understood exactly what the pit fighter was talking about.

I, however, kept my distance. Eventually Gumm offered to take some of the older children to a tavern. When they asked me to come I declined, and when I did, Gumm stared at me from across the flames. Perhaps he had sensed something about me, I don't know. But I had little to lose, so I stared right back at him. To be honest, I turned away first. He was a pit fighter after all.

Those who didn't follow Gumm wandered off as the older children departed and I was left alone at the fire. I watched them through the flames as they passed under the yellow-eyed ashwood houses, and ambled down the sandy road, growing smaller and smaller under the fluttering plumes of the night watch torches.

The few times I went by the tailor's shop that week, Dahl was either out or did not have time to talk. Then one night he showed up at the Den while I was working. He was at Gumm's side. Just the two of them.

I remember the night well because Roal, the Den's proprietor and my guardian and master, had given me a daunting task. With the departure of the bazaar a week prior, our patronage had swelled two-fold, and what's more, it was the end of the market week. When Roal wasn't buzzing nervously through the crowd, he was barking orders at me from across the room.

Most nights I worked from morning until well past midnight. Roal was, at heart, a slaver. He wore a doughy mask of a jovial face, framed with disparate patches of stringy hair that fell along his shoulders in streaks of iron and white. When he first took me in, I thought he was a good man, as he rarely chastened me and was always grinning. But after sleeping among the vermin in the cellar for a few months, I decided he wasn't a kind man at all and that the ready smile was merely a means for attention, gold, and ultimately more food to fill his swollen gut. But I didn't hate him. He merely was who he was. Yet, on those nights when I worked well into the morning, I did resent him a great deal.

On this particular night, Roal had tasked me with quieting the Orlethe brothers. The three were resident combatants. Roal boarded them in a rickety shack that ran along the length of the tavern. The trio's bearing flipped like a coin. When slated for a fight, they appeared at the Den flint-eyed and grim. On off-nights they reeked of drink and more often than not got themselves into a brawl. This was an off-night.

Approaching young Phip Orlethe with my hands open, I caught sight of his brothers, the hulking twins, Goesoothe and Woesoothe Orlethe. Shadowed in the near dark behind him, the twins were engaged in some sort of sparring game, the rules of which seemed to involve slapping each other in the face and giggling.

"Roal says that you either quiet yourselves or leave. He's afraid you're going to brawl again."

Young Phip stood on par with my chin, yet I'd seen him in the pit more than a dozen times and thus bore a healthy respect for his person.

He stroked back a swath of raven hair. "Inform our patron—"

There was a meaty smack, and Phip's head canted to the left, his eyes lit with rage.

Deep laughs harmonized from the shadows: "Har-har-har-har."

Phip swung back towards his brothers. "Do it again and I'll kill you both!"

Feigning gasps of fear, the twins hugged one another.

Young Phip turned back to me and, letting out a short sigh, closed his eyes and said, "Inform Roal that my brothers and I will have one more—"

Smack!

Phip's eyes looked as if they might burst from his tilted head.

And again: "Har-har-har-har."

There was a short hiss. Phip clutched a dagger in his small fist. He grunted once, then leaped at the two shadows. Chairs fell, burst into splinters. Shouts sounded from the crowd gathered around the pit.

"The Orlethe brothers!" someone bellowed.

Men jumped from their tables and the crush stamped towards me. I seized hold of a wood column and swung myself out of harm's way. I saw them then, sitting by themselves at an otherwise abandoned table—my good friend Dahl and Hortice Gumm. They were laughing.

It took only a moment for Roal to end the melee and shepherd the crowd back to their seats. He simply shouted: "You'll not be paid!" The three brothers quickly gained their feet, brushed themselves off and ambled towards the front door.

Glowering at me as he stepped from the crowd, Roal nodded towards the tables surrounding the pit and I dashed into the kitchen to fetch a tray.

Waiting on the two of them—Dahl and his pit fighter mate out for a night of drinking—was nothing short of humiliating and I was suddenly taken hold by the notion of tossing my smock into a corner and taking flight out the tavern's back door. Instead, I poured, filled a tray, and cursed my lot as I made my way back into the hall. My old friend barely acknowledged me as I served him. He nodded his head in my direction, then turned away. Gumm stared into the hole in rapt silence, occasionally throwing a fist, no doubt in unison with the action in the pit. After threading my way back through the crowd, I stopped outside the kitchen to lean my head against the wall. And I remember wishing that I was, if only for a moment, somewhere else, when I heard the voice—a heated whisper as though someone was hushing me to silence.

Is it that you do not like me?

I turned around quickly, but I was alone. As I turned a second time, I saw Hortice Gumm, his face contorted under a watery sheen that seemed to pass through the air before his face. The crowd had their backs to me, but Gumm, standing among the crouching onlookers, was staring directly at me. Then, jerking his head to one side, he turned and sat back down. The twisting of my vision disappeared, leaving me shaken and dizzy.

I found myself wandering into the kitchen oblivious to the bustle around me. When I returned, they were gone.

I went by the tailor's a few days later and the master told me that he'd not seen Dahl in a week. He said that if I saw Dahl I should tell him to go back to his parents' farm and get ready for the winter—a nasty bastard that tailor. I went back a week later and the master told me that he'd not shown his face.

Neither he nor I ever saw Dahl alive again.

But I did see Hortice Gumm.

On a long night near the close of the market week, Hortice Gumm showed his face again. It was late. Only a small crowd of stragglers were left in the Den. Roal smiled at me as I dragged myself to the tables, lugging platters clanking with bottles and flagons. Two thin rogues were engaged in a knife fight in the pit. As I navigated through the crowd, I caught sight of Garoden Ange and stopped in my tracks, which is what most men did when they saw him.

Garoden Ange was by far the largest man I'd ever seen. The table at which he sat was a toy beside his monstrous form. And though the man had seen more than forty winters, his arms remained thick and sharply hewn. But more than this, he was Garoden Ange, Sovereign Champion of the Pit, and every baron, merchant and farmer from the city of Roan to the Valley of the God's Hand knew his name. And though it had been more than a dozen years since he'd been challenged, it was known by all that he fought with the preternatural skill of a demon. In truth, there were those who said that he was possessed of demoniac spirits.

Yet, there were hosts of rumors and superstitions surrounding those who worked in the pit. I once overheard an older man say that in the city of Scaithe, he'd seen Rhiin, the pugilist, transform into an ape and rend his opponent in two. And once, a local merchant told me that Roal had sent his spirit into his bedroom at night to demand payment for an old debt. What's more, it was not uncommon in those days to hear tell that men who spend their life killing for coin stand in danger of becoming the substance of their worst desire— shades, creatures that thrive on terror and devour children whole.

But the times being what they were, I gave little heed to such talk, and never feared the pit fighters as most men did. Of course, Garoden Ange inspired fear for more tangible reasons. But I didn't fear him. For whatever reason, the Sovereign Champion of the Pit bore me a certain measure of respect.

The great man was brooding into the pit as I approached. Sometimes it seemed to me that Garoden hated the Pit. Frequently, when I placed a drink on his table, I'd find him glowering into the stone hole. Then he'd shake his head and say something like: "Neither finesse, nor style."

I always tried to reply. I'd say something like: "No, but he's fast."

Then, sometimes, if I were lucky, he'd grunt.

Or murmur to himself: "The Pit has fallen, there's no honor . . ."

Or sometimes he would point vaguely at the two men engaged and say something like: "Pugilists are ruining the Pit."

Or sometimes it was swordsmen or pikemen who were ruining the Pit, but nearly always someone was ruining the Pit, and he never made it clear exactly how they were ruining the Pit. And I never asked.

The small crowd suddenly erupted with cheers. I walked over to the rim. One of the rogues circled the pit with his arms in the air, a triumphant grin emblazoned upon his sweaty face. The other lay in the sand holding his stomach, a red slit in his leather jerkin. I glanced at Garoden. He looked disgusted. A few men jumped into the pit. Others leaned over the edge to help carry the wounded man out of the stone hole. *He'll live*, I thought, *and I'll finally sleep.*

"Challenge!" a voice called from the crowd.

Every man in the tavern turned towards the sound. It was Hortice Gumm. He walked to the rim of the pit. He wore his black, studded armor and a pugilist's gauntlet, a glove made from heavy leather, reinforced with a bar of iron embedded across the knuckles.

The rogue in the pit looked alarmed. "Knives," he said.

"My challenge." Gumm sneered. "A free bout."

"Then what?" the rogue asked.

Gumm raised his gauntleted hand and grinned.

The rogue unsheathed his dagger. "Then you will lose."

Gumm threw his arms up and jumped into the pit. Sand dust billowed like smoke around his feet.

Roal walked to the arbiter's platform at the edge of the pit. Though it was used only half-heartedly in an official capacity, the wooden platform, jutting a few feet off the edge of the stone hole, was meant to serve as means for the arbiter to oversee and if necessary judge the fights. To its rear stood an iron rack overburdened with a vast assortment of weapons.

Roal held his fist out, a smooth white owlstone locked in his grip. "This will be a free bout! Fight until quarter is given or one man drops! Fight with honor! When the stone falls!"

The stone plopped into the sand and the two men began circling one another. Side-stepping, Gumm moved with the measure and grace of a champion. I wasn't the only one who noticed. Though the rogue maintained a flinty bearing, his eyes belied real fear.

Gumm grinned as he began back-stepping slightly, an attempt no doubt to draw the rogue into a proximity where fists might trump a blade. The pugilist favored his right hand, but kept his left open. *Foolish*, I thought.

My shoulders jolted forward. I turned and looked up into the scarred face of Rhiin, the Den's resident pugilist. He held my shoulder in his considerable paw and grinned at me, rakishly. Rhiin, you see, fancied himself a dashing rapscallion, which was somewhat absurd. Years of batterings had left him with one hollowed-in cheek and a badly mangled nose.

Running a pinky finger through his oiled black hair, Rhiin studied my face. "Urias," he said with a silky lilt.

"Yes."

Lifting his scarred chin, he shifted only his eyes towards the two combatants in the pit. "A new pugilist, it seems."

"It looks that way, Rhiin."

"This one," he said, raising a crooked finger as if to instruct. "I will bounce this one's hindquarters across the lunar cycle." Then he nodded and narrowed his eyes as though he'd just imparted some valuable bit of wisdom.

This sort of comment was common for Rhiin. He was rather insane.

"Urias!" someone shouted from the crowd.

Glaring at me, Roal motioned his head towards Garoden Ange's table. I rushed into the kitchen and fetched a cup of ale. When I arrived at his table, Garoden took his drink without looking at me.

"Pah!" he shouted, spitting hugely on the floor. "I could sit in any alley in the thieves' quarter and watch this. Dragging the Pit into the gutter, boy. Into the gutter.

"Look at this. Just look at it. Blades . . . the blades they drop into the pit these days . . ."

The rogue swung his knife at Gumm's middle. With the slightest shift, Gumm dodged the blow. *He's fast*, I thought. As the rogue's blade swung wide, Gumm bore in on him with a wide cross. The rogue yanked his head back, the blow just missing his face. Gumm turned with the swing, his fist reaching into the air. Then, just as the rogue's lips curved into a grin, Gumm's elbow came crashing down hard and square on the rogue's temple. The rogue fell solidly to the ground.

Gumm jumped into the air and landed on the stunned man's stomach with both feet. The rogue's head and legs bounced in the sand and his eyes shot open.

Garoden Ange kicked his chair over and stomped off towards the door. I walked away myself then. As I entered the kitchen, I heard the sound of flesh impacting flesh through the open door.

Later that night, as I prepared a bed upon one of the tables—I had long ago given up trying to sleep in the basement—I heard a tapping sound. I walked across the hall and opened a window slat. It was Hortice Gumm. My heart began hammering.

It was near sunrise, yet he was wide-awake; a damp sheen glazed his face. "Come, get a drink with me."

"No, I don't think so," I said.

"Then let me come in and have a drink."

"No," I said.

"Did you see the fight tonight?" He raised his eyebrows.

I said nothing. My breath came heavy.

His black eyes darted back and forth. Then he looked at me closely. "I need a second—to keep arms—learn the trade. Might give you a try. You have something . . . finesse, something. . . . Would you like this?"

I felt a curious mix of horror and exhilaration, giddy that a pit fighter claimed to have seen something of quality in me, horrified that the pit fighter was Hortice Gumm. His offer was, in truth, a secret wish known only to me and one other.

Something tightened in my throat. "Where's Dahl?"

He winced like he'd been struck. "Why, I don't know. . . . What do you mean?"

"You do! I know you do! Where is he?"

His eyes flashed. "I'll come in, we'll talk about it."

He reached for the side of the window.

I stepped back. "If you do, I'll raise the alarum. The fighters will pour in here and the watch soon after."

His face twitched.

"What happened to Dahl?"

"If you let me in, they will not come."

"What happened to him?"

He cocked his head like a puzzled dog. "Hmmm. . . . You've lost your friend. That is sad. Very, very sad. . . ."

I closed the slat and walked back to my makeshift bed.

Then I heard his sneering whisper, mingling with my thoughts. *Oh, he's wounded me. Wounded me. . . . Wants to see his friend again. So sad. . . . But maybe not. Maybe not. Yet as I've shown him something of me, he and I will see one another again, of that he can be sure.*

Although I didn't hear the voice again that night, I lay awake until long after the slatted windows cast glowing lines across the Den's dark, wooden floors.

The best pit fights were held at the close of the market week. If one arrived early enough, they might see some of the Den's resident fighters contesting in the great stone hole. If not, one was at least sure to see some of Anu's most promising combatants. Gumm was now considered such a fighter.

After appearing at the window, I did not see him for a few nights. Then, at the end of the market week, he arrived at the Den for a ranked pugilist match.

There must have been talk about Gumm because all of the resident fighters were in the Den that night. Garoden Ange sat, as always, at his table on the edge of the pit. The three Orlethe brothers stood along the rim. Strangely enough, they appeared sober, yet it was still early in the evening. Rhiin, the pugilist, stood upon the lip of the pit as well, admiring himself in a small hand-held glass and gently massaging his oily beard.

I was serving drinks as men began driving thick poles into the sand for the pugilist match. Once secure, the two poles would then be anchored by binding them to spikes hammered into the sandy floor at opposing angles. The fighters are then tied to the poles, facing one another. When the stone drops, the two fighters pummel one another with closed fists until one of them asks for quarter, passes out, or dies.

Gumm and his opponent entered the pit as I handed a flagon to Rhiin, who watched Gumm with keen interest.

"This one will fight me next, Urias," he said as he glided his small fingers through his gleaming beard.

"So I've heard."

"Do you have any idea of what I will do to him?"

"No, but I'm afraid you're going to tell me," I said, knowing that Rhiin wasn't listening to me anyway.

"Crown and hindquarters shall be cuffed, first left, then right." He began making punching motions, his face utterly grave.

"Then, with one final and unmerciful blow, I shall send his buttocks spinning high into the air, until at last it settles in the sky forming its own perfect constellation."

"Indeed," I said.

Rhiin's eyes narrowed. "Indeed."

As the workers tied Hortice Gumm and his opponent to the poles, Gumm looked over in our direction, but not at Rhiin. He grinned at me, and against my will I quivered, as though a cold hand had slipped around my spine. I looked around at the audience. Garoden Ange was staring at me. I became addled then and stepped back into the crowd.

Roal announced the fight as I drifted towards the kitchen. Leaning my head against the door, I tried to slow my breath.

"Look busy, boy!" Roal bellowed as he strutted from the arbiter's platform. I paced into the kitchen and filled a platter with ale and wine.

When I returned to the edge of the pit, Gumm was finishing off his opponent. Although the fight was veritably over, the crowd continued to jeer. All movement around me slowed.

Gumm stared up at me. And the voice came then, becoming slowly discernible, like a whisper in a dream, telling me how "unfortunate" I was. I yanked my head to the side, and my vision cleared. And then the blows fell upon the southerner's head, Gumm's arms moving like the legs of a galloping horse. Blood was everywhere.

I walked straight out the back door and if it weren't for the cool of the night air, I probably would have retched onto the grass.

When I returned to the hall, the fight was over. Some men were carrying

Gumm's opponent out the door, whether it was to the physic or the house of ashes, I couldn't tell.

Gumm had climbed from the pit and was swaggering towards the tables at the center of the Den. A portion of the crowd followed, talking busily around him as he seated himself beside a table. When I noticed Roal, he gestured towards the small crowd and my heart dropped.

When I returned from the kitchen with a full tottering platter, Roal followed me with his eyes. I walked directly into the crowd surrounding Gumm.

A gaunt pauper in rags shouted: "Ale for the pugilist!"

As I carefully stepped through the small knot, Gumm, leaning back in his chair with one foot propped up on the end of the table, winked at me, gesturing towards the spot where his boot lay. As I leaned to place the tray down, he lowered his foot and one of my legs jolted backwards. I fell forward and all of the flagons and bottles on my tray spilled onto Gumm's lap.

"*Cretin!*" he bellowed.

The entire Den fell silent.

He seized my collar and pushed his face into mine, his stubble grating my skin. "*Clean it off, whelp!*"

Everyone was staring at me and my heart raced over the hills. But at the same time I was furious. Yet, I knew full well that I was a servant of no means, who either worked in the Den or begged on the street, so I grit my teeth and nodded my head.

Hands pressed against my shoulders and chest; then I was falling backwards over chairs. My head struck a table and I fell to the floor.

I heard laughter around me.

Gumm bared his teeth. "You keep this dog, innkeeper!" he said as he tugged on his leather gauntlet and marched towards me.

"Let me help you train him!"

"Challenge."

I thought that I had said it quietly, but suddenly I heard the word shifting through the crowd.

"Challenge. Challenge. The boy said, 'challenge.'"

Gumm's mouth hung open. Abruptly, Garoden Ange's ruddy face appeared above mine. He held out his hand and lifted me to my feet.

"Pugilism," Gumm said.

Garoden turned and slapped Gumm lightly on the forehead. "It will be a free bout. Now get yourself in the pit."

I felt like my insides were being throttled. Garoden seized my shoulders. "Fear will undo you now, boy, as sure as you stand. You'll either lose it or die."

He peered sidelong at Gumm and whispered. "You're faster than he is, and you certainly possess more wit, and endurance, I'd imagine, as young as you are. You'll use a sword—a short sword. And he'll most assuredly use his hands. Avoid him. Run. When he grows weary, strike deliberately."

For a moment, I stared at Garoden.

He shook me, his voice a harsh whisper. "You will be deliberate or you will die."

Garoden led me to the arbiter's platform. He turned to Roal. "Short sword," he said.

Roal reached into the weapon rack behind the platform and drew a wide-bladed short sword. Garoden grabbed the weapon by the guard and held the hilt out to me. "A good weapon for you. Listen to me now, don't even *attempt* to strike until he's winded. Now, breathe deep. In through your nose and out through your mouth."

I did.

"Good," he said. "Continue that."

I nodded then climbed down into the pit. As Roal announced the match, I looked at the sand around my feet and breathed in deeply.

The stone fell.

Gumm paced towards me sideways, slowly, like a cat, the gauntleted hand open, the other knotted in a fist.

The pit is the length of five men, I'd have little room to run, but run I would, as soon as Gumm passed the center of the sand floor.

He charged. I bolted along the wall. As I passed him, his knuckles rapped the back of my head, knocking me off balance. I fell sideways into the sand, rolling over my shoulder and onto my back, my feet in the air. As I pushed my hands into the sand, he was upon me. I bunched my legs against my chest. He fell onto my feet and raised his fist high. I pushed my feet up and sent him flying backwards.

As I had done, he rolled with the blow. But his roll was uncanny; he tumbled over himself backwards and leaped onto the soles of his feet.

I had enough time to get up and run to the other side of the pit.

Gumm punched his open hand and sneered, the gap in his teeth opening like a wound as he grinned. He chased me around the walls. I could hear his hand swishing through the air as he reached for me. Abruptly, he changed di-

rection and tried to cut me off by running across the length of the pit. I pivoted quickly, hugging the stone wall as I ran. Then, cutting through the center, he threw himself onto the ground, his outstretched hand momentarily grasping my ankle, and I stumbled. Pain and white light flashed through my head as my skull slammed against the stone wall. For a moment, all I saw was blackness.

The first thought that occurred to me as I ascended was that I had dropped the sword somewhere. When my vision cleared, I was almost level with the crowd, huddling around the rim of the pit. Everyone was staring at me. I began spinning. I caught sight of Garoden. He was saying something.

Roll.

Then the stone wall was coming at me. I shifted, hit it with my shoulder. Searing pain shot up my neck as I tumbled down the wall.

Gumm straddled my waist, held my neck, his hands hard as iron pincers. He peered into my eyes as I groped in the sand for the sword I'd dropped. Spittle dribbled onto my face as his features blurred under a watery sheen. The whisper rasped inside my head.

The friend was sad too.

He's with us now. Here with us as—

"*Pugilist!*" someone shouted.

When Gumm turned, I seized the back of his neck and smashed my forehead into his face as hard as I could.

His head snapped back, a sucking whine escaping his lips as he stumbled backwards and fell onto his haunches.

And there, between us, as though some generous spirit had left it as a prize, lay the short sword, its wide blade half-buried in the sand.

I snatched it as I leaped to my feet. Eyeing his chest, I lunged; the thrust ran high, puncturing his throat above the collar. It stuck there. His skin peeled from the blade like sepals from a budding poppy; but he didn't bleed—not a drop—and I glanced something dark, trembling beneath the tear in his skin. When his eyes went white, I began backing away, fixated on the wound, on the eyes, utterly dumbfounded.

Shouts rang out.

"*White eyes! A shade! A shade!*"

I didn't see him get up or pull the sword from his neck, I only saw him rushing towards me.

I thought to lean out of the way, but he came too fast. His body crashed into mine and I fell. Jamming my neck against the floor, he choked me with one hand, raising the gauntleted fist and screeching like an animal in its death throes. The sound reverberated through the hall. As if in response, the crowd erupted with shrieks and bellows.

"*Daemons! Shades!*"

His fist fell, I tried to dodge it, but it hit me square in the head and my vision edged with black.

When the walls of the pit appeared again, I saw Gumm flying away from me. Garoden had him by the wrist, the huge muscles in his arms bulging as he swung Gumm through the air. The pugilist hit the stone wall with a solid thump.

As the pugilist quivered against the wall, spindling black hairs wormed their way from his arms and neck; the skin on his face slipped from his body like a damp cloth, revealing something black and wet underneath.

Lifting a huge war axe from the sand at his feet, Garoden turned to me, his face darkening. "*A shade, boy! Get yourself from the pit now!*"

I jumped to my feet, grabbed hold of the supports of the arbiter's platform and pulled myself up.

The den was in chaos, so I remained crouched on the rim of the pit. Lamps had been turned over in the tumult, throwing a good part of the tavern into darkness. Sounds that will follow me to my death resounded through the room. Desperate shouts pealed from a silhouetted crowd cramming into the doors leading outside. Two men rolled under the tables by the kitchen doors, grunting almost rhythmically as they pummeled one another, and over and above it all, Gumm's screech—punctuated by what I could only hope were blows being landed by Garoden Ange—rose from the stone hole, filling the hall and reverberating against the distant walls of the Den.

Having just won back my life, I wasn't about to lose it by dropping my guard. Some intangible menace, driven by the sound clamoring from the pit behind me, hung about the air. I felt it. Though battered and weary, a tight sensation seared in my gut, making me want to quiet the mob, restore order by force. Like never before in my life, I wanted to kill something.

On the other side of the hole, a small pile of debris lay smoking, just off the lip of the pit. It looked like a heap of discarded clothing, yet all of it was the distinctive color of human skin.

Beyond it, something moved.

For a moment, I thought that the thing that hovered just outside the cusp of the lamplight might be an exceptionally tall man. But as it moved into the dim corona, I began to make out a form like a bear standing upright, yet with arms that reached down below its knees. And though I remained perfectly still in the near dark, it turned and faced me, and below the echoing cacophony came a growl, like a dog warding off an enemy, only deeper.

Suddenly, Phip Orlethe, the youngest and quickest of the brothers, came sliding across the floor on his knees. He yanked a war axe from the weapons rack and tossed it over his shoulder.

"Woesoothe!" he called.

He pulled a double-bladed axe from the rack and threw it behind him.

"Goesoothe!"

I turned to see Goesoothe lightly snatch the axe from the air. As I gained my feet, Phip, without so much as looking at me, pushed a long knife into my hand. Then he pulled a two-handed sword as long as his person from the rack and began slowly cat-stepping towards the creature.

"Saw him change!" he shouted. "Saw it all! I tell you, it's Rhiin, boys! Rhiin, the pugilist, and he's a hairy-arsed bastard of a blood-sodden shade!"

I fell into line with the twins and we kept pace a short distance behind Phip. As we approached, the thing rose to its full height, its head reaching up to the rafters, and as it roared, the floorboards rattled around our feet as though from a tremor in the earth.

Then it was running, its paws sweeping the ground as it bounded across the floor.

"Ready yourselves, boys!" Phip bellowed.

Phip dashed, tumbled to the floor, and rolled into its legs. The beast toppled. The Orlethe twins appeared beside me, and as I thrust my blade into its side, they hammered their axes into the creature's back. Black blood geysered under the lamps.

I left my blade sticking in the creature. It shuddered as I backed away, then went still.

A hand fell on my shoulder. It was Garoden Ange.

He studied my face. "How is it with you, boy?"

I was at a loss for words.

Phip Orlethe walked up and shrugged at Garoden. "Two of them only. . . ." He gestured at Rhiin's shaggy remains. "Vanity, I suppose." Then he pointed at the black mangled body lying on the sandy floor of the pit. "Enmity, no doubt. One defended the other I'd say, but what of the third? There are always three. That's what they say. *Three.*"

A white arm dangled from the black thing's torso.

"Like passions and maladies, daemons always come in three." Phip leaned towards Garoden, his face bright with agitation. "I mean, it's a diabolical number. That *is* what they say."

Garoden tapped Phip on the forehead with the flat of his hand. "Always illuminating, young Phip."

Phip looked pained. "Well . . . I like to think so."

Garoden gestured towards the remains inside the pit. "Your comrade," he said evenly.

With half the lamps down, the inside of the pit was unusually dark. The dead thing there had a man's shape, but curved like an insect where its parts met. Black hairs as long as timber spikes protruded from its limbs. Its head was gone—a shapeless mass spread out against the stone wall. From a wide crack at the center of the corpse came a pale, thin arm—a boy's arm. Upon the wrist was a leather bracer. The other half of the pair we'd bought at the Harvest Bazaar. Absently, my hand smoothed over the one that I wore on my wrist. My shoulders hiked up and my face clenched as I covered my eyes and wept.

Garoden laid an arm over my shoulder and guided me away from the pit. "We'll bury what remains of your friend. Always sad to lose a companion, I know."

I wiped my eyes with the back of my hand. "Yes," I said. "Thank you."

When I looked up again, Garoden was looking at me in a way that only my father had many years before. "You did well," he said at last. Then he turned away and peered into the corner of the room as though searching the darkness for something lost. "Cheap-jack!" he bellowed. "I think I'll train this one."

I hadn't noticed Roal's approach. He stood just outside our company, wiping his neck with a rag.

"Well," he said, his eyes flitting nervously. "It's not as though I can easily find someone to replace him."

"No, I imagine not. I'll pay you."

"And I have cared for the boy—cared for him since he was small, raised him like he was my very own."

Garoden scowled down at Roal. The tavern keeper crinkled his nose and said, "Well, I'll come up with a figure then, but it is up to the boy now, isn't it?"

"What say you, boy? My life grows dull and you do have some native talent." He looked around the Den. "And perhaps I'll buy this place as well."

"I lost to Gumm," I said. "In the end I lost."

"Count yourself lucky you're not in pieces. A shade, boy! Not a man! You performed masterfully well." Garoden folded his arms and eyed me askance. "And what's your surname?"

"Toom. My name is Urias Toom."

"Ah, Toom . . ." he mused. "A formidable name for a pit fighter."

I don't know what inspired me to say what I said next, only that, as sometimes happens, words fell from my mouth without a scrap of forethought. "My father always said that pit fighters are worse than whores." Instantly regretting the comment, I glanced up at Garoden.

"No," he said, "not at all." Then, for the first time since I'd known him, Garoden Ange smiled like he meant it. "We *are* whores. All of us. But like a good whore, a good pit fighter has some smattering of honor."

Maybe everything that I had been through that night released what had long lain buried. I only know that a thrill coursed through me like I'd plunged into the cool waters of the channel on a sweltering day, and I said, "I'd like to train, Garoden. I'd like to live in the long house and fight in the pit at the end of the market week. I'd like—"

"Well," he said. "Train first. But good. I'd well hate to be proven wrong, but I think you might bear a stitch of honor yourself . . . Urias Toom. Not like this incorrigible dung heap!" And he booted the furry remains of what had been Rhiin, the pugilist.

Then he looked down at me and his eyes paled and his face blurred and shifted as though he were looking up at me from underwater. Inside my head I heard a hushed whisper.

Pugilists, it said. *They're dragging the Pit into the gutter.*

A Plant's Scream

Christine Welcome

Rosalynd Brooks always made me think of one of the exotic plants she became so famous for painting, just as someone else might resemble a pug, or a fox, or some species of bird. At the age of forty she was as striking as ever—tall, slender, golden brown flecks dappling her pale skin, and always cool despite her mass of orange-gold hair . . . and she possessed, as always, a lily's calm.

Thinking back over twenty or so years, I realized I'd never seen Rosalynd cry or scream or swear, though she was always willing to listen to anyone's problems and help in any way she could. And, just as it was as hard for me to believe that a carrot being pulled from the earth would shriek in a tone so high that the human ear could not detect it, I could not imagine, say, Rosalynd Brooks making passionate love.

Which is why I suppose it struck me so funny that I'd just been discussing with Rosalynd whether plants scream, and it was she who had insisted they did. "Science," she said, "has proven beyond a shadow of a doubt that, not only do plants emit sounds the human ear can't quite hear, but cabbages, when being cut from the stalk, shrink away from the knife."

I jabbed at the contents of the bowl before me and nearly laughed aloud at a sudden mental picture of myself, plump and bookish middle-aged woman that I am, decked out as a cartoon cannibal savage giving my salad—poor amputated roots and stalks, shredded, decapitated leafy plants—a final toss.

What, I wondered, not for the first time, would make Ros so inhuman? Did she somehow bottle up all of her anger, frustration, and desires? She must once have had a relationship that stepped beyond friendship, mustn't she? Ros had, in her travels, accumulated not one or two but at least a dozen friends, people like me and my husband, Harry, who thought the world of her. Yet not one chance or arranged meeting had ever blossomed for her, as far as I knew, into romance and certainly never heated passion. Hence, of course, her reputation among those who didn't know her well, as being cold, bloodless, inhuman . . . a walking plant.

I looked up at her wonderful painting, a very valuable one now indeed, which she had placed with her own hands on my kitchen wall. Purplish jungle orchids swayed against a background of jewel-green leaves. Something indefinable made those orchids more than what they first appeared and made hot tears rise to my eyes. I was pondering for the umpteenth time on just what that might be, when Rosalynd's heartbroken cry issued from my parlor where I had left her just moments ago. Startled into dropping my salad tongs with a clamor, bits of green spraying the counter top and floor, I rushed to the doorway.

Rosalynd was sitting just where I'd left her on the couch, but she was bent forward, her long thin hands covering her face.

"Ros?" I knelt hastily before her and saw the glistening of tears that escaped her fingers and streaked down her chin, her wrists. Hesitating to touch her, I looked about, searching for the reason for my friend's sudden, startling grief.

The room was perfectly peaceful in the last of the spring sunlight that streamed in through the open drapes. Nothing disturbed the quiet of the hundreds of books, shelved or otherwise, the worn brown carpet, or the easy chairs, except a sob from Rosalynd and the steady drone of the television.

My eyes fixed on the screen, and I stared at a grainy news photo of a plane crash in the depths of a tangled jungle. Before I'd left the room to finish dinner, I had flicked through the channels to find something that might interest Ros and had stopped at a program called *Discoveries in the Green World*. The changing views of emerald green leaves and alien flowers had seemed like the right sort of thing.

"Ros?" I said softly. She gasped and, reaching out blindly with fingers of ice, clutched my hand so tightly I felt the bones grind together.

The picture on the television had changed and I now found myself gazing into the eyes of a gray-haired man, his expression stony with grief. "Rob," he said, "always called it 'going off into the Green.' And each excursion, all his discoveries, his very life's work was merely incidental to his quest for . . . well, I suppose I can only call it . . . true love."

The picture switched to a close up of his questioner, a bland-faced gentleman who had put on the profound expression of understanding common to all television interviewers. "Robert Swift's discoveries in the field of experimental medicines derived from tropical plants have saved and will continue to save hundreds of thousands of lives. He was the epitome of the unsung hero. Your son's true love for mankind—"

"No," Robert Swift's father said firmly. "I didn't mean true love symbolically, I meant it specifically. All my son's discoveries were by the way of the one thing he was looking for with all his heart and soul."

The interviewer leaned forward in his chair, and so did Rosalynd. Realizing that the answer to the mystery of my friend's scream lay somehow in the story being told, I leaned forward, too.

"It's a very odd tale," the father said, shrugging his shoulders and looking down at his hands. "When he was a teenager Rob worked for a big mail order herb company down in Florida, where we lived at the time. They packaged and sold dried herbs and herbal mixes, pills and potions, shipping them all over the country, and they had several extensive greenhouses in which they cultivated common household herbs and some of the more exotic variety. The building Rob worked in was called simply 'the Green' because of the masses of living things that crowded it, pressing from the inside, turning the windows solidly green. And each day after school Rob pedaled over on his bicycle and spent the better part of four hours immersed in the Green's steaming, fertile depths, harvesting leaves and petals and seeds from the more unusual plants.

"One night he came home and the boy was absolutely entranced, grin a mile wide, mind off in space. His T-shirt and the knees of his jeans were smeared with mud and green and there were leaves in his hair. It was entirely unlike him. I remember I had to ask him more than once what on earth he'd been up to that night before I got his attention.

"'Dad,' he said. 'I found a girl in the Green. The most interesting, wonderful, strange girl.'

"I thought at the time that she must be someone working there with him and that this was a teenage crush. Well, that's a normal enough phenomenon for a seventeen-year-old boy to experience. The leaves in his hair worried me a little, but Rob had always been such a sensible kid, I decided to keep quiet about it. For a month or more Rob was deliriously happy, animated, enamored of life and then, suddenly he broke his heart, or had it broken for him. It seemed the girl was gone. Vanished.

"When I asked him about it, he shrugged me off and subsided into what I thought was a morass of self-pity that lasted much, much longer than it should have. Weeks, months went by, and Rob went around with his shoulders slumped, his eyes lusterless and red-rimmed. He took to shutting himself up in his room. Finally I'd had enough.

"I went to blast him out, but when I opened his door, I found him sitting at his desk, his head bent over a schoolbook. The eyes that he raised to mine were not those of a boy being foolish, they were those of a man struck by grief.

"He had searched for her. Oh, yes, he had. Hours and hours in the thick, steamy, tangled interior of the Green. She was no fellow worker there, as I had assumed. She wasn't, Rob supposed, even fully human. Which puzzled me a great deal, but he wouldn't explain. He didn't know her name, but no one, he said, with those new eyes that knew loneliness and loss, would ever replace her. And, if it took him a hundred years, he would find her . . . she had to be somewhere, didn't she? And if she were no longer in the glassed-in structure called the Green, then where else could she be but in some forest, some jungle, some place in the Green out there?

"And so my boy arranged his life in such a way that he would spend it searching the hearts of forests and jungles where other men seldom, if ever, went, discovering new forms of plant life along the way, bringing back samples, but always and forever looking for *her*."

The interviewer cleared his throat. "And your son never found this woman?"

The father smiled bleakly and shook his head.

"Well, Mr. Swift, thank you for being here today and for that unusual insight into the life of your son. Unfortunately we're about out of time. Next week our show will focus on Dr. Alan West who'll tell us how an actual witch doctor, a tribal shaman in Africa, pointed the way to his greatest, if most controversial, medical discovery. But here, before we go, is a picture of the young Rob Swift, Robert W. Swift whom we honor today, perhaps the man who made the greatest discoveries to date in the Green World, who tragically met his death two days ago at the age of forty-one in a plane crash in the Zambezi River basin."

The boy stood, tall and lanky, before a two-seater plane, his hand raised in a farewell wave. I looked away from his lopsided grin to Rosalynd's face, tear-streaked and open-mouthed as she stared at the late Rob Swift in a photo taken more than twenty years ago.

It wasn't until after my Harry came in and made her drink whiskey that Rosalynd leaned back against the couch cushions, her eyelids closed, her vivid hair spread against the back of the couch like the streaming petals of a wilting flower, and told the story of the young girl she once was.

Rosalynd dropped her book bag on the front steps to pull the catalog out of the metal mailbox. The pages were unevenly cut, and the black print, when she fanned through it, had a peculiar odor, bitter and smoky. She looked again at the cover. "Beautify and slenderize naturally with herbs." Although the gummed label was addressed to Mrs. Tarp, the elderly woman on the third floor, Rosalynd stuffed the catalog into her bag, along with wet gloves and an open roll of breath savers. Mrs. Tarp would never miss it. Nothing could ever beautify or slenderize her, and she was half-blind anyway.

It was always difficult getting beyond the kitchen. Invariably, her mother was there cleaning up, or cooking or reading at the table. And there were always the same questions, "How was school? Do you have homework?" It made it hard to breathe, living as they did, the two of them in such a small, crowded space.

"Homework," Ros mumbled to her mother, as she entered the room, made steamy with stew bubbling on the stove.

But, even as her mother opened her mouth to ask her inevitable questions, Ros was saved by a loud hiss and the unpleasant scent of meat burning as the stew pot boiled over. Her mother rushed to turn the burner down while Rosalynd hurried away to her own messy room. Before shedding her coat and kicking off her shoes, she dumped her overstuffed book bag on the floor amidst a crumpled T-shirt, a scatter of colored pencils, several unfinished sketches of pea plants she had started for her botany report, and her latest unsatisfactory painting of a horse galloping.

A flood of books, squashed tubes of water color paint, sketch pads, gum and makeup slid out from her bag, the herb catalog on top.

"Rosalynd?" came her mother's distant voice. "Did you get your laundry together for me yet?"

Taking one look around her room and seeing clothes draped and thrown on every visible surface and angle, Ros called back, "I will in a minute." Grabbing the catalog, she hurriedly escaped into the bathroom. Locking the door, she started the hot water in the roomy, footed tub and gave a sigh.

It wasn't that her mother was so bad, or that her life was so hard. It was just. . . . Pulling her sweater over her head, she looked at her face in the mirror, watching it cloud over with steam. She shrugged. There were too many details and not enough time; people always wanted something done and. . . . Stripping off her other clothes and leaving them in a soggy lump on the floor, she stepped into the tub.

The herb book left black marks on her fingers as she reclined in a mass of bubbles, turning its ever dampening pages. The smell of the print mixed with the sweet scent of soap to create a curiously appealing mix. For a moment Rosalynd's head swam and she closed her eyes. With a start she found she'd been sleeping and had nearly dropped the catalog into the bathwater.

Sitting up straight with a slosh, she again began to peruse the catalog's pages. In addition to vitamins and shampoos, there were some very odd items indeed. "The South American miracle herb that protects your immune system. Restore your love life with Super Potency Formula #99. Try Tranquility and lift the strain on your brain with our newest formula. Contains skullcap, passion flower, catnip and other all-natural mystery ingredients. Have a real adventure in your bath and leave all your troubles behind."

She had some money left from Christmas and baths *were* her favorite escape. Her mother was barred from entrance by the locked door, and in the warmth and steam of the bathroom you could close your eyes and dream, at least for a little while.

The package was wrapped in brown paper and only as long and wide as her hand and perhaps three inches deep. It weighed nothing, with no mark except the return address, so carelessly stamped that half of it was illegible. Rosalynd held it gingerly, noticing that there were round holes in the cardboard all the way around as though it contained some small, living creature. She held the box up to one eye, seeing only blackness inside, but she could have sworn something shifted in there with a whisper of papery sound. She caught a breath of perfume and then the same odd, smoky scent of the print on the herbal catalog. Surely that had to be some living thing brushing itself against the inside of the box? A truck rattled down the street behind her, backfired, and Ros nearly jumped out of her skin.

Not until she was safely behind the bathroom's locked door, did she dare to open the package only to find a plastic bag with the inert pills inside. She counted thirty of them and then she picked one up and examined it more closely. It was huge and brilliant green, as unnatural and inedible as one of the plastic gems that adorned rings in the coin machines at the supermarket. Surprisingly, the hand-printed instructions read, "Take three per day with meals, steep as tea, or dissolve one in bathwater." No, she would not dare to swallow one of those things. Who would? "Poison!" The word hissed coldly through her mind, making the hairs rise on her arms. But she would try one in the tub.

The worst thing that could happen would be her skin turning green or itching.

She ran the hot water and placed one green capsule beneath the steaming flow. Almost immediately a heady perfume, only hinted at previously, pervaded the room. The water filling the tub remaining reassuringly clear and untainted, Rosalynd, with a shrug of her shoulders, stepped in. Lying back, she shut her eyes and felt the perfumed mist enclose her as the hot water rose. With her right big toe, she clumsily turned the faucet off and drifted gently, completely away.

Into the Green.

"Of course," Ros told herself, "it's only a dream. It *has* to be only a dream!" The water had cooled and she'd woken with a start to find her flesh had risen in goose bumps. Shooting up to a sitting position, she had cried out soundlessly and hastily flattened the wavering fronds of ferns and reeds of the tenderest green before her. The pool of water she was immersed in was a portion of a clear, rippling stream, the bed of which consisted of round, multi-colored pebbles. To her right and left, before and behind her were green living things, layer upon layer of lace and leaf. Shifting specks of sunlight flickered and shimmered on her bare skin and the scent of tiny purple orchids depending from vines and branches above her formed an exotically scented, living canopy. What at first had appeared peaceful she now saw was the opposite. There was a rush of busy life everywhere. Specks of crimson beetles ascended and descended a decaying stump. Feathered creatures whirred and flashed at the edge of her vision. Things called out in alien voices in the hidden distance and branches creaked, underbrush rustled.

And somehow Ros was in every drop of water, every bug, every serrated leaf and smooth blade. They were all extensions of her body and mind in the same way her hair was part of her, or her breath, or her thoughts.

And those who chattered in the treetops and sniffed the air suspiciously from behind not-too-distant rocks and trunks would not hurt her or fear her.

The jungle, she found, was the loveliest and most interesting place she had ever been. There were not only surprises that were heartbreakingly beauti-ful, waterfalls with rainbow mist plunging into unfathomable gorges, flocks of crimson birds, opalescent bugs lighting on her fingertips and in her hair making her glow in the shade, but shocks of such icy terror that she lost her breath. The snakes, of course, made her heart jump even though she knew they could not poison her. And some of the bigger animals, the cats especially, had extremely sharp fangs and claws and came very near with their blood-warm breath. She was, however, the queen of this lost world, and it was, after all, only a dream. She knew this because, while she was there, all her many words began slipping away from her, like a multitude of bright, little fish in a stream, only one or two of which she could catch. And because, after an hour or a day or sometimes even longer, she would open her eyes to find herself in the bathtub with her mother knocking on the door.

After the first few journeys, she found that, in some mysterious way, the jungle was getting into her. The green of her eyes was greener. Her skin was softening and tanning and in some lights, greening. Her hair grew more than an inch in less than a day and a night. Her voice carried the lilt and squawk of birds, the dots of light flickering through the green entangled canopy freckled her arms. She became a part of the jungle in the same way a motionless green and brown lizard on a tree trunk was indistinguishable from the mottled bark.

When she was angry at the apes for carrying a joke too far or at herself for forgetting where a particular fruit grew or perhaps at some stray thought intruding from that other place, the jungle roared and prowled, struck and killed, and torrential rainstorms burst with great white bolts of lightning, leaving her nostrils filled with the scent of ozone. When she was tired, deep night came and there was a cave or tree bole or netting of vines in which to curl up and rest.

It was like being the Peter Pan of her own Neverland, but she had no Lost Boys, no Wendy, and she was so lonely. Even if she could somehow bring them with her, her friends would never fit into the Green. The girls didn't care for bugs or even a single night's camping trip. The boys she knew were all too young somehow, too awkward or silly or rough. Her tears fell in the afternoon rain.

On her sixth venture into the other world, while she lay reclining in a clearing, there was a sudden rustle of branches. A young man in jeans, sneakers and a T-shirt broke through the surrounding vegetation to stand absolutely still upon seeing her. Ros sat up as quickly as any startled wild animal and bared her teeth. The stranger quickly looked her up and down, his mouth slightly open, but Ros, who belonged in the Green, did not cover her nakedness. He gave a sort of surprised snort then and bared his teeth back at her, which made her burst into laughter.

His eyes were as blue as pieces of the sky she saw if she scaled a very tall tree and peered through the thick greenery at the top. And the muscles in his arms rippled like those of a big cat. There was also light in his eyes showing he had brains, and when he moved he flowed. He was perfect, this boy who kept pointing to himself and saying, "Robert Swift. Rob. And you?"

All he had to do was look around to see the answer.

She was so happy he had appeared that her mouth kept wanting to stretch, her lips to part. "Smile," she remembered. The word was "smile."

"Smile," she said, baring her teeth a second time. And he did. The jungle was fast taking her over, her memory overrun with its tangle of flowers and creepers. This was the last word to surface before the language of that other place was lost to her entirely, overwhelmed by bird's cries, the drip of water, hiss of serpents, predators' roars and the rustling of an infinity of leaves.

Often after that she tried to imitate the many sounds he made. She would open her mouth but nothing came out because nothing would coalesce in her mind. It was frustrating, a memory that kept slipping away. Sometimes it made her growl. And that made him laugh. She loved it when he made the laugh sound, it felt like eating honey.

They had many adventures together, good, frightening, mysterious. Often she had to save him, because the snakes could poison him, and he could bleed. But he was in tune with the place; she could sense his respect and love for the Green. And he was brave.

They became entwined and it was indistinguishable where one began and the other ended, as impossible to separate as the subtle entanglements of vines miles long growing together in the tops of a multitude of trees.

Rosalynd held the last capsule up to the bathroom light, and realized it was more precious to her than any emerald. The catalog had disappeared. She'd searched her room frantically, turning her book bag inside out, ransacking her locker at school. She'd dumped the contents of the garbage bag out onto the kitchen floor, thinking perhaps her mother had tossed it away, and then, the tears dripping off her chin, she had to scrape up the unsavory contents of broken jars and opened cans, the catalog still horribly gone. The address on the box had been, even when she'd first gotten the pills, partially unreadable. She'd called information in the town in Florida and had been told no such business existed. She'd gone to the library and searched through Florida telephone directories with absolutely no luck. How could it have gone out of business in just the passage of thirty days?

Rosalynd woke into the Green. Each second, each breath was precious because she remembered this was the last time. With the camera of her eyes she tried to record each scene, each frond, each feather. She savored each pungent scent and tried to record the sounds of the jungle in her heart. She sat quite still hoping to make the time stretch by her inactivity, and when he came, she made him sit still, too. Puzzled, he looked into her face and she tried by her very will to slow his breathing, but the time passed ever and ever swifter. She couldn't tell him with sounds he would understand, but she put her hands together and pulled them apart, she pulled him towards her and then pushed him away, but her actions only confused him and made him unhappy.

She was losing him forever, and she couldn't tell him. . . .

Taking his hand fiercely in her grip, she went with him to her favorite place, the rainbow falls, and stood watching the eternal water cascade into the depths below. If she thought hard enough, she could make it freeze, couldn't she? He leaned against her, his fingers entwined with hers and she felt his warmth. Closing her eyes for a second, she desperately searched her mind for some way to make the moment, their love, the Green itself last forever. There must be something she could do, mustn't there? And then there was a knocking on the door. "Rosalynd, Rosalynd, wake up," her mother called. "You're asleep in that bathtub again!"

The very next morning Rosalynd called the Better Business Bureau of Florida and was informed that the herbal business had been sold and its name changed, but it was still at the old address. She took down the information and frantically dialed the phone number to order a new catalog. What arrived was a glossy, vividly colored listing of items without mystery. There were no green pills to put in the bath, only something called Jungle Scents. What she got when the packet arrived was a very nice sweet-scented bath.

Her mother was on a tight budget, so tight that food shopping was sometimes a luxury. There was no money to pay for a ticket by bus from Rhode Island to Florida, nor could she have ever explained to her mother why she needed to get there. Ros contemplated hitchhiking, but a particularly gruesome news story at the time scared her away from that risky venture.

The artwork Rosalynd did from that point on took on the qualities of the Green. Once during her second year of art college, she was taken on an archeological dig to document finds and visited a real rain forest. "It was the same," she told Harry and me, her brow furrowed with pain, "and not the same, of course. The snakes could poison me . . . and I was more lonely than I could bear because I looked for him, even though by then I'd convinced myself I'd dreamed him up. I looked for him, and I never, never saw him again. . . ."

Now that I know the answer to the mystery of Rosalynd Brooks, I finally see what is hidden in the painting she gave to me. It was camouflaged like a child's picture puzzle with hidden objects blended into a complicated background. Here are the orchids, the rich background of leaves, the wild, uncontrollable death and growth of unspoiled jungle and inseparable from them is a boy's sparkling eye; here is a freckle, here the whorls of his fingerprint. He is all there if you look the right way, his essence forever inhabiting her lost world. But the real secret to Rosalynd's painting is its silent cry of loss.

Healing Hands
Aliette de Bodard

Ianthos, chiseling at the face of a statue, heard the incessant wailing of the citizens of Aenors rise in intensity when the men entered the shop. He heard them through the keening voices of women in mourning for the husbands and sons they had lost to the plague, and, of course, through the weeping for the loss of Liadhes. To Ianthos it was all of little concern: the only sounds he could be preoccupied with were the soft moans from upstairs, where his daughter Rheana lay dying of the plague.

Nevertheless, he rose, for one does not keep customers waiting.

There were four men in white tunics, with tanned, impassive faces. A fifth man—portly, with flushed cheeks—carried himself with an air of command. He was dressed in purple, and walked between the statues in the workshop as if nothing were there at all—not the soldiers with drawn, menacing swords, or the women with their mouths curved in coy, inviting smiles, or the men in tunics that seemed to rustle in an inexistent wind, the marble rippling like cloth.

"Strategos Charenas," Ianthos said, bowing.

The strategos acknowledged the gesture with a curt nod, before coming closer to look at the statue Ianthos had been working on. He ran his fingers across the smooth marble surface—as if he were just examining a block of stone at the marketplace, and not a piece that had taken Ianthos days of work.

Ianthos suppressed the urge to strike the man's hands away from his work.

"Beautiful," Charenas said. "It is a true likeness, Ianthos. I can almost hear her speak." It was a statue of Aenora, the goddess who had given her name and protection to the city, as well as the spring on the cliff that was now inside the holiest of shrines. Ianthos, working from an old memory of a vision, knew it was a failure, that he had only sculpted someone else, molded someone else's soul into stone. The goddess remained beyond his reach.

"It's not yet finished," Ianthos said, wishing that the strategos would go away. Rulers of the city had no place in his workshop, and no right to pry into his makings.

Charenas nodded distractedly. "You are wondering what I am doing here. Your reputation has grown since you first started to sculpt."

Ianthos, his hand still around his chisel, said nothing.

"I have a commission for you, Ianthos. One of utmost importance to the welfare of Aenors. You will be paid well." Charenas's hand went to his belt and patted a pouch that tinkled with the familiar sound of coins clinking together.

"Who'll sit for me?"

"Liadhes."

Ianthos felt a sharp intake of breath burning his lungs. "He's dead. The city mourns his passing."

"He died of the plague. But that is immaterial. He will be buried at night in four days, and a statue of him will be unveiled then. You will sculpt it. Liadhes will give one last message from beyond the Night Waters to the people."

"What message?"

Charenas's eyes glittered dangerously. "What he would have wanted. The plague has struck us hard, but Dakeniais has been weakened militarily in the previous years. We must strike now, put an end to the war between us, and free the other cities from their tyranny. Unite the peninsula under one rule."

"I don't work with dead men," Ianthos snapped. "My gift is to see into the souls of the living."

Charenas raised his hand, and for a moment Ianthos feared that the strategos would strike him for having had the temerity to refuse, but then the man smiled. "You will find a way. I shall send someone to fetch you and the statue in three days." Charenas whirled round and left, followed by his escort.

Ianthos remained standing where he was for a long while. No trace remained of their passage, but he knew better than to pretend they had not come. Charenas. He had no choice. Charenas ruled Aenors now. Liadhes had been carried away by the plague. Wise, kind Liadhes, whose vision had guided the city for more than ten years—a rarity for a people who elected their rulers for only two years. He had presided over a period of unequalled prosperity, and now lay in the shrine of Aenora, washed and garbed for his funeral.

But . . . Charenas. Not a man to be crossed. Ianthos thought of leaving, of going into voluntary exile with Rheana before it was too late, but knew he could not. Charenas would find them eventually.

But he could not sculpt a dead man.

Long ago, a gift had been granted to him. The statues he made seemed alive because he saw beyond the masks of flesh of those who sat before him, gazed into the recesses of their minds, and translated every flicker of thought into stone or wood. Some claimed to have heard his works speak to them, and that was what Charenas sought, no doubt: an illusion.

But how could you find the soul of a dead man in his corpse? Aenora and her brothers would have long since carried it away. Nothing would remain but a blank face, distorted by the plague.

Gently, Ianthos laid the chisel on the ground, stared at the flawed statue. He had no choice. He would have to try.

"And you'd sculpt a lie?" Rheana's pale hands clenched her sheets; her voice brimmed with barely contained anger. "Just because that toady Charenas pays you enough?"

In the face of her indignation, Ianthos felt almost embarrassed. "Not a lie. Charenas said it was what Liadhes would have wanted."

Rheana inhaled sharply. Her face, still that of a child, was starting to bulge with sores, and every movement she made was accompanied by a grimace of pain. "If you believe that, you might as well believe that Aenora is coming back to cleanse the city from the plague."

"I saw Aenora once," he said.

Her eyes were still clear and merciless. "You did. And look at what it brought you."

"You don't believe me." It was an argument they had had many times since Rheana was old enough to question her father's religious tenets. In many ways, she was like her mother, although she had never known her. She had certainly inherited Farha's acid tongue and skepticism.

"I don't know," Rheana said at last. "They say he had healing hands."

"He received a gift in the sanctuary, the same way I received mine. Aenora spoke to him and taught him how to lay hands on the sick and on the dying. He healed dozens of people when the plague started. But he's dead now."

"So am I," she said, shivering. "Dead and buried. But he shouldn't have died."

"What do you mean?"

"You know perfectly well what I mean. He had powers. He could heal people with a touch. Why did he die of the plague?"

"Perhaps he couldn't heal himself."

"Or perhaps Charenas slipped him some poison. It'd be easy enough, if you know the right people. And he couldn't fight both things at once: the plague and the poison."

"You shouldn't talk like that."

Rheana's face was white, as grave as those of the gods in the temples. "He can't hear us. I wish you wouldn't take the commission."

"What else do you think we can do? He'll have us killed if I don't."

"He wouldn't. He couldn't even kill Heragew. He had to have him banished on some ridiculous pretext. For ten years. The nephew of Liadhes, and he can't even be here at his uncle's funeral or he'll be killed. It's all wrong. Although they do say that he is coming back with an army to oust Charenas."

"You have been listening to Mera again." The old woman had been in his service for twenty years; she had taken care of Rheana ever since his wife died, and had proved an invaluable help when the plague struck his daughter. But Mera had an ear for gossip and liked to share it.

"I have nothing else to do," Rheana whispered, staring at the closed shutters around which he had wrapped thick linen cloths so that the cold winds of the night would not worsen her condition.

How long did it take for people to die of the plague? Forty days for Liadhes. Ten for the infant daughter of the neighbors. Rheana had been sick for thirteen days.

"We won't talk about the commission again," Ianthos said, hoping to give the illusion of firmness. He sensed her slipping beyond his reach already, retreating into another world, where he meant but little. The dead had no allegiances or family ties, the priests said. A fierce longing filled him. A longing to go back to the days when they had been happy, both of them, when he had sculpted those who wanted to see the truth of who they were, and when she had been taught by Mera all a wife needs to know to keep a husband.

Over now, he thought, dully, without bitterness. He walked back to his room, and lay in his bed, trying to find something to cling to. Finally, he drifted to sleep, clutching a dream of Aenora which held no truth.

In the morning, he went into his workshop to choose the wood for the statue. Black blocks, ready for his sculpting, lay side by side. He had already decided that he was going to use ebony, for nothing else would do Liadhes justice, and also because he had died of the plague, which turned a man's face black in the hours before he expired.

Ianthos ran his hands over each block, feeling for imperfections, for hidden flaws within the wood which he would not see until he uncovered the core. He felt nothing; his gift was not for that. He picked one at random and, vaguely frustrated, went to the shrine of Aenora.

It lay at the top of a plateau on the outskirts of the city; the steep path leading to it started at the end of the street on which he lived. As he walked, the thatched houses with white-washed walls and painted wooden shutters became marble, sandstone, and granite. The earthen path transformed into a large, paved road. Small temples to lesser gods and heroes littered the ascension. He stopped to sacrifice a black crow to Yrger, patron of artists and messengers, and resumed his climb. The sun had risen and was mercilessly burning the skin of his exposed back. He wished he had taken more than a short tunic for the day, but he was too far away from his home for it to matter. He thought of Rheana, cared for by old Mera, and suddenly realized that the city which lay before him had been silenced by the plague, reduced to a shadow of itself, and that the death of Liadhes was only one more step towards decline.

What are you thinking? We survived the tidal waves and the barbarian invasions; we lived through harsh weather and fires and rebuilt our city. The plague can't harm us. We'll live on. Some of us will.

The air above Aenors was pure, crisp, and left a tangy taste on the tongue, as if the plague had not reached there yet, as if the goddess still watched over her shrine, if not her city.

The central temple to Aenora, which housed the miraculous source, was usually crowded with pilgrims from all over the peninsula. But there was no one there but a few men praying to the goddess with fervor, their heads bent before the massive statue of Aenora that occupied the eastern end of the temple. They were all speaking the same words, from the Great Prayer composed centuries before, when the first settlers of Aenors had been decimated by the harsh summer and by uncounted diseases: "That you would spare us from the sickness that lies all over the land . . ." Their almost pathetic eagerness—the desperate calling on a goddess who likely had little time for them—made Ianthos uncomfortable. He walked until he found a priestess in an alcove, kneeling before a statue of Aenora.

She was middle-aged and as thin as the spear that the statue of the goddess held aloft. She prayed silently, mouthing words that Ianthos did not recognize. He waited for her to finish, staring up at the face which had been sculpted anew fifty years before. It was not a true likeliness—no other sculptor had been granted a vision of Aenora—but there was something in the cast of the eyes, in the set of the jaw, which spoke of matters beyond man's consideration. Much better than the one he had tried to sculpt.

The priestess rose, gazing at him serenely. "Yes?"

"I'm Ianthos. I wish to see the body of Liadhes. I was told that he was in your keeping." Something in her distant gaze reminded him of Rheana, but he quashed the thought. *I must not obsess over that. Then again, what else do I have to be obsessed with?*

"I will ask the high priestess," she said. "Wait here."

He stood before the alcove, shifting his weight and watching the room, not sure what he should be doing. The atmosphere of the temple grew stifling, and the prayers of the pilgrims sank to an unbearable drone; over it all were the expressionless eyes of Aenora in her glory, looking down on her scattered pilgrims—always watching over them. And was that not terrifying, in a way? That she saw the suffering in her city, and did nothing?

The priestess came back with a lamp. "The strategos warned us that you might come." She gestured, beckoning him out of the alcove, towards the upper reaches of the temple. "Though I'm not sure why," she said as she led the way up a winding flight of stairs. "There is nothing to see here."

The small door at the top of the stairs creaked open when she pushed it. Inside, the air was thick with the smell of incense and herbs. "In here," she said. "I will be waiting for you downstairs."

He watched her retreat, and then turned his attention back to the room. Under the cloying smell lay another, far more disturbing one, sickly and acrid: the smell of death. He stopped. He did not move for a long time, and then, abashed at being frightened for nothing, walked in.

The room was dark, with the shutters closed. At first he saw only the outline of a sarcophagus, with the lid resting on the ground nearby. And then he saw the body. The face. The eyes.

Still. Everything was still, frozen in some parody of life. The eyes had not been closed, and stared at him with a vacant expression. The face was contorted with pain and covered with sores. The skin was black, the lips purplish, rolled back, exposing the teeth. There was nothing to say what the man might have looked like before the disease. How he might have lived.

Ianthos shuddered and left.

He spent the afternoon in the palace, staring at the sculpted busts of Liadhes until the other's myriad faces filled his thoughts. Not one sculptor had given him the same look, and yet there was something in all those marble eyes which had not changed, but he could not pinpoint. Not one sculptor had seen beyond appearances.

He talked, with Charenas's blessing, to the servants, to learn what sort of man Liadhes had been. A patriot, they all said. He cared more for Aenors than for himself. Someone who could be ruthless and sacrifice people to the welfare of the city, and someone whom the widespread plague had devastated, seeming, as it did, to be the judgment of a god.

"This city has become corrupt," one old woman said, darkly. Her eyes were on the wool she was spinning. "We were judged, and Aenora found us unworthy of her trust. People like Charenas were elected because they paid for votes. We all share the guilt." She looked beyond her shoulder as she finished her speech, with something close to fear.

"He was a good man," she said, finally. "I hope you do him justice."

I cannot, Ianthos thought, leaving her sitting in the sun in the courtyard. *I do not know what justice would be.*

When he exited the palace, he saw soldiers running everywhere, and caught a glimpse of the stout figure of Charenas amidst his bodyguards. It did not concern him; there was a statue to be made.

He went back to his home through the desolate, plague-ridden streets, not looking back. The block of wood he'd chosen earlier sat in his workshop, cold and unfeeling. Someone—Charenas, no doubt—had left a bust of Liadhes sculpted in the later years of his rule. The white eyes stared at him, weighing him. Judging him.

Ianthos sighed, took his tools, and started chipping away at the ebony until he had created a rough human silhouette. He did not know how to represent Liadhes. He closed his eyes and thought of the rare times he had seen the strategos, from far away, at festivals, awarding prizes to playwrights and to fighters. Depositing the laurel crown on a kneeling person's head. Yes, that would have to do.

When he was finished, he knew without looking that the physical resemblance might be there, but it was bland, without fire. It did not speak to him. It would not speak to Charenas, although perhaps the strategos would imagine that it did. The statue possessed Liadhes's stern, bearded face. The hands extended, slightly curved, having just let go of the laurel crown, in a gesture that could have been a blessing. But any other sculptor could have made that lifeless image, anyone with the skill of carving but without his gift might have produced that portrait of Liadhes.

Three days left.

Rheana broached the subject of Liadhes after her evening meal. She picked at the food Mera had brought her, and when she raised her right hand he saw that the little finger was twisted out of shape by a suppurating sore. Shadows already moved upon her haggard cheeks. He thought of Liadhes's face, and said nothing.

She waited until the old servant had shuffled out of the room before she spoke in a low voice.

"Have you started on the statue yet? I saw the wood in your workshop."

"Yes," he snapped, irritated. "But I can't sculpt a dead man." And then what she had said hit him. "You shouldn't have been out of bed." She shouldn't have dragged herself downstairs, following the gods knew what foolish ideas—she was sick enough as it was without weakening herself.

"I wanted to see. To know how he truly died."

"What does it change? Charenas was lawfully elected, and you can't take that back."

"Haven't you heard? You've been so busy seeking his soul that you missed it."

"What?"

"The rumor was right; Heragew is back, with men to support him. Charenas had to leave to negotiate with him. They say Heragew accused him of murdering his uncle."

"And what did he say?"

Rheana shrugged. "He blanched when the first reports of Heragew's army reached him. I wish he had dropped dead on the spot. He almost wasn't elected because of his weak heart."

Ianthos said nothing. It was public knowledge, and Charenas's flushed cheeks were enough of a clue for those who saw him.

"Perhaps Charenas's heart will finally give out in battle, and we'll be rid of him."

He thought of the double siege: Heragew's, and the other, more insidious, the plague's. "You should stop daydreaming," he said at last, containing his fear. "You're a grown woman now."

"I don't dream," Rheana said, her voice loud and annoyed. "Or if I do I can't remember. It's just unfair that this city should have to endure Charenas, believing him to be such a great man. I hope Heragew wins."

"Life isn't fair," Ianthos said. He wanted to add, "and the city is dying." What for? Once again, it isn't fair. It's just the way things are. He was not sick, and yet it was only a matter of time before the plague got him as well.

After dinner, he went down to the workshop, carefully keeping his gaze away from Liadhes, took his chisel, and smoothed the cheeks of the statue of the goddess. It was flawed, but he had put so much time in it that he could not envision leaving it unfinished.

The final touches took a few hours. When he was done, he stepped back, and a woman striking water out of a rock with her spear stared back at him. Not a goddess. A woman. And, looking at her, he finally understood who he had sculpted as the goddess: Rheana, before she became ill. Rheana, under the traits of Aenora, as if by doing this he could ensure her immortality, could make her free of all earthly ills. And because he had sculpted her so well, he heard her speak, clearly, a voice in his mind:

"Don't worry for me, father."

His eyes stung with tears.

She was dead already, as she had said. He would be the one who would put the coin for the ferryman under her tongue, who would wash her hair and garb her in white. Her face would be darkened by the plague, her teeth shining white under the contracted lips.

He shook his head. He could not afford to be morbid. He should have been finishing the other statue, not that one. But he could not help it.

Ianthos sensed the presence in his workshop long before he actually saw it. There was no noise. There was no creaking door, no footsteps. But a smell that had no equivalent on earth filled his nostrils, and the air seemed to become infinitely softer.

He had witnessed these signs once already. He turned slowly, and stared into the face of the goddess. It would not yield to his gaze, kept shaping itself around some odd detail, blurred and yet throwing everything in the room into insignificance. His knees gave way under him, but he did not fall; she held him up without a gesture.

She was dressed in a blue tunic that hid her feet, and leant on the spear that was her symbol. In her other hand she carried a water pitcher brimming with an iridescent liquid. Her scarf, like her face, perpetually shimmered out of focus, and fluttered in a wind that was not in the workshop.

"It is a good likeliness," she said, and her voice filled Ianthos to bursting. "Not a true one, but then, you will never be able to sculpt that." She fell silent. Her dark, huge eyes waited for him to speak.

"I had hoped—"

"I granted you one gift already," Aenora said. "There is not much that I can do, Ianthos. And it is not permitted for mortals to look upon the true face of gods."

"I don't want that." He forced the words from between lips rigid with fear. "I want—"

"To see a dead man's soul. Your daughter would like to see it as well."

"I—"

"You used my gift well, Ianthos. I will give one more thing to you." Her voice filled him with rapture; he was hardly aware of the world around him; all that mattered was her radiance. But she was fading; moving away from him until his eyes, blurred with tears, could see nothing beyond the familiar jumble of statues littering his workshop. Everything in her wake seemed to grow dull and colorless, as if she had taken all the meaning in things as she left, leaving nothing but a throbbing ache in the air, a sadness. Just as she had done before, when Ianthos saw her standing by the side of the sacred pool in the shrine, and had dared ask for a gift.

That night, as he slept, Aenora came for him. She said nothing, only smiled—he could not see her face, but the light that surrounded him was warm and comforting. He walked with her past the room where his daughter lay, down the stairs into his workshop, into the streets. The sky shone with a hundred stars, and the city was filled with a deathly silence.

They walked past the walls of Aenors, into the countryside ravaged by the war, past the charred dwellings of peasants, contorted and blackened olive trees, herds of goats roaming wild without shepherds, and deserted crossroads. They did not speak. As they moved away from the city, the landscape flowing past them twisted and changed, becoming harsher.

Ianthos did not know when they left the countryside of the peninsula; all he knew was that, tearing his eyes from the shining figure of Aenora, he saw a bleak plain of black stone before him, cut by a river circling a huge island. On the other side was nothing but endless darkness, as if the world stopped once one had crossed.

When they reached the banks of the river, Aenora spoke. "He will come to you."

Her eyes overwhelmed him, but he found the strength to ask a question. "Why?"

She laughed, and her laughter was a terrible thing to hear. "Aenors needs Liadhes, Ianthos. Did you think I would let my city be consumed by the plague?"

She walked away, on the water, towards the island, gliding over the dark writhing waves, her radiance driving out the shadows. He watched her; in that black place that was the Netherworld, she was the only thing he could cling to.

She did not come back. Instead, a weaker light on the river grew closer. Only when it was almost upon him did Ianthos see what it was: a lantern affixed to the bow of a boat, with a tall, hooded figure holding a pole and steering emotionlessly. When the barge reached the shore, someone disembarked. Every part of Ianthos's body seemed to have gone numb; every thought had been banished to some faraway place.

"Sculptor," Liadhes said.

Ianthos bowed without looking at the other's face. One did not look in the eyes of ghosts. "Strategos."

"Here, I am but a man," Liadhes said, shaking his head. His voice was bleakly amused. "Raise your eyes, and look at me."

"I can't."

"What harm could I do?" Liadhes asked, his voice slightly bitter. "The dead have gone past that."

He raised his gaze. The other's face was not as it had been sculpted; a few subtle changes in the features made a completely different man from the one he had imagined. The eyes were dark, without pupils or irises, and there was a hint of the plague on the cheeks.

"Tell me how my city fares, Ianthos." The voice was distant, bored almost, as if it were something utterly unimportant, a subject of conversation, nothing more.

"The plague still has us, my lord. It will kill us all the way it killed you." He did not ask the unspoken question, the one Rheana would have asked were she in his place, but Liadhes seemed to read his thoughts.

"I do not know what I died of. I suspect poison, but of course it is easier than acknowledging that my gift of healing failed."

"Charenas?" Ianthos asked, forcing the word out from between dry lips.

"Perhaps. Now he seeks to exploit my death; that much is certain."

"He said you would want to invade Dakeniais while they were weak."

"If I were alive, undoubtedly. We have been for too long at each other's throat, and all the cities of the peninsula make up nothing but a squabbling bunch of children. And while we squabble, other countries move to invade us, or hope we will sink into a war so great we will exhaust our resources."

"There is the plague."

"Yes," Liadhes said, holding his hands in front of him, staring at something beyond Ianthos's shoulder. "There is that. Aenors must be cleansed before we can rise. And you would see into my soul to sculpt a statue for me, Ianthos. I will give them a last message."

They talked, standing before the river after which there is nothing. Later, only the first things they had said remained clear in Ianthos's mind. That, and the way Liadhes moved and spoke, which were the only things that mattered for him to use his gift. Images sank into his memory. He remembered kneeling, and shaping out of mud, with his bare hands, the statue as he would sculpt it, and adding all the details that were missing, until it seemed that there were two Liadhes standing under the dull light, staring at each other.

"You have a gift," Liadhes said. That, too, he remembered. And then nothing beyond the flickering radiance as Aenora came to him, and walked him back into the real world. Into the city of the plague.

He shut himself in his workshop all day. Mera knocked at the door, increasingly panicked, and then gave up. He hardly heard the old servant, except as a distraction from the work at hand. Even the thought of his daughter was not enough to drive the fire from his soul. Chips of wood flew around him, and the ebony seemed to part under his chisel, as if it were eager to give birth to something living.

Beyond the shutters of the workshop, the light dimmed; he lit the torches in their sconces and went on working.

Rheana found him late at night. "You have finished," she said from the doorway. Surprised, he whirled round, took in her pale, drawn face, her waif-thin body, the white shift covering the sores on her chest.

"Get back to your bed," he said.

She stood still for a while. Then, gently, carefully, as if each move would break her, she stepped away from the doorway, and progressed into the workshop, clinging to statues.

"You should—"

"I'm past the time when you could give orders to me," she said, standing before the finished work. She did not speak for a while. "He frightens me," she whispered at last.

"Why?"

"Because you have sculpted a dead man. We change after we die, don't we? Charenas won't like it. It says the wrong things."

"What things?" Ianthos asked.

She shook her head. "If you don't see it, then perhaps I am wrong."

"I only sculpt what I have seen."

"I know," she said, shrugging, as if it did not matter. She was staring at Liadhes with an odd hunger in her eyes, one he did not fully understand.

He did not know what woke him up that night. A noise, perhaps? The house was utterly silent; the white-washed walls shone in the light of the moon. It occurred to him that he had forgotten to close the shutters before he went to bed. He listened again. Nothing. Or perhaps, at the cusp of hearing, a faint noise, a voice, calling a name. His? No.

He rose, laced his sandals, put on his tunic. It was foolish. He was imagining things after the visions he had had. *Aenora save me from madness.*

The landing was deserted; there was no light in Mera's room. The moon shone on the stairs and outlined the open door facing his.

"Rheana," he breathed, and the house seemed to echo her name, the inaudible voice growing stronger, feeding on the syllables he had uttered.

The bed was empty, the sheets pushed back. The smell of the plague filled his nostrils as he moved within the room, searching for her, knowing she would not be there. He threw open the shutters, and stared into the night. Only the rattle of the death-cart, loaded with the corpses of those who had succumbed, and the wind moaning through the empty streets. Why would she leave the house?

He went downstairs. A terrible, irrational fear seized him. She was dead. He had not even had time to say goodbye to her. He had nothing of her beyond a flawed statue, and a smell that was not hers in an empty room. She was—

The workshop door was ajar; he pushed it, heard it creak under his touch. No answering noise came from within.

A faint light spun in the room; the shutters were open at the far end. He moved between the living statues, his breath the only one he could hear.

Moonlight shone on the statue of Aenora, throwing it into sharp relief; the marble seemed to drink it all in, giving nothing back. The statue of Liadhes, on the other hand, shone with that cold light, glinting like polished metal. The former strategos stood over the prone body of Rheana. The hands extended over her head.

And, in that light, he finally understood what his daughter had meant. Liadhes's hands were not reaching out, but rather it seemed that at any moment he would pull away, withdraw his blessing and his protection, would turn away from the viewer and leave nothing. Dead men change. They have no ties, no allegiances in this world. It was a cold, unforgiving sight, and one that chilled the blood.

This city is corrupt, he thought, desperately, remembering the old woman. *It banished Heragew on a false accusation five years ago; it allowed itself to be bought to elect Charenas. The plague is killing us. Liadhes is abandoning us.*

He bent down, touched Rheana. She was unaccountably warm, but something had changed, something he was not sure he could pinpoint. Her arms lay by the side of her body, her hands palms up like a supplicant. Her hands—

Which finger? he wondered. One of them had been distorted by a sore only the previous night; he had seen it. But both hands were smooth-skinned, if a little emaciated, the fingers straight, intact. There was nothing.

With mounting panic, he pulled the tunic away from her, fumbling to get it over her head, and finally tearing it in his haste. The skin was unbroken. Her chest, which he knew was covered in sores, was smooth under his touch, warm. Healthy, almost.

He could find no traces of the plague. Kneeling by her side, looking up into the dark and unfathomable eyes of Liadhes, staring at the hands extended over them both, he thought, *it is a true likeliness. It has his powers.* What else had sprung from the work of his chisel?

He rose after a while, closed the shutters. He arranged the torn tunic over Rheana, lifted her, surprised at how little she weighed, and carried her upstairs without a backward glance for the statue, which still shone with a suppressed light.

Rheana was still weak the following morning. Ianthos sat on the porch of his home, looking at the sun as it rose over the city, wondering what would happen. After a while, he stopped brooding and went to the marketplace to find a veil to cover the statue of Liadhes—he could not have left such work for Mera;

like the wood, the veil had to be right. Besides, he needed to be away from his house. It seemed to him that the world had changed, that his gift had evolved into something he did not want to think about. Aenora had her own reasons for helping him, and while he knew that she cared for her city, the thought of a goddess interfering in politics made him uneasy. Like the dead, the gods had an opinion on the world that was far removed from that of the living.

The marketplace was abuzz with rumors of the battle. Heragew had apparently moved below the walls with his army. His men had been mustered from Dakeniais; the other city was only too glad to foster discord in her old adversary. Some said that Heragew had betrayed Aenors, and others that Charenas was the betrayer, that by sending Heragew into exile on a false accusation, and by murdering his uncle, he had broken the laws, both human and divine.

Strategos Charenas was still on the city walls, overseeing the defense of Aenors; he had spent the night with his commanding officers, hardly sleeping. Some said that he had collapsed at dawn, clutching his chest, but that he had recovered not much later—if one could recover at all from a weak heart. Ianthos chose his veil amidst snatches of news, watched the seller fold it: a lean woman with rings under her eyes.

"You look tired, good woman," he said.

She shrugged. "My son and my husband both have the plague. I do what I can."

Waiting for their deaths, he thought, and then remembered that Rheana had been healed. The event had an unreality to it, as if a mere word would be enough to shatter it. He felt a compelling desire to see her, to check that he had not dreamt the whole thing and that she had been saved by the work of his hands.

When he reached his house, Mera was waiting for him on the doorstep. She had received a message from the palace: a wax tablet, which he stared at for a long while before recalling what the letters stood for. Charenas was busy defending the city. The veiled statue would be picked up by his men, and transported directly to the site of the cemetery. The funeral itself would take place that very night. Ianthos was requested to come with his work. He left the tablet downstairs and went to see his daughter.

She was resting, her back propped against the white-washed wall. He watched her without a word. Her face was pale, both hands unscathed, healthy. She had tied her torn tunic around her left shoulder; the area over her right breast was free of sores.

"So it is true," he said.

"Yes. I had to try. I dreamt that he was calling me."

"He wasn't." Ianthos remembered the gesture Liadhes made: one of withdrawal. And yet Rheana had clung to those hands, as if beseeching him to come back, and he had heard her. In a fashion. "And you don't believe in that sort of thing."

"I believe in your talent," she said. "The gift was part of who he was, and things once given by the gods are never taken away." She raised her hands, stared at her skin, caught in the wonder of it all. "When does Charenas come to see the statue?"

"He doesn't. He'll have it delivered to the cemetery."

"So soon? But—"

"The funeral is tonight. I have to attend."

Rheana's face grew pensive. She finished eating, set the plate aside carefully. "Tonight? So he can be sure that Liadhes is done for, surely. Heragew won't have time to plan something. And Charenas will be fresh back from the battle, ready to crow his victory to the citizens."

"What could Heragew have planned?"

"I don't know. Something like an accusation, I think. He'd only have to say the word, you know, and enough people would believe it."

"Even if it's not true?"

"Do you think Charenas incapable of murder?"

Ianthos had looked at enough souls to know. "No. He is ruthless."

"Nevertheless, Heragew may try something," Rheana said.

"How do you know?"

She shrugged. "Intuition. And he knows that the only thing he can lay at Charenas's feet is that."

"And his banishment."

"The banishment might have been a true judgment on him. And he won't risk having his own part in this questioned. Everybody believes that Liadhes was murdered."

"I know," Ianthos said.

Rheana was silent for a while. "Promise me something," she said at last.

"Yes."

"Be careful."

"Why should I be careful? Heragew is not inside the city."

"Charenas is. And he has asked you to be present at the funeral."

"What of it?"

Her gaze was distant again, as if the plague had returned to take possession of her. "Because he needs a scapegoat if things go wrong. And who better suited than you?"

"I've done nothing."

She smiled, without joy. "I know that. He doesn't. And the statue is not something that will please him, even if it's only wood."

He said nothing as he left to cover the statue with the veil he had purchased. He stood for a while, staring at it. *It's not wood*, he thought. *It lives. And I don't know what I have sculpted anymore.* As he draped the veil over Liadhes's features, he saw the inscrutable eyes of the statue of Aenora stare at him, and wondered why he felt such a sense of doom. His work had been done; now it remained for Charenas to stir the population. It did not matter that Heragew's siege rendered the whole question of attacking Dakeniais moot, since Dakeniais was instead the one assailing Aenors through Liadhes's nephew. None of it mattered. He was a sculptor, and he had done his work.

The men came for the statue at nightfall. Ianthos, sitting in a corner of his workshop beside the veiled, dark mass, watched them move it into the street, and into a waiting cart. He followed them, amidst the creaking of the wheels, lost in his own thoughts.

In the cemetery, the coffin was open, displaying the grotesque face of the plague for all to see in the light of the dozens of torches surrounding the gravesite. A few Aenorians had already gathered there; Charenas was nowhere to be seen. In the flickering light, Ianthos moved behind the men as they unloaded the statue and laid it to rest on a pedestal. He stood to one side of the veiled mass that had somehow ceased to belong to him, watching faces he did not know change as the light danced over their features.

"You are the sculptor?" a voice asked behind him. He turned, surprised, and saw a priestess he did not know. She wore the scarlet robe characteristic of the high priestess. He bowed.

"I have that honor," he said.

The high priestess's face did not move. "I hear that you saw Aenora once."

"Like Liadhes," he said, curtly. The goddess's ever-shifting, inhuman features filled his mind—her face turning away from the city as Liadhes had done. He quashed the frightful thought before it could overwhelm him.

"It can be a terrible thing to see a god. And it is said that those with a divine gift are beyond our understanding."

He shrugged. "That is what they said. What news from outside?"

"There was a battle today. More than that I do not know."

She stopped speaking then, for a squad of soldiers had entered the cemetery. One of them was supporting Charenas, who was limping, and who appeared annoyed at his inability to move by his own means. Even in the light it seemed to Ianthos that his face was far more flushed than would have been expected. He thought back to Rheana's words: perhaps Charenas's heart will finally give out in battle. . . . No. They couldn't afford the chaos which would follow the death of the strategos.

"Sculptor," Charenas said, approaching. His gaze shifted to the high priestess. "I trust that everything is ready."

She nodded and followed him to stand beside the veiled statue. Ianthos remained where he was. A sizeable throng had gathered, but the faces were lean, haggard, with the shadow of the plague all over them. Aenors was mourning its dead and its dying, whether in battle against Dakeniais or against the sickness.

The high priestess started the ceremony with prayers to Aenora, entrusting the soul of Liadhes to her. Ianthos stood by her side, listening to the drone of her prayers and knowing them to be useless. Liadhes had already reached the Island on the Night Waters. What did it matter, this rigmarole? As her prayer grew to a climax, he found his attention wandering—all he wanted was to go home to speak to his daughter, to revel in the gift of life, and not to dwell on the other, far more dangerous gift that Aenora had granted him.

Nevertheless, he was aware of the precise moment Charenas stepped forward, walking on shaking legs, but without the help of a soldier. He addressed the people in a stentorian voice, "Citizens. We stand at a difficult moment in the life of this city. The plague has depleted us. A usurper is at work spreading malicious rumors, and stands below with an army, thinking he can enter the walls of Aenors, which have not been breached since its foundation. But we stand firm.

"The plague carried Liadhes off in his prime. But let that not dismay us, for we believe that our city will be protected by Aenora, as it has always been. We know that she has never abandoned us, even as we lie besieged and dying. We know that Aenors will always be great.

"We do but say farewell to a great man, and know that what he built in life will not be destroyed so easily. The walls that he restored still stand; the temples are untouched, our treasury is full, and our army will be victorious. Even as I speak, our soldiers are killing Heragew's men. We shall prevail, never fear. When we are done with the usurper, Aenors will be free to move against Dakeniais and to unite the peninsula under one rule."

There were no cheers; only a few dull looks from the citizens.

Charenas went on, oblivious. "I now call upon the sculptor Ianthos to unveil the statue he has sculpted in honor to a great leader."

Ianthos, as if in dream, moved forward under Charenas's predatory eyes. He reached out and pulled the veil. It fell, billowing around him, so that for a while his vision was obscured, filled with the darkness of the cloth, and the only sound he heard was an intake of breath from the crowd as it stared at his work.

There was silence. Stunned eyes gazed at him, at Charenas. Ianthos saw all this only dimly; all he could see was Liadhes, slowly withdrawing his hands, slowly walking away from the city, turning his back on Aenors, going further and further into death. He could not speak. He could not move.

Someone shouted, "Liadhes is abandoning us!"

The same cry traveled through the crowd, repeated over and over as the people turned to Charenas. More cries rose up.

"This is your fault!"

"No one can replace Liadhes!"

"We should have known . . ."

"Aenora watch over us!"

It wasn't quite a riot: none of them had the energy for that. But they were moving towards Charenas with raised hands, with clenched fists, their eyes gleaming with anger.

"He turned away from you, murderer!"

"You're unfit to rule . . ."

"Ianthos!" Charenas, suffocating with rage, his face flushed redder than ever, pushed him roughly, both hands going for his throat. "You dare sculpt this— thing! It should have been burnt before it even was begun, gods take you!"

Ianthos took a step back, arched against the smooth surface of the statue, felt it start to shiver under his weight. His hands, scrabbling, somehow found a grip on Charenas's wrists, and forced the strategos's arms apart, slowly. He had to—had to survive—if he could turn the struggle to his advantage.

He bent forward, pushed the strategos to the ground, trying to prevent him from regaining a hold on his throat—trying to hold Charenas down, to keep him from struggling, from pushing at his hands. . . .

When Charenas grew still at last, he rose on shaking legs, to see to see everyone watching him. The soldiers stood, frozen, their eyes flickering between him and the mob: his fight, which had seemed to take such a long time, had in fact taken place in an eye blink.

"Murderer . . ." someone whispered with satisfaction, but it wasn't Ianthos they were addressing.

Ianthos, still trying to make sense of the last few moments, looked down at Charenas, and saw the face of death staring up at him. The bulging eyes and grey, still face, were enough to tell him that Rheana had had her wish at last, that the exertion of overseeing the defense of the city, topped with the frantic fight, had finally been too much for the strategos's heart.

"He's dead," Ianthos said.

The silence that followed did not last for long. "We're lost," someone said, and the sentence spread within the crowd, was transformed into an ugly noise made up of thousands of different voices uttering different words, hurled back at Ianthos. "He got what he deserved. . . . He killed Liadhes. . . . Liadhes has abandoned us. . . . This city must be cleansed of all corruption. . . ." He was unable to move.

A soldier stepped towards him, and was pulled down in a clatter of metal by two men from the crowd. And then, with a great sigh like the release of an unknown tension, the throng moved forward, picking up torches and assaulting the soldiers and the high priestess. They fought back. Ianthos, caught in the melee, buffeted from side to side, could do nothing but watch as a deflected torch caught the statue of Liadhes; it started to burn, and smoldering embers reached the coffin.

The crowd, moving forward, pushing the soldiers out of the cemetery, left him behind. He stood, shivering. He watched the dancing lights move away. He watched the statue, which had been a gift of Aenora to her city, being reduced to ashes. The city was now vulnerable within its unbreachable walls, which would do nothing beyond shut the mob in.

When the first thatched roof went up in flames, he started running. He ran through crowded streets that shone vaguely with the reflections of fire. He reached his house, breathless, and rushed inside.

"Master," Mera said, staring at him. The old woman's voice was fearful.

"Later," he snapped, "Come with me." He rushed upstairs.

Rheana, lying in her bed, raised her eyes, looked at him in silence.

"The city is burning," he said.

She did not answer. He took her in his arms, carried her to the threshold, Mera in tow.

He walked all the way to the shrine, with his daughter huddled against his chest, her breath mingling with his. The smell of burning things lay all over the city, but the temple complex was untouched: stone would not be destroyed that easily. Some people had started to understand their predicament, and were walking on the same path as he, but he paid no heed to them. He was intent on getting away from the fire.

He stopped just before he reached the entrance to the shrine, looked down. From the place where the temples of stone became houses with thatched roofs, to the walls, the city was a writhing shadow in the fire. The pulsing lights danced before his eyes, claimed more streets. He said nothing. Rheana stared at the desolation. She pressed herself closer to him without a word.

Priestesses had gathered below the carved stone gates, looked at the new-comers, and directed the plague-stricken to the infirmary, which stood far away from the shrine. They did not stop him.

He laid Rheana below the statue of Aenora—not the greater one, but the one where he had found the priestess two days before. His daughter sat up against the wall on the right side of the goddess, shaking, while he told her what had happened. Mera had vanished; presumably the servant had joined the crowd praying and chanting before the monumental statue of Aenora at the eastern end.

"Charenas deserved it," Rheana said.

"We'll never know."

"I was right. It was a terrible statue."

"Not anymore, I think. The fire destroyed it."

"It's destroying everything else as well," Rheana said. She looked at the statue of Aenora, and asked, in a lower voice, "What will we do now?"

"I don't know," he said. "Shelter here, and then . . ."

He had no answer, and she had turned away from him, lost in her thoughts.

A priestess came to see them later, to bring them some food and water, and to ask them if they needed anything. Ianthos shook his head. She told them that the whole city was now on fire; the high priestess had died in the riots, and the gates had been opened by the people so that they could flee into the countryside. Heragew's men had used the opportunity to enter Aenors, heedless of the fire, and were fighting the supporters of Charenas in the burning streets. It seemed that Heragew had the upper hand, although nothing could be certain anymore.

War, Ianthos thought. *Liadhes brought war in this city. It was not Liadhes who turned away from us. No. Aenora was the one who made the city burn.*

"It should be over by tomorrow," the priestess said, before she left. "If Aenora wills it." She sounded tired, and discouraged.

Ianthos looked at the goddess who had healed his daughter and who had set the city on fire through the work of his hands. He saw, suddenly, the healing of Rheana as a gift in exchange for what he had done later with the statue of Liadhes, in exchange for Charenas's death.

"Do you think I would let my city be consumed by the plague?" Aenora had asked. And now, too late, he understood what she had meant. He thought of all those who had been incapacitated by the plague, and who had not had the luck to live near the shrine. He imagined the fire sweeping through the houses, burning everything away, including the statues he had made and the room where his daughter had lain dying only the previous night; he saw sparks jumping from roof to roof with the wind, flames gripping shrunken bodies. The city must be cleansed. Of the sickness. Of the corruption.

He thought of Liadhes, burnt twice, once as a corpse, and once as a statue. He had had, as Rheana said, healing hands. And sometimes the act of healing involved destruction.

"Tomorrow it will be over," he said. Rheana did not answer.

Tomorrow. . . . Tomorrow the air would be clear and fresh, and the wind would carry through the streets the ashes of the plague-stricken who had not been able to move from their houses in time. Tomorrow Heragew, Dakenian soldiers by his side, would speak to the citizens in the assembly, would begin the rebuilding of the city. In the morning Aenors would rise, and be great again, as it had always done in the past.

We were healed, Ianthos thought, his gaze lost in the unfathomable eyes of the goddess, and wept.

Dragonfly Savior

David Walton

If anyone else had asked, Hickory would have refused. But he'd never been able to resist Marigold. Not even the time she dared him to ride a bullfrog and he ended up in the river.

"There's nothing to it," she said this time. "But if you'd rather not, Dewdrop and I can go alone."

That decided it. He knew the sort of looks Dewdrop gave Marigold. There was no way they were going to spend the afternoon alone together, not if he could help it.

So here he was, perched on a dragonfly on the highest, thinnest branch of the pine tree that grew over the river, looking down at the roaring speck of the waterfall below. The branch swayed sickeningly in the breeze.

"All right, boys." Marigold held two pine nuts, one in each hand. "First one back gets a kiss."

Hickory felt his face grow hot. He'd never been able to banter and tease with Marigold like Dewdrop could. He just got embarrassed. At least his darker complexion kept his blushes from showing. Most of the time.

"A kiss," Dewdrop said, tossing his blond mop and winking at Mari. "High stakes."

"So drop them," Hickory said.

"Okay, okay. Here goes." Mari let go.

The two dragonflies under Hickory and Dewdrop's sway took off from the branch after the falling pine nuts, leaving Marigold behind. As soon as they took to the air, Hickory forgot his embarrassment. He was good at this. Bonded to the creature's mind through his touch, he controlled its body, feeling the rush of air through its four wings as if they were his own.

Freefall wasn't fast enough; he used his mount's wings to accelerate his descent, trying to overtake his target in time. The trouble was, Dewdrop was good at this, too. They caught the pine nuts at almost the same instant, using their dragonflies' hooked legs to snag them out of the spume just before they hit the water. Hickory concentrated all his skill into the wings, willing them to beat harder, fighting against his momentum. Finally, laboriously, he rose back toward the tree branch.

But Dewdrop was above him! Hickory tried to rise faster, to take the lead, but his dragonfly was at the limit of its strength. Dewdrop reached the branch first, victorious.

"Ugh," Marigold said. "Did it have to be you?"

Dewdrop grinned. "Who else?"

Hickory landed, glumly watching his two friends flirt. He and Dewdrop had grown up together, had always been the best of friends . . . but sometimes Hickory wished he'd just go away.

"I suppose a promise is a promise," Marigold said, feigning a martyr's sigh.

She sauntered over to Dewdrop's dragonfly, clambered up behind him, and kissed him on the cheek.

"Yuck," he said. "That's my prize?"

She mussed his wet hair. "Ungrateful."

Rather than watch, Hickory focused on the deepening shadows of the trees around them. "It's getting late," he said. "Let's go back."

Mari turned to face him. "What, Hickory," she said, batting her eyelashes ridiculously, "jealous?"

He flushed hotter this time and knew his complexion wouldn't save him. He wished he could play the game the way Dewdrop did; he knew that's what she wanted. But he could never come up with anything clever enough to say.

Mari slid down from Dewdrop's dragonfly and walked along the swaying branch toward Hickory, holding her arms out to her sides and tilting back and forth, as if she might fall any moment.

Hickory said, "Be careful," and then instantly regretted it. Stupid, parental thing to say.

But then she reached his mount and climbed up beside him. That close, she seemed to radiate energy. Hickory swallowed.

"The loser needs something," she said. "A consolation prize. What do you think?" she called to Dewdrop.

"Maybe you should kiss him, too," Dewdrop called back. "But no, wait— that would be more of a punishment."

Marigold's lips set determinedly. "All right," she said. "I'll punish him, then."

She grabbed Hickory's head and kissed him on the mouth. Before he recovered from his shock enough to respond, it was over, Marigold still looking into his eyes, holding his head between her hands.

Thoughts crashed through his mind like the waterfall below them. Was that for real? Was it meant for him, or was she just teasing Dewdrop, to make him jealous? Should he kiss her back? But before he could do or say anything, she shoved him right off the dragonfly.

He shouted, scrabbling at the bark of the branch, slipping once but then managing to hold on. He tried not to look at the water far below. Was she crazy?

"Are you trying to kill me?" he shouted.

She raised her eyebrows. "Don't be ridiculous. If you'd fallen, I'd have caught you."

Hickory heaved himself up into a sitting position. "Come on. A pine nut's one thing . . ."

"Don't think I could?" she said, her eyes alight with defiance. She fluttered her dragonfly under another branch where a baby pine cone hung and began swinging it, trying to break the stem. "This is about your size, wouldn't you say?" Her eyes dared them to disagree.

Hickory and Dewdrop traded looks, suddenly allies. "You can't," Hickory said. "It's too big."

A bad choice of words.

"Can't?" Marigold repeated the word like it was an insult. Then the stem broke, and the pine cone hurtled downward.

"You win!" said Dewdrop. "Now let's—"

With a whoop, Marigold and her dragonfly plummeted toward the falling cone.

In an instant, she reached it and caught it perfectly, snatching it out of the air with both hooked legs at once. She pulled up, fighting for altitude, and for a moment seemed to be gaining. But not fast enough. As Hickory and Dewdrop watched, helpless to do anything, a spray of water from the waterfall struck, drenching her, knocking her nearly into the churning water.

"Drop it!" Dewdrop shouted, although there was no way Mari could hear him.

She wouldn't do it anyway. She'd never admit to herself she couldn't handle something, wouldn't allow the possibility of embarrassment. Miraculously, she kept above the water, unable to rise, yet refusing to fall. She reached the bank, then crashed ungracefully into a clump of reeds.

Dewdrop and Hickory relaxed, laughing a little too hard at her crash, relieved she hadn't landed in the water. Mari would be hard to live with for the rest of the day, but at least she was still alive. They waited for the reeds to part, for her to emerge with that fiery glare, threatening certain death or worse to anyone who would dare to laugh at her.

The reeds swayed lightly in the breeze. Their laughter trailed off into a silence as long as the shadows. Marigold did not appear.

Coriander had let them go, and she regretted it already. She'd seen Hickory and Marigold and Dewdrop heading for the river and had known what they were up to, but hadn't told anyone. After all, she and her friends had pulled stunts like that before they were army age. No big deal. Kids, especially talented ones like those three, weren't content with the ants and snails they were allowed to sway. They wanted more excitement.

But now, watching her unit stretch and measure the fresh snake skin they'd found, she wished she'd acted differently. There hadn't been a snake this size in the valley since before she was born. Snakes, with their ability to mesmerize victims, were the fielding's greatest threat. And a large snake meant one whose craftiness had kept it alive a long time. When she reported this, the army would go on full alert. It was no time for kids to be playing in the forest.

Kids. Cori smiled at her choice of words. Only two years older, and she thought of them as kids. The army changed your perspective.

Of the three, only Hickory didn't seem like a child. Physically, with his height and dark complexion, he looked more like a man than the others. Even when they'd played together as young children, he'd seemed ahead of his age—more like her group of friends than his own. And in some ways he seemed so mature—he thought before he acted, most of the time, and didn't fall into the sort of stupid mistakes common to his peers. But in other ways, like his infatuation with that spoiled brat, Marigold, he seemed hopelessly childish.

And remembering that it was Marigold he was with, Cori decided to return to the fielding right away, and if they weren't back, send out a search party. With anyone else, she'd trust Hickory to keep out of trouble. But with Mari, there was no telling.

Raspa hung motionless, dangling from a branch high above the clump of reeds, watching the two creatures search for their friend. They were so weak. So tiny. How could such pitiful things exert so much control over other animals?

She pulled herself back up to the branch, feeling with pleasure the working of her taut muscles. One of her slave-husbands lay near the trunk, half-asleep, but not relaxing his hold on the she-child trapped in the center of his coils.

Raspa twitched her tongue in delight, savoring the sweaty smell of the girl's terror. Did she think her two friends would rescue her? Or had she already despaired? How Raspa would love to encircle the child herself, to constrict inch by inch, tighter and tighter, until the luscious crunch of bones snapping . . . but no. Patience. Practicality first, then pleasure. The girl would be useful.

She slithered forward, letting her tail unwrap as she moved. The she-child turned her head away, her terror-smell heightening. Raspa slid closer, waiting, eyes wide.

It didn't take long. This child was bold. Inevitably, her eyes flicked toward her captor's, and in that moment she was caught fast like a fly in a web, unable to turn from Raspa's unblinking gaze. She cried out and squirmed and gritted her teeth, but couldn't tear away. No other huntress had eyes as powerful as Raspa's.

"Now listen, sweet," she said, drawing out the sibilance.

The girl shuddered, then relaxed, fully mesmerized.

"Listen carefully. . . ."

"It's no use," Hickory said. "She's not here. We've got to get help."

Dewdrop didn't answer; he just kept pushing through the forest of reeds they'd searched three times already. He'd grown more frantic and less reasonable ever since they'd landed. Hickory was about to give up on him.

The first thing they'd found had been her dragonfly, its abdomen cracked and oozing, its four wings shredded, its head mashed. Certainly not the result of a crash.

The second thing they'd found was a swath of bent and broken reeds, obviously caused by something much larger than Marigold.

"Maybe it was a beaver," Dewdrop said, pushing through more reeds. His guesses had become more ridiculous the longer they searched.

"Too low to the ground." Hickory was losing patience. They both knew what it was. "We need help."

"No."

"But if it's a—"

"Stop it," Dewdrop said. "If it were . . . just forget it."

Hickory left him there. Marigold's life was more important than not getting in trouble. He'd just have to get help alone.

Once clear of the reeds, he made a chittering noise, calling the three tame praying mantises they'd ridden from the fielding. The creatures became visible only when they moved, abandoning their camouflage to stalk forward on their long legs.

He mounted one, glanced back to see if Dewdrop was following, then swayed it into flight, back toward the fielding. Mantises generally made excellent mounts, so sensitive to sway that they became tame after a few rides. Camouflage and the ability to stand perfectly still kept the rider safe from larger animals, and the jagged spikes on the mantises' forearms were a match for the more dangerous insects. But this late in the day, when the bats were in the air, Hickory would gladly have traded him for a beetle, or even a cricket.

The mantis sensed them before Hickory did, diving suddenly in a crazy, zigzag pattern toward the ground. When faced with a natural predator, sometimes instinct could overcome sway. It didn't know the bats were sentries, ridden by soldiers guarding the perimeter of the fielding. Hickory guided it to the ground, where it could walk the rest of the way. A few moments later, he felt the rush of air, heard the flap of leathery wings, and knew he'd been sighted. A silhouette of bat and rider momentarily blocked the waning light from above, then merged back into the shadows of the trees.

The steady, careful gait of the mantis on the ground was frustratingly slow. He reached the grass fields and plunged through. A farmer Hickory knew was driving a team of ants through the field, their front pincers reaping the long stalks.

"Hickory! What news?" the farmer called, but Hickory just drove his mount on.

He passed the row of hollow prison gourds, the grass mills, the aphid pens. At the corner by the marketplace, he narrowly missed overturning a cart of sunflower seeds, but kept sway over the mantis and veered toward the barracks, a hollow log with two bright lights shining at its base.

To Hickory's surprise, he found a force already assembled there. He had expected to have to rouse the general and form a search party. Instead, a trio of gigantic weasels pawed the ground to the left, each with ten soldiers on its back, while to the right a full dozen mantises stood in motionless rank, twelve pairs of forelimbs clasped together under twelve glinting pairs of black eyes.

At the entrance to the log, flanked by two soldiers holding fireflies under sway, stood General Hoarfrost. The general and his army existed for the protection of the fielding against the many threats of the forest, a job he did not take lightly. Hickory and his friends spent most of their time avoiding the general, who always called them "private," and seemed to consider them under his authority, even though they wouldn't reach army age for another year.

This wasn't the time to be squeamish. Hickory dismounted and presented himself before the general, back straight, head high.

"Sir, Marigold and—"

The general seized his jaw with a grip like an ant's pincers. "Make it quick, private. Where are they?"

"Sir, at the river. Where it bends by the big pine. We—"

"Still alive?"

"Yes, sir. That is, Marigold . . ."

Hoarfrost stepped past him and signaled to the lead rider of one of the weasels. The weasel trotted forward, and the general swung on behind the last rider, shouting instructions to the leader. Before Hickory could close his mouth, the weasel shot off toward the river, followed closely by the other two. The phalanx of mantises held their ground, too slow to join the chase, but a cloud of bats erupted from the barracks, followed by a leaping chaos of crickets. One of the crickets landed almost on top of Hickory, legs splayed. Its rider was Coriander, General Hoarfrost's daughter.

"Hop on, kid," she said. "You can tell me what happened on the way."

Hickory clambered aboard, glad she couldn't see his blush in the dark. Cori had been a childhood playmate, and was gorgeous besides, but he couldn't think of her as a peer. Even though she wasn't much older, as an army officer she seemed already an adult—he always felt like a little boy around her. As they half-hopped, half-flew through the trees, he told her what had happened to Marigold.

"Stupid girl," Cori said. "Why didn't you stop her?"

Hickory was wondering how to explain the impossibility of stopping Marigold from doing anything when they burst into the river clearing to an incredible sight. In the dim gloom on the bank, an enormous snake thrashed, throwing up gouts of sand with its tail. It lunged and snapped at something Hickory couldn't see. Then, as the cricket reached the peak of another jump, the whole scene became clear.

Dewdrop, astride his mantis, was leading the snake away from the river, dodging its lunges and slashing out with his mount's spiked forelegs. There was no hope he could hurt it. Hickory wondered why he didn't just try to escape. Then he saw the other mantis behind the snake, its body crushed, and beside it, a slumped, motionless form. Marigold. Dewdrop was leading the monster away from her, making himself the target of an enemy many times his size.

The snake moved with deadly grace, as smooth and fast as the water falling from the rocks behind it. The battle could not have been raging for long, or Dewdrop would have been dead. The snake lunged again, just as Dewdrop was slashing forward, and he was thrown from his mount. The snake opened its mouth, fangs bared, to finish him, but at that moment the weasels attacked. They tore into its unprotected throat; the snake writhed, ripping itself away, but fell twitching, belly up, onto the sand. By the time Hickory and Cori arrived, it was dead.

The soldiers helped Dewdrop to his feet, clapping him on the back. They draped Marigold, still alive but unconscious, over one of the weasels to send her back to the fielding.

"That girl will kill somebody one of these days." Cori kicked at the ground so hard that Hickory jumped a step back. She relaxed just as suddenly, though, laughing a little at her own emotion. "I'm just glad it wasn't today," she said.

Raspa still clung to her branch in the growing darkness, watching in glee as the little people congratulated their young hero. Let them think themselves victorious. Her slave-husband had performed his role superbly, though of course he hadn't known it would mean his death. She didn't grieve him; she could always find other husbands.

Raspa remained motionless for some time, waiting for the little people and all their animals to leave. It didn't bother her. Waiting was something she did very well.

The general looked like a flooded river about to erupt over its banks. Coriander smiled and sat down next to him. Though sitting next to her father at political events often meant getting an earful, she enjoyed the rare chance to spend time with him.

"He didn't even tell me," Hoarfrost growled. "I should have killed him long ago."

He was talking about King Wheat-Tip, who stood on the platform draping a medal around Dewdrop's neck. The crowd, except for Hoarfrost, bellowed and whooped their approval. Cori found it funny to hear her father rant against the king, something most people would be terrified to do. But he and Wheat-Tip had been boyhood friends, had even fought over the girl who had later become Cori's mother. Hoarfrost had been offered the throne first, but had refused it. Now he complained at least once a week that he should have accepted, to save the fielding from Wheat-Tip's incompetence.

The crowd cheered again, as a medal was draped around Marigold's neck. Hoarfrost's annoyance was not that the three youths were being honored, but that they were being honored with military medals. In order to give them, the king had conscripted Dewdrop, Marigold, and Hickory into the army a year early. Without consulting the general.

"I can't trust them," he said. "They've been with the snakes."

"Fighting them is hardly spending time with them," Coriander said.

"We don't know what happened. One of them might have been mesmerized, might even now be under the snake's influence."

"But the snake is dead."

Hoarfrost's frown deepened. "Didn't you see?"

"See what?"

"The snake was male."

Cori drew in her breath. No wonder the snake had been so easy to kill. She'd assumed any fighting snake would be the female. But then where was she? And what was she planning?

The third medal, for Hickory this time, drew only lackluster applause from the crowd. The story being passed around was that Hickory had run away, leaving Dewdrop and Marigold to battle the snake alone. Cori knew this couldn't be true—there was no way they could have survived against even a male snake long enough for Hickory to ride to the fielding and bring back help. But Marigold was playing the lie well, the way she gazed at Dewdrop with unmasked admiration while completely ignoring Hickory. She wondered if Hickory knew he'd done the right thing.

"I'm putting them in your command," Hoarfrost said. "I want you to keep an eye on them."

Cori was surprised at her own reaction. She should have been horrified at the prospect of trying to maintain discipline with someone like Marigold in her unit. But instead, seeing Hickory's handsome, serious expression as he accepted his medal, she felt only elation. She wondered how long she'd been so attracted to him.

He didn't think he deserved it, but Hickory was glad to be in the army. In less than a week, he'd learned how to keep sway better than he'd been able to manage before, as well as the rudiments of swaying larger creatures in tandem with other soldiers. And Coriander's unit was a flying unit, which meant bats and dragonflies. But being in Cori's unit also meant almost continuous lectures about snakes.

"It's like being under sway," she said, stalking back and forth in front of them. "Never look a snake in the eyes, no matter how distant. She can mesmerize you before you blink—make you lose control of your animal, or run away, or even turn against your friends."

"Why are we drilling on snakes?" Marigold said. "Isn't the snake dead?"

Cori stared her down. "Because while you're in *my* command, you're under my sway." She looked as fierce as her father. "You drill when I say drill, you march when I say march." She turned to the whole group. "And because snakes are our most dangerous enemy, clever, quick, venomous, and immune to sway."

Hickory could see why most of the army, even other officers, didn't like Coriander, despite her beauty. She was tough, no-nonsense, and, probably worst of all, the general's daughter. Anger at the general's policies or gruff demeanor translated into resentment of her, not to mention jealousy at her promotions.

Yet she led well. Hickory suspected she was qualified for even higher rank, but had been held back to avoid the appearance of favoritism.

He watched Marigold glare defiantly at Cori, clearly incensed at being put in her place, and probably smarting over having a superior officer in the first place. Hickory bit his lip to keep from smiling. Marigold wasn't used to admitting anyone was superior in anything. It would do her good.

But thinking of Marigold reminded him of how little time he'd spent with her lately. It had been weeks since they'd had a proper conversation. Hickory longed to get her alone sometime, to try to mend the relationship he felt slipping out of his grasp. He hadn't forgotten the tender touch of her lips on his just moments before her dive. He imagined the two of them touching in the dark, her lips finding his. . . .

Similar thoughts haunted him all day and into the night, making it difficult to concentrate properly on his first sentry duty. He was far from accustomed to the bats' strange way of bouncing sound off objects to see them in the dark. Although he could use the skill, the bat's natural reflexes were suppressed under sway. More than once, Hickory had to swerve at the last moment to avoid collision. Thinking constantly about Marigold didn't help matters.

He'd been given the northwest post, which tended to be the quietest. Not far away, a more experienced soldier flew skillfully through the trees. He made the rounds among the green recruits to check on them, make sure they kept to their posts, and double their watch. With a snake in the area, no one was taking any chances.

The ground past the perimeter was bare except for where the river entered the fielding, and anything under the water would be kept out by the sluice gate. Hickory made another pass along the perimeter, expecting to find nothing, as he had every other time. But this time the sound coming back to him reflected something by the sluice gate that hadn't been there before. The fielding's most common nocturnal threat was from raccoons or opossums just blundering through, but this shape seemed too small for either. He wheeled and dove closer—there! Someone walking along the river. Maybe Coriander, checking up on him?

Whoever it was, Hickory decided to show him he'd been spotted. He swooped quietly down, as close to the ground as he dared, then circled around to approach from the rear. When he reached the spot, he strafed it with the bat's cries, able to see the scene clearly then with its strange vision. The intruder, who had been leaning on the winch for the sluice gate, shrieked and dove for cover as Hickory shot past.

He saw her clearly. The intruder was female, but it wasn't Coriander. It was Marigold.

Hickory gasped when he recognized her. It was as if his constant thoughts of her had swept her out of bed and materialized her there on the bank. What to do? He ought to report her, to sound the alarm and bring the army crashing in. But hadn't he been hoping for just such a chance to spend time with Mari alone? It was Marigold, after all, not some criminal—she probably had a perfectly good reason to be wandering the perimeter in the middle of the night. The least he could do was ask her.

He brought his bat down for a landing. It sprawled on the ground, gracelessly. As soon as Hickory dismounted, it took flight again, no doubt returning to its home in the barracks. He should have had it stay and wait for him, but it was too late. His watch was nearly over anyway.

"Mari!" he whispered. "It's me, Hickory!"

She stepped out from behind a reed. He could barely see her in the dark, but she looked confused, even frightened. He couldn't remember ever seeing her look that way before.

"You're not going to call the guard, are you?" she said.

Hickory took a step toward her. "No, I should have done that already.

But I figured you'd have a good reason for being out here." He paused to let her explain, but she just looked at him. "So, why are you here?"

She still seemed confused, as if she didn't quite know herself how she'd gotten there. "I couldn't sleep. The dreams. If you had dreams like mine . . ." She wrapped her arms around her body, hugging herself tightly. "If you knew . . ."

Hickory touched her on the shoulder. The touch seemed to melt her; she buried her face in his shoulder, her arms still wrapped around herself, suddenly crying. "Snakes," she said into his shirt, "the most horrible . . . whenever I shut my eyes."

He soothed her, stroked her hair, and kissed the top of her head, astonished that she was opening up to him. He'd been right not to report this; what was more innocent than nightmares after the ordeal she'd been through? Now, instead of humiliating her, he could help her through her most frightened, vulnerable time.

Just then, behind her, Hickory thought he saw something move in the middle of the river. The water was black, so he couldn't be sure, but it was probably just a ripple on the surface, or the shadow of a tree branch shifting in the breeze. The sluice gate would keep anything dangerous from entering by water. Hickory closed his eyes and rested his head on Marigold's, breathing in the scent of her hair.

When she finally left him to try again to sleep, he stood there by the river awhile, enjoying the quiet. There was no use going back quite yet; his watch was over by now, and he had a lot to think about. But not two minutes later, the sound of someone's voice in his ear startled him out of his thoughts.

Coriander finally found Hickory by the river.

"Your bat returned to the barracks alone," she said. "What's wrong?"

He whirled around when she spoke, as if she had discovered him in some indiscretion.

Hickory wiped his brow. "Cori! You scared me."

"What are you doing here?"

"I was investigating something. Something I thought I saw."

She waited.

"And it turned out to be nothing."

She was suddenly furious with him. He didn't realize the trust this assignment meant. What was he hiding from her?

"Listen," she said. "You might think since it's your first duty, I should go easy. But you remember that snake you ran away from?" She knew the snake hadn't really shown up until after he'd left, but she didn't care. "That snake was male."

No response. He had no idea.

"Male, Hickory. Male snakes are just vassals of the females. They never act on their own. We can't afford to have a gap in the perimeter. His mistress is still out there somewhere."

The dressing down seemed to have no effect; Hickory was staring off to the side, as if thinking of something else entirely. She followed his gaze, and saw the sluice gate winch. A chill ran through her body. The gate was open.

She looked back at Hickory, who was now looking at her guiltily. Why had he opened the gate? Only one answer made sense: the snake *had* been there before he ran for help, and he'd been mesmerized by her. Now she'd used her power over him to breach the fielding's defenses. There was no time to lose.

"I didn't realize it was open," Hickory said. "Maybe someone forgot to close it." He started to move toward the winch.

"Come with me," she said, putting as much steel in her voice as she could muster. "We've had a perimeter breach; it's too late to—"

A scream of pure terror interrupted her. A scream coming from inside the fielding.

"—close the gate." She grabbed his arm and ran toward the sound. "You'd just better pray this isn't your doing!"

Raspa fought the urge to break through the wall and eat the fool she-child. Why did it have to make such an awful noise? She had entered the child's dreams, and could see it in her mind, the vile thing shaking and screaming. Its screaming stopped, though, in its dream as well as reality, as soon as its eyes flicked to Raspa's, where they stuck fast as if in a bog. The girl flared her eyelids wide and tried to move, but couldn't break the gaze. After a moment, she relaxed, and the dream faded. That was when Raspa spoke into her mind, telling her what she wanted her to do.

Raspa slid through the shadows of the village, avoiding the army, seeking out the children. Children were so suggestible, so easy to control. Their sleeping minds were easy to invade, to insinuate with the image of herself and her powerful eyes. It would be lovely to kill them now, but much sweeter, in the end, to follow her plan. Her patience would be rewarded.

Once alerted, the army reacted with impressive efficiency. By the time Hickory and Coriander reached the scene, the excitement was just about over. The entire fielding had been combed. Nothing had been found. The girl who had screamed sheepishly explained that she'd had a nightmare. No one else reported seeing anything unusual.

Relieved, Hickory slipped away while Cori was talking with another officer. He thought about finding Marigold again, but she was probably sleeping. Had it been she who opened the sluice gate? Or had it been carelessly left open by someone else? He'd promised Mari he wouldn't tell anyone she'd been there, but circumstances had changed. He wasn't worried about taking the blame, but if Mari were in trouble, then as a friend he should get help, no matter what he'd promised.

But now, he just felt exhausted. His watch was over. There was nothing anyone could do this late at night anyway. He looked forward to catching some sleep—drifting off to memories of Marigold nestled in his arms. And maybe he'd been right not to tell anyone, despite the scare. It had turned out to be nothing, after all.

He was just stepping out of the barracks when General Hoarfrost caught him by the ear.

"A word, private?"

Hickory didn't try to resist, and found himself half-dragged out of the barracks and under an empty turtle shell the general used as his command center. In its shadow sat several of the general's aides. A few moments later, Coriander joined them.

Hickory sat uneasily. Apparently Cori wasn't going to let this incident slide.

"I understand you abandoned your post," the general said, pacing in a circle around the group.

Hickory thought this a bit harsh; he'd been investigating an intruder on his watch, not running off to catch a nap. But of course, they didn't know that. He hadn't told them.

"I'm sorry, sir," he said.

"Yes. And now you're going to tell us why."

"Why, sir?"

"Why you left your post."

Hickory clutched his knees, trying not to make nervous movements. Could they know about Marigold already? Were they testing him?

"I thought I saw someone by the dam," he said finally.

"And had you?"

Hickory hesitated. He realized at once that this was a mistake; unless he denied it immediately, they'd know he was hiding something. But it was too late.

General Hoarfrost crouched in front of him. "Look, son. People's lives are in danger. I can't protect them if I don't have all the information. Now who or what did you see or do by the dam?"

Knowing he was doing the right thing, and yet feeling like a complete traitor, Hickory told them about Marigold. In her defense, he told them she'd just been out walking, unable to sleep because of a dream. At this, the general leaned so close it seemed impossible their noses didn't touch. Hickory could see the pockmarks and wrinkles of his face.

Emphasizing each word, the general said, "What was her dream?"

"She had nightmares about snakes," Hickory said. "It's only understandable, given what she—"

"Bring her here!"

The general's bark was so authoritative that Hickory leaped to his feet before he realized the command wasn't directed at him. An aide scurried off to find Marigold.

"Sit down," the general said.

Hickory sat again. He rested his face in his hands, wanting to be anywhere in the world but there when Marigold arrived.

When she first ducked into the shadowed room, she looked more frightened than Hickory had ever seen her. As soon as she spotted him, however, her face hardened. When she sat next to him as instructed, he whispered, "I'm sorry. They . . ."

But she swiveled her head toward him, narrowed her eyes, and hissed, "Never speak to me again."

The whole movement was so serpentine that Hickory gasped aloud. He remembered Coriander's warnings about mesmerized victims. But Marigold hadn't seemed this way by the dam! What was wrong with her? He was suddenly glad he'd told the general the truth.

General Hoarfrost crouched beside Marigold and grasped both her wrists. She fought to free herself, but he held her fast. She writhed sinuously, throwing her body to the floor and even flicking her tongue in and out of her mouth. Hickory saw General Hoarfrost's look of concentration and realized he was *swaying* Marigold like an animal.

Soon it was over; the general relaxed his grip, and she tore away, backing away from him in sudden sobs. Hickory reached a hand out to touch her, but she glared at him and scuttled farther away. Though obviously angry and terrified, at least she moved normally now, not like a snake.

"What did you do?" Hickory asked, shouting. "Is she all right? Did you help her?"

But the general was already outside with his aides, sending them scampering with shouted orders. Coriander, who had watched everything, helped Hickory to his feet.

"He wasn't trying to help her," she said.

"But—"

"She's been mesmerized. The only way to help her is to kill the snake."

"But what—"

"He was using sway as a tool. Through the same sort of mind connection you can have over a swayed animal, he could see the snake's mind. Determine her plans."

Hickory shook his head. He wasn't sure he understood.

"Come on," Cori said. "My father must know where she is. You can help Marigold by fighting."

"Where will they take her?"

"One of the prisons, probably." She helped pull Hickory to his feet. "It's the safest place for her."

Hickory nodded. The prisons were dried gourds, hollow on the inside, with holes carved in the top. There was no climbing out of them without help.

Cori touched his shoulder to guide him out. "As long as the snake's alive, Marigold's in her control. All the more reason to attack now."

Hickory couldn't help noticing that Cori's attitude toward him had changed. At the sluice gate she'd acted like the furious commanding officer; now she was treating him as if he'd done something well. He didn't see why—he'd just betrayed a friend's confidence. Why would she approve of him for that?

Reluctantly, he let Cori lead him away, leaving Marigold slumped on the floor.

Coriander and Hickory joined their unit, which took to the air on dragonflies with the task of forward reconnaissance. These were huge, military dragon-flies, bigger than those he'd swayed by the river.

They found the snake easily. Long and pale and gigantic, she lay coiled in an open field, facing the fielding, as if expecting them.

"Remember the eyes!" Cori shouted as the snake lifted her head to gaze at them.

After circling over her, they veered back toward the oncoming army of weasels, rats, and mantises, and confirmed the sighting. When the army reached the field, the snake hadn't moved.

Neither did she move when the army approached—not until they were nearly close enough to strike. Then she slowly reared her head, looked out over the force arrayed against her, and made a dry, rasping hiss that could only be interpreted as a laugh.

The sound carried disconcertingly over the squeaks and growls and beating of wings from their animal army. Turning a tight circle over the snake's position, Hickory simultaneously heard the sound and saw the reason for it. Behind them, marching slowly across the field, came another army. An army of children. They carried pitchforks, knives, ant mandibles—anything they could find with a sharp edge. As they grew closer, Hickory could see that their eyes were glassy, their mouths set. They weren't coming to help fight against the snake. They belonged to her.

Coriander recognized the implications at once.

"Follow me!" she shouted. "We've got to disarm them!"

From his dragonfly, Hickory could see the whole horrible battle unfold. The children, ranging from toddlers barely walking to some of Hickory's peers, fought viciously, the little ones attacking legs and feet while the older ones fought hand-to-hand. They would have been no match for professional mounted soldiers, if those soldiers had not been facing their own beloved children. The soldiers fought defensively, at a disadvantage, trying only to disarm and capture, but not harm.

On the other flank, the snake attacked as well. She proved more formidable than her mate. Three weasels had taken him easily, but she was a huntress: quicker and stronger and smarter. She would appear to retreat from an attack, then suddenly strike, forcing the attackers back, never letting them get around her. The army, which had expected to surround their quarry and win by superior numbers, instead found themselves in the middle, beset on both sides.

Hickory's unit concentrated on the child army, swooping down from the sky to grab weapons, or sometimes even the fighters themselves, and carry them away from the battlefield. One flier came too near an older child, who slashed at her wings with a scythe. One wing tore, and the dragonfly tumbled into the crowd.

Watching in horror as three children tackled the downed rider, Hickory didn't notice an older girl leaping from a boy's shoulders until it was too late. The girl landed on his dragonfly's abdomen, dipping the mount dangerously backward. Hickory kept both hands in place to maintain sway, but he could hear her scrambling up behind him. He stole a glance behind, and despite the hollow look in her eyes, recognized her immediately. It was Marigold.

Had the children pulled her out of the gourd, or had she escaped herself before they could put her there? He realized now that she must have been mesmerized by the snake ever since that first day by the river, and was now responding to the snake's call with the rest of the children. An analytical part of him wondered how thoroughly she was controlled by the snake; did it command her every move, like with an animal under sway, or was it simply her will that was influenced, leaving her to carry out the snake's commands as she would? Was her direct attack on him influenced by her resentment? As far as he knew, she wouldn't hesitate to kill him. He had to find a way to get her off.

Clasping his legs tightly around the join between his mount's thorax and abdomen, Hickory flew away from the battle, keeping low to the ground. Just as he heard Marigold's breath behind him, he swerved, turning the dragonfly upside-down. Mari cried out, but didn't fall. Hickory's emotions seemed to turn flips, too—hearing her cry made him want to protect her, to hold her close. But he knew he couldn't do that.

With difficulty, he used the momentum of the roll to pull them upright again. Marigold grabbed him around the middle and tried to wrest him off the dragonfly. Hickory rolled again, but again she stayed on. Finally, just as she was about to pull one of his hands from the mount, he rolled a third time. Marigold lost her grip, tumbled off, and landed hard on the ground in a cloud of dust.

Hickory circled again, terrified that he'd killed her. But she jumped to her feet and ran for the battle again, without even looking up. There was no anger in her gait, no determination, just obedience to the call. There was nothing he could do for her now except fight her mistress.

He wrested his eyes away from her and back to the battle. General Hoarfrost's strategy had changed; instead of trying to fight on two fronts, he'd concentrated all his forces on the snake. It was working well—fighting for her life, she couldn't direct the army of children. That left the real army free to attack her. The weasels, growling and snapping, had her pinned against the trunk of an oak tree.

Then Hickory spotted Marigold running straight for the tree. Before anyone else saw her, she slipped between two weasels and clambered up onto the snake's neck. The weasel riders drew their mounts back to avoid harming her, leaving the snake free to coil her way around and up the tree, taking Marigold with her. Because of Mari, the weasel riders dared not follow.

Again, the children attacked. Besieged from behind, the army could no longer concentrate on what to do about the snake. A quick glance around told Hickory that most of the other flying soldiers had been pulled to the ground or had crashed. He saw Dewdrop, still aloft, dropping a toddler gently into the grass away from the battle. When he turned, their eyes met.

Hickory looked up at Marigold, high above on the snake, and then back to Dewdrop. He pointed at himself, then up at Mari, then at Dewdrop, then to the ground under the tree. Dewdrop nodded, understanding. It was up to them.

Hickory lifted his dragonfly high in the air, making a wide circle around the tree. There was no time for a better plan. As the snake's hostage, Marigold was temporarily safe, but the snake would rather kill her than let her escape. Hickory aimed directly for them, picking up speed as he flew. He thrust aside his doubts; this was the only way to save her. The only way.

Just before he reached them, the snake twisted around, lashing out at him with an attack designed to protect her vulnerable throat. But Hickory wasn't aiming for her throat. He was aiming for Marigold.

He collided with her at full speed. With no handholds to grasp, Mari was knocked cleanly off the snake and hurtled toward the ground. Hickory veered his dragonfly and tore down after her.

It all happened in an instant: Marigold dropping like a pine cone toward the ground, Hickory plunging after her. But where was Dewdrop? Hickory had known his momentum would carry him too far; he hadn't turned fast enough to catch up to Mari. She was falling fast. What if Dewdrop hadn't understood? What if his signals hadn't been clear?

No! He pushed the dragonfly harder, willing it to fly faster, but he couldn't force it beyond its own physical strength. He watched Marigold, out of reach, plummeting toward the ground, the moment stretching forever. But at what seemed like the last possible instant, another dragonfly swooped over her, scooping her up perfectly with both its legs and carrying her to safety.

Dewdrop! He'd understood after all. Hickory watched as the dragonfly dipped with the sudden extra weight, wobbled, nearly righted, then rolled over and crashed into the grass. In a moment, Dewdrop and Marigold were back on their feet, apparently unharmed.

The weasels charged up the tree, converging on the snake before she had any chance of escape. They tore into her, jaws snapping. She took one with her as she fell, its bloody jaws still sunk in her flesh when they hit the ground together.

The moment after the snake struck the ground, the battlefield filled with sounds of crying. All the children, no longer mesmerized, found themselves in a strange place, bruised and tired, with little idea what had happened to them. The soldiers dropped their weapons and searched through the crowd, finding their own loved ones and holding them close.

Hickory landed near to where the snake had fallen. A crowd had gathered around her, a few soldiers making certain she was dead, and the rest gawking at the size of the monster. Hand in hand, Dewdrop and Marigold came toward him through the grass. Hickory ran to them, intending to hug them both, to share in their elation and thank Dewdrop for catching Marigold when he couldn't get there. But halfway to them, he saw Marigold's face and stopped. She stared at him with unconcealed disgust.

He stood there, unbelieving, as they passed him by without a word. Dewdrop didn't even turn to look at him, as if he didn't exist, but Marigold actually glared. He wanted to shake her, to tell her that without him she'd still be with the snake, or dead. Didn't she realize that he'd pushed her off intending for Dewdrop to catch her? But maybe Dewdrop hadn't told her, or had told her something else. Obviously he was willing to let himself appear the hero, and Hickory the fool, yet again. And Marigold was willing to believe him.

From now on, he realized, things would be different. And not just with Dewdrop. Watching Marigold, Hickory realized he no longer thought her beautiful. It wasn't just that she was dirty and disheveled from the battle. Nor did it matter that she had fought for the enemy; she couldn't help being mesmerized any more than the children could. It was just that, since joining the army, he'd come to see her in a different light, though he hadn't entirely realized it until now. What had seemed exciting and daring about her before had, around Coriander and the other soldiers, struck him as foolish or immature. As was her anger with him now. Hard as it was, what he had done would have been right even if Marigold hadn't survived. It had allowed them to win the battle.

Not that he expected anyone else to see it that way. Once again, when he did what was needed to save his friends, someone else would get the glory. But it didn't matter. As long as they let him stay in the army, he'd be content.

He'd become a soldier, learn the craft of war, commit himself to protecting the fielding. To protect and save, even if no one appreciated him for it. He didn't need love; the camaraderie of his fellow soldiers would be enough. Besides, as a soldier he wouldn't have time for romance.

Just then he felt a hand slip into his. He turned to see Coriander, a smile on her face and admiration in her eyes. She understands, he realized. She thinks I did the right thing. As they turned to walk together back toward the fielding, Hickory decided to revise his resolution. Perhaps he'd make time for romance after all.

Deathless in Manhattan

Hank Quense

A slight change in air pressure alerted Ida to the approach of a subway train. Was it worthwhile to jump in front of it? Whether the train destroyed her or not, it would surely ruin her dress.

From her vantage point, she saw three people milling around in the 68th Street station, a hundred feet away. She ignored the rank odor of the subway with its components of dust, ozone, and rodents and stood up from the wooden plank covering the electrified third rail of the south-bound Lexington Avenue subway line. She pressed herself against a steel column between the tracks, ready to leap in front of the train but it slowed as it approached the station. A local wasn't any good. She needed an express train, one that would zoom through at high speed.

She heard a sob and cocked her head in the direction of the noise. Nothing. She sat down and reviewed her reasons once again, still searching for a counter-argument. Three hundred years was long enough to exist in this state. Even in Manhattan, with its vibrant undead community, her existence was a crushing bore. Menial labor—at less than minimum wages—just to pass the time. Living in abandoned steam tunnels. She couldn't remember the last time she had a date. It might have been before she fell into the vat of shellac and drowned. A decent employer would have simply buried her since she was an orphan. But not her rotten boss. He had her animated to work as a slave laborer.

She heard another sob.

In her first attempt at self-destruction two weeks ago, she had jumped in front of a delivery truck leaving the Holland Tunnel. *That* had been an experience. The traffic was so dense that seven other cars and trucks ran her over before someone noticed and diverted traffic. By the time the Emergency Medical Service squad delivered her to St. Vincent's Hospital, she had completely recovered. Who knew her animation spell was that strong? The

EMS workers, angry at wasting their time, chased her out of the hospital and down West 12th Street as far as Fourth Avenue before they gave up. Meanwhile, she hadn't been able to remove the tread marks from her jacket.

More sobs. She walked towards the sound on the north-bound side, where a little boy huddled against the tunnel wall, sucking on his thumb.

"Whatsa matter, kid?"

The boy took his thumb out of his mouth and said, "I'm lost." He wiped his snotty nose on his wrist.

Ida bit her lip. She should return the kid to his parents, but that would wreck her plans for the day. The most considerate time to jump in front of the train was at least two hours before the homeward-bound commute began. That way, the Transit Authority could clean up the mess before rush-hour. She'd never get the kid home and make it back in time.

"Where do you live?"

"By the park."

Ida sighed. Manhattan had a lot of parks. "Do you know what street?"

"Yes." The kid snuffed his nose.

"Well?"

"I live on East 71st Street." The boy talked with a lisp because of his missing front teeth.

A breeze brushed her face. A north-bound train approached the station. "Come with me so you don't get hit." She took his hand and led him to the south-bound side. The wind from the train whipped her clothes as it roared passed them. An express. Just what she needed before the kid showed up.

"What's your name?"

"Alex."

"How'd you get here?"

"I ran away from Daddy to play a joke on him."

"And you came down here to hide?"

"Yeah. Daddy was talking to someone and didn't watch me."

It was possible that no one was around to stop him. During off-peak hours, the platform was frequently empty. "Okay. Let's get outta here."

She led Alex up the stairs at the end of the platform where a middle-aged woman glared at them. Ida was used to people doing that.

On the surface at Lexington Avenue and 68th Street, the brilliance of the sunlight blinded her for a few moments. Once she regained her sight, she scrutinized the boy. The blackness of his hair accentuated his pale skin.

Brown eyes peeked out of an almost handsome face.

When they reached the corner of 70th Street, two squad cars from the Nineteenth Precinct pulled up, each with a pair of NYPD cops. One jumped out of the first car and said, "Back away from the boy. Do it." The cop had his right hand on the butt of his revolver and made an effort to position himself upwind.

Great! The cops were busting her for helping a lost kid. She was proof that no good deed went unpunished.

"I was tryin' to take him home." Ida released Alex's hand.

A policewoman got out of the second car and took him by the shoulder. Alex stuck his thumb back in his mouth.

Ida's shoulders sagged as she watched him get in the car. The kid was having a rough day. But not as rough as hers.

At the station house on East 67th Street, Ida sat in a cell and brooded on her pathetic existence while devising new ways to exterminate herself. She rejected self-immolation, afraid she might end up as a walking pile of ashes and bones. None of her clothes would fit.

A cop took her out of the cell and into a conference room where a tall, thin man sat. He wore an expensive pin-striped, three-piece suit.

"You found Alex?" the man asked.

Ida nodded.

The cop, holding a handkerchief over his nose, motioned for her to sit in a chair.

"Thank you for helping my son. My name is Fedor Kosloff."

"Fat lot of good it did me."

"Hey!" The cop shrugged. "Some lady called on her cell phone about you and the kid on the subway tracks. We had to check it out, but you're free to go."

"Come with me," the man said.

Ida followed Alex's father outside where an ancient and dented white limo sat at the curb, motor running. A small green, white and red flag flew from the front left fender. Fedor opened a rear door for her. After Ida climbed in, he shut the door and went around to the other side to sit alongside her. "We'll go to my house, where I can repay you for your trouble. You see, Alex told me the whole story. It was quite stupid of me not to pay attention to him for a few minutes."

"Look, I'm kinda busy, so drop me off and I'll go away." That's what everyone wanted her to do; just go away.

"Please." Fedor smiled. "Alex never had a chance to thank you. He really wants to."

The limo stopped in front of a three-story brown-stone on East 71st Street between Madison and Park Avenues. Fedor led her into a living room filled with old, scarred furniture and threadbare oriental rugs.

Alex ran over and hugged her legs. Ida's mouth opened and shut a few times. Alex released her, scampered out of the room and thumped up a flight of stairs.

"I can't tell you how grateful I am," Fedor said. "Name your reward and I'll try to fulfill it."

"I don't need a reward."

"Nonsense. Such neighborly assistance must be rewarded."

Alex came back with a plastic model of a space ship. "This is my best one," he lisped. "If you want it, you can have it."

"It's a great-lookin' ship." Ida smiled at the lad. "But I don't have any place to put it. Can you keep it for me?"

"What kind of work do you do, Ida?" Fedor stared at her and she felt uncomfortable under his gaze. Not many people could look at the undead with their unnatural light-gray skin color without getting queasy. Their characteristic smell—like curdled milk—disgusted most people.

"Mostly, I work in a laundry. Washin' and ironin' clothes. At night, after the store is closed."

"That's really the best you can hope for, isn't it? The undead are definitely discriminated against in New York." He sighed. "But, that's to be expected. The last census recorded, what, ten thousand undead? Not enough to have any political clout in a city of eight million."

Ida nodded at Fedor's sympathetic tone of voice.

"But I can understand why you undead like New York City. With its great diversity, you can almost blend in." Fedor cleared his throat. "I'm the UN ambassador for Romoslavia, and I'm raising Alex by myself. I'm concerned that the troubles in my homeland will spill into New York. I need someone to look after Alex. The job is part nanny and part bodyguard."

Ida raised an eyebrow. A job? Her heart would be beating fast, if it still worked.

"Please?" Alex looked at her expectantly.

"You're an ambassador and you don't have bodyguards?"

"I have an office staff at the UN but Romoslavia is a poor country. It owns this house—which needs a lot of work—but if I want a personal staff, I have to pay for it."

"You'd let an undead take care of Alex?"

"Romoslavia has a long cultural history of undead as well as vampires and werewolves. In my experience, these beings are no different than everyone else. Some are evil, some are good, but most don't bother to be either."

"I'm kinda tied up right now."

"Aww, c'mon Ida." Alex tugged on her slacks. "We can have fun."

"Three hundred a week and a room in the house." Fedor grinned at her.

Ida gulped. That was more than she made in two months. And a real room! No more steam tunnels. She could live in luxury until she figured out a way to destroy herself.

So far, none of the usual methods had done anything except wreck her wardrobe. Like the time she jumped off the roof of a ten-story building. She landed on a fruit-and-vegetable stand and the juice from the squashed pomegranates had hopelessly stained her best dress.

"All right. Only for a while."

Alex jumped up and down and shouted with joy.

The kid's exuberance gave Ida a lump in her throat.

That night, Ida put Alex to bed and retired to her third-floor bedroom across the hall from Alex's. Her room had an attached private bath with a cracked mirror and a tub with a dark ring around the inside. She filled the tub with hot water and took her first bath in several decades. It felt so much more relaxing than a shower under a busted cold water pipe.

She dried herself then dressed in a robe she found in a closet. It didn't quite enclose her girth. In the mirror, she observed the curls in her brown hair. They resulted from her attempt to electrocute herself. With each foot in a bucket of water and her left hand clamped onto a metal water pipe, she stuck a finger into an empty fuse socket. She blew a transformer and left a five-block area without power. It didn't kill her, but it did curl her hair, a nice improvement over her previous hair-do. Ever since she fell into the shellac vat, her hair had stuck out in unmanageable spikes.

She promised herself that, once she got some money, she'd buy make-up. A little eye shadow and people wouldn't notice the black bags under her eyes.

She tip-toed across the hall, opened Alex's bedroom door a crack and peeped in. He was snuggled up and quiet. She smiled as she watched him for a few moments. She closed the door and turned towards her room when she heard a strange voice downstairs.

"—support the Fatalist Movement of Romoslavia and the Exalted Prelate," the visitor said in a strident voice.

"A bunch of degenerates." Fedor's voice. "Justly executed for crimes they committed."

"The Exalted Prelate is determined to stop this persecution by your biased government."

"By revolution? The government was democratically elected."

"The Romoslavian undead were denied the vote." The voice sounded hysterical. "The Exalted Prelate teaches us that government is too important to be left in the hands of the living. Only the undead have the wisdom to rule. The movement rejects your democracy which is only for the living."

"Your logic makes a mockery of rational thought." Fedor sounded like he was losing his temper.

"I demand that you issue a statement supporting the Fatalist Movement."

"I want no part of your idiotic movement."

"I warn you. Unless the statement is released within twenty-four hours, you will regret it."

The front door slammed. Ida wondered what the threat meant. She had a sudden, ugly thought. The threat could affect Alex and endanger her new lifestyle.

Two nights later, Fedor left the house for a dinner engagement. Ida, wearing the robe, relaxed in her bedroom with a romance novel, picturing herself as the blouse-busting heroine. Footsteps and a creaking floor in the hall caught her attention. She opened the door. "Hey! Who're you? What're you doin' by Alex's bedroom?"

The stranger jumped then looked at her and sucked in his breath.

He was cute in a craggy sort of way, but her instincts told her he was trouble. Perhaps he was the man who threatened Fedor. She had to do something. "You better leave." She put her hands on her hips and stared at him.

He didn't move.

She would have to resort to stronger measures. "Fedor isn't home." She sauntered closer to him, swiveling her hips. "But . . . maybe you're lookin' for someone else."

The man backed up and licked his lips.

"What's your name?" She admired the pinkness of his tongue, so unlike the unnatural dark color of her own.

"You're undead." The man's voice came out as a croak. "And . . . you're a woman."

"Guilty on both counts." Ida batted her eyelids.

"You're an abomination!"

"Damn straight I am." She gave him a lascivious grin. "Us abominationists have some pretty neat moves, you know." She took another step closer while loosening her robe. "Come inna my room and you can have your way with me."

"Back off, you unclean bitch." The man drew a gun. "You'll defile me."

"Oh, please. All a gun'll do is put holes in my robe."

The man ran passed, charged down the stairs and slammed the door on his way out.

Unfortunately, that was how all men responded to her moves.

When Fedor returned an hour later, Ida told him about the intruder.

"From your description, his name is Pasha Popov," Fedor said. "He's a thug from Romoslavia and he's a sympathizer of an undead political party called the Fatalist Movement."

"Wow. An undead organization. They got it together in Romoslavia, don't they?"

"No they don't. It's a quasi-religious group of undead male criminals. Men who pass the initiation tests are killed then animated. They claim an undead woman is an outrage against nature. All the members have to avoid undead women or they're considered defiled and expelled from the party."

Ida blew a raspberry.

"They want to take over the country and run it according to the dictates of their leader, who is a fanatic." Fedor's face assumed a stern expression. "Ida. Listen to me. Please don't let the boy out of your sight. I'm the ambassador and if I support the movement, it'll give them a measure of respectability. Pasha will use Alex to put pressure on me so he can impress the Exalted Prelate and join the undead."

So Pasha wanted to kidnap Alex. How dare that jerk threaten her cushy job? Besides, she liked playing with Alex and taking care of him. If she saw this Pasha creep again, he would regret it.

The next day, Ida and Alex left the house for Central Park, a few blocks away. The mild spring weather was perfect for an outing. They planned to have lunch near the 79th Street entrance where Alex could watch the model sailboats on the lake. She carried a large shoulder bag crammed with food and bottled water. In case of trouble, an aluminum softball bat stuck out of the bag.

The pair strolled west on 71st Street. Ida wore a new blouse, walking shorts and sneakers, purchased with a salary advance from Fedor. She noticed that most people didn't give her dirty looks as they passed. The new clothes gave her respectability and her step had an unaccustomed bounce to it.

Close to Madison Avenue, an idling van sat by an open manhole while two guys fussed around the back of the truck, oblivious to the traffic problem they caused. Out of the corner of her eye, she glimpsed a man poking his head out of the manhole.

"That's them." The man pointed at Ida and Alex. "Get the kid."

Pasha! The two men moved towards her. They looked like the typical low-lifers that could be hired anywhere in New York City for a few bucks.

Her anger surged. For the first time in her existence, she lived comfortably, and these jerks threatened to end it. She grabbed the bat and placed herself between the men and Alex.

The thugs hesitated when they saw the bat. One moved to his right to get around Ida. She jabbed the bat into the gut of the other man. He doubled over. Ida kneed him in the face. The man stumbled backward and fell by the manhole. She closed on the second man and swung the bat, connecting with his shoulder. He moaned and fled towards Park Avenue.

Ida turned to Pasha who had watched the fight from the manhole. She dropped the bat, leaned over and, grunting from the effort, shoved the manhole cover toward him. Pasha's eyes widened and his jaw dropped. He ducked his head below street level while hanging on to the edge of the manhole with his left hand.

Ida rolled the cover into place, crushing his fingers. The cover muffled most of Pasha's scream.

"Let's go to the park, Alex," Ida said, "and have some fun." She giggled, thinking it would be a long time before Pasha tried to screw with her job again. To her surprise, she realized that she had worried about Alex's safety. How strange.

"Gee, Aunty Ida. You're better than the superheroes on TV. That was really cool what you did."

Alex's praise gave Ida a warm glow.

When Fedor came home that night, Ida told him about the incident.

"Pasha called this afternoon and gave me an ultimatum," Fedor said. "He threatened Alex unless I issued a statement supporting the Exalted Prelate."

Ida punched one hand into the palm of the other. Damn it! Why was a complete stranger trying to mess up the best job she ever had? She wanted to stay with Alex.

"I also received a report on him from my government. He's a ruffian with a long prison record."

"Is he actin' on his own?"

"Most likely. In any event, he's a danger to Alex. Please be extra cautious if you have to go out."

Ida nodded, then excused herself to read Alex a story before he went to bed. This was now her favorite time of day.

After Alex went to sleep, she pondered how to end it all. Just in case Pasha ruined her job. She had an idea that getting her head under the business end of a pile driver would do the job. But how to get on a construction site? She may have to join the union.

After staying inside the house for three days, Alex displayed symptoms of cabin-fever, and Fedor gave Ida permission to take him out. Close to noon, Ida and Alex walked down Lexington Avenue on their way to the Children's Zoo in Central Park. Ida basked in the warmth of the sun, her new status and the presence of the child. This was the best time of her entire three-hundred-year existence.

They passed Hunter College on 68th Street and came alongside the red-bricked Seventy-Ninth Regiment Armory when an SUV screeched to a halt a few yards in front of them. The doors flew open and four men jumped out. Pasha, with a cast on his left hand, was one of them. His brow furrowed and the veins in his neck bulged.

The threat transfixed Ida for an instant. The softball bat wouldn't do much good against four men. One of them would surely grab Alex while she fought off the others. Her anger surged. Pasha had threatened her once too often. Now she would end it and she knew just how to do that.

She sent the bat windmilling at one of her assailants and dropped the shoulder bag, then scooped Alex into her arms and fled north. At the corner of 68th Street, Ida ran down the steps of the subway entrance, pausing until she heard a stampede of footsteps not far behind. She grinned and sprinted across the entrance area. She jumped the turnstiles while Alex trembled in her arms.

Ida ran to the edge of the platform. Nothing moved on the tracks and several people yelled in alarm when she leaped from the platform to plunge into the darkness of the tunnel. More shouts told her the men followed her lead. She heard them cursing in the gloom. Down here, she had an advantage. Whenever a few undead got together in New York City, they used the tunnels to play Subway Chicken or Hide-and-Seek. She knew these tunnels and Pasha didn't.

She sensed the men falling behind as they slowed down, confused by the darkness and wary of the danger of electrocuting themselves.

Ida stopped between the tracks and screened herself behind a girder. "Listen to me, Alex," she whispered. "I want you to hide for a little bit."

"I told Daddy I wouldn't hide in the tunnels again."

"I hear 'em," a man yelled. "This way."

"You have to do it this time, Alex. It's an emergency. Okay?"

"Daddy'll get mad at me."

The slow, steady footsteps of her pursuers sounded closer. "I'll straighten things out with your father." Ida hurried over to the tunnel wall and set Alex down behind a signal cabinet. She patted him on the head. Alex popped his thumb into his mouth.

With Alex safe, she turned from prey to predator.

Ida melted into the blackness and let them move about twenty yards beyond her before beginning to stalk them. She went for the one who brought up the rear, placing her left hand over his mouth and her right arm around his chest. She held him close while she whispered in his ear, "Hey, Studly."

The man struggled to squirm free. Ida tightened her grip.

"Let's you and me get it on." Ida chewed his earlobe.

The thug made mewing sounds. When she licked his ear, his body stiffened then went limp. Ida dropped him between a pair of steel girders and moved after the next one.

This time, she grabbed the guy, spun him around and planted a kiss on his lips. He gagged. Ida pushed her tongue into his mouth and pulled back an instant before the man vomited all over himself. She dumped him on the tunnel floor and left him convulsing with dry heaves. Ida continued up the tunnel. She could track Pasha by his ragged breathing.

A train roared past. Ida moved in under the cover of its noise and threw a choke-hold on Pasha, squeezing until he went limp.

The fourth guy turned and took a step towards her. Ida waved a fist. "You're next if you're still around when I'm finished with Pasha."

The man fled down the tracks towards the 59th Street station.

She hauled Pasha's inert body across the north-bound tracks and found an equipment room. She opened the door, dumped Pasha on the floor, shut the door and flipped the light switch. A single bulb showed the room half-filled with cable reels, boxes of spare light bulbs, and tools.

Pasha groaned and sat up, his face distorted by fear.

"Hi, big guy." Ida smiled. "Let's have some fun."

"Please." Pasha's eyes went wide. "Don't hurt me." He threw a cast-covered hand in front of his face.

"Hurt you?" Ida smiled again. "Not a chance."

Pasha gurgled and shoved himself backward.

"I saw the way you looked at me in Fedor's house. I know you're interested in findin' out what undead chicks have to offer."

"N . . . no!" Pasha crawled into a corner of the room.

"C'mon. Let's do it."

"I'll be defiled. I won't be able to join the Fatalists."

"Oh please. Lie a little. Don't tell them about the fun we had."

"You don't understand. The Exalted Prelate uses torture and drugs on candidates. I'll end up telling him."

"Too bad." Ida blew him a kiss.

"I won't bother you again."

Ida stared at Pasha, letting him sweat it out. Finally, she said, "Why should I believe you?"

"It's true. Leave me alone and I'll leave the kid alone."

"All right. Here's the deal. If I ever see you again—anywhere in the city—you're gonna be my boy-toy."

Even in the dim light, Ida could see Pasha go pale.

"You . . . you're kiddin', right?"

"No, I'm not. You and me'll get real close and friendly."

"I . . . I'll go away."

"Good choice." Ida opened the door a crack. "Don't forget to turn out the light when you leave."

She walked over to where Alex waited. "C'mon Alex. Let's go to the zoo." Ida took the boy's hand. "Mind the third rail."

She smiled at the realization that not once during the attack did she worry about losing her job. All she thought of was ending the threat to Alex. It felt pretty good.

"That was fun," Alex said. "I always have fun with you."

After taking a bubble bath that night, Ida went into Alex's bedroom to read a story. He sat on the floor using a remote control to maneuver a robot around the room. Ida stood in the door and watched, realizing that she had not pondered how to destroy herself in days. She didn't want to end her existence anymore. She had found the ultimate counter-argument. She wanted to see Alex grow up and mature. She wanted to see him go to his high school prom and later get married.

After that, there would be time to find a way to end it. Unless Alex wanted her to watch his children.

A Night on Pope Lake

James R. Cain

God knows why Dad decided to go fishing that night. Pope Lake was twenty clicks beyond Bodie, down a rugged drainage channel that passed for a road on Water Board land. It was not an easy place to get to; not on the tourist map, anyways, but Dad knew the mountains well. He used to visit Pope Lake as a kid, and told me about it more than once. I guess that was the attraction of the place, though, wasn't it?

It was an ideal place to be alone.

It was an ideal place to die.

I know he was depressed. Mum was dragging him through the courts for child support for my kid brother at the time—the usual trumped up shit. That woman held a chip on her shoulder. She felt cheated that Dad had left, maybe, and took every opportunity to make his life hell. Dad needed to escape, I guess. I get that way sometimes. It gets so that solitude's the only thing to clear your head.

Dad's aluminium boat and rusted Ford turned up six days after his disappearance. A Ranger stumbled upon them while looking for noxious plants. The boat floundered in the reeds, with an Esky of warm beer, and a bottom strewn with emptys. There'd been a maggoty bag of worms beneath the seat. Dad's fishing rod was recovered from the mud on shore. Its hook and sinkers were missing. The line had been snapped.

It was assumed Dad had stumbled overboard and drowned. The mountains around Bodie are pockmarked with limestone caves, and the emerald waters of the Pope bleed in from an underground stream. Police dragged the lake and sent down a diver but found nothing. Pope Lake plummets in the middle into an underwater chasm, or so they said.

One of the locals, an Aboriginal by the name of Indigo Jim, informed me the lake was barren of fish. Guy had only one yellow tooth, a crooked grin, and his breath stank of turpentine. He sidled up to me in the Innes Hotel, put his arm around my shoulders like I was an old war buddy, and breathed heavily into my ear.

Dad's death was common knowledge you see.

I squirmed out of his embrace.

"All you can catch are eels, mate," Indigo Joe said and asked me to buy him a drink.

A chuckle began in my throat, and this grew into a sort of laugh. I laughed until tears formed in the corners of my eyes and the tears stung as they crawled down my cheeks.

Dad hated eel, you see. He couldn't stand the taste. In the early days, Mum cooked eel soup once—only ever once. Dad had tasted it, and promptly dished it to the dog, our old Labrador named Sue. Furious, Mum had hurled a mug of tea at Dad's head and it shattered on the wall.

I wiped my eyes with the back of my hand and shouted Jim that beer. I thanked him, although I don't quite know why. With drink in hand, he shuffled away.

The funeral was a quiet affair, but I'm sure Mum was grinning as they lowered the empty coffin into the grave. That made me mad.

To spite Mum and somehow remember Dad, later that week, I got a tattoo on my shoulder. The tattoo artist was a biker with more ink than skin on his arms, and I think he tried to make it hurt. He made wisecracks every time he stuck in the pin anyway, and told me to take in the hurt. The tattoo was of a crucifix with Dad's name etched above some thorns and a tangle of roses. This pissed Mum off to no end when I showed her. She screamed that I'd desecrated my body.

She hurled a cookie at my head.

I smiled at that. Making Mum angry made me feel as if somehow Dad was around.

That's probably why I agreed to my cousin's hair-brained idea of a fishing trip on the anniversary of the accident. I told Roger all we'd catch were eels. That didn't matter to Rodge though. He claimed he was in it for the sport and seemed set on the idea.

I knew Rodge had been down. He was always fighting with Aunt Patsy, and there was the usual trouble with fighting and drinking at school. Aunt Patsy flushed his stash of weed when she discovered it in a shoebox in his cupboard, and Rodge was pissed about that one; let me tell you. So, what the heck? I agreed. Rodge said he needed to talk to me about something, which might be something or nothing at all—Rodger's full of shit at the best of times. He sounded pretty grim though. I suspected he was in some sort of trouble.

Rodger was only seventeen. I didn't want him ruining his life. He was fast on the way to flunking out of school.

So, there we were.

Fishing.

In Dad's old boat in the middle of a lake full of eels at 10:30 at night, shivering our balls off in our parkas and jeans, sipping bourbon straight from the bottle. We faced each other with me in the back and Rodge in the front with the bottle between his knees. I was depressed. The alcohol filled my skull with warm fuzz.

Rodge brought the booze. I don't know how he got it. I knew better than to ask, with him being underage and all. Rodge was doing his utmost to get spiked, so I figured what he was about to tell me had to be something important. *Maybe he's knocked up some chick?*

But then Rodger started to speak.

I couldn't have been further from the truth.

"Jay." Rodge took a deep breath, all serious, and sounded like he was gargling whisky. "I have something to tell you, and it's real. This is no b-s."

Here we go, I thought, but out there, in the cold and with shit-all to do, I couldn't help it, my interest spiked. Rodge's news had to be more exciting than looking for eels in the dark. The moon was full. I could hear those eels slapping about the boat, leaping out of the water surrounding us. An eerie sound.

Rodger hunched closer toward me. "Don't laugh, but I gotta tell someone, or I'll go mad. You know we've always been close . . ." He paused for effect, I guess gauging my reaction, but I hadn't had one. I was just listening to those eels, *slap, slap, slapping.*

"I'm gay."

I didn't reply. I didn't even fucking breathe, at first. But then I laughed. I laughed so hard I almost toppled backwards off my seat.

Rodger chugged bourbon, and came even closer. He came so close I could smell his breathe, and his breathe was bittersweet. "Don't laugh, you bastard. This is no joking matter." I kept laughing. Rodger hooked me with a stare. "I love you, man."

My laughter died. I sort of felt queasy as if maybe I'd been snacking on the bait in the dark and had a belly full of worms.

An eel leapt and landed close to the boat. It wet my face with a spray of ice.

I cursed and started reeling in my line. Rodger was silent, and all I could see were his eyes glistening, waiting, soaking up the moonlight.

Watching me, watching him.

And forever waiting.

But, I didn't say anything.

"Well?" he asked.

"What can I say? You're sick. I'm your cousin, man."

Something bumped against the bottom of the boat. A sound like a fist punching the hull.

"Freakin' eels must be getting hungry." Rodger gave an uncertain smile. "Maybe I'll throw them a worm?" He tipped out a shot of bourbon into the water.

"That ain't tequila. Save it." I stood as I reeled. I didn't want to fathom exactly what Rodger meant when he'd said he loved me. Plus I was thinking: *What will Aunt Patsy say? Hell, Rodge's stepfather was not a man to be taken lightly. Pete's built like a Sumo and has a shit tempter to boot. This is the last thing he'd share with his mates down the pub. How his son has a preference for arse.*

"How do you know?" I stared at Rodger, hoping that maybe this was my cousin's drunken idea of a joke. "I mean have you ever had a girlfriend?" My hook came out of the water. The bait was gone—freakin' eels! "Have you ever had a boyfriend for that matter?"

Rodge suckled bourbon, and watched the lake with a crazy look in his eye that made me think that maybe he was about to leap overboard just to escape me. I felt panicked.

"Of course I *know*," Rodge said between sips. "It's just the way I am, but I've got to tell Mum and Pete. I thought you could help."

"Shit, no." I threw my rod in the bottom of the boat. "This is a lot to ask, man. You know what Pete's like. He'd more likely punch me in the head than listen, and excuse me if I don't plan on having his steel-caps dance on my face."

Rodger looked up at the moon.

Another eel head-butted the boat, then another, slightly louder this time. The boat rocked. I swayed, putting my arms out to keep balance. "Think these stupid eels did this to Dad? I mean, makes sense. Dad's off his nut fishing. Along comes this greedy-assed kamikaze eel, rams the boat. Dad falls ass over tit into the drink." A tight knot constricted my heart. "Sure that's it. Has to be." I gritted my teeth—but there's nothing you can do to get payback on eels.

Rodger was crying. He tried to conceal his tears by burying his nose in his sleeve. I sat next to him, and put an arm over his shoulders like maybe a big brother should.

"Let's go home."

Rodger nodded. "I gotta piss first."

I withdrew my arm. "Can't you wait till shore?" I said this more harshly than I should have and immediately regretted it. "Shit, I'm cold, man." I said this as way of apology.

Rodge pulled away, tossed his rod and crab-crawled down the end of the boat. "Whatever."

"If I don't go, I'll pee myself." Rodge stumbled over the back seat and nearly tripped. "Don't worry, I don't expect you to hold me." He opened his zipper and stood at the back.

I reeled in the second line, and turned away. The eels were splashing around us. They were hitting the boat quite frequently. It reminded me of B-grade horror movies, the really bad ones with piranhas and shit. "Give these eels a taste of booze and they lick themselves into a frenzy, hey?"

Tinkle, tinkle. Rodger was peeing off the boat.

The thrashing of eels was a maelstrom around us—slapping about like a school of sharks that have just been thrown a bucket of chum. They were whacking the metal, and the boat was rocking. Rodge was swaying, probably too drunk to realise and then *wham!* The boat rose out of the water, and I was Ahab in his whaling boat rammed by Moby Dick. I tumbled airborne and plunged headfirst into a liquid nitrogen kiss. I sucked the chilled water, and cold bloated my belly, and contracted every pore. It shrivelled my scrotum into a pea. All I saw were strands and strands of eels, a weed bed of eels, circling, spinning, dragging me down, ever down into the deep.

Cold and the black crushed in upon me.

At least Rodger doesn't have to tell Pete he's gay now.

At least I'll see Dad.

And that was somehow sorta nice.

I came to into light, a brilliant, sunburst light that throbbed from the roof of a cave. The air was stagnant with a liquid-metal tinge. It was humid, and stank of old urine, like one of those public toilets in the park—a really bad one with shit on the floor.

I shook my head.

I rubbed my eyes and peered about.

The place was a cavern of pink-hued stalactites and stalagmites. It was warm almost, which was just as well, as I was near naked on the stone. My Parka, socks, and jeans were sitting in a pile by my side. Water leaked out of a crack in my shoe. I was in my T-shirt and jocks. Light throbbed from a particularly large stalactite in the centre of the roof. To the right, on a platform of stone, three figures sat around a rickety table the wood of which was patchy with starbursts of lichen.

Rodger sat in his underpants on a metal bucket with his back to me, and beside him Dad perched on a rock, his clothes spotted black with mould. The third figure caused me to scrabble away, and shake my head in disbelief. I blinked and stared and rubbed my eyes.

Was I dead? Was this an oxygen-starved dream?

An impossible giant was hunched across from Dad at the table. His head was a shrub of matted moss that tumbled down into a beard that lay in a heap on the floor. Jutting out of the hair were two large ears, pointed like spear tips. His yellowed teeth were spikes, a bear trap of ivory, and his eyes were prominent, more like the suckers of an octopus than eyes. They blazed a furious light—the orange of wind-blown coals. The creature snorted through its trunk of a nose and picked at its chin with a nail.

"Deal!" it said and tossed Dad a pack of worn cards.

"Dad?" I asked and came closer. "Dad? Is that really you?"

Dad paid me no mind and shuffled. He started to deal.

Rodger also seemed oblivious to my presence, entranced by the game.

"What's up?" I asked, taking courage at the absurd normality of the scene. They were like three old mates on a card night and nothing more. I came to the table.

Dad glanced up at me then, but his expression was grim, and his face was drawn and tired. His eyes were bloodshot as if he'd not slept for a year, and I began thinking that maybe he hadn't.

"Eel?" Dad asked and indicated a heap of raw eel in the table corner.

"I'd rather puke. No." I grimaced. "You hate eel."

"You'll get used to it." Dad flicked cards around the table.

"Hi, Jay." Rodger seemed only to notice me now. "Hope you don't mind the clothes, but I didn't want you catching the flu." He nodded to the empty side of the table where a hand of cards lay.

The giant scooped up his own cards in a sledgehammer fist, and I noticed he was male. He was naked, and fat, and his skin was an unhealthy flour-white. He looked at me with those fire eyes and grinned before his attention returned to the game.

"Where are we?" I asked, and squeezed water out of my T-shirt. In the floor there was a still pool, a trapdoor of black water. Was this how we'd entered the cave? I went to Dad's side and put my hand on his shoulder. He shrugged me off.

"Shhhh," he hissed. "Concentrate. Important to concentrate."

"Better. Game better now." The giant guffawed. "With four I'll 'ave a change of eats. Up da ante to yer life." And he sneered—a malicious smile—a grin that was all teeth with eel guts dangling from his gums.

Dad motioned for me to get seated on a rounded stalagmite. "Now pay attention," he said speaking quickly. "Vod here likes to gamble see, and you'd better learn fast. We've been playing hands for like, forever, keeps him amused, company and all, and you'd better learn, because with two it's different than three or four. Vod's upped the ante as he said, and if you lose, you're a snack, a meal, eaten anyway, gone and kaput."

"What?" I placed my hand on Dad's wrist. "I don't understand a thing you're saying."

"Listen, Jay," Rodge said. "This here bunyip or elf or whatever likes to gamble and the stakes are high. Like Russian Roulette, ok?"

"Bullshit!" I looked at the giant, thinking that this was a joke. The giant winked, and I took notice of his tree-trunk biceps, and a webbed tail that ran down his back and twitched behind his fat arse on the floor. There were spikes growing from his skin, spikes of razor-sharpened bone, and I knew, *knew*, this thing could not be beaten in a fight, not by me. Such a thing could not be outswum or evaded in the cave.

I had no choice. I'd have to play, except I didn't know the game.

"Listen hard and fast," Dad said. His left eye twitched. "Game's euchre, cut throat, first to eleven wins." He placed the pack in the centre and flipped the top card.

It was the ace of diamonds.

I noticed something then. Each of us had two cards in front of us—counter cards—a five and a six to make eleven, except old fish bones didn't have any counters. "What's up," I asked, tapping the table. "How come he's got no counters?"

"Vod can't lose, and the deck only has three suits besides," Dad said with an expression like a collage of dog shit. "Hearts, diamonds and spades. No clubs, you see, and Vod can't lose, so what's the point? The one of us who wins, Vod's agreed to set free, *if* we can swim our way out. The other two, the one who loses by the most becomes fish supper, the other stays and plays cards till they drop."

I swore under my breath. How long had Dad been there? A year? And all the time playing cards and eating eel? He should have drowned.

"Diamonds up." Vod reached across and took the ace.

"Oh, by the way." Dad paused with a sigh. "Vod always gets to make suit and always gets to lead."

"House rules." Vod clacked his teeth.

Vod was a cheat, but I dared not voice this aloud, because I noticed at the back of the cave was a mound of bones, mouldered and heaped in piles. Human bones. The remains of settlers and aboriginal natives that used to live in the region from ages past, most likely. The skulls were stacked like Lego bricks and bone shards lay in criss-cross piles with femurs, and rib bones all split and sucked of marrow. Maybe Dad had been lucky that Vod was a lonely freak, or he would have been eaten for sure?

So we played. Vod cheated like the Devil's grandmother. He stashed cards in his beard, and hid jacks and aces under his rump. Of course *we* didn't cheat, although I was sorely tempted to try, as I was losing. Dad must have read my mind though and whispered repeated warnings in my ear.

Six points, seven points, eight points down. Dad tried to throw the game. He played like he'd never seen a card in his life, even though he must have been pretty sharp with the game by now. Vod won hand after hand and began to assign points indiscriminately as he saw fit. These went mostly to Rodge and as far as us humans went, Rodge was winning. Dad had five points and I had two. I felt like bait in a bucket must. My heart was doing an Irish jig inside my rib cage. All I could think of was becoming a meal.

"Hand." Vod trumped my ace of hearts with a seven of spades. Of course spades was trumps and the bastard had euchred me in three tricks.

Vod gave Rodge two points and that made ten. One point to go.

"Damn!" I held my face in my hands.

Rodge tapped my hand. He nodded to me and smiled.

"You dog!" I lunged at Rodge but Dad caught me and held me back. "This is your fault, and you think this is funny?"

"I'm not to blame."

"Yes you are. You brought me out here. You with your confession. You with your secret. Big news Rodge! But it's not anything you're gay. So what? You're still the same. Mostly though I want to hit you for peeing off the boat and tipping us into the drink." Dad let me go when I said that, as if maybe he'd done the same sin and that's how he'd ended up here. I threw my punch at Rodger.

Vod caught my fist. His grasp was cold and clammy. His gaze looked beyond me, as if he was seeing something beneath my skin—my soul maybe?—and he gave me a twisted grin.

Vod pushed me back down. "Deal." He exhaled the stink from a drain.

I looked at the black pool in the floor. "I'm sorry, Rodge." I knew then I'd be making a runner come the end of the next hand. "I'm just venting, ya know?" If I was going down, I decided to do it on my feet.

"Wait a minute," Rodge placed his hand on Vod's paw.

I mouthed, "What?"

"This is hardly fair," Rodge said in a sing-song voice. "You guys play all the time, and then we turn up and are expected to beat you? I'm only winning because of you, although God knows why you're making me win? It's sweet though."

A deep growl vibrated in the base of Vod's throat. Dad made cutting motions across his own neck.

"What have you got to worry about, Rodge?" I stared into Vod's blood-moon eyes. "I just hope you're planning on at least cooking me, ya bastard. Wouldn't like to think you did me raw."

Vod licked his lips.

"Let's play," Dad said and swept up the cards. "Let's make this interesting, old buddy. Let's play doubles."

Vod patted his stomach. "Deal!"

We went silent and all I could hear was my heart. "Whatever. Hey, Rodge. Not that it matters, but concerning your personal question, when you get out of here, tell your parents yourself and stuff 'em if they don't listen. You're a pretty special guy, and they either love you as you are or they're fools, and you're better off without them."

"DEAL!" Vod slapped the table and blew cards onto the floor. His fists opened and closed and his nails did this *click, click, click.*

"So tell me," I asked as Dad picked up cards off the stone. "I gotta ask. Why no clubs?"

Vod roared into my face with his mouth all jagged with teeth.

"No, no, no, no, no!" Dad pressed his thumbs into his own sockets like a blind man fitting marbles for eyes "Clubs are reminiscent of a certain un-mentionable religious symbol which shall not be named—*ever*, never."

"You mean a crucifix?" I asked, being a smart ass, I suppose, and formed a cross with my fingers.

Vod punched me in the mouth. His bone spikes tore up my chin and shattered the jaw bone. I dropped like a sack of spuds.

"Stupid, stupid, son!" Dad knelt by my side. Blood gushed from the wound in my face, spilling across my chest, reddening my top. Dad pulled off my T-shirt, and tore it up into bandages, and Vod went upright and bellowed. He started waving his arms as if he were batting away blowflies.

I dimly saw the giant staring at my shoulder, at the tattoo of the cross on my arm with Dad's name inscribed. He backed away at the sight of the crucifix.

Dad dragged me across the chamber to the pool. He called to Rodger, but Rodger turned towards the giant. He lifted his arms and went to Vod who at this stage was smashing the table against a rock, obliterating it into a rain of splinters that flew out across the floor.

Then we were in the water and swimming. Dad pulled me through the dark. I passed out, whether from shock or the cold I don't know. I do know my body shuddered from the black-ice of that underground current. I was dragged along like a puppet on elastic string.

I awoke in a hospital some time after. My jaw was wired. Mum sat by my side reading the *Woman's Day*. I mumbled after Dad, and she began to cry. I mumbled after Rodger.

She told me Rodger had drowned. She looked at me with an expression I could have taken as hateful. She hurried from the room.

I found out later, that everyone assumed I'd driven myself to the hospital after the accident in which I'd smashed my jaw. The boat was recovered overturned and submerged in the waters of Pope Lake. Rodger's body was never found. Popular opinion was he drowned like Dad a year before. The papers reported it as a double family tragedy, but they didn't know the truth. A reporter tried to interview me—I punched him in the eye.

Dad, well Dad never showed up. He turned up two years later, after my college graduation. He gave me a hundred bucks, shook my hand, then gave me a postal address, a PO Box in Tasmania. He said not to tell Mum. The world was better off with him dead. He never knew my younger brother anyways and the kid was better off without him, he said. I couldn't say I disagreed.

I asked Dad about that night, and he turned with a wild-eyed look.

"We both share the blame of Rodger's sacrifice," I said. "Rodge was a nobler soul than either of us."

And to think Rodger was only seventeen.

I never did tell Rodger's parents his secret. They never knew him anyway, and I didn't want to risk Pete the bastard re-breaking my jaw. With Rodger dead, I'm sure that's what he would have done. To hurt me would be easier than accepting the truth.

As for Pope Lake, I never could reconcile the memory of that night with reality. Weeks, months later, I began to wonder if I'd saved Dad, or if Dad staged his disappearance and vanished on the night of his first trip? After all, the card game and the cave seemed so surreal. I attended counselling; the psychiatrist convinced me my fantasy was a product of the cold and the booze. He said I'd driven myself to the hospital in shock after the boat overturned and Rodger disappeared.

Maybe?

Maybe?

Maybe he was right, but I'm not so sure. Because in the drawer by my hospital bed I later found something—a crunched playing card—an ace of diamonds. I asked a nurse about it. She told me the doctors had to pry open the fingers of my fist to get it. It had been pulped within my grasp.

It was still damp with the waters of Pope Lake.

Renewal

Robyn A. Hay

We woke to a restless morning, consciousness overwhelmed by anxious voices witnessing a strange passing. Subtle at first, the summoning crept through the forest, plucking strings of an ancient lyre left untouched by practiced hand for generations. A band of energy without focus, it was wild in form. It pestered and prodded upon our edges, the message passing from one ear to another. Flowers twittered and branches cracked until awareness descended upon a single entity.

A cloak governed by leaves and brambles dropped solicitously down upon his shoulders. A ready–made staff awaited his first steps, its base tightly secured in the earth. His eyelashes fluttered; his neck craned from side to side as if to ease an ancient crick.

Ferro opened his eyes but snapped them shut again, unable to handle the onslaught as every plant and tree chorused their welcome. Fallen leaves rustled happily on the damp ground, bellowing that the sun would soon shine brilliantly.

Ferro tilted his head upward, his wooden eyes opening a slit to study the darkened sky. "Be careful children," he said, with a smile. It was a stiff smile, but familiar. "You'll wake the dead."

The leaves refused to be still, already gossiping of something else. Children were children no matter if an eternity had passed. Still, we knew he couldn't concentrate with all their jostling. We siphoned the energy from the beetles and spiders, stilling their movements for the seconds it took to bellow a shout for silence, shaking the land itself.

"Now, see what you did." Ferro laughed. "You made the forest angry."

The leaves tittered with him. Inevitably, their impatience overcame caution and again offered information in droves until something caught his attention.

"What plea for help?" Ferro raised his hand to command silence. *That* they listened to. He paused, tilting his head, ears cocked. "There is untamed magic in the forest, one that grows more desperate as it moves north."

We mentioned that it began in the east, at the weakest edge of our territory with sounds of metallic clashing, human shouts and a cry so full of panic we had no choice but to wake him.

He shuddered, gripping the staff tight. "Yes, something terrible happened there. Something blasphemous."

He shook himself, coming back to reality. "But it is always better to deal with the living before the dead." He pulled the cloak more tightly about him, turning away from the dark emotions. "I will judge that one later. Keep him contained to the east. Do not give him reprieve. As for the other trespasser . . . I will decide his fate now."

He flexed his toes, snapping off the tendrils that dug deep into the soil. He leaned on his staff for support and easily pulled one foot, and then the other, free from the earth. He left the grotto, soon moving with an ancient grace that belittled his long years of dormancy. He followed the winding path that hadn't existed a minute ago, whistling all the way.

"How long have I been asleep?"

We didn't know. We don't record the passage of time.

"A century or two, perhaps? Long enough for you to grow restless." He easily evaded the branch that moved to intercept his movements. The path was folding back in on itself, despite our efforts to keep it open. "This is Harlan's doing. That man was far too paranoid."

In more than one way, we were glad that Ferro had been the awakened sentinel. Siobhan had difficulties dealing with humanity, holding grudges against any species that had trespassed through and against the wood. A sentinel's power is formidable even if the knowledge of their existence is not. Like guardians, their nuances hold great purpose. Harlan was our last guardian. He had died years ago, too distrustful to go in search of an apprentice. His failings had left us unkempt for far too long and his power, that beloved power, had been lost into oblivion. Siobhan never forgave him. Had it been up to her, we would have grown savage, tameless.

Ferro's steps slowed until he came to a mass of twisted thorns and discarded branches woven into an impenetrable barrier. "Apparently, I am needed nearby but in which direction? Can you—"

A frightened voice rang out, quickly suppressed by angry cursing and a tree screaming in agony.

Ferro swiveled, trying to locate the source. There was a flash of green light to his right, followed by a strange stirring as we instinctively responded to the call of a forest child. Our consciousness shifted away from Ferro, touching a mind far more erratic than we expected. His fear awakened a dark menace that wove its way into our trees like the sap that sustains them. We saw a fully armed man hacking away at the protective cocoon a tree had formed around the boy.

"Help me!" he screamed, feeling our presence.

Being what we are, we couldn't help but respond to his frightened plea. The branch stuck hard and fast, merciless.

Ferro pushed his way through the thicket, only a moment before we pulled free from our enemy. An axe lay embedded in the roots of an ancient elm and a shield belonging to King Menotek lay discarded nearby.

Ferro glared at the bloodstained limb, though his anger was at us. "Why bother waking me when you choose your own form of judgment?"

We cringed in shame, although a small part of us, the part that had gladly shattered the bones of that man, rejoiced at the vengeance a guardian had granted us. Ferro was too compassionate.

Moving cautiously, Ferro braced his right shoulder against the trunk to look inside.

Wild eyes stared back at him. The boy shoved himself further back.

"He is so young," Ferro whispered. "Far too young for such responsibility."

Ferro rested his full weight against the tree and the hole opened a little more. The boy's fear spiked, power flashed and we were afraid of what he might ask us to do. The tree warred with the conflicting commands of master and adjudicator.

"Your pursuers are gone and shan't return," Ferro said gently.

The boy relaxed slightly.

"I am called—"

"Ferro," the boy rasped. "Yes, the forest spirit just told me. You are a sentinel, a pillar of wood given life to act as judge." His shoulders slumped. "At least, that's what I was taught."

The boy looked around the hollow, frowning at the makeshift cocoon, and started to disentangle himself.

Ferro stepped back, obviously troubled. "So young. Still . . . from a single sprout, a forest might grow and thrive."

We agreed, but added hurriedly that he might wish to tidy things up a bit.

Ferro flicked a cursory glance at the body. "No, that certainly won't do."

He tapped the ground gently with his toe and watched the earth open up, swallowing the man until only a glimpse of purple cloth remained. He hastily pressed the bit of tunic deeper when the boy emerged from the tree, brushing off bits of twig and dirt. He paled slightly at the sight of the axe and shield.

"The forest can hide many things," Ferro said. "Unfortunately, forged weapons must remain exposed."

The boy swallowed roughly.

"Come, I will take you somewhere safe."

"There is no safe place." The boy looked around sadly. "I can't stay here for long. More will come. Menotek leaves none alive who might oppose him."

To our delight, Ferro didn't recoil but took in the words with his usual joviality. "Last time I checked, we rarely have human visitors who enter and leave the woods intact." When the boy simply stared at him, he added, "Our last guardian was rather harsh, you see."

"How long have you been alone?" the boy asked, tremulously. "And without care?"

"Too long, child. We have missed the songs your kind sing." Ferro flicked a sidelong glance at the boy. "Can you sing?"

"I know some music," the boy said, brightening slightly. "My master was teaching me before we were forced to leave our home."

"Why did your master choose to come here? A cursed wood isn't a suitable place for anyone."

Though we knew Ferro was teasing, we bristled with indignation. That is, until we saw the boy's expression darkening again, but with sadness rather than anger.

"Either way," Ferro added quickly, "you are welcome here."

We chorused our approval.

"My name is Tivon," the boy said abruptly. "Son of Matilda and Jerome Stolt. Inheritor to Soray's power. My master," he added unnecessarily.

Ferro smiled, feeling our combined satisfaction at this small show of courage. There was strength in that voice, promise. "And I am Ferro, as you already know. Come, it is getting dark and my time is short. Let me take you to a place we might rest, though it hasn't been used in some time."

We waited for Tivon to make a choice and tried to feel as harmless as possible. Finally, he nodded his acquiescence.

Ferro led him back toward the grove. Tivon followed close to the sentinel's heels.

Created to offer peace and safety for those who cared for us, the clearing beckoned them onward. Fruit trees planted in three corners, and a small cabin, overgrown with moss and home to a rather chatty family of raccoons, rested in the center. A rotted door, hinges and all, lay on the stone walkway. Portions of the roof caved in and were scattered across the furnishings within. Nearby, a small garden overgrown by weeds and ferns begged for tending.

When the duo arrived, Ferro stopped too abruptly and Tivon bounced off him. "I'm afraid my kind forgets the ravages of time. I hope this is satisfactory. We haven't tended to anyone for a while."

Tivon shrugged. "I've stayed in worse places."

Obviously embarrassed by the condition of the hut, Ferro pointed with his staff to the east corner. "The earth there is groomed for sentinels. Because of our presence, there is no safer place for you than this grove. The cabin was home to Harlan. There is a well around back and the fruit trees bloom year round." Finally, Ferro asked the question that had plagued us since we'd felt possible renewal arrive. "Will you stay here with us?"

Tivon looked to the place that still demanded judgment, to where beasts and a maze of foliage contained our quarry. "There really isn't anywhere else for me to go."

Though we felt his pain, we surged with anticipation. We would have a new guardian, even though he was a bit younger than we had expected.

Nothing is ever easy. Words to remember when exploring a new path in life and believing everything will fall into place. For some, selection for a prestigious position is proof that they are special, that possession of a superior quality will help them outshine the competition. Tivon had a place of power in the world, not in wealth or family, but in understanding and maintaining the beauty of wilderness. Still young, he struggled to emerge from an awkward and gangly shell, refusing to give in to despair but uncertain how to accomplish the goal. If he'd been older, the transition would have been easier and we might not have suffered so much.

The humming moss blanketing the walls vibrated and flared bright red. Every one of our boundaries heard their wails of anguish. Some flora expressed their sympathy, while others raged, begging Ferro to end the folly of teaching a prepubescent the language of trees. Our thousands of voices demanded silence, maddened that our only choice sat in front of Ferro, bellowing in a voice that threatened to bring the entire cabin down.

Ferro clamped his hand over an ear and pressed the other against his shoulder. "Stop! For the sake of my sanity, please stop!"

Tivon sputtered to silence, flinching when he noticed the effect his voice had on the most harmonious, gentle plant in the forest. "I don't think I've quite caught on to this, Ferro," he said, voice cracking.

The moss trembled as he spoke, an echoing effect from their recent torture.

Ferro dropped his hand to his lap, bewildered that a forest child could possess such little harmony.

The boy's eyes followed the movement, and then shifted to the sentinel's right shoulder, finally noticing the absence.

"Your arm," Tivon whispered, eyes flashing.

Ferro tried to smile reassuringly though his ears still rang and sap tried to force itself from his eyes. "We all are made from our experiences."

"Did it hurt? When they cut it off?"

Ferro blinked, surprised by the boy's brusqueness. "Yes, it did. And still does when the weather changes." He studied Tivon carefully. We could see the swirling power of protectiveness in those young green eyes. "But it is no great matter and not one to mull over. It happened ages ago. I don't usually miss it."

And there certainly wasn't time to discuss it. Dead patches of moss lay strewn across the ground while the living contemplated suicide. We prodded Ferro until his hand reached out and caressed the soft plant, humming the song that had proven so difficult for Tivon. It instantly faded to yellow, knowing an experienced being was reaching out to soothe its distress, and then settled back into its typical, luminous green.

While Ferro worked, we considered Tivon. We never knew training a pupil would be quite this troublesome. Still, the boy had taken in Ferro's long, dirt-encrusted robe and tangled beard without scorn, met his wooden eyes without flinching, and not fled screaming in terror, as other prospects had, when faced with our great supremacy. We'd held no doubt about Tivon, until now. Singing should be instinctive for a forest child. How could a prospective guardian possess so little ability? How could his master have missed *this*?

"A guardian's voice should ease the soul of the forest," Ferro said, our irritation making his voice sharp. "It does not condemn it to death."

Tivon stared at the soft boots encasing his feet. "W–what did you sing to the moss?"

Ferro smiled wryly. "At least you noticed a difference. It was the song you tried to sing."

Seeing Tivon's instant dismay, we thought perhaps it might have been the wrong thing to say. Ferro shifted his hand away from the wall and let it rest on Tivon's thin, drooping shoulders.

"Don't worry," Ferro said, adjusting his grip to pull the boy to his feet and then brushed small pieces of singed moss from his clothes. "It takes time to find balance with a forest. Nevertheless, you have to be careful, for it is alive as you or I. The adjustment might have been easier had the responsibility not been thrust upon you, but in time, you will find the proper harmony. Just use less zeal."

Tivon nodded, eyes travelling from the newly exposed beam of the cottage to the dead moss that once covered it.

Ferro led Tivon away from his failure and into the sanctity of the warm day. Our land would soothe his distress far better than Ferro could. When his thin shoulders began to straighten and his stride no longer lagged, Ferro casually reached out to stop the boy. Surrounding them were dozens of ancient trees blocking out the sun's rays with overgrown branches and thousands of multicolored leaves.

Ferro winked at him. "Watch this."

Tivon nodded and followed the sentinel's gaze up to the canopy.

Ferro took a deep breath and sang a short elegy. The notes expressed sorrow and requesting forgiveness on the boy's behalf for hurting a part of us. A tremor went through Tivon's body, followed by a gasp of astonishment.

Leaves rained down, an offering of peace and understanding. A rainbow of foliage encircled them, as comforting as an autumn quilt.

Tivon smiled, gratified by our gesture, and tilted his head up to the sky, opening arms to embrace the fallen. That is, until the branches overhead shook, sending down bits of dust.

His eyes snapped shut. "Could you ask them to stop doing that, Ferro?" he said, rubbing his eyes with his fingers.

We responded to the boy's command and stopped, feeling distressed for causing the boy injury.

Tivon glanced at Ferro. "Thank you."

Ferro spread his hands wide and smiled. "I did nothing."

When Tivon just stared at him, Ferro explained, "The forest is not here to be at anyone's command, but simply wishes to thrive in your care. If you give respect, it will love you in return. Just remember that the forest didn't grow in a day. Nor will a poorly sung song destroy it. Ask what you wish from it . . . gently, and it shall build you a kingdom."

Tivon laughed shortly. "I suppose that I should practice singing more, but Soray used to kick me when I tried to practice the scales."

A single leaf floated down, serving as a reminder and warning.

Tivon watched, while Ferro let it come to rest upon his open palm. The leaf was green, etched through with red.

"I'm not doing very well, am I, Ferro?"

A subtle green aura surrounded the boy. It was the exterior embodiment of his newly acquired magic as were, to a lesser extent, his green eyes. Specifically, Tivon could unlock the mysteries of the forest. Because of this light, we knew he belonged to us despite his inability to harmonize.

"Your voice will come in time, child." Ferro felt our touch of disquiet, our irrational fear. He slipped his left hand within the length of his cloak, hiding the small tremor. "But this has nothing to do with you. Let us return to the cottage. You still have much to learn."

Typically, one learned to chant before learning the more intricate lessons of the wood. Believing Tivon and the moss needed time to heal, Ferro shied away from the music drills and instead explained the natural cycles of life within the forest. During the next afternoon, they took a rambling walk. Ferro showed him the varying breeds of plants that grew within our borders. It was important that Tivon recognize the name and purpose of each. He absorbed the knowledge like drops of water in a lake.

Everything Ferro taught returned to the art of creation and building a connection. We believed Tivon needed to find the correct melody and understanding would follow.

"Again," Ferro said.

Sweat dripped off Tivon's nose. He reached forward with trembling hands and touched a wilting ghost flower. She was a short, blooming albino plant that grew only in dark, wet places. For this lesson, he did not have to sing, simply whisper a command. He spoke softly but with fervid intensity. The flower strained to respond, but outwardly, she remained lifeless.

Seeing this, every doubt we'd had dissolved. For decades, our kingdom lay unprotected. Yet, that is better than leaving it to someone unsuited for the task. We'd already made that mistake once with Harlan. Apparently, one didn't necessarily have to sing to tame the wilderness. Sometimes a simple touch can express everything.

Disappointed when nothing happened, Tivon sat back with a sigh and rubbed sweaty palms on his thighs. He shook his head in exasperation. "I'm never going to get it right."

"Yes, you will," Ferro said softly. "When helping a plant find strength, you must become one with it. Each has its own name, an incantation if you will, but every forest has its own melody. Choose your words carefully and follow the same tune. If you manage this, you will have taken a giant step toward becoming a guardian. Try again. Open your mind."

Tivon reached out toward the flower, and did as Ferro asked. He murmured a word and she straightened. "I did it."

Despite his victory, Tivon seemed more troubled.

Ferro frowned, feeling our concern. "What's wrong?"

He hesitated a moment before responding. "I feel kind of uneasy. My bones feel itchy."

"And what does this tell you?"

Tivon examined the area. His eyes darted back and forth, trying to read the subtle shifts of the foliage. They jostled, trying to voice the source of their discontent. He glanced up toward the trees filled with their own expectant tension.

A rumbling sigh escaped Tivon's lips. "They tell me nothing. I can feel the land stretched thin, and that a restless energy waits just out of reach. It bothers me, Ferro."

"What do you feel in the air?" Ferro said quietly.

Tivon opened his mouth, tongue sticking out. "It feels heavy, moist. Like a storm is coming from the east."

"Crude but effective," Ferro said. "And you are absolutely right."

Tivon grinned, pleased with this small victory.

"I have some business to take care of tomorrow," Ferro said abruptly. We jostled our foliage in agreement. It was time for settling debts. "Will you be alright by yourself?"

Tivon studied Ferro's face, a frown wrinkling his youthful features. "Where are you going?"

Ferro didn't reply.

Finally, Tivon nodded. He rose to his feet and they began the long journey back to the grove. Tivon didn't say a word, despite Ferro's attempts to lure him into conversation. When they arrived at the clearing, Tivon simply entered the cottage and climbed into bed.

Ferro kept watch all night, sitting in a chair fashioned from a tree that freely gave its life for simple comfort. The boy's mind fell open to us when he slept. There was a darkness lurking in his dreams and we worried that he might draw us back to a place similar to the time of Harlan. Whatever was going to happen, he wanted reprisal badly.

"If you doubt him, simply remember his touch," Ferro told us. "There was gentleness there."

A ghost flower twittered her agreement.

Ferro left before dawn, leaving the boy to his destiny.

It didn't take long to find the spot; the eastern forest had been constantly moving for three solid days, growing more impatient and strained from the activity. In a patch of thorns not far from a brook, Tivon's master lay on the ground. Arrows protruded from his chest, neck and shoulders. Dead eyes stared up at the sky. The leaves were oddly still about him.

"Why are you so quiet, children?" Ferro asked, as he knelt by the body. "A sign of reverence or a warning?"

His hand stroked the dead man's brow. Time meant nothing in that moment. This man, this Soray, could have been ours. Instead, we had Tivon, a quiet and awkward youth who, with our help, would bloom into a force to be reckoned with. Still, we grieved for what might have been.

Ferro waited patiently as our mind, body and soul slowly lured our quarry to justice.

It didn't look as if the three days in our wood had been kind to him. Sweat and dirt streaked his face and clothes. The smell of his unwashed body tainted our air. A sword hung from his belt, and he held a bow in his hand.

He started at Ferro's appearance, nocking an arrow. "What are you? Speak, *creature!*"

Ferro ignored him, hand still moving back and forth across cool flesh. With every pass, Tivon's need for vengeance seeped up his arm until Ferro disappeared beneath our wrath. We wanted to touch the infiltrator, feel his skin and bones crushing in our grasp.

Our eyes, Ferro's eyes, trained upon the man standing before us. He stepped back, body trembling from fear and the strain of three days of no food, water or rest. We knew what he saw, a depth of rage so inhuman it was incomprehensible.

Shunk!

A branch wrapped around the man's wrist, too slow to stop him from releasing a shot but effectively stopping him from making another. We glanced down at the arrow embedded in Ferro's chest and calmly pulled it free. Another notch marking him as ours.

The man swiveled to look at what held him, mouth working as he tried to comprehend that a tree had stopped his attack. He struggled viciously but we were too strong. Within seconds, the branches had taken hold of the rest of the man's body, stripping him of weapons. They fell to the ground, useless. The man thrashed, but only managed to exhaust himself. His useless attempts to break free stopped when Ferro's hand settled on his neck and lifted him off his feet. He watched us wide-eyed as the hand tightened.

"You should have known better," we said simply.

Incomprehension filled the man's filmed eyes, tainted as he was by his contact with Menotek. The words could never reach him. All he heard was the crackle of shifting wood and the whistle of wind between the leaves. We watched the man's chest heave, striving for breath; his limbs twitched and then went limp. Our hand opened and the branches released him simultaneously. The rumpled, discarded flesh hardly seemed a threat now. The tree swayed harmlessly in the light breeze, never knowing what part it had played.

We returned to our weightless body and crooned our thanks to Ferro.

He stumbled back, away from the body and us.

Roots erupted from the damp earth and worked to loosen the soil. They twined around Soray's body, pulling it deep under the earth. We left the murderer's body exposed. The animals would find the flesh and make use of what we couldn't stomach. Until then, it would serve as a warning to others who might enter to cause harm.

We chattered our thanks again; but Ferro shook his head, refusing comfort.

It was only then we'd realized our mistake. We'd never used him to act before, only judge. A sentinel was a kind, benevolent being. They came by their decisions through the greatest of philosophies; however damaged a soul might be they considered all options. To him, we'd just forced him to commit murder.

We watched him flee, unsure how to help him.

For hours, Ferro locked himself away from us, stumbling and drunk with guilt. We asked him, begged him to return to the grove and take his place opposite Siobhan. Mostly, we wanted him to rest. He'd done more than enough.

The boy remained silent during this time, absently stroking the head of a mother raccoon. Her cubs played happily at his feet. Since he didn't seem too concerned, we gave Ferro his solitude. However, we maintained a careful watch on him, directing his movements only when he swerved too close to the periphery of the forest.

Tivon said nothing when Ferro appeared, only watched as the cloak fell from Ferro's shoulders and he dove his feet deep into the earth, into blissful dormancy. His mind entered ours and we grieved together.

We felt a hand reach out and heard a pleasant, soothing melody. Tivon spoke to us of peace, of a forest embarking on new growth under his protection. His anger was gone and all debts were finally paid. Though his words comforted us, his touch was all the reassurance we needed.

Chaos Theory

Brandon Alspaugh

An execution.

At the Ivory Tower of the Silver City, they're not uncommon. Or particularly spectacular. What they *are* is mandatory.

Michael raised one powerful hand, and the assembled host quieted. "Azrael," he said, spitting the name out like a curse, "has transgressed against His Law. His thoughts have deviated from the orthodox. He has committed acts contrary to the Divine Plan. He is a traitor. Now he is subject to the mercy of the Creator." The metallic light of the City glinted from his blade. With a single fluid motion, he drove it through Azrael's heart. The condemned angel's body dropped to the ground.

Gabriel never understood executions. Michael, and through him the Creator, punished traitors. But why would anyone turn against the Creator? Even if they escaped His gaze, evaded the all-pervading eyes and ears of Michael and his Dominions of Seraphim, why work against Him? To what purpose?

He was careful to take wing and leave the Ivory Tower with the others. Each angel flew seven abreast, eventually breaking away to their respective places of service. Gabriel spared a quick glance upward. In contrast to the terrible brilliance of the Silver City, Creation peered at him with tiny pin-pricks of light.

"By the Creator." Gabriel's alabaster hand tightened about the scroll he was carrying. "What a thing to behold."

He lowered his eyes and continued. Creation was to be completed, not admired.

"Two plus two equals four," Saraquael said. "It is one of the basic principles from which we are trying to build this . . . this . . . ah . . ."

"Universe," Gabriel said.

Saraquael shot him an annoyed look.

"A linguistic detail . . . not our concern," Gabriel said. "I only happened to hear it the other day at the Cathedral of Syntax."

"Nevertheless," Saraquael said, "the variable order should be sufficient to the Creator's needs, to maintain the balance . . . and it must all be able to be expressed mathematically, or we can't hope to track . . ."

Gabriel listened intently, used to Saraquael's infatuation with the sound of his own voice. His orders were crucial to the work of the Creator, which was, of course, more than enough reason. Higher Mathematics . . . it was a highly desired post. An assignment given only to those angels who had proven their devotion to the Creator with the greatest sincerity.

Slowly, with an effort, Saraquael concluded, ". . . and so our measurements must be confirmed within Creation. I am permitted to bring an assistant."

Obviously none volunteered. If they did, they would be implying they were more worthy than their brothers. But all craved it, nonetheless. As of yet, there was no mathematical expression for desire.

"Fractals, you know," Saraquael said, ruffling his wings, "that's really what it all is. Too many of the Host compare the vacuum between masschunks to Chaos, which is a gross generalization at best. For one thing . . ."

Gabriel shivered at the mention of Chaos. It licked at the edge of Creation, looking for the slightest breach. Behind the devotion and serenity of each angel, even one as blusterous as Saraquael, was the memory of the Creator snatching their flailing form from Chaos, preserving them from destruction.

(Don't be a fool!) Gabriel recited equations in his mind, going from two plus two to more complex expressions, gradually reclaiming himself. He forced aside thoughts of an imperfection in Creation. (If anyone noticed. . . .)

He turned back towards the body they were circling. The Creator had asked for it to be studied in particular, and everything set properly to rights, with no unknown variables. Hundreds of the host circled the blue-green orb, each performing their own unique function. Each was wholly indispensable. Each was also completely replaceable.

Saraquael drew his attention to the violet neighbor of their primary focus. It hung closer to the system's star, and roiled with thick clouds of methane. "Make sure the gravitation of that masschunk doesn't interfere with this globe's integrity."

Gabriel glided on ivory wings towards the planet, so joyous in the simple state of being. The planet before him seemed to shift; for a moment he felt a deep connection with it, this inanimate bit of swirling gas and dust. It made him feel curious and yet satisfied.

He didn't even notice the second rustle of wings until another figure dropped in front of him.

"Samael!" Had she noticed his temporary lapse of concentration, or. . . .

She didn't immediately respond, but instead gestured towards the purple globe, silhouetted against the planetary system's only star. "Isn't it absolutely stunning, precious?"

Gabriel blinked, but he couldn't focus on the planet. His eyes were transfixed on Samael, the line of her, her muscles swimming under porcelain skin. (Idiot! Look at the blasted planet! 2+2=4+2=6. . . .)

"Very much so," he said. "We just need to make sure there are no adverse affects from its gravi—ah!"

Samael whirled about in a prismatic flourish and spread her wings. She flew by, her wingtip barely touching him. Gabriel winced as it seared his skin, leaving a small dark place on his right shoulder.

"You don't say! Mathematics? Oh, but I can't pretend to be interested in anything that *dreadfully* boring right now! You're *such* a dear, though! Ta ta!" Moments later, she vanished into the void.

Owing not a thing to the thousands of degrees radiating from the nearby star, Gabriel felt a strange heat ignite inside him.

Every cycle in the Silver City was much like the next. Gabriel glided towards the Cathedral of Higher Mathematics, careful to stay abreast of the others and neither speed nor slow himself.

"Gabriel!" a voice vibrated as soon as he entered the Cathedral.

"Saraquael."

"You were with Samael the Firstborn yesterday. This was not one of your appointed duties."

"Apologies, Saraquael," Gabriel said, only half-hearing the overseer. Like a creature split in two, he was a thing half-devoted to his master and half-devoted to his own mad desire.

"And what did the Creator's Chosen have to say of my work?"

"Only the highest praise."

It was hardly a gamble. Saraquael would never challenge the truth of a compliment.

(This talent . . . deception? Why in Creation had it suddenly come into play? What was wrong with him?)

Gabriel felt as if he were forbidden to scratch a deep, prowling itch. He had spent the remainder of the previous cycle and the entirety of this one resisting the urge to examine the burn on his shoulder. If anyone saw him acting so strangely, the consequences could be dire. He cringed from the memory of the harsh light reflecting from Michael's sword.

For a time, he considered reporting himself to Raphael, to see if her healing powers might help him. But something, the same un-angelic spark which led him to mislead (he lied!) Saraquael prevented him. And now it contracted his focus to the mark on his shoulder.

Impossibly, in the center of the thin red welt, he made out two words:

COME ALONE

Gabriel quickly slid his tunic over the burn again. He had to integrate much of the recently developed calculus methods before he was free to do anything.

Do anything? He wasn't seriously considering. . . .

But before he even finished the thought, the spark had already spun out a plan.

It had to be done carefully. He couldn't afford the slightest mistake.

Angels required rest . . . it made no sense, Saraquael had explained to him once, to have an angel be needless in any aspect, because any capacity which was infinite was the Creator's, and the Creator's alone. And when a cycle was ended, each was expected to either pursue work on their own initiative or return to their dwellings for rest.

In less than a breath of quicksilver, he was borne in the air, two angels to his left and four to his right. Certain none noticed, he angled towards the residence of Samael.

If any were to ask, the spark told him, he was to say he was exploring some quantifications of 'beauty,' a subject Samael was renowned for her knowledge (and possession) of. But none would dare ask.

The other half of his fractured mind railed against what he was doing, pleaded with him to return to his duties. But he wouldn't. The spark drove him inexplicably onward.

He alighted in front of her dwelling, his bare feet taking notice of the cool marble, so different from the metal and porcelain of the City proper. Another oddity: there was some kind of blockage in the point of entry, barring him from entering directly. Gabriel had no time to ponder on the significance of this. The portal disappeared as if it never was, and he was pulled inside.

Before he said a word, he felt a cruel pain explode onto his lips. Her face was pressed against his, her mouth on his, and for a moment he stood there, frozen and burning.

Samael released him. "Darling! You came! And alone, too!" She laughed. "Won't you sit and join me? Oh, of course you will, what am I saying? Come, sit, sit!"

Gabriel sat obediently in the leftmost of the two chairs in the pale room. Another oddity. There was a certain . . . blast, what was the color designation? Pink . . . that was it. A pink ambience to the place. Very odd. Almost deviant.

"Samael . . ."

She offered him a cool chalice of honey-sweet nectar, which he gratefully took.

"This is all too much. If Michael or his Seraphim learned of this . . ." He blinked his eyes. The strangeness of her home was almost painful.

Samael laughed again, but it was a lower, more constrained sound. "Michael! What a dreadful bore that one is. 'Here we have a betrayer' he'll say, and then chop! No sense of theater or drama at all." She paused to take a piece of ambrosia from a golden basket on the table next to her chair. Gently, she patted him on the cheek. "You're frightened of me, aren't you, precious?"

Gabriel nodded.

"Well, you shouldn't be. I'm a wave function . . . a repeating motif. Inevitable, even though that's a concept most angels haven't grasped yet."

"I fail to grasp the significance, Firstborn."

She crooked an ivory finger at him. "That, right there. 'Firstborn.' It's accurate, I suppose . . . I was the first of His host. In the beginning," she said, smiling, "He was just plucking us out of Chaos left and right, you know. And we all had our points of view . . . it's why He built this place, so we didn't get too out of control and wreck things. We needed a baseline."

"Point of view?"

"Of course, precious! Look at Creation . . . do you think you see the same Creation I do?"

"Creation is defined on strict lines of design. Of course I do."

She shook her head and finished her fruit. "Never mind. Well, look at the thing then . . . have you ever asked yourself what holds it together?"

"The Will of the Creator—"

"Don't be silly." She kicked his leg playfully. "It's atomic bonding. All of those little pieces joining with others like them. It's Divine Attraction. It's Love."

"Love?"

Samael sat up then and leaned over, her face scarcely a few inches from his. She took his hand. The burning was cool now, almost pleasant. Pleasure and pain. . . .

"Love is the part of Chaos He had to hold onto in order to make His whole Creation work properly. I remember the earliest stages, when it was only myself and Michael and Raphael and a few others . . . try as He would, He couldn't will the universe into a desired shape. It always collapsed. Creation by its very nature is solitary, cruel, and selfish. Love is the ultimate randomizer. It forces things into union despite all reason to the contrary. Love . . ." she said, shooting him a piercing sidelong gaze, "is what makes someone believe two plus two doesn't always equal four."

Gabriel stood up straight, feeling himself go numb. "Samael . . ." he managed to say, but his voice choked. He had never known such pure horror. To imply a limit on the Creator was like claiming. . . . ($2+2=5$? No, that's not right! It's. . . .) "I . . . that's . . . you can't . . ."

"Shh . . ." She took hold of the hair on the back of his head and drew him closer. Again he felt her lips on his, the taste of cream and syrup. His hands found her smooth body, caressing, seeking, adoring.

A tormented fragment of consciousness tried to recite equations, restore him to himself. But try as it might, it could not seem to make two plus two equal four.

Later, when his exhausted body had collapsed on the bed, Samael looked upon what she had wrought. And she saw that it was good.

Good enough, at least.

"Oh, you're awake! How simply exquisite, don't you know."

Gabriel felt as if Chaos had taken hold in his brain. His thoughts and feelings were a torrent of conflicting impulses. He looked up and saw Samael fastening her belt around her waist and sliding her tunic over her shoulders. The alienness of the room pounded behind his eyes.

"Samael . . . by the Creator, what—"

She put a finger to his lips . . . he scarcely felt the scorching contact. "Shh, beloved. In a moment."

He sat up and grabbed for his own tunic, thrown carelessly (and since when was he careless?) on the floor, and dressed himself.

Samael took his hand and led him out of her chambers into the foyer.

"This is important, beloved. I know you are frightened. But if you act as if nothing is wrong, no one will notice." She looked upwards for a second and smirked. "His Eternal Eye has a few more cataracts in it than you know. But you have to leave now."

The one half knew this, knew he had to report soon for his daily work. The other threw his knees to the floor and wrapped his arms around her legs, and he felt his chest heaving, throbbing around an impossible pain.

"No! I will be with you! Damn it all and everything! I . . ."

(2+2=4. . . .)

And it was gone. He stood and straightened his tunic. "I'm sorry . . . my behavior has been very indecent, Firstborn."

Samael sighed. "And we're back to Firstborn now, are we? Oh well. A little dichotomy is good for the mind, I suppose. For the part which spent the previous hours ravishing me," and Gabriel flinched, "I'll leave with an invitation to join me at the planet we both admired after this cycle ends. His Most Holy of Blowhards wants to gauge how much Chaos remains in that system of darling celestial bodies. Mind you, I prefer *your* celestial body. . . ." She ran her hand down the length of Gabriel's chest.

"I . . . that is, good day to you, Firstborn!" Gabriel forced his shaking feet to carry him out the door. Without even waiting for any others, he took to the air, gliding towards the Cathedral of Mathematics.

If he was a little distracted in his tasks during the day—if triangles ended up not equaling 180° on a sphere as they did on planes, or a proper square root of -1 was not established (making for a great deal of trouble down the road)—it's really quite difficult to blame him.

"I remember the day the big lummox opened His eyes for the first time," Samael said, running her feathers playfully over Gabriel's face. "That's when He 'created' me . . . Michael and Uriel came shortly after, but I was the first."

The two of them darted through the boiling clouds of the second planet from the system's star.

Gabriel laughed. "Opened His eyes? Surely there must have been more to it than—"

"Oh hush, beloved," Samael said. "It's all that was needed, what He was the first to provide . . . a point of view. Don't you see me differently than you did before?"

"I do," he said. He arced upwards and drew his flight abreast of hers. His hand caressed her powder-white face for a moment, and then she dove. He followed. Amidst the tumult of the planet's atmosphere, they danced.

"It's all He was . . . the first point of view. It's what creates the things we experience . . . He didn't make a blessed thing. He was just the first to notice it, and it all fell into place the way He saw it. Quite simply," she said, "it's His universe. We just live in it."

Samael smirked. "When I saw you next to it, I saw it in your eyes. Your mind was *wandering*. You were seeing things for *yourself*. Do you know how gratifying it was? To find someone who doesn't buy the Celestial Party line? Who has their own darling little opinions?"

Gabriel rolled and twisted, soared through the milky-white ammonia clouds. "I suppose not."

"Don't you adore this planet, by the way?" Samael dove and climbed, a delicate release of joy.

"I do . . . it reminds me of you. Wild, untamed fire."

"I think I'll claim it. Over in Linguistics they call it the Morningstar. It's a beautiful name, isn't it?"

"I have but one standard of beauty," Gabriel said, "and against her, any name pales and falls short." He halted, hovered for a moment. He still didn't understand.

She looped around; now she flew above him. "Oh, do ask already. I've been waiting for at least two blessed minutes."

Gabriel's mouth formed a thin white line. "My love . . . where did He come from, then? Are His capacities, like His span, not infinite?"

At that, Samael went into freefall, laughing so hard Gabriel feared it tortured her. After a moment, she righted, expanded her wings, and regained enough of herself to respond.

"You're working on mathematics, love, so I suppose I can explain it. You've got all of Chaos out there," she said, gesturing towards the sky, "all of it roiling and boiling in senselessness. But Chaos is infinite . . . and at some point in infinite Chaos, a segment of perfect Order has to occur. That's Him. That's where He came from. And us, really. So no, He's not infinite. He's not even very big, to be frank. Just first out of the box, is all."

Gabriel's elation was marred only by the searing pain in his skull, the battle fought between the part of him rebelling against the heresy which was dripping from her lips, and the knowledge he would do anything, anything, to taste her warmth. "And so, mathematics . . ."

"Is dangerous. So very dangerous. If He manages to define everything in strict, mathematical terms . . . eliminate the bit of Chaos He had to retain in Creation, then what place has Love? Or me?" She took his hand and drew it to her lips, the kiss like an explosion. "Or us?"

Gabriel stopped in place. She wheeled about, bringing them face-to-face. "Do you understand?"

Though he felt his skull splitting in two, he couldn't look away. "Whatever . . . whatever I can do."

She nodded, her face all the grace and beauty he could desire. "I know you will. But His deplorable cycle approaches its beginning, and you've got such a lot to do today, don't you know."

"I do. But I shall return. . . ."

"Three cycles hence." She stood and ran her fingers through his thick blonde hair. "I'm sorry dear . . . I know you're dreadfully disappointed. But we have to be careful. It won't be long before we're ready to move against the Creator Himself. If He were to find out, or Michael . . ."

"I know," Gabriel said, and he caressed her jet hair. Again the pain! Again the rebellion! Again the final certainty: against all reason and logic, he meant it.

"And with the differential equations project underway, we can all expect a great deal of extension to be done on previous work." Saraquael droned on.

Gabriel shook his head. The pompous windbag (what are you thinking?) was always quick to expound on the obvious. If he could get away with pointing out the Silver City had a noticeably silver tone in its colouring, he would. (He's your appointed overseer!)

Gabriel was busy, one hand sketching solution sets to his assigned linear approximations, the other casually working the theory of Chaos into mathematics. It was surprisingly easy . . . circles inscribed with crystal formations of ever-growing complexity, indeterminate ratios for circumference measurement, his own innovation of a thing he called game theory . . . all of it quietly slipped in to the manuals.

And because no one was supposed to notice, no one did.

(By the Creator, what are you doing? You can't!)

"Gabriel!" a voice thundered.

He looked up from his tablet, forced a smile. "Saraquael."

"Have you finished those linear approximations?"

"Nearly complete. I had a bit of trouble. . . ."

"Trouble?" Saraquael asked, and Gabriel knew he'd made a mistake. Saraquael leaned over Gabriel's workstation.

Gabriel panicked and tried to hide his Chaos work with his hand, but he needn't have worried; Saraquael was predictably focused on proving his superiority in the matter of all things linear. Ego begat myopia, in his case.

"You see," Saraquel said, "when the line approaches its zenith—oh, blast. Can I use an inscriber of yours? I'll never be able to explain it simply enough without a demonstration."

"Of course. Here . . ." His voice died to nothing as Saraquael reached for the stylus, his tunic slipping.

Exposing the scorch marks of long, slender fingers.

Fingers he knew.

$(2+2=\text{~~Love~~})$

"Gabriel!" Saraquael tried to shake Gabriel's sudden, impossibly strong grip on his right arm, the stylus snapping in half against the drafting table.

Three angels surrounded Gabriel. He twisted around, throwing off their arms. As he did, he saw it on each of them; the burns and welts, the mark of her.

The pain seared his mind to nothing. Without even a thought, a single equation to right his descending madness, he flew straight, a lightning bolt of ineffable pain.

Pain.

And vengeance.

Gabriel descended into the grounds surrounding the Ivory Tower. He hadn't even known where he was flying to, but something compelled him here. And he knew what it was as soon as he saw the insignia of the Seraphim, the stained grounds of the courtyard.

Michael.

"Michael!" he called, the sound raspy and high-pitched. The pain had lodged itself in his chest like a tumor, crushing his body from the inside. He could barely speak. "Michael!"

Two Seraphim, each bearing spears, alit on the ground next to him. "What business have you with Michael?" the shorter of the two said.

Gabriel fell to his knees. His hands feebly grasped at the robes of the confused Seraphim. "You must tell him . . . Samael plans to . . . the Creator! Warn the Creator!"

"Better let Michael deal with this one personally. If he's afflicted with insanity like Baal . . ."

The larger one nodded his assent. Each taking one of Gabriel's arms, they escorted him inside.

"I had suspected as much," Michael said, slamming a massive fist onto the polished metal table. "Samael has always been a non-conformist. But the Creator has always been lenient with the Firstborn. . . ." He shook his head. "How many are involved?"

"I don't know," Gabriel said, shaking his head. "I saw the burns on so many . . . I barely had the presence of mind to come here."

"The burns . . . oh, right. It was some odd condition of hers . . . originally why the Creator put her in charge of lighting all of the stars in Creation. Lightbringer, she was called." Michael pulled his sword from its case and sheathed it. "Well, we'll make short work of this insignificant rebel cabal."

"Michael!" A Seraphim crashed through the doorway and almost lost his balance, reaching out to steady himself on the metal table in front of the burly angel.

"It seems this is a day for breathless interruptions by hysterics. What is it, Abdiel?"

"A rebellion! Samael is at their head . . . they're striking all through the streets and causeways!"

Michael snorted. "So? Take a legion of Seraphim and be done with them."

Abdiel shook his head. "We cannot! Many of the Seraphim have joined the rebellion . . . as have others! At least a third of the Host are in revolt!"

"A third of the . . ." Michael's features lost all expression. When he spoke again, his voice was confident, authoritative. "Send Uriel to inform the Creator." He secured his breastplate and drew his sword. "I shall deal with Samael personally."

Gabriel seemed forgotten in the midst of all the excitement. But he stared at Michael's sword, and the pain was replaced with terror. Terror and sickness. He remembered the way it gleamed with Azrael's blood, with the blood of so many others. And soon Samael's. . . .

His heart hardened. She chose this fate as she did her lovers . . . carelessly, and without thought to the consequences.

(2+2= . . . I don't care. Not anymore.)

He collapsed, trembling in agony. This, his mathematical mind thought, must be the inverse function to Divine Attraction. The part that's left after Love has (betrayed!) departed.

He shut out the horrible death-cries already ringing through the metallic towers and cathedrals. For centuries after, the polished metal surfaces of the Silver City would reflect nothing without a crimson hue.

"Samael?" he whispered. The planet, only an angel's breath away from the Morningstar, had been the focus of the Creator's attentions for the past several cycles. He remembered, so long ago, he and Saraquael ensuring its integrity, remembered the hundreds of angels so intent on it. This was the result.

There were peculiar green and brown growths over much of it. Occasionally, Gabriel even discovered bizarre things which moved with a life of their own. These he avoided.

"Samael?" he whispered again. "I can't see you, but I know you're here. I need to talk to you."

He waited for a moment, heart sinking. She would not forgive him. Which was no surprise, since he would not forgive himself. He had so wanted—

A long, slender creature dropped onto his left shoulder. "By the Creator!"

"Shh! Gracious, darling, you were always a screamer, but really . . . this is neither the time, nor the boudoir."

"Samael?" Then he remembered. "Samael . . . I . . . I'm so. . . . I didn't mean to . . ."

She made a cooing sound. "Shh, shh. I . . . was wrong, Gabriel. I never realized . . . never really appreciated Love, what it would do if it wasn't guarded jealously. . . ."

"But . . . the rebellion. And a third of the Host . . . and you, cast from the City. . . ." He could barely keep his voice down.

"Still a stuttering mess." She smiled; despite the fangs, Gabriel found his heart fluttering. "It's all right. Really. Besides, this is my big moment. See through those trees? The two bipeds?"

Gabriel pushed aside some of the green growth and looked. One had odd fat deposits on her chest, while the other seemed to have an eleventh finger protruding from his waist. "What about them? They look like everything else on this world . . . odd and misshapen."

"That's the Man and the Woman. The Creator has given them this world in exchange for their total obedience and worship. But the insecure idiot left, as He always does, a reassurance for His own Infinite Ego. A delightful apple tree which they're forbidden to eat from."

"So? They won't eat from it. Look at them! They don't even have the sense to clothe themselves!"

"Don't be silly. Now," Samael said, inching her way up the tree, "me and the Woman are going to have ourselves a little girl talk. Once I've peer-pressured her into taking a bite, you'll see. He'll see, too. The Man's love for her will compel him to eat it too, even though he knows it means his destruction, because—"

"Two plus two can equal five," Gabriel said, with a small smile.

Samael laughed and leaned out, flicking his cheek with her tongue. Gabriel closed his eyes and savored the searing heat of it.

"I suppose you have to be getting back to the City. . . ."

"They've taken to calling it Heaven now, but no. As part of my—" his voice cracked again "—rehabilitation, I've been forced to set foot upon the base clay. I'm His envoy in this portion of Creation."

"How positively lovely! We'll be neighbors." She peered through the branches. "There's my gal pal now. Back in a tick, dearest."

She slid through the branches like mercury. When she dangled above the Woman's head, she cleared her throat. The Woman looked up, a blank stare on her face.

"Honestly, darling, have you tried the apples today? They're *absolutely* scrumptious."

Stephanie Pui-Mun Law lives in Oakland, working as a freelance artist in the fantasy publishing and game industry. She has also authored books on drawing and painting techniques for fantasy (*Dreamscapes*, and *Dreamscapes II*), while also exploring her own concepts and projects, including the Shadowscapes Tarot. She has become known for her sinuously elegant watercolor paintings, pencils, and ink drawings delving into the realms of the unconscious and the fantastical demesnes of the otherworld.

Michail Velichansky lives in Pittsburgh where he now writes young adult and middle grade books with his wife, Rachel. Their latest, *Claws*, is based on the short story found in this anthology, though it takes the idea in a completely different direction. Michail works as a web designer and developer; he recently decided to return to school in order to study nursing.

Maggie Slater lives and writes in Portland, Oregon. She has had numerous works of fiction published in small press venues, but *Fantastical Visions IV* was her first notable sale. She currently moonlights as one of the submission editors for the sci-fi/horror e-zine *Apex Magazine*. For more information about her and her current writing projects, visit her blog at maggiedot.wordpress.com.

Jeff R. Campbell's addiction to genre fiction causes him to write mystery, horror, science fiction, and fantasy. His work can be found splattered across a wide variety of publications including—but not limited to—*Wax Romantic*, *Spinetingler Magazine* and *Challenging Destiny*. In addition to the printed word he also provides scripts for radio's *Imagination Theater* and *The Further Adventures of Sherlock Holmes*. Risking the wrath of his fellow scribes, Jeff recently crossed into the shadowed realms of the Editor-Kings, co-editing an anthology of stories mixing fantasy fiction with the world's greatest detective. The result, *Gaslight Grimoire: Fantastic Tales of Sherlock Holmes*, was recently nominated for Canada's Aurora Award. His next editing project will be another mash-up, this time pitting Sherlock Holmes against the fiendish imaginations of horror writers. Look for *Gaslight Grotesque* on bookstore shelves before Christmas 2009.

Scott Huggins has written several short stories over the years, including "Giantkiller" in the anthology *Heroes in Training*, and "Bovine Intervention" in *Andromeda Spaceways' Inflight Magazine*. He currently teaches history to high-schoolers at the Independent School in Wichita, Kansas, where he lives with his wife Katie, and son Tristan. Fans are encouraged to send chocolate and coffee.

Margaret Yang is a full-time writer and parent who lives in Ann Arbor, Michigan. Her favorite things include coffee, cooking, and computers. (If she had a flying car, that would be her favorite thing, but she doesn't.) More about Margaret and links to her published short stories can be found on her webpage. http://yangandcampion.googlepages.com.

Todd Austin Hunt was born in the mountains near Gatlinburg, Tennessee and grew up in central Kentucky amidst a parade of seven brothers and sisters. As a young child, he wanted to be an inventor, but all his inventions were ridiculously impractical. Thus, with the aid of reading writers like Roald Dahl and Stephen King, he turned to writing speculative fiction. He attended University of Kentucky and subsequently Eastern Kentucky University to obtain his Masters. He was first paid for a piece of writing when 10 years old, but he didn't see another check until 16 years later. Hunt has been published regularly since, appearing in anthologies such as *New Growth: Recent Kentucky Writings* and magazines such as *Morpheus Tales*. He won an Honorable Mention in the 2003 Annual Ray Bradbury Contest and was nominated for the Pushcart Prize in 2007. He now lives in Charleston, South Carolina.

Greg Beatty lives with his wife in Bellingham, Washington, where he tries, unsuccessfully to stay dry. He writes everything from children's books to essays about his cooking debacles. Greg recently published his first poetry chapbook, *Phrases of the Moon*. It is available from Spec House at spechouseofpoetry. blogspot.com.

For more information on Greg's writing, visit www.gregbeatty.net.

M. T. Reiten's fiction has appeared in *Baen's Universe*, *The Writers of the Future XXI*, and *All the Rage This Year*, the Phobos Award anthology. His experience in Oklahoma and Afghanistan with the US Army shaped the stories that appeared in The Yard Dog Press anthologies *International House of Bubbas* and *Houston, We Got Bubbas*. After earning his Ph.D. in "lasers," M.T. left Oklahoma for a job in Maryland that paid substantially better than fiction writing. He finds it ironic that a former Army soldier now works within rock-throwing distance of the US Naval Academy. He's also upset they took away all his rocks.

Michael Penncavage has been an associate editor for *Space and Time Magazine* as well as the editor of the horror/suspense anthology, *Tales from a Darker State*. One of his stories has recently been filmed as a short movie.

His fiction can be found in approximately 60 magazines and anthologies from 3 different countries such as *Alfred Hitchcock Mystery Magazine* in the USA, *Here and Now* in England, and *Crime Factory* in Australia.

Organizational affiliations include the Mystery Writers of America, the Horror Writers of America, and the Garden State Horror Writers.

Jason S. Ridler's fiction and poetry has appeared in *ChiZine*, *Nossa Morte*, *Andromeda Spaceways Inflight Magazine*, and other fine venues. His short story "Billy and the Mountain" is forthcoming from *Tesseracts Thirteen*, edited by Nancy Kilpatrick and David Morrell. His nonfiction has appeared in *Clarkesworld*, *Dark Scribe*, the *Internet Review of Science Fiction*, as well as such academic journals as *War, Literature and the Arts*, the *International Journal of Canadian Studies*, and *Canadian Military History*. A former punk rock musician and cemetery groundskeeper, Mr. Ridler is a graduate of the Odyssey Writing Workshop, holds a Ph.D. in War Studies from the Royal Military College of Canada, and is a columnist for Fearzone.com. He is also a founding member of the Homeless Moon writing community. Visit him there (homelessmoon.joskinandlob.com), or at his writing blog, Ridlerville (jsridler.livejournal.com).

Alex Jackson teaches or hangs out with his family when he isn't writing. He lives in Philadelphia, Pennsylvania, with his wife, Suzanne, and three sons, Caleb, Lucas and Cole.

Christine Welcome is a writer of fantasy stories and/or a paralegal in a real estate office. Her writing tilts toward the dreamlike and the dark side, while her office work is nothing but mundane. She lives in a cottage on a small island in the middle of Narragansett Bay, Rhode Island, and/or in a condominium unit in the heart of the city of Providence—a sort of country mouse and city mouse combined. What moves her is her deep respect and admiration for the natural world, her love for the unusual and doors. With a past littered with unpublished work, her future is yet to be determined.

Aliette de Bodard lives in Paris, where she holds a job as a computer engineer. Her short fiction has appeared or is forthcoming in *Blood & Devotion* (also from Fantasist Enterprises), *Realms of Fantasy*, *Interzone*, and *Orson Scott Card's Intergalactic Medicine Show*. She is a Campbell Award finalist for 2009. Visit www.aliettedebodard.com for more information.

David Walton is the author of the novel *Terminal Mind*, which was nominated for this year's Philip K. Dick Award, and the winner of the 2008 Baen Memorial Award for short fiction. He lives in Pennsylvania with his wife, five children (none of whom have reached double digits in age), and one gerbil. By day, he works for a large defense contractor on classified government programs, which not even the gerbil is allowed to know about. The rest of his time he spends storytelling, sword-fighting, tower-building, diaper-juggling, and otherwise taking care of his children. Since he doesn't actually have time to write, he's trained the gerbil to do it for him with a combination of Morse clicks on its drinking bottle and cleverly-arranged pellets. The gerbil has produced quite a few published short stories over the years, which have appeared in *Analog*, *Baen's Universe*, *Cosmos*, and elsewhere.

Hank Quense—assisted by his faithful mutt, Manny—writes science fiction and fantasy stories (along with an occasional fiction-writing article) from Bergenfield, New Jersey. All of these stories are humorous or satiric because he refuses to write serious genre stories. He feels that folks who crave serious fantasy and SF can get a full measure in any daily newspaper.

In the spirit of disclosure, Hank reports that all of the story ideas (the good ones anyway) come from Manny. Hank merely translates the dog's ideas into a manuscript. Hank can be reached via e-mail at hanque99@verizon.net while Manny refuses to get an internet address until someone develops a paw-friendly keyboard.

The pair has sold stories to *Andromeda Spaceways, Cyberpulp, Fantastical Visions, Neo-opsis, Afterburner SF, Faeries* (France), *Electric Spec, Scyweb Bem, Glassfire, Darker Matter Flash Fiction Online* as well as several anthologies. *Fool's Gold* is a recent novel available in both ebook and print.

Visit their website at www.hankquense.com.

James R. Cain has had stories and poems published in over 130 publications and is the editor of *Dark Animus* magazine (www.darkanimus.com). His novel *Ek Chuah* is available from Active Bladder (USA) or the Dark Animus site. You can learn more about him at www.jamesrcain.com.

Robyn A. Hay has spent most of her life daydreaming in the shadows of the Rocky Mountains. Driven to understand the dynamics of the world, she obtained a degree in Earth Science but decided to create and explore her own realities instead. Her writing has appeared in the ezines *Deep Magic* & *Nanobison*, as well as the anthology *Wicked Little Girls*. She currently lives with her young family in Alberta, Canada.

Brandon Alspaugh is a graduate student in Middle/Near Eastern studies with an emphasis in Hebrew, Greek, and Aramaic languages. As far as he knows, he is the only child whose second grade teacher insisted his mother attend a parent-teacher conference to discuss his 'excessive reading,' and imagines they preferred he find a street corner somewhere to hang out on.

W. H. Horner is Publisher and Editor-in-Chief of Fantasist Enterprises, an independent publishing house specializing in fantasy and horror short fiction anthologies, novels, art, and music. He holds a BA in English and a MA in Writing Popular Fiction. William is also the founder and director of the First Writes, a writing group that meets in Wilmington, Delaware. For more information about William and his freelance editorial services, please visit www.whhorner.com, and to learn more about his projects with Fantasist Enterprises, please go to www.fantasistent.com.

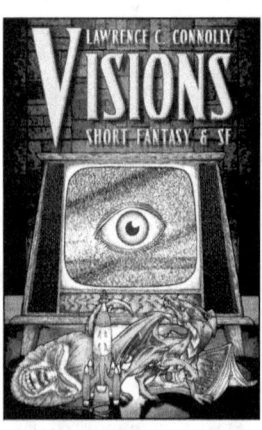

AVAILABLE NOW

Fleeing from what should have been a perfect crime, four crooks in a black Mustang race into the Pennsylvania highlands. On the backseat, a briefcase full of cash. On their tail, a tattooed madman who wants them dead.

The driver calls himself Axle. A local boy, he knows the landscape, the coal-hauling roads and steep trails that lead to the perfect hideout: the crater of an abandoned mine. But Axle fears the crater. Terrible things happened there. Things that he has spent years trying to forget.

Enter Kwetis, the nightflyer, a specter from Axle's ancestral past. Part memory, part nightmare, Kwetis has planned a heist of his own. And soon Axle, his partners in crime, and their pursuer will learn that their arrival at the mine was foretold long ago . . . and that each of them is a piece of a plan devised by the spirits of the Earth.

A finalist for the 2009 Eric Hoffer Award.

Nominated for the 2nd Annual Black Quill Award for Best Small-Press Chill.

Appeared on the Preliminary Ballot for the 2008 Bram Stoker Award for Superior Achievement in a First Novel.

Trade Paperback • 260 Pages • 8 Illustrations • $15.00
ISBN 13: 978-1-934571-00-2 • ISBN 10: 1-934571-00-8

www.VeinsTheNovel.com | www.FantasistEnt.com

Fasten your seatbelts and prepare to take your reading experience to a whole new level. With *Veins: The Soundtrack*, author and musician Lawrence C. Connolly provides a series of instrumental soundscapes inspired by themes and scenes from his critically acclaimed supernatural thriller *Veins*. Performing with his band, Connolly delivers a mix of trance, rock, and ambient compositions designed to complement the novel.

The CD also includes two music and spoken-word bonus tracks, each showcasing a complete story from *Visions*, "Aberrations" and "Echoes."

Packaged with Star E. Olson's distinctive cover art and including a synopsis and full production credits, *Veins: The Soundtrack* is a must for every dark fantasy reader.

Read the book. Hear the soundtrack. Enter a world where fantasy lives.

6 Tracks & 2 Bonus Tracks • Total Run Time: 38:13 • $10.00
UPC: 700261267371 • ID#: FE-934571-00-2

Available Now

An aging wizardess learns more than she expected as she hunts down the last dragon in "The Singing Dragon," while a demoness who has seen the error of her ways must still pay the price in "Blood of the Blade." "Affliction," concerns a surgeon who takes on a disease of mythic proportions, while an elven thief tackles the forces of darkness in "Thick as Thieves."

From heroic to tragic, light to dark, fanciful to painfully real, *Fantastical Visions III* contains these stories and more tales of fantasy and wonder that explore the many facets of the genre.

Trade Paperback • 220 Pages
14 Stories • 28 Illustrations •$13.00
ISBN 13: 978-0-9713608-3-9
ISBN 10: 0-9713608-3-9

Featuring the art of Stephanie Pui-Mun Law

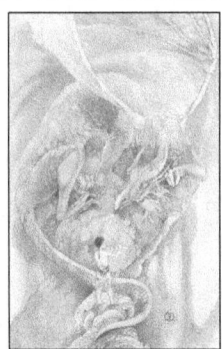

Available Now

Polish your cutlass and prepare your spells for what awaits on a journey across leagues of unimaginable adventure. Ride the waves to mystery and magic.

Featuring 28 stories of mermaids, pirates, and magic beyond your wildest dreams as well as an afterword by Mark Summers & John Baur, creators of International Talk Like a Pirate Day, *Sails & Sorcery* is beautifully illustrated by Julie Dillon.

Trade Paperback • 456 Pages
28 Stories • 42 Illustrations • $23.00
ISBN 13: 978-0-9713608-9-1 • ISBN 10: 0-9713608-9-8

www.FEBooks.net

The life of an adventurer isn't all piles of treasure and damsels in distress. There are sights to see, quests to complete, and jokes around every corner. So grab your giant axe, vorpal sword, or mystical grimoire and prepare to meet your destiny with a smile on your face.

Bash Down the Door and Slice Open the Badguy features 24 stories that will tickle your funny bone while quenching your thirst for adventure.

Trade Paperback • 276 Pages
24 Stories • 29 Illustrations • $17.00
ISBN 13: 978-0-9713608-5-3 • ISBN 10: 0-9713608-5-5

Available Now

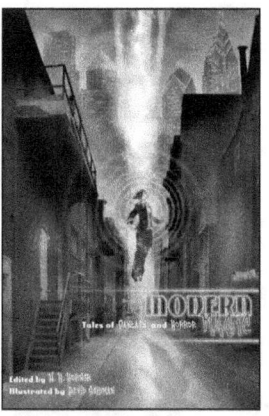

Magic surrounds us. The Enlightenment did not kill it with science, nor did the Industrial Revolution extinguish it with mechanation. Elves may feel cramped in the big city, but they get by. The wild lands disappear, but werewolves still find time to hunt, though with care.

Explore 26 worlds of mystery, wonder, danger, and horror in *Modern Magic*. You may find them to be not unlike the world in which you live.

Trade Paperback • 280 Pages
26 Stories • 35 Illustrations • $17.00
ISBN 13: 978-0-9713608-4-6 • ISBN 10: 0-9713608-4-7

www.FEBooks.net

Some elves thrive in the darkness, stalking their victims for their own twisted pleasure. Sometimes they hunt and kill for the mere thrill. Sometimes their motives are beyond all human understanding.

In *Cloaked in Shadow* you will find elven assassins, kidnappers, and conspirators. And you will also find human beings caught up in the games that the Sidhe play, both sides struggling to survive.

Trade Paperback • 256 Pages
22 Stories • 35 Illustrations • $16.00
ISBN 13: 978-0-9713608-2-2 • ISBN 10: 0-9713608-2-0